# Blood Lands

USA TODAY BESTSELLING AUTHOR
STACEY MARIE BROWN

# ALSO BY STACEY MARIE BROWN

## Contemporary Romance

**How the Heart Breaks**

**Buried Alive**

**Smug Bastard**

**The Unlucky Ones**

**Blinded Love Series**
Shattered Love (#1)
Broken Love (#2)
Twisted Love (#3)

**Royal Watch Series**
Royal Watch (#1)
Royal Command (#2)

## Paranormal Romance

**A Winterland Tale**
Descending into Madness (#1)
Ascending from Madness (#2)
Beauty in Her Madness (#3)
Beast in His Madness (#4)

**Darkness Series**
Darkness of Light (#1)
Fire in the Darkness (#2)
Beast in the Darkness (An Elighan Dragen Novelette)
Dwellers of Darkness (#3)

Blood Beyond Darkness (#4)
West (#5)

## **Collector Series**
City in Embers (#1)
The Barrier Between (#2)
Across the Divide (#3)
From Burning Ashes (#4)

## **Lightness Saga**
The Crown of Light (#1)
Lightness Falling (#2)
The Fall of the King (#3)
Rise from the Embers (#4)

## **Savage Lands Series**
Savage Lands (#1)
Wild Lands (#2)
Dead Lands (#3)
Bad Lands (#4)
Blood Lands (#5)
Shadow Lands (#6)

## **Devil In The Deep Blue Sea**
Silver Tongue Devil (#1)

To my characters and readers,
Hope you will forgive me...

# Chapter 1

Let the games begin..."

This resonated through the arena, riding over my chest in deadly strides. The call for battle. The declaration of war.

A war I would not win.

There was no winning here and no survival in any sense, especially not for my soul. But I realized there was a line I would stop at. One where I'd choose death because I wouldn't be living, even if I survived.

What Istvan Markos was doing was horrific—pitting us three against each other in his newly updated version of the Games to see where our true loyalties fell.

My attention went from Hanna to Scorpion, terror and disbelief holding them like statues. They could never have expected what was really happening. The ultimate choice they would have to make.

One I already had to make tonight.

Zuz's dead body still laid at my feet; her blood had sprayed over me and soaked into the dirt around her corpse.

"Fight!" Istvan ordered us, jolting both Hanna and Scorpion, their eyes going wild. "Or you *all* die."

Through red-tinged lashes, my gaze went up to my old guardian, steady in my fury. The bloody hairpin dropped from my fingers, plunking in the dirt.

Istvan's lip pulled up, his hand digging into the arm of his new young fiancée, Olena, the princess of Ukraine. I guess with Caden gone, Istvan strategically took the opportunity to gain Ukraine instead, easily replacing Rebeka.

"I said, fight soldier," he barked at me. His happy pretense with his new bride dissolved as he pulled away from her, leaning on the railing. "I gave an order."

"That's the thing, Istvan," I called him by his first name to others, but very rarely to his face. He demanded respect for his title, even from Caden when we were in public, and by his expression, he didn't like the informality of it. "I'm not your soldier. Not anymore."

Markos's shoulders rose at my insolence, his lids lowering into slits.

"Then I guess you die." He gripped the railing tightly.

"It's what you wanted anyway, right?" I snipped back. "Me to be killed by fae so you could manipulate Caden's emotions? Twist him into the biggest advocate to destroy the fae no matter the costs… to avenge me?"

Where was Caden? I'd figure as his new right-hand man, he'd be here, making sure I *"got what I deserved."*

Istvan straightened up, his mind probably going back to the private conversation he had with Kalaraja in his office months ago, when I was hiding behind a curtain. The realization hit him that they had not been alone, and I had overheard everything.

"Now I don't need to." He quickly recovered any momentary surprise, his mouth quirking in arrogance. "You did it for me by taking him hostage, didn't you? Now he despises you. Turned his back on you." The jab hit harder than I let on. "Wants you dead."

Caden protected me that night. He could have told Istvan I had the nectar, but he didn't. Why? And why wasn't he here if he wanted to watch me die? What was going on at HDF?

"Then where is he? Is it awkward now you're fucking his fiancée?" I motioned to him and Olena. Her cheeks reddened, hate streaking her beautiful face. "Where is Rebeka, Istvan?"

Anger flamed in his face. "Kill her." He nodded at Scorpion and Hanna as if they were his personal assassins.

"Fuck. You." Scorpion sneered at him with a vengeance that would frighten anyone. The man was intense—tattoos covered almost every inch of his over six-foot frame. Dirty, scruffy, and scarred, with his brown hair knotted back out of his face. But all I saw was someone I cared about. Loved. I wouldn't say exactly like a brother, because he was damn hot. Our

2

connection made him family to me, someone I would kill for. I could never hurt him, just like I could never hurt Warwick.

They were a part of me.

Istvan kept his expression even, not allowing himself to respond to Scorpion. His gaze moved to Hanna. "Guess it's up to you."

Betrayal and hate shone brightly on her face, her head shaking as she stepped closer to us. "No."

"No?" Istvan's eyebrow curved up. "Are you sure?"

Hanna's mouth thinned as she jutted up her chin. I saw Scorpion's gaze slide to her. She didn't even look back at him, but I felt something there. Istvan must have sensed something as well, his focus darting from one to another, an eyebrow curving up, his nose wrinkling.

"I see." Istvan's features hardened. "You might want to rethink that, my dear." His head lifted to the stands, his chin dipping. A scream pierced the hushed room, where everyone had been silent, watching the drama unfold. Commotion stirred up in the seating area; a man hollering... as he was moved into the aisle.

Familiar faces came into view, my stomach sinking with dread at the understanding of what Istvan was doing. It took Hanna a little longer to comprehend—for her eyes and mind to register what she was seeing was real.

Two guards held guns to her parent's heads. Nora and Albert Molnár, standing petrified, staring down at their daughter.

"Mom? Dad?" Her head wagged in confusion as truth slowly ebbed into understanding, her gaze darting back to Istvan with fear and hate.

"Still no?" Istvan pinned his lips, flicking his head back at the guards. "Kill them."

"Noooooo!" Hanna bellowed, her back curving as her worst nightmare played out, guttural pain streaking her face. "No! Please don't hurt them. Please!" She begged. "Please!"

His self-satisfaction bloomed in the air, as rancid as body odor. It was an inconceivable choice he just laid at her feet, but one she would have to make.

"If you kill them," he gestured to Scorpion and me. "You and your parents live. If you refuse, you all die."

Tears streaking down Hanna's face, she turned to look at both of us. I could see the agony and torment. I understood it. I also knew who she would choose.

"Please," she beseeched Markos, her glistening eyes going up to her parents. "They've done nothing to you. Let them go!"

"You have two options, Hanna. Choose one. Or I will do it for you."

A cry from Nora snapped me back up to them. The soldier holding her cracked the handle of the gun across the back of her head, and she stumbled to the side.

"Stop, please!" I heard Hanna wail, but all I could focus on was the guard. His eyes were wide and crazed, his body twitching with violence, as if at any moment he would turn feral. He was itching for blood, craving carnage.

"Just me!" Instead of Istvan, it was Scorpion's voice that boomed out, jerking my head to him. His shoulders spread, chest puffed. His eyes were on Hanna, indicating he would be the sacrificial lamb. "Hanna can fight me… leave Brexley out of this."

She stared back at him, expression unreadable, though her chest pitched in and out with distress and grief.

"You dare tell me what to do?" Markos barked, anger reddening his face. "You are nothing, fae. You think I care anything about your life or death? You are here for amusement only." Istvan twisted his attention to Hanna. "I thought you would want to kill him, Hanna. He was the one who guarded you when you were being held prisoner. That is what you told me, *right*?" His question was a challenge. A single hitch in his tone.

A test.

Confused, Hanna's mouth opened and shut.

No doubt she had told Istvan everything when she was being debriefed, being the perfect obedient soldier. It was what we were trained to do. No questions asked.

She didn't know it was her death warrant and would be used against her. He got whatever information he needed out of her, and now she was worthless to him. Something to discard. Especially now if he thought her in any way *"compromised."* And because her parents were imprisoned, Hanna's return was a gaffe he couldn't have. She wouldn't have accepted their disappearance or whatever story Istvan claimed about them. She would have been a thorn in his side. Another reason to dispose of her.

"Here is your chance, if you really meant what you said, private Molnár. You stated you hated the fae, especially him." Istvan motioned to Scorpion. "Wished him dead. Here is your revenge. Kill the vile trash."

Hanna glanced over at Scorpion, their eyes meeting for a moment. Her body shifted with hesitation.

Weakness.

Istvan could smell it from miles away.

4

"Do not tell me you have grown soft for these monsters?" Istvan clutched the railing, baring his teeth. "Have they tricked your brain into thinking they are human like us? Have you become a traitor fae lover as well?"

"No-no." Hanna's head wagged, her voice cracking in half before her expression locked down. "No, sir."

"Then prove it." He waved to us. "You prove yourself... here, now, and not only will your parents live, but you might be reinstated back into HDF."

"Hanna, do it! Do what he says." Albert yelled from the stands, and Hanna clenched her jaw even stronger.

"He's lying to you, Hanna." I shook my head. There were so many dog whistles Caden and I learned to recognize when many did not. People only heard what they wanted.

He didn't say her parents would be set free or even be treated well, just that they would live. And the strategic game of *might be reinstated* meant the chances were probably zilch.

Istvan's glare went to me, his amusement ebbing, while Olena stirred at his side as if she was getting bored.

"Enough talking. Kill them, or you and your parents die miserable deaths. No one will remember you even existed."

Hanna hesitated, her weight shifting nervously from foot to foot.

It was slight, but I caught the dip of Istvan's head.

*Bang!*

The gunshot sliced through the arena, my attention jolting back to the stands with a harsh gasp. Blood from Albert's head sprayed over Nora, his body falling hard to the ground.

Nora and Hanna's shrill screams pierced the air with horror and grief.

Hanna collapsed to the dirt, deep wails sobbing through her, while a guard held Nora up, her body almost limp with trauma, her arms out, trying to reach for her husband as if there might be a chance to save him.

No remorse or reaction came from Istvan at murdering an old friend in cold blood. Istvan never had much substance before, a man solely driven to gain more power, but now he was becoming a replica of a cruel dictator. A narcissistic psychopath who only feels something when others suffer. And like with any drug, it would have to keep increasing to get the same high off it.

"Better decide quickly, Hanna," Istvan warned, as the guard with Nora practically was salivating at the idea of killing her.

Hanna tried to fight back the sobs, struggling… to move.

"Lil' viper." Scorpion's voice came out low, barely skimming my ears, almost intimate as he crouched near her.

*"Last time I dozed, the little evil viper bit me."* The memory of him calling her that when she was chained up in the base came back to me.

Her sobs shuddered through her body, but she quieted, her blue eyes lifting to his. "Dig deep. I know you got it in you. You gonna keep crying worthless tears, or you gonna come and get me?" He rose back up, looming over her. "Here's your chance. Were you all talk about kicking my ass? Think you got it in you? I personally think you are just a weak, *pathetic* human."

It was a taunt, pushing her to get up and fight, turning her anguish to anger. Saving her mother's life…

Hanna sneered, taking the bait. She sucked in, climbing to her feet.

"That's it, come on." He opened his arms, beckoning her to come and get him. "Show me what you got, Little Viper. I like the way you bite."

Darting quickly, Hanna swiped up the hairpin I dropped, a sneer curling her lip, going into fighter mode. How fast Scorpion was able to get her to compartmentalize her grief and turn the energy into something operable.

But instead of Scorpion, it turned on me.

Stepping around him, Hanna swiped her arm at me, the dagger of the pin only a breath away from my skin. "This is all your fault."

I darted back.

"No! Come after me." Scorpion growled, trying to regain her attention off me. "I'm the one who kept you handcuffed to a pipe."

"You are just a *mindless* soldier. Doing what you are told." Hanna's eyes never left mine, her pain twisting into fury, but I saw Scorpion flinch at her words. "*She* is the reason for all of this. It always comes back to her." Hanna tried to cut me again, but I dodged out of her reach. "Little did I know that someone I considered a good friend would destroy my life and everything I cared about. You took *everything*." A flash of agony went across her face. "My father…"

"She is not the reason your father is dead." Scorpion moved in, creating a triangle, his hands up. "The real person to blame is the man right up there."

"Does it matter?" Hanna's lip trembled, no matter how much she tried to hide it. "I won't let my mother die as well. I—I can't."

Fuck, did I understand.

"I know." My teeth gritted together, my own eyes filling up.

Scorpion's head swung to me, his eyes wide. I don't know if it was the tone in my voice or if he was able to pick up on something, but I saw the "no" start to form around his lips, his head shaking.

I was a fighter. A survivor, but I realized with Istvan, there would be no end to the suffering. He would force me to kill each of my friends, leaving me a husk even if I made it out.

If I died, I hopefully would take the most powerful object in the world with me. It needed me. If I was dead, I felt in my gut the magic in it would wane. No one else could ever use it for their own greed and power.

If it wasn't Istvan, it would be someone else. There would always be another wanting to possess it, to use its power.

I knew what I had to do.

Without hesitation, I whirled on the person standing next to me. My knuckles smashed into the side of Scorpion's neck, striking the vagus nerve, the exact spot I was trained to hit to knock someone out cold. I couldn't have him part of this fight. He would only try to stop me.

Scorpion toppled to the side, grabbing his neck, his wide eyes meeting mine in bewilderment.

I hoped in time he'd understand.

Striking again, I hit the pressure point. He tried to gasp for a breath before he fell over into the dirt. Unconscious.

"What are you doing?" Hanna gaped at me when I turned for her.

"Now, it's just us. Your chance to finally take me down. Don't tell me you didn't wish every day in training for this. Just as the rest of our class did." I leaped for her, my fist cutting across her jaw. Not enough to break, but enough to fire her up. To piss her off.

And it worked exactly as I was hoping it would.

As Scorpion was doing earlier, I wanted to turn all her sorrow into fury. Blind her to what I was tricking her into doing.

"Come on, bitch. You think you can finally challenge me? I always kicked your ass. Do you think now will be any different?"

She bellowed, coming for me, our bodies colliding and falling back into the dirt.

I put up enough of a fight to sell it, flipping her over me onto her back and jumping up. Dancing back away from her, I egged her on. I hesitated and gave her opportunities to strike. This was for show. Exactly what Warwick did with me when we were fighting the final time in Halálház. He could have killed me instantly, but he batted me around, got an arousal out of me.

7

I swear I could feel him slinking in around me now, but it wasn't warm or soothing. It bristled with irritation and anger, like, *"What the fuck are you doing, Kovacs?"*

"I'm sorry," I muttered under my breath to him, not ducking when Hanna's fist collided into my kidney. My frame buckled over as stabbing pain echoed in my back, forcing tears to spill down my cheeks. A boot struck the back of my knees, my face smacking into the dirt, my head dizzy. As Bakos had taught us, Hanna didn't hesitate, jumping on me. The girl was fierce, and I adored that about her.

She punched the back of my skull, and bile heaved up my throat, my eyesight blurring as the hits kept coming. I no longer had to feign weakness, my lungs struggling to breathe. My body wanted to curl up on itself and disappear. Blackness crept over me like fog.

Once again, I was positive I could feel Warwick's energy stab at my skin like nettles, his anger and fear pressing in as if he could feel me giving up, realizing my plan.

I hoped he would understand eventually.

A violent roar rumbled the pit, vibrating the walls of the arena, pulsing through every cell in my body.

Livid.

Savage.

*Deadly.*

*"Don't you even fuckin' think about it, Kovacs."* Warwick loomed over me, his expression burning with fury. His hazy form was next to me in the pit. It didn't matter if he was a hallucination or not, I let myself believe, perishing with a tiny bit of happiness. *"Get the fuck up. You will not die as some fucking sacrifice."* His ferocity thundered through me, making me gasp.

"I have to," I think I whispered. "It's the only way."

*"The hell it is, Kovacs!"* He grunted, crouching down, eyes blazing. His fingers skimmed my face. It felt so real, even the buzz of energy I felt from his touch, a numbness easing the pain in my body. The darkness cleared with a rush of adrenaline searing in my veins. *"Get the hell up, or I will tear through this place and fucking kill her! Do you understand? I will kill EVERYONE to get to you. I will spare nothing!"*

"STOP!" A sharp voice boomed, forcing me to blink up into the seats, knowing it wasn't the Legend who had ordered the cease.

Hanna stopped, the entire place going still.

"Take me instead!" Andris had pushed himself up to the barrier, talking directly to Istvan. "Wouldn't it be far more worthy than two young girls you've known since birth, Istvan?" Andris glared at my old guardian. "This is beneath even you."

Istvan shifted on his feet.

"You know you would much rather have my death. Wouldn't you love to kill the man who turned his back on you? *Betrayed* you? Who purposely chose the fae over you?"

My stomach dropped, realizing what he was doing. With terror, I shoved Hanna off me, climbing unsteadily to my feet. Somewhere in the back of my brain, I understood I shouldn't be able to stand. I definitely shouldn't be coherent after my fight with her and Zuz, but nothing mattered except my uncle at that moment.

"No." It came out a whisper, my head shaking vehemently.

"What do you do, *old friend?* Let them go. This isn't about them, anyway. It's always been about you and me." Andris paused for a moment, Istvan staying silent. "When I knew you, you weren't someone who toyed with children. You played with those who could actually fight back. Is this what you've become?" Andris motioned to the three of us in the pit.

Istvan's jaw locked down, his face turning a deep red. Finally, he dipped his head. "Fine, you want to play, Takacs?" He peered down at Samu and Joska behind the gates in the pit. "Take her and that fae out." He pointed at Scorpion and Hanna. "But she stays." He motioned to me.

"What?" Andris shook his head. "That's not the deal. This is about me! I said just *me.*"

Istvan let out a laugh. "There's where you are wrong, *old friend.* This isn't just about you."

He rubbed his hands together, close to the railing, seemingly to forget the woman beside him.

"And you have no say here." Istvan's creepy smile tugged on his lips. "But I will honor part of your wish. Now it's you and Brexley who have to fight to the death."

# Chapter 2

I think I screamed.

I know I begged.

Terror and panic scooped out my insides, plopping my heart outside my body, leaving it to break in my hands.

Guards dragged Andris into the ring, tossing him forcefully into the dirt, slamming the gate behind them.

On his knees, Andris's head lifted, his eyes finding mine. A sorrow so deep burned his gaze as he shakily pushed himself up, pain etching his expression, "sorry" mouthing from his lips.

"Only one of you lives," Istvan declared. "If you forfeit, you will both be burned alive in the firepits." Istvan motioned to the large flames set in the arena; this time, I understood what the pole in the middle would be used for. To chain someone to it and let them be seared alive. "Both of you chose fae over your own kind, and you will burn just as the soulless magic sorceresses used to be back in the day."

"Noooooooo!" I felt the sound tear up my throat, my body collapsing to the ground, my gaze meeting my uncle's.

He had no fight in him. Just grief and something that looked like remorse.

"Brexley…" He spoke my name like a melancholy song, taking a step toward me. I could hear the melody, the timbre of his resolve. The decision he already made for the both of us.

I became a terrified wild animal, not able to think. I could taste the panic on my tongue, the sharp, bitter fear and vomit searing up my throat.

"No. No. No." My head shook, the word on repeat. I went from having to kill my friends to having to kill the only man left in my life I considered family. I destroyed the most powerful object in the world, ripped away my own power to bring him back to life. He was everything to me. Without a doubt, I'd do it again.

To lose him now and be the one to do it?

No.

*"Drágám."* One word was all it took to break me. Because it wasn't the word, it was the thousands of moments we shared, the times he read me stories, or when he gave me the stuffed animal, Sarkis, to watch over me. It was the sound of family, of my father, of comfort, and times of safety and happiness.

Andris was my touchstone now. The man who represented the time in my life when I still had my father. And deep inside, the dark part of me understood if my own mother or my real uncle Mykel were also in this ring, I know who'd I save. The one who had been part of my family and life since I was a baby. And this recognition merely made me sink further into bleakness.

There are those times when you get to a location, but you can't recall how you did, your mind receding far into itself, blacking out time. That's how I felt. Nothing seemed real.

*"Drágám?"* He spoke to me again, my head rising to look at him, stilling when I realized Andris hadn't opened his mouth. He stared at me from yards away.

I could make myself believe the moments with Warwick had all been in my mind, needing the connection so bad he was with me, but not Andris.

*This can't be happening.* My heart was bleeding all over the ground, my grief heaving so hard in my chest, blackness dotted my vision. I couldn't breathe, sobs wrenching through my soul.

In the distance, I heard Istvan's voice, my uncle's, even my own wild wails, sounding like a wounded animal, though nothing penetrated my despair.

*"Kovacs."* His voice was the only thing that cut through, piercing the barrier and yanking me back into myself. *"Brex, look at me."* The feel of a hand brushed at my chin, my face turning up. The fierceness of Warwick's eyes slammed me back to earth, a calmness sweeping over me at his touch. His heavy gaze gave me a tether to the world.

Air caught in my lungs at seeing his ghost-like form. It was nowhere near as solid as it once was, but now I knew it was real. The magic was coming back.

*"Use me."* He growled. *"Do whatever it takes to survive this. Mentally and physically."* My heart thumped against my chest, feeling him skim over my skin. *"Don't let Markos break you."*

"Brexley?" Andris's call sliced through Warwick, his vision disappearing, turning my focus to my uncle. He fell on his knees in front of me, both of us ignoring the outburst from the crowd and Istvan. Only a handful in the crowd were on our side. The rest wanted the show; they wanted death and blood.

*"Nagybacsi,"* I croaked, my heart splintering when his hands cupped my cheeks. Did he feel the extra bond now? How could I ever hurt him? I gave everything to save him. "I-I can't."

"You must." His eyes held so much sorrow, but I could feel a resigned strength in him.

*"You don't get much say in the way you die, but you can choose how you handle it."* My father's voice came back to me. *"Always hold yourself with honor. Especially in death."*

Andris lived by the same motto.

"N-n-no!" I shook my head, tears spilling down my face. "I can't lose you; don't you get that? It's why I brought you back. And I would do it again without question."

"You don't know how much I love you for it. You gave me time to say goodbye, even if I didn't realize it then."

"You are *not* saying goodbye."

A sad smile hinted at his mouth.

"I think we both know I am…" He lowered his head to mine. "You gave me such a gift, *drágám*. People don't realize *time* with those they love is the most meaningful thing in the world. No money or riches could ever match it. I should have been dead the night of Samhain. But your love, your magic, gave me another chance. Now, it is my turn to sacrifice for you."

A noise balled up my throat, my head shaking more.

"It's not something we can stop." He held the side of my face tighter, running his palm over my tresses. *"Please, let me go…"* His voice circled my ear, his eyes penetrating mine, his mouth closed.

A small gasp came from my mouth, his hand squeezing mine, his head dipping with acknowledgment of what was happening. The payment for saving his life. I had told him all about Warwick and Scorpion. He seemed to realize the bond that was there. What we shared.

"Look at me, my girl." He forced me to look at his features. "There is no question I'd give my life for yours. It's not even a choice."

"N-no." I sobbed, my head wagging.

"I love you so much. You are a daughter to me. I would do anything for you." He held me closer. "But I don't belong here. I don't want to be here without her… to live a life without Ling."

"But—"

He hushed me, his pitiful expression forcing a sob from my gut.

"The only thing I hate is what this will do to you and having to leave my people. But I know they will be in good hands. You are a natural-born leader, Brexley." His eyes pierced mine as if he was trying to convey more. "I wish it didn't have to be this way. I love you so much. But please know you are doing me a favor. I want this. I'm not meant for this world anymore." He tucked hair behind my ear. "All I can hope is I did enough with my time here, made enough difference. Now, it's for you to finish it."

"You can't do this to me," I howled. My fingers balled into his shirt. "You have to stay. I can't do this without you."

"You can, and you must." He bowed his head. "I hate all this falls on you, but it does. You are strong, caring, smart, and resilient. You are so similar to your father. He would be incredibly proud of you, Brexley, of the person you have become." Andris croaked out, tears sliding down his cheek. "And so am I. You have so many who love you and will fight by your side. I couldn't be prouder or love you any more if you were my own."

"Please…" My shoulders sagged, heavily under the weight of my grief.

"I never thought one day I would be in love with a fae and leading a rebel army. Sometimes the cause chooses us." He kissed my forehead before leaning back. "I do not regret a moment of my life. It all led me to what I was supposed to do. Finding my soulmate, my fight. And it eventually brought you back to me."

The boos and hisses were growing louder around us. Clanks from the gates tore my attention to the sentries stomping out, ready to pull us apart.

Panic flew up my throat. "*Nagybacsi.*" I cried as Joska ripped me away from my uncle while Samu grabbed Andris, hauling us closer to the fire.

"Istvan! Don't do this!" Andris tried to thrash against Samu, his petrified glance jumping from Markos to me. "Don't you have any soul left? You've known her since she was a baby."

"And she betrayed me." Istvan pointed at me in fury and disgust. "As you did. As her father did."

13

*What?* I craned my neck to look at Istvan. What was he talking about?

"You don't want to kill her, Istvan, I promise you." Andris shook his head wildly, glancing from me back to him, his tongue sliding over his lip. "She's *special*."

My limbs froze, my eyes widening as our gazes met again. I could feel it; Andris was going to tell him about me in hopes of saving my life.

If Istvan found out what I was, what power I contained, the entire game would be over. No one and nothing would survive.

I shook my head. *"No."* My shadow whispered to him.

*"I'm sorry."* His shade stood next to me. *"I have to. I won't let you die."* He cut the link, his attention going back to Markos. "You don't realize what she—"

"You're a worthless piece of shit, Istvan," I screamed, flailing against Joska, creating commotion to override whatever Andris was going to say. "You are a coward! A pathetic, weak man who can only get power by killing, cheating, or bribing people."

I knew how to strike his ego, knocking Andris's words into the air.

It worked too well.

"Enough!" Istvan yelled, ire streaking his cheeks. "Burn them both! Him first!" He ordered our guards.

"No!" I screamed, watching Joska tug Andris closer to the roaring flames. "Istvan, please!"

"I gave you your option, Brexley. You chose to not use it."

My insides drowned in acid and bile, my attention darting back to Andris and the stoic way he held his chin as they carried him toward the trench and flames.

Death came in many ways. Some so quick your brain didn't even register pain before you died. Most laid somewhere in the middle, where you suffered for a moment, but peace took you fairly quick. Then there was the slow, excruciating way, where torment ground through you so deep and piercing it would mark the earth forever, echoing your screams and pain for lifetimes to come.

Being burned alive was the latter.

My brain began to shut down again, reducing me to my most feral instincts.

I could feel Warwick's roar through the stadium, his energy eclipsing the chants and pitch of the crowd. I could sense him trying to get to me.

A phantom whisked in my peripheral, biting into my bones.

*"Use me, Kovacs!"*

I didn't think or question, my mind was primitive, zeroing in on one thing.

I let him in. Latching on like a leech, I pulled all of Warwick's energy into me. It wasn't even a quarter of what I got at the train station, but it was enough.

Slamming back into Joska, I jostled him and took him off balance, giving me a chance to lurch forward, twisting out of his hold. With a grunt, my arm swung out in a right hook, smashing into his throat. Choking and gasping, he fell back, clawing at his neck.

Whirling around, I sprinted for Samu, using the vigor Warwick pumped into my muscles. I dove into Samu, taking him to the ground, punching and kicking resembling a frenzied beast, as if killing him would release serenity through me like an endorphin.

Is this what Warwick meant when he said, *"nothing but killing made me feel anything."*

"Kovacs!" Joska's strangled voice hacked through the air, the memorable cock of a gun whipped my head around.

Joska stood next to Andris, his gun pressed to his temple.

"Get off Samu. Now." His eyes were wild, his stance reminding me more of a gorilla than a man.

My lip curled, slowly rising to my feet, my eyes on them. I could hear Samu choking and sputtering in his own blood. Unfortunately, I was sure he'd live, especially since he was on those new pills Istvan created.

"There's no way out of this." Joska seemed to struggle to form and speak his words. He pushed Andris closer to the fire. "You both are finally getting what you deserve."

It was only a second. A single moment. A smirk.

Joska shoved him into the ditch of flames, my uncle's clothes instantly ablaze. Andris's guttural screams shredded through every tiny molecule, ripping, tearing, and demolishing my heart and soul. He fought to climb out; the agony of his torture howled through me.

My legs moved without thought, the need to save him overtaking any logic.

Joska jumped out in front of me, stopping me.

I heard a crackle of lightning in the distance, matching my roar of fury. My instinct was to attack anything between me and the person I loved, like a mama bear. Yanking what was left of Warwick's energy, I went for Joska. As he swung to me, I ducked under his arm, popping up, my knuckles striking his temple with such force. He stumbled to the side, his head

15

dipping while my knee slammed up into his nose with a crack. Joska crashed into the dirt with a groan, blood leaking down his face.

Zipping past, I ran for my uncle, stopping short in a horrified gasp.

He had crawled out, but I no longer recognized the body lumped on the ground. His skin bubbled, oozed, and blackened, reminding me of what Warwick looked like on the battlefield the night I saved him.

"*Nagybacsi!*" I collapsed down next to him, sobs racking up my spine and back down again. The smell of burnt flesh making me dry heave.

He wheezed for air, his lids barely open.

"You will be okay. You can heal." I rocked next to him, no longer understanding what I was saying.

A louder wheeze came from him, and I realized he was trying to speak. "What?" I leaned in closer.

"Please…" He gasped. "I beg you."

A sob broke free when I realized he was begging me to kill him. "I can't."

His body was violently shaking, and I knew he was in so much agony. *"Please,"* his shade whispered next to me in agony. *"Do it."*

I peered back at the gun on the ground next to Joska, who was starting to regain consciousness. Swiping it up, I held the cool metal in my hand.

My head bowed as a cascade of tears trailed down my face, landing on my uncle's.

His disfigured and crisp hand reached up, touching my face. "Let me go. I need to be with her."

Hiccupping through my wails, I rose, my legs wobbling violently. My arms trembled as I lifted the gun.

Andris's eyes looked into mine, a plea… for me to end his suffering. *"I love you, drágám. Never forget that,"* he said through our link.

"I love you too. So much." The words barely made it out, cracking and breaking my heart.

*Bang!*

The bullet went right between his eyes, killing him instantly.

The gun dropped from my hands. A wretched cry tore from my chest, my shoulders sagging as I took in my uncle's dead, burnt face. I could see serenity in his expression, a slight smile on his lips as if he were finally at peace.

I was the opposite. Beyond any hell I could ever imagine. The grief was so acute, so excruciating, my brain could no longer compute anything else. His death wasn't just emotionally painful, but I could actually feel the bond we shared rip out of me, death's scythe cutting the connection.

I had just killed my uncle. Even if I was ending his pain and suffering, it didn't take away the notion his blood would forever stain my soul.

Whatever will I had left vanished from my body. Everything drained from me in a wave of grief. Curling into the dirt, a wrenched wail howled from me like a tempest.

Until I heard clapping behind me, I hadn't realized the arena had been silent.

Istvan's applause was slow and mocking, giving life to a deep wrath in my bones. "Well, my dear, deep down I knew you had it in you. I guess those years of training didn't go to waste."

I couldn't move or acknowledge anything around. I was empty.

Joska grabbed the gun next to me, and I almost begged him to take me out too. Because I knew the shock was only temporary. The calm before the storm. The numbness before the fall.

We all had ideas about who we were. What we think we would do and wouldn't do.

It was all crap.

Even to ourselves, we could be strangers. The moral ground you were so sure about became nothing but crumbled ethics and shattered beliefs in a single moment. A sturdy boat in the middle of the sea you were sure would never sink… until it did.

Hands grabbed me under the armpits, hauling me up to my feet. More guards had entered the pit, seizing me. My gaze found Istvan. His fiancée righteously peered down at me as if I deserved it all and more.

"You did what needed to be done." Istvan dipped his head at me as if he were prideful of my actions. "I'm pleased with you."

"Fuck you," I sneered, spit spraying from my mouth.

"Ah-uh," he tsked me. "Be careful. I am *allowing* you your incentives. Be grateful to me you get to live another day. Next time I might not be so generous."

The feel of the gun still echoed in my hand, and anger at myself for letting it go tightened my shoulders. If I had only pushed myself beyond my grief and thought about the man who made all this happen. He might not be standing here anymore.

I would never let that opportunity pass again.

"Next time, I might not be either," I replied evenly as the guards hauled me out of the arena.

Craning my head right before they pulled me into the tunnel, I glanced back at my uncle's body. It was empty now, his soul gone. I hoped wherever he was, he was with Ling.

I was just afraid that in sacrificing himself—no matter the reason—he took a vital piece of me with him.

My humanity.

Four guards towed me from the tunnel, their grips digging into my arms, dragging me up the stairs to the lavatory.

"Your lucky day, 839." One strolled closer, licking his lips, his eyes bright. "You earned a shower." He twitched abruptly, his tongue constantly flicking over his mouth. Something felt off about him, his mannerisms abnormal. It took me a moment to recognize it was Kristof. The guy who taunted Rosie. The one from the marketplace who almost caught me.

Two other officers ripped off my boots and socks before shoving me into the open running shower stall. The water soaked my soiled uniform, making it cling to my frame.

"Now strip—slowly," Kristof sneered. The other three cackled, moving closer to me, their voices and movements reminding me of a clan of spotted hyenas getting riled up. "Last shower time with you, me and my friend here didn't get to participate." He motioned to a lean, blond soldier on his right. By his statement, I took it they had brought me up from the hole. When I came out, I had no understanding of anything around me, including myself. They were all just faceless figures. "We can't look as if we don't take our job seriously enough."

The four of them inched nearer to me, circling like predators around their victim.

"Think it's about time I get a taste of the so-called princess of Leopold." Kristof mocked. "The girl who could ensnare noble men and leaders with her beauty."

Why did people think just because men were noble or leaders, they weren't just as infallible as every man with a dick? I found their egos and entitlement made them more so. Weaker to praise and admiration.

"Yeah, I know you. Heard about the stunning and perfect Brexley Kovacs for years now." He smirked at me. "Look at you now. Pathetic piece of fae-loving trash." He snarled at me. "Your fae friends shot my buddy. Think you need to be punished for it." Kristof's shoulders rolled, hostility perfumed off him in waves, affecting the three around him like a drug. "Though we all did get promoted and treated as heroes for protecting the market." He waved around to the group, and I realized all of them had been at the market that night. "Now we get to watch *puncik* get wet every day."

Knowing Istvan as I did, he wouldn't promote any of these lazy shit-dicks because of the market. They were being used as test subjects, knowing or unknowing. To Markos, they were discardable. Easily humored with a pat on the back while he was the one fucking them over.

"Strip!" Kristof yanked his baton from his belt. "And face us while doing it." His eyes ran down my figure, the men around him stirring and making wild, shrill sounds.

Men in groups fueled by testosterone could be terrifying enough in situations, but the way they looked at me, the way they moved, their energy bouncing off each other, building, raked terror down into my bones. They weren't right, as if the pills were creating a chemical imbalance or something in the fae essence was turning them feral.

Unhinged.

"Now!" Kristof ordered, already rubbing at his crotch.

I peered down at the blood, dirt, and charred streaks smeared across my wet gray uniform. Flecks of ashes from my uncle's burnt skin stuck to my top like confetti of death.

"Fucking, spoiled bitch! When I order you, you do as I say." Kristof swung his baton, stomping for me.

Tonight, I stabbed a comrade in the chest with a hairpin, watching her suffocate on her own blood, oxygen leaking out like a balloon. Knocked out one of my best friends to keep him alive, almost died at the hands of another. And then witnessed my uncle being burned alive before shooting him in the head. The remains of him are still on me, on all of them, staining deeper than the fabric.

Now, these little boys were trying to take what was left of me.

Water dripping off my lashes, I lifted my onyx eyes to Kristof. The lava roiling deep in my gut bubbled and spat. I could feel nothing inside me but hate, rage, revenge, and empty darkness which could never be filled. They could do nothing to me. I was already too far gone.

And when you have nothing inside, other lives become insignificant.

The four came at me, their frenzy feeding off their arrogance and ego. Not one of them believed, even after seeing me kill, I could possibly take them down.

Men never understood a woman's strength, the carnage which would paint the world when she broke. I had no more fucks to give. No more fear, pain, or grief.

Once again, my brain stepped out of my body, my ingrained training taking over, striking out first. A loud crack clapped off the tile walls as my fist struck Kristof's nose. My mind centered to such a point nothing existed outside of my movements, each one exact and lethal.

I didn't want to walk the shadows of death. I wanted to *be* it.

*The Grey.*

Cold. Meticulous. Precise.

Kick. Punch. Hit.

Swing. Duck. Strike.

They ripped at my clothes, struck at my face, my body, their shrieks and howls of anger growing louder, bouncing off the tile.

One of them grabbed at my breasts, his hand trying to slide down my pants.

The fire inside roared with a vehemence.

I tasted their blood which sprayed over my face, felt their skin split across my knuckles, heard the crunch of bones, and watched each one crumble to the floor. The sharp smell of blood and bleach stung my nostrils, my breath heaving loudly in my ears.

Staring blankly at the four men sprawled across the bathroom, red liquid trickled past my bare feet, trailing to the drain. They were alive— though they wouldn't be getting up for a while.

I wanted them dead, to feel their lives expire, their pulses weakening against my palm.

"Kovacs?" I heard my name, trying to tug me back to myself. I didn't want to go. I wanted to stay where I was. Where there was no emotion. No conscious. No pain.

Let the darkness consume me.

*"Brexley..."* The power of my name curled and wound through me. His dominance forced my head to lift, my gaze landing on him.

The *Legend.* The *Wolf.*

Like the first time he found me in the bathroom at Halálház, Warwick stood inside the doorway, bloody and bruised, his knuckles cut open, looking as if he had fought his way to get to me. The string of unconscious or dead soldiers trailed a path to us, and it was only a matter of time before they came for us.

His aqua irises penetrated my barriers. Thick and corded, he dripped with feral virility. His power and strength dominated the room, soaking up the air, peeling away my skin and bones, finding the tiny bit of my soul still left inside.

His shoulders rolled back, his focus on me, ready for battle.

Except this wasn't a battle of fists.

I saved his life, dragged him from the abyss, forced him to breathe, taste life, and see color.

He came for payback.

# Chapter 3

"Fuck. You know how to make me hard, Kovacs."

Warwick's attention drifted over the unconscious, beaten bodies on the ground. A low growl vibrated in the air as he turned his focus onto me, shocking emotion through my entire body. You were never prepared for Warwick, and the ruthless way he seized and engulfed you, giving you no choice but to bow to your own downfall.

And my demise was my emotions, the burden of my actions, seeing the faces of my victims. Two lives were ended tonight by my hand. One I sacrificed to live, and one who sacrificed for me to live.

The image of my uncle engulfed me in so much agony, it felt as if our link was being seared off, and I had to carve out a bit of myself, dumping it on the dirt like pumpkin guts. I couldn't breathe, wanting nothing more than to claw my way out of my hell. My lungs clenched, suffocating me.

"Warwick." His name barely made it out, splitting between a plea and a warning.

"What do you need, princess?" His tone was direct, telling me he would be whatever I needed to help me survive the moment. A rock for me to hold on to or one I beat myself against.

"I need you. Make me forget." I whispered hoarsely, not able to stand one more second in my grief. "I can't breathe."

His eyes darkened, the intensity drilling into me. Lust. Passion.

Violence. It was alive, weaving and threading through the air between us. I don't know how I ignored it before. How I thought it could be my imagination. The connection was subtle, but it was there, pulsing and needy, returning so gradually it was hard to recognize.

The ghost of his tongue licked between my thighs, causing a gasp to catch in my chest, snapping the last wall of my defense.

And his.

We moved for each other like prey. Our mouths and bodies collided in a turbulent storm of desperation, where our battle would leave everything around us in shambles. Sensing it was the last thing I wanted, he wasn't gentle, his mouth claiming mine with ferocity, dragging me kicking and screaming from the abyss. Tearing the numbness from my body, pouring frantic emotion into my veins.

The need to taste him, feel him inside and out, dominate and rule with a primal instinct.

Growling, Warwick seized my ass, easily lifting me up, my legs wrapping around his waist as he slammed me back into the tile, the water cascading down over us.

Anger. Grief. Devastation. I was broken into pieces, losing myself to the pain.

He drove need through my soul, flaying me open and exposing me. The unemotional shield I found myself in was stripped by his hungry lips, his ruthless hands. He ripped my top and sports bra over my head, the fabric slapping to the ground. His starving gaze tracked over my breasts, the bruises, cuts, and scars which marked my skin like tattoos.

His tongue flicked over my nipple before his mouth covered my breast, sucking and nipping. My spine arched, my core throbbing, as I felt the light brushes of his presence gliding over my skin.

His mouth claimed mine again, creating more urgency.

It wasn't a want—it was a necessity.

The ground under my feet was sliding away, and he was my one tether to life. The only way out of the void. My survival. My escape.

Tearing his shirt from him, I groaned as my hands moved down his ripped torso, shoving his pants down, my hand wrapping around his girth while inside my mind, my tongue licked up his shaft. It was faint, but I could feel the throb of his cock, tracing the vein, tasting the pre-cum on my tongue.

"Fuck." His cock twitched and hardened to my imaginary touch. Warwick sucked in with a grunt, eyes meeting mine with intensity. He felt it. Knew what it meant.

His nose flared. Something in him snapped. I could feel it—a chain breaking.

The man was gone; it was only the wolf. The legend who would annihilate and pillage.

He dropped me back to the ground, kicking off his boots, and yanking down his pants. His thick cock and unbelievable physique had me touching myself, my shadow sucking his dick as I watched him undress.

A noise came from him before he shredded the pants and underwear from my body, his huge palms lifting me back up again under the stream of pelting water. His wet naked skin rubbed against mine.

There were no words needed. We needed carnage. Blood. Pain.

Clawing and scratching at his skin, he didn't give me any warning. He thrust into me, so deep and hard both of us bellowed out, overcome by a zap of electricity running down our nerves.

The temperate water cascaded down over our hot skin as he pulled almost all the way out, driving back in so forcefully, he pinned my lower back to the wall.

"Oh, fuck!" I screamed, losing all ability for logic. I needed more. Tightening my legs, I tipped back, feeling him sink in deeper, his rhythm picking up.

The hint of his mouth on my breast, up the back of my neck, between my thighs, teasing my ass. It only made me more feral, tearing into his flesh like it was my meal.

He pounded into me, his hands running through my hair, clutching the back of my scalp, holding me to reach even deeper. "I can't seem to get close enough. To be deep enough. I want to destroy you, claim every last bit of you."

"Do it!" I grunted, riding him harder. The need to crawl inside him, to feel him take me over, to end my sorrow. The sensations he was driving through me were worse than any drug. I knew I would crash and burn, and the fall would break me into pieces, but I couldn't stop the desperate need for him to completely consume me.

Grief, anger, fear—I took it out on him, demanding punishment, requiring cruelty. I was my own judge and jury, and I needed him to be my executioner.

He grabbed my arms, forcing them to grip the shower head above me, stretching and curving my torso as his hand clasped around my neck, squeezing just enough my nerves danced with elation, turning the sensation even higher. The hints of an orgasm squeezed my pussy around him. The wolf roared, letting him completely free.

Savagely, he plunged into me over and over. Merciless and brutal. My eyes watered at the exquisite pain. The sounds of his dick thrusting into me, slapping and wet, mingled with our groans bouncing off the walls.

The deep guttural noises coming from me only increased his frenzy, spurring him on to choke me harder. His other hand tugged roughly at my hair as I felt teeth nip down on my core.

*"Sotet démonom."*

I screamed. My climax hit me so hard, my vision went black.

Lightning zapped, energy crackling the air.

I had a vision of us fucking on the battlefield, surrounded by the smell of blood, dirt, and death. We strolled across a field together, side by side, covered in gore, dead bodies strewn around us. Cries of war rang around us while we were still under the spray of the shower. It was brief but vivid in color and detail.

"Fuuuuccckk!" I heard him roar, his hot cum spurting inside me, carving his signature even deeper into my bones, waking something deep within me. This time I could feel the tentacles that linked us wrapping and coiling around me, knitting us back together as he filled me.

*"Life connects you, but death binds you."*

It took us several minutes to come back to ourselves, the thrumming of his energy around me growing stronger. Not quite where it was before, but there was no denying it now—our connection was back.

Slowly, I lifted my lashes and found him staring at me, both of us heaving and gasping. His expression was unreadable, but I could sense the emotion underneath. To my shock, it wasn't resentment or anger.

It was relief.

Serenity.

He watched me for another beat, as if he was making sure the bond was really there again, before he grabbed my face, kissing me so deeply and passionately, he shredded through any strength I had left.

Pulling out of me, he lowered me onto my shaky legs. The sensation of him leaving my body made me gasp for air. As if he were my barrier, my wall of defense, his body my shield from the pain. The moment he slipped out, the pain and agony attacked.

Pictures of my uncle, stretching from when I was a small child to seeing his scorched face, flashed in my head. The lost connection was excruciating. His raw voice and pleading eyes begging me to end his life punched me in the gut. Without me coming back into his life, he and Ling would still be alive. Happy. Together.

The grief hit me like a train, knocking the oxygen from my lungs. A howl struck my heart, emotion clobbering me under its force. Warwick didn't speak, only drew me to his warm chest, his arms engulfing me, keeping me on my feet. My frame shook with sobs, sinking beneath the guilt and anguish.

Losing Andris was losing my father all over again. I may have found a blood uncle and a mother, but they were practically strangers to me. Andris was my family. He'd been there on my birthdays, every holiday, even when I lost my first tooth. He played games with me and bandaged me when I got hurt. My dad, Andris, and Rita were my security growing up. Those I trusted and turned to.

Now they were *all* gone.

Being buried alive under the weight, my sobs turned to violent wails. The pain seemed never-ending.

"Use me." Warwick's deep voice stroked my ear. "Don't let the darkness take you from me." He brushed my tangled, wet hair from my face, his mouth grazing my neck as water sprayed down on us. "Use me, Kovacs. Feed off me… take whatever you need to get through this."

I understood what he was telling me. Giving me permission to latch on to his power, ease my pain, absorb his strength similar to a vampire. Whatever it took for me to breathe. To get through the crushing agony.

A better person might say no. A stronger person would want to do it on their own, but I was neither. I was twisted and fucked up as he said I was. And similar to a junkie being offered a hit, I was too desperate to turn down the notion of feeling numb again, especially when the other option seemed like endless pain, anguish, and darkness.

Going off instinct, I let my soul dive into him. I could feel for a moment he wanted to wall up against the intrusion, but he took a deep breath, allowing me fully in. The intimacy that twisted between us was excruciating discomfort and unbelievable desire. It pulsed every nerve, made both of us groan as another climax built up.

Erotic. Forbidden.

I took. I became gluttonous with need, the lightness of my heart, my soul. Insatiable to the ease of my grief. Voracious in absorbing his strength.

"Brexley, stop." He growled in my ear, his hands landing on the wall by my head as if he needed a little help to stand.

I couldn't stop. I was rabid. Insatiable no matter how much I took.

"Enough!" He shoved me back into the wall; my lids burst open. He watched me as the high evened out. I still felt heartache, but it was distant, livable. My physical pain was gone entirely.

I felt no guilt for wanting more.

A smirk hitched the side of his mouth, his legs a little unsteady. "Fuck, princess. You have a ravenous appetite."

"I do." I didn't wait for his response as I dropped to my knees. There was no foreplay. I wrapped my tongue around him, sucking him as far back as I could into my mouth. His size made my eyes sting.

"Fucking hell!" He hissed, one hand staying on the wall, the other threading through my locks, pushing farther down my throat. His erection hardened and grew, choking me.

Wetness dripped from me as his fingers dug into my head, my fingers curling around his ass, pushing in. My shade curled around him, licking down his back, taking his balls into my imaginary mouth.

"Fuck! Fuck!" His eyes rolled back. The total power I wielded over him hardened my nipples, lighting my skin on fire.

He quickly flipped it on me. The feel of his tongue slipped inside my pussy, making me groan loudly around him.

Grabbing my head, he tugged it back, yanking me up to my feet.

"I wasn't done." I frowned.

"Neither am I." He flipped me around, pushing my breasts into the cool tiles as he parted my legs. I was so ready, and he slid inside, his girth hitting every nerve ending, causing me to fist and claw at the tile, my head spinning. "Gods, I missed this. Missed you." He rumbled in my ear, thrusting in again. "I never want to stop being inside you. Whether with my cock or whatever this connection is between us. Don't ever cut it off again." His pace was steady and deep, making sure I felt every inch of him, striking me with electricity with every thrust. "You're mine, *sotet démonom.* Forever."

Every time he called me that, desire sprung on me like a beast.

"And here I thought you didn't believe in marriage," I verbally poked.

"I don't." He hoarsely grunted in my ear. "Who said anything about marriage? With fae, mates go way deeper."

"So, you think I'm your mate?" I groaned, our bodies moving together.

He balled up my hair in his fist, pulling it back as he rammed in deeper. Grabbing the soap, he lathered it, rubbing it through my tresses and over my body, cleaning the blood and dirt from me as he steadily fucked the hell out of me. His rough hands slid over my nipples, gliding through my folds.

"Think we go way past *mates*." He growled against the back of my neck, going harder. His hands kneaded at my breasts. The feel of his fingers rolled over my clit as a tongue slipped between my ass cheeks.

27

My voice rose so loud he crushed his mouth to mine to keep my cries muted.

*"Harder! Fuck me until I can't breathe! Until I am nothing but particles."* My shade nipped at his ear, biting down on the curve of his neck.

He pumped into me, pushing my bones against the wall with a bruising force, moving me up and down the wall.

He unleashed. Pounding ruthlessly into me, where I felt nothing but him. Bringing me back to life and destroying me at the same time.

Life and death.

"Warwick!" With a blackout roar, we both came together. His cum filled me so much, it spilled down my leg.

Lights flickered, and I felt the links of our bond cinch into an unbreakable knot, exploding my orgasm through me like fireworks.

Deep inside me, fire and power came roaring to the surface. For a moment, I could see the nectar, glowing steadily, then it suddenly flared with power, singeing the edges of the box it was in as though it felt the energy coming from Warwick and me. Our connection filling it with life.

My senses were flooded with the magic I experienced the night at the castle. I could taste and feel it again. The name I'd heard called to me, but slipped from my conscious, came crawling from the depths.

Warwick fucked me in color, but he just unleashed…

*The Grey.*

The name hummed in my veins, a power I didn't even realize yet somewhere inside me, but this place kept it dampened. Quiet.

For now.

The fae formula the human guards were on was able to slip past the spells blocking this prison of fae magic. Warwick and I seemed to be another loophole. From Halálház to Věrhăza, the spells in the prisons couldn't seem to prevent our connection. Though this time I could feel the wards trying. Killian put thicker enchantments on this place. Like a weighted blanket trying to hinder our mobility, the spells couldn't entirely eclipse the power between us. I had this rooted feeling nothing could.

Pulling on a fresh uniform left out on the table for me, my limbs quaked severely from the aftershocks of Warwick, of the intense surge of power knotting us together. The peak of my high was starting to slide down the mountain. My grief was distant, though I knew it wouldn't stay there, the pain slipping steadily toward a tar pit of darkness. For this moment, I was thankful it was dulled down.

Thoughts and ideas rolled around my head, and by Warwick's silence, I knew the same were going through his. He was guarded, trying to put up a barrier, but I could still feel him, and if I pushed hard enough, I could break in. Like he could do the same to me.

We would have to lay down some rules later, but right now wasn't the moment. With four guards laying at our feet, one starting to stir, our time was limited.

"It's back." I twisted my long, wet hair over my shoulder, squeezing out the water.

Warwick huffed. *"No shit, princess."* His voice growled into the back of my neck as he stood in front of me.

I sucked in a breath, my lashes fluttering. How much I had missed that. The intimacy was profoundly sensual and comforting. His shade bumped into the back of me as the real man stepped closer, sandwiching me in between the two.

He was redressed, but my gaze wandered over him, wondering how easily we both could be naked again. My body warmed with the fantasy of both him and his phantom inside me.

Warwick smirked, sensing my thoughts. *"Dirty girl."* His spirit nipped at my ear. *"You want a threesome, Kovacs? To fuck both of me at once?"* The actual man stood over me silently, predatory. We had done glimpses of it, touches, licks, and bites from our shadows at the same time, but never solidly both. And Warwick's other self was almost as real to me.

A moan from a few feet away broke me out of our haze, where our hunger for the other seemed to take away all rational thought. The guards started waking up. We had nowhere to go or run. It was a matter of minutes before I'd have to face what I did.

"The nectar." I jumped back on topic, a rush of terror bleeding through the euphoria. "It's back as well."

Warwick's demeanor shifted in an instant, his jaw clenching, head dipping. "I know. I saw it too."

"If it's found…" I swallowed. I had no idea where it was, if it had been dumped, picked up by scavengers.

"Istvan can use it," he muttered.

To be both happy and terrified over our connection returning pitted a war inside me.

29

"I think it's been slowly coming back to life since—"

"We fucked at Kitty's," he replied bluntly.

It was the first time we had been intimate since I burned through the nectar. We brought it back; our connection balanced and strengthened it. And it seemed to get stronger each time we were together.

Guilt over finding pleasure just after killing my uncle and taking Zuz's life dropped the high I was on to the floor. Despair gurgled up my throat, and emotion started to pour in.

"Stop." He stepped up to me. I gulped back the sob wanting to take over, fighting back the emotions that were becoming louder. He didn't ease them, and I didn't ask. "Hating yourself is an insult to him. To all of them. Andris wouldn't want that. You gave him time. Most humans don't seem to cherish it even though they have just a blink of it in the scheme of things. Appreciate the extra time you got with him. Don't let your ego get in the way, Kovacs. Don't make this about you and *your* guilt."

My first instinct was to lash out, to tell him to fuck off, but deep down, I knew he was right. My uncle could have died a month ago, under the rubble, but he lived, had more time with his family, with me, and with Ling.

A guard groaned from the floor, drawing us to him. He reached for something on his belt, a type of walkie-talkie. "Help! Level 5 latrine," he gurgled and hissed into it. "Code one!"

Warwick's boot slammed into his head, knocking away the device and the man out cold again.

But it was too late.

Commotion echoed from a distance. They were coming.

*Fuck. Fuck. Fuck.*

Anxiety funneled into my bloodstream, adding to growing panic, skirting me closer to the edge. Instinct always made you want to run, but there was nowhere to go here. After what I'd done, I knew where it would lead me, which speared my panic higher with thoughts of the hole. I was strong, but I didn't know if I could make it through again without bending completely to Istvan.

"Hey." Rough hands grabbed my face, forcing me to look solely at him. "Look at me. Whatever happens, we make it through, right?" He gripped me harder. "We fight."

My nostrils burned with unshed tears, the hollers growing louder.

"No matter what." He gritted through his teeth at me. "Right?"

Nodding, my voice cracked. "What are we going to do? What if someone finds it? I know Caden is out searching for it. What if he does and hands it to Istvan?" We were screwed.

"We do the only thing we can. We take it back."

"How do we do that?"

"We find a way out of here and kill everything standing in our way."

The pounding of feet and yells jerked my head to the doorway. A group of soldiers led by Boyd came through the large doorway, their gazes going from the guards strewn on the ground to us.

"About time you boys showed up. I was getting bored. They broke way too easily." Warwick stepped away from me, putting up his arms as if he were the one who attacked the sentries.

Oh shit...

"Seize them!" Boyd pointed at us. Men with batons, guns, and whips surged for us.

Warwick's focus stayed intently on me.

"No." Fear tumbled down into my stomach at the realization of what he was doing.

He winked, a glint of mischievousness in his eyes, right as he whirled around on the few soldiers grabbing for him. The crack of his fist splintered across one's face. His quickness and skill punched about five of them before their clubs reached him, dropping Warwick to his knees with the spiked batons.

"No! Stop!" I pitched forward, but a handful of sentries seized me, their faux-fae power holding me in place as I thrashed and fought to reach Warwick.

They continued to dice and chop into his skin, kicking and beating him until his face and limbs were bloody.

"Please!" I begged.

The moment Boyd approached, they all backed off, letting their leader move in.

"If you wanted back in the hole so bad, you should have asked me." Boyd leaned over Warwick, smiling creepily. "Need to get away from the missus that bad, huh? And here I thought she had a magical pussy, able to get so many of you to trail after her like schoolboys." Boyd glanced back, leering at me. "I didn't get a full taste last time. Maybe I should sample it again."

*"Warwick, no!"* I cried through our link. Boyd was purposely poking the beast. And it worked.

Warwick pitched up, his head slamming so hard into Boyd's, the guard went sailing back, smacking the tile floor with a thud, as The Wolf spat and growled, climbing to his feet. Warwick parted his bloody lips, his saliva tainted red, sneering and moving for Boyd.

*"Warwick, stop!"* My shade touched his chest, trying to get his attention. He peered down at me, heaving in and out.

"Take him to the hole," Boyd screeched, wobbly on his feet, touching the blood dripping from his head. "You will rot in there, Farkas."

Without fighting, Warwick let the guards cuff him and start herding him for the door. It was what he wanted in the first place. For him to take the blame, not me.

*"Warwick!"* I cried out, though my mouth didn't move.

He didn't respond. His gaze latched onto mine, the feel of his mouth claiming mine hungrily, his fingers digging into my skin before his body was dragged from the room, shutting down the link between us.

Again, I knew if I pushed, I could break in, but before I could even contemplate it, Boyd was in my face. I tightened my shoulders, my jaw crunching together. The fresh wound on his forehead still leaked out blood as he patted it with a handkerchief.

"You have been nothing but a pain in my ass since the day you entered Halálház." His disgust curled his lip up. "Farkas never caused a problem until you arrived. Even my lord changed when he took you in. You corrupt men's minds, distort their beliefs, warp them. And now look, they are all either in prison or dead."

"How easily you flipped on *your lord* for a pocket full of coins." I sneered back. "Talk about warped beliefs. You are now working for a human."

He stepped closer, his lip hitching higher, voice dropping so only I could hear. "Let them do all the work, set the stage for us, then we come in to take it all."

"Why not just take it back now?"

"Because what they are going for, we want as well. A complete takeover. Humans think themselves so much smarter." Boyd's attention flashed to the four soldiers being helped up by other human guards. He watched with a smirk on his face, clearly not bothered about them being attacked. "We are predators. We lie in wait until our victims willingly step into our mouths. This fight has just begun." Abruptly, he moved away from me. "Get this bitch out of my sight. Take her to her cell."

My mind still wheeled with his claim as officers dragged me back to my cell, tossing me roughly inside and slamming the door.

While one game was playing in the arena, another one was being played outside these walls, and it would be far more brutal and complex than I'd first thought.

With the nectar back on the board, a deadly game of chess was now being played, and the stakes were everything.

Tonight, I would let myself cry and wallow for Andris, but tomorrow, I would shove my heartache away and focus. We had to learn everything we could from every soldier here, gossip from the outside, their routines, weaknesses, their loyalty.

Not only was our country on the precipice, but so was the world... and there were only a few of us who could stop it from falling.

## Chapter 4

"No, he didn't seem to enjoy waking up to you sucking on his fingers."

*Chirp!*

A groan hummed in my throat as their voices pierced into my head, stirring me from a shallow sleep.

"Nor did he like you licking his ears."

*Chirp!*

"It wasn't me!" I could feel Opie's foot stomp into my leg, my dried salty lashes parting fully.

*Chirp! Chirp!* Bitzy chewed him out from the pack on his back.

"I didn't nibble them either." Opie huffed. "Total misunderstanding."

This morning their outfits were faded beige cotton, and judging by the identical fabric I had in my bathroom locker, someone was missing a towel this morning. Opie had designed it into a one-piece with strategic shapes cut out, leaving very little to the imagination, and a snake puppet with inked-in eyes and teeth covered his crotch. His hair was loose with thin braids at the front plaited in with his beard. Bitzy had snake puppets over her ears, her face twisted in irritation, her fingers flipping the world off.

"Should I even ask?" I rubbed my eyes.

"Do you like it? Needed a little whimsical fun today." Opie twirled, showing me the thong back. "I mean, the color is so drab, so I wanted to make it fun. When I walk—look—the snake bobs and weaves."

34

I groaned, rubbing my eyes harder as he pranced up and down my leg, showing me what he meant. "Not that I wasn't scarred enough, but it's not what I meant."

*Chirp!*

Opie rolled his eyes. "Stop putting this on me. You were the one who wanted to see him."

"Who?"

"The pretty one with the mushrooms."

"Ash?" I sat up quickly, making Opie stumble.

"Yeah." Opie centered himself on my thigh, his palms up. "Let me warn you, contrary to the noises he makes before waking up, he does *not* want his fingers, toes, or ears being sucked on."

"And why were either of you sucking on them?"

"I wasn't. She was!" Opie pointed at Bitzy.

*Chirp, chirp!* Bitzy motioned her middle fingers back at Opie.

"Leave Ash alone," I scoffed.

"Wasn't me!"

*Chirrrrrrp!*

"It wasn't either of us. I was *just saying*, with no reason at all, there is a good possibility he doesn't like it so much."

*Chirp!*

"Right, he didn't mind it when he was asleep." Opie nodded to Bitz. "But again, I have no real reason or reference to saying this. Just an arbitrary passing thought."

"Why were you there?"

"Oh, no reason." Opie and Bitzy blinked at me innocently.

Probably hoping Ash still had remnants of mushroom on him. I wanted to believe it was because they cared about him also. They were checking in on our twisted, crazy family.

"He's okay?"

"His vocabulary is in serious question. The names he called her? Wow." Opie thumbed over his shoulder, shaking his head.

*Chirp-chirp. Chirp, chirp-chirp! Chirp!* Middle fingers flared through the air. Bitzy sounded as if she were spitting out every curse word under the sun.

Opie's eyes went wide. "See? She shouldn't hear such things—so impressionable at this age."

I snorted. Bitzy was probably dozens of centuries old.

"But yes, Blondie is fine. Before he so rudely told us to vacation in a warm place, he asked if you and the big man were okay. Where is the walking grenade launcher, anyway?"

My shoulders sagged, my thoughts going to Warwick. I could still feel the remnants of him inside me, causing my body to crave more. I tried to reach out to him several times, but he was able to keep me back as if he didn't want me to see him in pain. The moment he slipped, I would push through his barriers, taking on his agony, numbing it enough to keep him together.

It was how we made it out before. I thought he was a hallucination, but our link had bled through last time. We had helped each other survive, and I wouldn't abandon him now. Or ever.

Last night he won the battle only because the drop of adrenaline, the dissipating of my numbness, crashed me to earth, tearing through, making me almost immobile. More pieces broke off, falling into the boiling pit in my soul. My howls of misery were drowned out last night by so many others who were grief-stricken.

I wasn't the only one who lost a father figure and idol. Andris was a patriarch, a leader, a friend to thousands of fae in the resistance. Their voice, their purpose. I couldn't be greedy in my suffering; many had shared my anguish last night, though I would always be the one who had pulled the trigger.

They also lost a friend and comrade. Zuz and I may not have been close, but she was to many at Sarkis's base. And again, most would always look at me as her murderer, no matter how much they said they understood.

"Master Fishy?" Opie spoke quietly, pulling me from my thoughts. Sniffing, I wiped at the renegade tear. It would be my last to be seen in the daylight.

I could have fallen apart, could have let Istvan break me, but in forcing my hand, he cut off another idyllic part of me—the part that wishes for someone to find them, that cries for others to help, to have pity.

That shit was just fairytales.

I understood Warwick even more than ever. The people you chose to be part of your family you protected by destroying and slaughtering the world to keep them alive. I had brought many people into my circle, and I would do anything to keep them safe.

*"Find a way out of here and kill everything standing in our way."*

A plan started to form in my head. Getting out of here was the first step, and I needed everyone to help, especially Killian. Time was of the essence, and it wouldn't be long before Istvan had him in the pit fighting to the death. The problem was, it was almost impossible for us to communicate.

My gaze went down to Opie.

"Uh-oh… your look worries me, Fishy."

"I think you would look terrific in a messenger's outfit." I tapped at my lip.

"Hell, yeah I would…" He paused, tipping his head, his head wagging, taking in my intention. "No. N-O. No."

"No?"

"Do you know what happens to the messenger?" He tossed out his arms. "They get killed, whacked, murdered, stabbed, shot, executed, beheaded, and chopped into little pieces every time. They are nothing more than a sacrificial lamb. So, no! No matter what, I won't do it. Absolutely one hundred percent—NO!"

"But you can wear a cute little hat and short-shorts."

His shoulders deflated. "Dammit, I can never say no to short-shorts."

"Luv!" Rosie greeted me the moment I entered the bathroom, her arms hugging me tightly. "I am so sorry…" Rosie was tough as nails, but she was also very empathetic. It probably was the actress in her, used to exploring a range of characters, emotions, and actions and taking them on as her own.

I was taught to never show my hand. To always hide the weakness of feelings. After all she'd been through, Rosie was so much stronger than all those men who hid behind their stoic walls, pretending to be tough and powerful.

"Thanks." I stepped back, my gaze jumping around to the guards along the walls, then spotting Lucas, Birdie, and Wesley. As Lucas came for me, Wesley and Birdie stayed in their spot.

I fought back the wave of guilt.

The absence of Zuz in this morning's group wailed through the room. She would never be again, and I could feel their reproach, their confusion of being happy I was alive but resentful I took not only their friend but also their leader from them. Even if they understood I had no choice, feelings didn't care about facts.

"Brex." Lucas hugged me tightly. He didn't bother to say sorry or anything else. No words could soothe what had happened.

It was brief, but I hugged him back, allowing him to chip at the burden I carried. Pulling back, I squeezed his hand, glancing over at Birdie and Wesley, forcing myself to move to them. My steps were solid, my chin high when I stopped before them.

"There is nothing I can say except I am sorry." I peered between them.

Wesley's head dropped, shuffling his feet. "I know."

"Let's be honest, Zuz was a real bitch, but she was our bitch." Birdie was solemn, but like me, didn't show any real emotion. "And Andris was more than a leader. He was our family."

My throat tightened.

"I know you get that more than anyone. I can't imagine being in your shoes. You did what you had to do... we understand." She motioned between her and Wesley. "Doesn't make everything okay right now."

My lips pursed. I got it. I really did, but...

"Too bad," I replied coolly. Both reacted in shock to my words. "We don't have the luxury of time, catering to personal grievance in here. If you thought it was brutal out in the Savage Lands, then just wait when you get put in the hole or are whipped beyond any limit your mind can take. When you are the one in the Games, fighting for your life..." I folded my arms. "It comes down to life and death. Time or emotions are privileges we don't get. Our only way to survive is to come together and fight."

"You talking mutiny?" Wesley's eyebrow lifted.

"Yes." I nodded. "But first, we need to find a way out of here. To know we *can* escape this place when that moment comes. Plus, we need to decipher who is on our side and who would turn us in. Just one turncoat will destroy everything."

"Who'd want to stay here?" Rosie huffed.

"You'd be surprised how many will go against their own best interests to become the inside snitch, thinking they'll be rewarded."

"Okay." Birdie dipped her head, fully turning to me. "What do we do?"

"Learn everything you can about every guard, every door they go in and out of, any loyalty they might have, especially the fae guards. Get them to talk, to slip any useful information. And tell others to do the same and get the information back to me."

"I see people lagging in the middle," a guard yelled out to us. "This isn't social hour."

"What if we can't?" Birdie whispered, all of us looking like we were moving away from each other. "We barely get a moment to talk to each other."

38

"Let me say, please don't kill the tiny messenger in short-shorts."

"Huh?" Lukas shot at me.

"I said move it," the same sentry bellowed out to us.

"If a brownie comes to your cell with a pissed-off looking imp… they're not there to clean," I said before dispersing, doing my business quickly.

A coup would only happen if we did this right. Killian would know the most about this place, but he didn't know all the guards nor what Istvan might have done to it since the takeover. We had one shot, and we had to be smart about it.

We were shuffled through to the mess hall. A lot of eyes on me, a similar response to when I won the first time in Halálház. Awed, angry, scared, and uneasy that a human won. This time, though, there were a lot more who struggled with anger and sorrow. Andris was a big hit for many. A light going out in the rebel fight.

I couldn't show any weakness, any nicks in my walls, even if I was a burning hot mess inside.

Settling down on the bench, my gaze caught Nora's red-streaked eyes from the table over. Next to her was Hanna.

Hanna and I stared at each other as strangers, though I remembered when she threw up Pálinka on her mother's favorite rug after the first time we got drunk with the boys and stumbled back to her apartment. We scrubbed and scrubbed the stain, but it never fully came out. We blamed it on their cat.

In all my grief, I had forgotten they had lost a father and husband last night.

But Andris's sacrifice saved Hanna and Nora's life.

"Before we start your yummy breakfast," Zion's voice took my focus away from them to the doorway. He strolled into the room, escorting a new prisoner dressed in gray. "Let me introduce you to the new fishy in the schoolyard."

Disbelief stilled my body. I blinked, making sure I wasn't hallucinating.

A sharp, guttural noise pulled my focus to Lukas across the room. He jerked as if he'd been electrocuted, his eyes wide with shock on the new prisoner. Sensing me, Lukas's gaze snapped from me to Kek, like he was making sure we also saw the same person.

A person who should be dead. We had all watched his execution.

"What the fuck?" I muttered to myself, my mouth parting as he was pushed toward the human section, his eyes meeting mine.

39

Tracker.

Was alive.

"Watch and learn, fishy, or your first day might be your last." Zion shoved him onto a bench across from mine. Tracker's lip lifted in anger, the alpha in him wanting to retaliate. He sat down, and slowly his emotionless gaze found mine again while my shock and bewilderment cracked and fizzed.

How was this possible? Where had he been this whole time? How did he survive?

The night we left him at the bridge entrance, I didn't even question that he was dead, otherwise, I would have brought him with us.

"All right, humans, get your privileged asses up to the food line now, or I will have the fae go first for once." Zion waved us up.

Collectively, we traveled to the food counter, forming lines. I cut and wiggled, making sure I was next to Tracker in the queue.

"Tracker." I breathed out his name quietly, my disbelief still not letting me fully comprehend he was here. "You're alive. How?"

He turned about to answer me, but I put my finger to my lips, wagging my head. His gaze darted around, picking up on the tense silence; only a murmur of voices from the guards and sounds from the kitchen buzzed the air enough to cover my whisper.

"How are you here?" I asked through my teeth.

"I could ask you the same thing," he muttered back, rapidly catching on to the danger around us, keeping his voice barely above a whisper.

"We thought you were dead."

"Yeah, I would have thought the same until I woke from a coma a few days ago."

We inched up the line. "Where have you been?"

"HDF. Guess they found me that night and realized I was still alive." He peered around, checking on the guards strolling up and down the lines.

I don't know why they would keep him alive. Even if he were human, he was still a traitor to them.

"The bullet should have been fatal. I shouldn't even be up and moving around so fast." Tracker leaned in closer. "What's strange, besides the bizarre dreams of being in some water tank, is waking from my coma. I've never felt better in my life."

Dread sank in my stomach like a boulder. Now I realized why he was still alive. Of course, Istvan would use him as a science experiment. What a perfect specimen to test on while in a coma. And if he died, no loss to Istvan.

Was he one of those in the tank I saw that night? Was he faux-fae now?

My eyes scanned Tracker; he looked the same as when I saw him pumping iron in the gym: healthy, ripped, young, and virile.

He shouldn't be if he was near death and in a coma this long.

I bit down on my lip. Right now wasn't the time to get into it, but I needed to learn more. Anything he could recall.

"I'm sorry. If we had known…" *we wouldn't have left you for dead.*

He shrugged, looking away from me.

"When you're at meals, stick with me, and when we go to the factory to work, stick with Lukas."

"Lukas?" Tracker's head snapped to me. "He's here?"

"So is Kek." I nodded my chin over to them.

They both stared at Tracker as if they hadn't even blinked yet, questions and bewilderment written in their gazes.

"Wow, the whole gang is here." He jerked his chin at them like he had seen them yesterday. "Well, almost."

"Sorry about Ava."

"Yeah, me too." His jaw tightened. Tracker was never a warm fuzzy, keeping everything inside. If he just woke up two days ago, it must be still so fresh to him.

After being handed our watery bowls of gruel, we had no more chance to talk. Tracker was an unexpected hitch, but he might be the very piece we need. Someone who might know more about what is going on outside the House of Blood.

Halfway back to the table, my bowl came tumbling out of my hands, spilling across the floor. I froze. My lungs clamped down as my senses went from normal to overwhelmed with pain. Bile coated my tongue, rooted terror exploding over my neurons.

Physically, I was still in the mess hall, but everything else was torn from the silent, dull room, now filled with piercing sounds and agony. I could feel the pounding in my head, filling with so much pressure, it felt like a tick about to burst.

His pain was acute; even taking on a little of it dropped my real body to the floor in the mess hall, vomiting on the floor while my shade stood in the hole with him.

Shackled up like a starfish and upside down, he was beaten badly with old and new bloodstains covering him. The chains could be cranked and tightened, stretching his muscles and limbs to the point they gave. Drawn and quartered.

41

*"Warwick!"* I cried, moving to him. The moment my fingers grazed his skin and laced through his hair; the agony tripled inside me. My teeth gritted together, trying to absorb the harsh punch of it in every muscle, nerve, and bone. The pressure in his head from being upside down, on top of the shrill noises, was the worst. It would break any human, mind, body, and spirit.

I didn't know how "death proof" Warwick and I were or if we had just been lucky. What neither one of us was immune to was losing ourselves mentally. If they couldn't break his body or will, they would crumble his mind.

*"Warwick..."* I leaned my forehead against his swollen, cut mouth. They had him hanging right at eye level—easier for them to beat him without him being able to do a thing.

A light groan came from the back of his throat.

*"Stay with me."* My nose rubbed against his, my lips grazing his forehead and cheeks.

Another moan. His lashes flickered; his puffy eyes only able to open into slits. Through the flashes of light, I could see his aqua eyes looking back at me.

And it almost broke me.

He had no fight in him. No will. He was slipping away from me. My heart pounded with terror at the thought of losing him. A world without Warwick Farkas?

No. *Fuck.* No.

There would be no world left. I would make sure of it.

My hands dug deeper into his hair, grabbing the back of his scalp, absorbing more of his pain. *"You don't get to fucking leave me, Farkas,"* I growled, my real body curling into a ball, convulsing. *"You don't get out of this so easy."*

"Easy?" The barest of sounds huffed into my ear, almost lost to the torture around us. But the more I pushed, the more it became further away. A barrier protecting us from the onslaught.

*"Yeah, asshole. You're stuck with me. I didn't drag your ass back from the dead for you to die here. So, no more getting yourself thrown into the hole. I forbid it."*

He snorted. "Whatever you say, woman."

*"Agreeing with me? Now I know you're losing your mind. Too much blood going to your brain."* As I cupped his head, his tiny slits of eyes watched me. A spark of life, lust flared in them.

"Get up!" A scream from where my real body lay wavered the link between us.

Grabbing Warwick tighter, reality starting to pull me away from him, my mouth covered his with desperation. Kissing him with everything I had—passion, love, life. My lips conveyed what I didn't say, what I felt so deep in my bones. I wondered if it had been etched into them from the day I was born.

I opened myself up, and he took, as I had with him many times. There were no polite manners or courteous etiquette with us. We were feral. Raw. Absolute. We cut past the bullshit of what was right and wrong. Black and white. We had no use for either.

"I said get up, 839!" I felt a guard kick me.

*"Whatever it takes,"* I demanded Warwick. There was no other option. *"Whatever you need to do, Farkas. Do it, but you will fucking survive this."*

With a harsh blow to my gut, the link was cut.

Gasping, I curled into myself as a boot kicked me again. The feel of the cold floor, my pants soaked with my breakfast, snapped me fully back to myself. My energy was almost nonexistent, and I struggled to get up.

"Joska, leave her alone," a girl's voice yelled out, the familiar tone spearing fright through my ribs.

Hanna.

Joska stopped, his beefy chest moving up and down as he lifted his head, his jaw cracking. "What did you say, traitor?"

My head jerked to Hanna. The only one standing at her table, she swallowed nervously, realizing what she had just done.

It had to be difficult for Hanna. Just *yesterday* morning, Joska and others here were part of her HDF family. Peers. We all knew each other in some way. We were once on the same side. Now, in a blink, it had flipped.

To someone like Joska, she was the worst of the worst—a traitor to her own kind, the same as me. Even if she did nothing, if Istvan claimed she was, then in Joska's tiny mind, she was, no question. She not only deserved to be here, but punished severely and killed for it.

"I just asked you a question, 1278," he barked, glaring at her.

Hanna's head tipped back just slightly, but it was enough for me to see. She wasn't a person to Joska anymore. She was a number. Any connection she had hoped to use with a fellow HDF soldier, I watched vanish from her face. Her expression shut down, but her gaze darted to me for a moment. Like, what the fuck do I do?

Her silence, the scent of her fear, riled him up like a savage animal. He scurried to her, and before she could react, he grabbed her by the back of the neck and tossed her with a ferocious grunt. Her frame flew way across the room as if she was a toy ball. Hanna smacked the ground with a pained grunt, sliding across the tile.

I had seen hints of what the pills were doing to them, but to see him throw her as if it was nothing? Even the true fae around the room gaped with awe.

Joska's face crunched up in fury, fists rolling together, skin reeking with aggression, muscles twitching violently. I could see the deadness in his eyes. He had no off switch right now. He would kill her.

"I said, answer me, you piece of trash," he roared, striding for her.

I didn't think. Leaping up, I darted for her, sliding myself between them. At the same time, a yell rang out. Scorpion was suddenly next to me, growling and snarling at Joska.

*"Faszkalap!"* Dickhat. *"You touch either one of them,"* Scorpion bellowed, but I knew Joska nor anyone else in this room would blink an eye.

Only I saw him.

My head jerked to where the real man sat across the room, his eyes widening when they locked on mine, realizing our connection was back. It wasn't as strong as it once was, fuzzy around the edges, but at the notion my bond with him was still there, relief I didn't even know I was holding came flooding out. Our connection survived and returned similar to Warwick, and I could feel the same response from him.

How fast we had become dependent on something we barely had time to get used to. It felt wrong when it was gone. Missing.

Now that I could feel the buzz of him, the link finally there, I felt home, but in a completely opposite way than Warwick. Scorpion, though sexy as hell, was more like a brother, while The Wolf was my equal. My lover.

*My mate.*

"Soldier!" Boyd's loud voice boomed into the room, jerking Joska's head over his shoulder. He almost didn't even look human, his skin sweaty, pallid, and twisted into crude and boorish features. "You can't touch those who are in the Games."

Joska snarled, spittle flinging from his mouth.

Boyd spread out his shoulders. "Take a break, soldier, or face me. And as much as you think you're ready to play at our level, you're not."

From the side, Samu stepped out, nudging Joska. "Come on, Jos. Let's go get some fresh air."

It took Samu another two tries before Joska's deadly gaze broke from Boyd, and he nodded, wiping at his nose. A streak of red smeared the back of his hand.

Tracking the threat across the room, my gut squeezed. The memory of being at the palace, seeing the woman at the end, blood leaking from her eyes, nose, and mouth. The sign of the end.

A defect in the formula.

I had a bilious sensation every HDF guard here would have the same fate.

Chapter 5

I hissed, sucking the drop of blood from my fingertip, glaring at the needle like it was another thing in here wanting to torture me. My fingers had been stabbed dozens of times as I handstitched the HDF logo onto the arm of military uniforms. Sweat dripped down my face and back while irritation weaved my hunger, body aches, exhaustion, and dehydration together in a knot.

The heat from the stoves had already caused two to collapse. The guards dragged them away, and I was terrified to think of what punishment they would get for that.

From across the room, I watched Ash and Lukas try to show Tracker the ropes, though Mr. Alpha wasn't taking to it with the seriousness he should. The human was arrogant and entitled, not understanding he was no longer the big man down here. I could see how frustrated and angry Ash was getting with him, because if he fucked up, it might come back on them too. Lukas wouldn't leave him, though, probably because he felt he owed him out of guilt. Deserting a comrade was almost a sin for special ops units, even if Lukas himself had been shot and clinging to life.

Kitty and Sloane were on another fire oven, Scorpion and Maddox next to them, while the rest pounded at the metal and worked the machines. I noticed the guards purposely put Killian in a position where he had to work the metal with his hands, the iron drooping his shoulders and blanching out his skin. He struggled to stand, the metal collar around his neck only adding to the torture.

To see them all in pain, every day their spirits dimming a little more, hope and fight leaking out of them, shattered me. It felt worse than any whipping I got in Halálház. Physical pain you could get past; it was the emotional and mental agony that utterly destroyed the will to live.

I had to get us out of here.

A choked cry jolted my head to the side. The human girl next to me, someone I had seen in the lab with Ling, gurgled up blood, her body jerking as red liquid poured down her neck.

The woman on the other side of her cried for help as I tried to understand what was happening. It didn't take long to realize she had stabbed her own throat over and over with the sewing needle, wanting to take her life.

She fell from the bench onto the ground, her chest instinctually heaving for oxygen, for survival. Her eyes glossed over as she stared up at the ceiling, jerking and twitching in her last throes of death.

On instinct, I scrambled down to her, her blood mingling with the vomit and gruel stains on my pants. The sound of the guards yelling and moving toward us became distant fog when my hands landed on her. I could feel her pain, hopelessness, the desire to no longer experience this much devastation, grief, and misery. Her emotions flooded me. And I felt the moment her soul left her body. The buzz of a spirit made the hair on my arms stand on end. This was the first time I really sensed the moment happen, felt her spirit break from her body.

I shook my head. "Don't give up." I acted without thought, a deeply embedded response taking over. Energy swirled inside me similar to a tornado, power dancing down my limbs, and I yanked on her ghost and shoved her back in.

The girl sat up with a swell of air. "Noooooooo!" She snarled at me, trying to claw out of my grip.

Terror forced me back with a gasp. The moment my hands let go, her body fell back to the ground with a thwack. Her mouth and eyes open, her body a shell. Empty.

Commotion moved around me, guards coming toward the dead girl.

Once again, like the ghosts in the church or graveyard, I felt her presence skating past me, and I felt relief come from her.

"Get the fuck up, 839!" A guard was suddenly in my face, snapping me out of my trance. He grabbed me, tossing me back onto my seat, slamming reality back into my face. I was overwhelmed with the loud sounds of the machines and peoples' stunned stares. Curiosity. Trepidation. Confusion. I could feel them from everywhere, so many wondering if they really saw that girl come back to life.

Feeling jittery, I peered around as other soldiers dragged her body away, no more than trash to them. My gaze landed on Ash and Lukas, but it was Tracker next to them who twisted my stomach. Most might chalk it up to the last throes of death or some other explanation, but his gaze pierced through me. He showed no emotion, but the way his jaw was set, the way his eyes held mine, it was as if he were saying, *"I see you."*

"I need someone to fill this spot," a guard yelled, twisting me back to my area, not even waiting until the girl's dead body was completely removed.

Nora stood instantly, moving from the overcrowded press machines to the vacated spot. Silently claiming it, her head bowed, picking up exactly where the girl left off.

The guard huffed, clicking his tongue. "Get back to work! All of you!"

Feeling Scorpion's shadow brush up behind me, my gaze met his across the room.

*"What the hell happened?"*

"Later," I muttered under my breath. I didn't have the strength to link or explain right now.

He nodded, turning back to his duty.

Nora cleared her throat, shifting next to me, her gaze going up, noticing most of the guards were chatting at the far end.

"You all right?" she muttered.

"Fine." I kept working, not physically responding to her question.

"You saved my daughter twice now." Every word was between her teeth, watching the movement of the guards while we worked. "I'm in your debt."

"She's my friend. Even if she doesn't believe it right now." I tried to still my shaking hands as I threaded my needle. "You all have been in my life for a long time. I'm sorry about Mr. Molnár."

Nora stiffened, her jaw clenching, holding back her emotion. She dipped her head with thanks, taking several moments before speaking again.

"You and Andris saved Hanna's life that night. It would be what Albert wanted." Her voice wavered. "I wanted you to know how much it means to me. And I'm sorry I believed the lies about you. I see clearly now. And I'm sorry for the girl who sat here... if you knew her."

I didn't, but sensing her soul, experiencing her pain, felt personal.

My gaze darted to the soldiers, still in conversation.

"Can I ask you something?"

"Anything," she replied.

"What is happening in Leopold? What happened to Rebeka?"

Nora sucked in, only pausing a moment on her stitching.

"Soon after Samhain, after Istvan declared the fae ruler was killed, things changed *quickly*. Rebeka saw it, but I was too blind to take her seriously. She had been having sleepless nights and episodes since Caden was taken. We were each other's solace at the time, afraid for our children and what was happening to them, if they were even alive. So, I chalked her paranoia up to exhaustion. She invited me to tea one afternoon and told me she was scared, that Istvan was no longer the man we knew, and if she disappeared, it was because she knew things she shouldn't."

"Did she say what?"

Nora shook her head. "No. She said she would not put my life in danger." Nora swallowed. "The next day she was gone. Just vanished. Her clothes and items were boxed up, her room emptied. That night, Istvan threw a party, announcing his engagement to Olena. He moved her in immediately, as if Rebeka never existed. Of course, I demanded he tell me what happened to my friend, that I would not stand for such a thing." Nora scoffed, her head shaking. "I thought years of friendship would mean something. As you can see, it did the opposite."

"That's why you are here? Because you demanded to know where she was?"

"Partly." She glanced over at the sentries still grouped up. Without Joska, Samu, and Boyd, the guards seemed less inclined to stomp around us continuously, instead enjoying their gossip time.

"Years ago, Albert was losing money in his factories. A lot. We couldn't pay for basic necessities, let alone Hanna's training. We were desperate. Istvan stepped in with a deal to save us. He took possession of the underground space and rights to the building in exchange for a bailout. We agreed, thinking he was our friend. Rebeka and I had been friends for years." A sadness watered her eyes. "Istvan made sure we succeeded. Albert and I stupidly looked away as money rolled into our bank accounts, while workers and other factories suffered at our expense." Her lips pursed. "I can't say I'm proud of my actions now, but we did what we needed to and continued to look away when things shifted at the factory. Albert was never good with money, so I would come in and do all the books. It wasn't just odd influxes of huge amounts of money in and out, it was people disappearing, factory workers found drowned in the Danube, trucks hauling in things late at night, and screams from deep below the office floor."

"Did you know what was happening down there?"

"No." She shook her head. "I see now I purposely kept my head down. Albert kept reassuring me all was fine. He was lying to me to keep me in a safe, protected bubble, but I saw his fear grow each day." She tied off her thread, starting on a new patch. "When Rebeka disappeared, and Hans and Petra also vanished, Albert confessed he knew what Istvan was doing below his factory, and he said he discovered a secret."

"What?"

"He wouldn't tell me. But whatever it was, it greatly changed his view of Istvan. He was petrified of what he would do to us. He wanted us to sneak away over the wall and disappear that night. I said no because of Hanna. At dawn, we were taken from our beds."

"It must have been terrifying." I glanced at her. "You don't know anything else about what Albert knew? Or maybe something you saw?"

Her lips pinched together.

"What?" I asked as we continued to work, talking out of the sides of our mouths.

"I saw a layout of the underground Istvan had built under the factory. At the time, I brushed it off." She paused as a guard broke from the group. The anticipation waiting for him to pass us knotted up my muscles, the soles of his shoes clipping up the back of my spine as he went by.

Once he was out of earshot, Nora spoke again. "There are three levels under the factory."

*Three? I saw maybe two.*

"Not only do they all join each other, but from the top level, the tunnel leads straight to the Ferencvárosi railway station."

My shoulders tensed at her news. Ferencvárosi was the largest train station in Hungary and was now only used to distribute cargo, heading to all major ports in Romania, Ukraine, Poland, Serbia, Czech, and beyond. How easy it would be to get the pills to the train station, load them, and send them out to your allies without being noticed at all. How far out had they reached by now? How many leaders were in possession of them?

How fucked were we?

"We were taken not just because of Rebeka's disappearance, but because Albert knew too much. Istvan made sure he was silenced. I'm afraid I am next." A noise came up her throat. "Please protect my baby girl. She shouldn't suffer because of our selfishness."

Hanna could undoubtedly take care of herself, but I nodded in agreement.

I didn't have the heart to tell her what horrible things Istvan was doing in that factory. The very thing they ignored in favor of protecting their family, for money, was already in their daughter's system. It could be too late for Hanna as well.

Nora's information shoved my need to escape this place into overdrive. Every moment, more and more shipments of the pills were being sent out. He wasn't doing it out of the kindness of his heart; it came with the agreement he now commanded your country if he said the word. How long until Istvan had control of the entire East? If he ever found the nectar or discovered it in me, we were screwed. Bringing that girl back today, it was clear my powers were not only coming back with gusto, but no fae spells could block them.

If he somehow procured them from me, he would have the power to take the Unified Nations as well.

We were running out of time.

Boyd and Joska always seemed to rile the soldiers up, get them in a primal state, their anger and hate rubbing off on the rest. The atmosphere was slightly less strained at dinner with Joska, Boyd, and a few others still absent. Even so, no one was suddenly skipping to other tables to say hi or doing anything out of line.

Rosie, Tracker, Hanna, Nora, Petra, and I sat together, our heads low, muttering between bites.

"We have to speed up our timeline. Listen and observe everything: schedules, habits, conversations, and get them talking if you can. Look out for hidden exits and *anything* else you think might help," I whispered to the group. "We also need to learn who is on our side. Be very careful who you trust. We can't have anyone turning us over before we even get a chance to overthrow them."

They all nodded their heads, someone constantly glancing around, making sure we weren't being overheard or catching the guards' attention.

"Wouldn't he know how to get out of here?" Rosie's nose wrinkled, flicking her chin to the man sitting by himself. Killian's regal demeanor still did not bend under the weight he carried on his shoulders, even with his energy being drained from the iron around his neck. He was breathtaking, even drained, but thinner and in soiled, ill-fitting clothes. "I mean, he built it." She glanced away from him with irritation.

"Because of our escape from Halálház, he told me he made sure this place had no weaknesses."

"Thanks for that." Hanna frowned, her body constantly moving, not able to sit still. Sweaty. As if she was coming down from a high.

"I will still try to get to him. See if I can get anything more out of him, which might be helpful."

"How do we talk to people if we can't really talk?" Tracker whispered, glancing over his shoulder.

"In the lavatory, in line getting food or water, in the factory, or the person next to your cell. Any chance you can get. We need to be spies and recruiters in one," I muttered. "There are more of us than them. If we can get a mutiny going, find a way out of here, we have a chance to escape."

"But *they* have power, right? Not the fae down here." Tracker leaned his arms farther on the table, curling his hands into fists, his movements smooth and graceful. Why did the guards and Hanna act like they were coming down from a heroin high while Tracker seemed different? He said he was in one of those tanks I had seen at the lab. What was Istvan doing with them?

"I need to learn more from the both of you. What you saw and experienced out there. What Istva—"

Out of nowhere, pain exploded through my body. My nerves burned with electricity, taking me down to the hole.

Warwick was now chained against the wall as Boyd electrocuted him. Other guards were clubbing him with their spiked batons. His agony crashed down on me, ripping the air from my lungs.

He felt me there, his head twisting. Our eyes met, and emotion choked me. I couldn't even get out his name before he slammed his lids shut, slicing the link between us.

*No!* I clawed to get back, but he locked me out tight, not wanting me to be there. To see his pain or to feel it—to take it on. *Stubborn asshole.*

"Luv?" Rosie held my arm, keeping me upright. Her voice snapped me back to my surroundings, sweat trickling down my temple, my limbs quaking. "You okay?"

The imprint of his distress still thrummed through me, but I nodded, swallowing back the sour taste on my tongue. Now I knew why Boyd wasn't here. He was too busy torturing Warwick.

"I still don't see how this information is going to get us out of here."

Tracker, oblivious to my episode, scooped slop into his mouth, his nose wrinkling with disgust. "How can we overtake them if they have all the power?"

Taking a few more gulps, revenge and fury churned in my gut, forging more of my broken pieces together.

I turned to Tracker, my voice full of conviction and promise.

"A swarm of bees can take down a herd if they are fighting for their lives."

# Chapter 6

*"Hope you're not jerking off to thoughts of me."* I leaned up against the cell wall, my real body back in my own cell. I grinned down at the occupant on the ground. *"That would just be awkward."*

"Holy shit." Scorpion jolted at my voice, scrambling to sit up, yanking his hand out of his pants and pulling them all the way up. His eyes met mine, and he huffed out a long breath. "Fuck, you scared the shit out of me."

*"Yeah, I could see you were... occupied."* I smirked, glancing down at his hand, then over his shirtless frame. The man was sensual—the kind of hot that unsettled you.

His lids narrowed. "You might have just ruined the only thing I had left here. Now, I'm paranoid you're gonna pop in at any moment."

*"And here I thought you brought me in."* I winked.

"You weren't who I was thinking of." He leaned back against the wall with a smug grin. "Not that you aren't hot as hell and great material, but I think Warwick would cut me into little pieces even having you anywhere near those types of thoughts."

I couldn't fight him on that.

*"Can I ask who you were thinking of?"* I lifted a brow.

"You can, but you won't get an answer." He mimicked my expression. I had an idea who it might be, though he'd never admit it.

Silence grew between us, and I realized we hadn't spoken since the night in the pit. Hadn't confronted what had happened when we were almost forced to kill each other.

*"I'm sorry…"* I bit into my lip.

"For?"

*"Everything. That night. Doing what I had to do and eliminating you from the equation. For… Andris."* Blinking, I looked down at my boots.

"Brex." His tone tugged my head up. "It would have been cruel to let him die that way. He made his decision to go in. You gave him peace at the end." He rubbed at his chin. "And if you don't think for one second the thought of losing you instead…" He tapered off, his hand moving over his face and into his hair. He shook his head, not finishing his thought. "Though punching me out? You will pay. Fuck, it hurt."

A choked laugh came up my throat.

Scorpion watched me for a while. His gaze was heavy and full of unsaid sentiment. I would never lie and say we didn't have something there—a spark—how could we not when we had this crazy link? But there was no contest. With Scorpion, I'd sacrifice myself to save him. With Warwick, I would sacrifice the world.

"We're back." Scorpion motioned to me, his voice low and quiet. He tried to hide the emotion behind it, but I could feel it.

*"We are."* I couldn't fight the joyous smile beaming over my face, which pulled Scorpion's mouth into the same happy grin. It was so rare to see; I felt tears building up in my throat.

We didn't touch or say anything else, but it was all there.

*Home.*

Scorpion would be part of my life, part of me, forever. Whatever fate put him in the way of my magic that night, I was so thankful.

"So, besides interrupting my alone time?" He pulled up his legs, dropping his arms over his knees with a wink.

*"What would you say if I asked you if you wanted to start a mutiny, overthrow the guards, and get the fuck out of here?"*

"I'd say it's about fucking time you asked." He went up onto his feet, rubbing at his bare chest. "Tonight good?"

*"Whoa, cowboy. We get one chance. I need you to get close to Killian tomorrow in the factory, learn anything you can about this place."*

"Why not ask him yourself? I mean through me, of course." Scorpion pounded on the wall. "Hey, your highness, you up?"

My mouth parted. *"Killian? Killian's next door to you?"*

"Ash is on that side." He nodded to the cell on the other side of me.

*"Ash?"* I whirled around to the wall like I could see through it. The need to see my best friend had me wanting to plow through it.

"Hey, fairy, someone wants to talk to you." Scorpion went to the corner, hissing into Ash's cell.

"For the last time, I won't give your dick a pep talk. It was a one-time thing," Ash muttered back through a yawn.

I glanced at Scorpion; eyebrow curved up.

"He's kidding." He cleared his throat, his head wagging.

*"Don't worry,"* I smirked at Scorpion. *"He's probably jerking off over there to both Kek and Lukas."*

Scorpion sputtered. "Both Lukas and Kek? Seriously? At the same time?"

"Whoa. Who the hell did you hear that from?" Ash was suddenly off the floor and standing at the corner of his cage.

"Wow, you *weren't* kidding?" Scorpion snorted, addressing me. "Interesting. And with *that* demon—she's fucking terrifying. Call me impressed."

"*Bazdmeg*." Ash sighed. "Brexley's there, isn't she?"

"Yeah, or I finally lost my mind." Scorpion scoffed.

"There is a good possibility of both," Ash replied.

*"Tell the asshole I miss him."*

"Brexley says you're an asshole."

*"Scorp!"* I smacked Scorpion. The sensation was like touching someone through plastic. Real, but not completely yet. *"Tell him."*

"I am not going to tell him that. I won't be your carrier pigeon." Scorpion huffed, stomping over just a few feet to the other side, hitting the wall connected with Killian.

I could see Ash's hands sticking out of the bars. Reaching over, I let my hands grasp onto his. Goosebumps covered his skin, his body jolting with a chill.

"Fuck!" He jerked back. "That's just creepy, Brex." He chuckled, shaking out his shivers, knowing full well it was me. Out of most people, Ash would feel the connection threading through the atmosphere, the energy tugging at the molecules connecting Scorpion and me. "Many people claim to have sex with ghosts... always been curious. Any takers?" I pinched him with my fingers, making him laugh louder. "Just putting it out there."

Strolling over to Scorpion, I chuckled to myself. Damn, I missed my boys.

"Hey, your highness? Wake up." Scorpion whispered toward Kilian's cell.

Silence was the only response. But I could feel he was awake, feel the brooding melody of his mood.

There had always been a connection to Killian from the day he brought me to his palace. I felt his presence from a distance, could sense him in an abstract way. It was vastly different from my link to my boys, but still substantial. Was it my magic, Aneira's power running through me, which made me feel his more acutely? He was at the level of a noble, a king if he declared himself to be. A queen would respond to this kind of magic—good or bad, enemy or ally, war or peace. Killian was an equal.

And that kind of magic attracted the same.

*"Killian."* I knew he couldn't hear me, but I wondered if he could sense me too. *"Killian, please, we need you. Don't give up. I can't do this without you."*

"I am not saying that either," Scorpion grumbled.

I glared up at him.

He blew out. "We need you, blah, blah, don't give up." Scorpion rolled his eyes.

*"Well, that was heartfelt."*

"It's all you're gettin'." Scorpion retorted. "Basically, highness, stop moping and help us out here, or your girlfriend is gonna nag me all night long. Drive me out of my skull."

"What do you want?" Killian's low, taut voice finally came through the dark. "And who are you talking about? I have no *girlfriend*." He spat the word, which sounded odd coming from him. It didn't fit him at all. Killian did not have girlfriends. It was too insignificant for him. He had lovers, or possibly a mate.

"Black hair, black eyes, magnet for danger, and a real pain in my ass."

"Mine too!" Ash piped from the cell over.

"Brexley?" Killian sounded like he sat up.

Both Scorpion and Ash burst out laughing.

"That obvious, huh? Didn't even have to think about it." Scorpion snickered.

*"All of you are dickheads."* I rubbed my neck.

"Why are you asking me about her? Is she all right?" Killian moved to the bars right where Scorpion's cell and his almost met.

"You all right, PIMA?" Scorpion asked me with a grin.

*"PIMA?"*

"Pain in my ass."

*"Oh, yeah."* I scowled. *"I'm fantastic. Besides being imprisoned, brutalized, starved, beaten, forced to kill my uncle, thrown into the hole for five days, and knowing Warwick is being brutally tortured every single moment and he's blocking me out. Sure, I'm fucking fabulous."*

"She says she's horny."

I couldn't fight the snorted laugh breaking from my lips.

"What do you mean *she says*…?" I knew if I could see Killian, his eyebrows would be furrowing in confusion.

"Yeah… well…" Scorpion licked his lip. "She's here with me now. Not physically, though to me there's not much difference. I'm not gonna get into it; she can tell you the whole story later. Just let's jump to the part where you accept the fact she's here, and we can move on."

There was a beat of silence.

"I believe you."

Scorpion tipped his head back in shock. "Really?"

"A lot about Ms. Kovacs seems to go against the norm. Defying convention." There was a slight smile in Killian's words. "I can't explain, but I sense her." He cleared his throat. "She's really there with you? You see her?"

"Can I see her?" Scorpion reached out, knocking my shoulder. "Oh yeah. I can feel and touch her too," he said salaciously, making me flick my eyes to the side.

*"Can we get to it?"* I threw out my hands. Linking with Scorpion took more energy than it did with Warwick, and I could feel myself getting sleepy back in my cell several rows below.

"I am your puppet." Scorpion leaned back against the wall again.

As I explained things to Scorpion, he relayed everything I told the group at dinner and in the bathroom earlier that morning to Killian and Ash. My plan to learn everything we could and quickly. Find a weakness and flip this place on its head.

*"We need to know anything he knows about the spells on this place. I mean the smallest detail that could help us escape."* I spoke to Scorpion, and he passed it on to Killian.

Killian exhaled with frustration. "Of course, this had to come bite me in the ass," he muttered. "I honestly can't think of one weakness. I made sure of it. I even had Tad double spell all doors and exits in the prison, so it was impossible to break out. Built it deeper in the mountain. I designed it to be impregnable."

Scouring at my head, I paced the tiny cell. There had to be a way. We would *not* die here.

"What about the gate up at the factory?" Ash hissed over to us. "They guard it the most."

"Tad spelled the gate," Killian responded. "But only once, since I never planned to use that floor for inmates. It was merely meant for trucks and supplies. It would be the weakest point here, though it is smart enough to know the difference between prisoners and everyone else."

That's what I had thought.

"Weakest point?" Scorpion restated.

"Yes, but it doesn't make it easy to break. Druid spells can't be broken by anything other than a Druid."

"Have any of those lying around?" Ash said dryly.

*"We did in Halálház,"* I muttered to myself. Thinking about Tad, a memory of what he said to me came back. *"Your family line at one time were Druids."*

What if it was possible? What if the spell recognized my family's Druid blood in me? Could I counter it?

*"What about me?"* I sputtered out.

Scorpion pushed off the wall. "What do you mean, what about you?"

*"My mother is a witch, but at one time, she was from a powerful Druid line. I also have the magic of a queen... I mean, my magic works down here when yours doesn't. What if I have the power to undo Tad's spells?"*

"Shit, I didn't even connect that your magic worked here." Scorpion shook his head, the notion finally hitting him. "You're *similar to them.*" Meaning those human-fae mutants.

*"No, they're trying to be me,"* I smirked at Scorpion, folding my arms.

"What is she saying?" Ash barked, all of us still trying to be so quiet, though the sounds of the prison, the clanging metal and howls, kept our conversation muted to guards.

"Brex's magic isn't blocked. She's wondering if she could break—"

*"More like loosen,"* I punched in.

"Sorry, *loosen* the Druid spell. Is it possible?" Scorpion finished.

Heavy silence came from both sides.

"I have no idea," Killian finally replied. "My first instinct is no. Tad is no ordinary Druid, and she has no training nor is she a true Druid, however, Brexley doesn't seem to follow the rules either."

*"We don't play by the normal rules, Kovacs. You and I make our own."* Warwick's sentiment from weeks ago vibrated in my chest, filling me with determination to at least try.

*"Are these locks spelled by Tad? Can I try on these?"* I reached out for the iron gate as Scorpion relayed my question.

"No!" Killian replied sharply. "The magic on these cells isn't Druid cast, only the main entrances and exits. But these *are* spelled to trigger an alarm if messed with."

*Figures.*

"There is warning on the main ones as well, but if we are escaping, it doesn't really matter if they are going off," Killian added.

"The Games are scheduled in three days' time," Ash muttered over to us. "If we do this, we should try to do it then. We're all out and together. Be a good time to start a coup. Before any more can die in the pit."

"Agreed." Scorpion nodded fervently, having had a taste of what it was like in the arena.

Terror gripped my stomach. We had so much to do in such a short amount of time.

*"So, I go in blind."* I had no idea if what I was planning was even possible, just a gut feeling, an intuition.

"It's worth a shot." Scorpion winked, shrugging down at me.

*"A shot might be all we get."*

"Then make sure we go out with a bang."

My plan spread through Věrhăza quickly. So quickly I started to worry the guards would catch on or overhear as we moved through the day. Bitzy and Opie had woken me up early with information they got from other inmates—positions of guards, their break times. Nothing groundbreaking, but it was a start.

"The cerulean creature says as long as she gets steak, sex, and a drink after she's all in." Opie folded his arms over his lederhosen, which appeared to be made out of an oat burlap bag and were so short they could have been bikini bottoms. His chest was left bare under the suspenders. He tied another burlap strip around his beard and wrapped his hair into a high bun, with carrot leaves springing from the top like a fountain. Bitzy had booty shorts and a bow tie in the same burlap.

"Sounds like Kek," I smirked. "Anything else?"

Opie peered down, ramming his toe into my leg.

"What?"

"I tried—"

*Chirp!*

"We tried," he corrected himself. "To unlatch some locks at the top... thought we could help."

"And?"

"I couldn't—"

*Chirp!*

"*We* couldn't." Opie's face looked pained. "The Druid spell blocks us too. We tried to find you when you went missing, but we were blocked."

Because Tad had spelled Killian's cabin too, keeping them from finding me.

"Oh." My shoulders sank. I wasn't relying on them, but damn, it would have helped. "It's fine. We'll find a way."

We had to. We didn't have a lot of time. Every day someone was beaten or killed here, and it was only days until the next Games. I had no doubt there would be even more death and new levels of hell in Istvan's plan for us.

Our goal was to do it the afternoon of, when we were all still in the factory and some guards were away, setting up for that night's event.

Purpose is a powerful thing. It bloomed hope—a reason to continue when you have no incentive to do so. This place quickly drains it out of you, swallowing you whole in horror, despair, and anguish. To the point death would be mercy.

Death himself was losing hope. As much as Warwick tried, he could no longer keep me out. Though it didn't really matter, he had receded to the far crevasses of his mind. Breathing, but no longer living.

Boyd and his merry band of dicklickers continued to torture Warwick in the most excruciating ways. They had his feet and hands bound together behind his back, curving the huge man into a painful position, drowning him in stimuli over and over again.

*"Warwick."* I kneeled next to him now, my hand brushing at his face. I could feel the blood, sweat, and dirt crusting his skin, beard, and hair. *"Please hold on."* I gritted my teeth, trying so hard not to cry. Hoping I was easing his pain.

There was no response. His eyes were too swollen to open, his black hair, almost red with blood, knotted over his face. His frame was nothing but old and new wounds, deep and oozing, some even infected.

He may still be alive, but I could feel him slipping away mentally. Even the Legend had a breaking point. I was scared if he did let go, I would never get him back, his mind lost to the darkness.

61

*"Please."* I leaned into him, my lips grazing his torn and swollen mouth. The wounds felt like braille against my touch. Heat radiated from his skin in a fever, sticky and clammy. *"We fight, Farkas. We survive. That's what we do. Whatever it takes, remember?"*

He was my world. And if this world took him from me…

I would burn it to the fucking ground.

# Chapter 7

By the next breakfast, if you could call it one, you could feel a spark in the air, a change in our demeanor. Which was not lost on Boyd, nor Joska and Kristof, who were both back, and appeared even more twitchy and filled with increased rage.

They could taste our hope, smell it in the air, feel it brush their skin. Boyd's intuition could sense it, but the fake-fae picked it up like smelling another animal in heat. It confused them. And when beasts get confused, they get angry. Agitated. They wanted to rip it out, beat it down, and remove anything that challenged their hate and wrath.

Boyd went around randomly clubbing people, having their beaten bodies dragged out of the room, only antagonizing the souped-up soldiers around him.

Somebody would break eventually.

"We have to hurry this up," I muttered to the group at my table.

"How?" Tracker hissed back.

So far, I found out most fae guards here were only in it for the money. They didn't like the humans but weren't faithful enough to their own side to refuse the money Istvan was giving them. And the HDF soldiers acted more as if they were in a cult than an army.

There was a thin line between the two, which could be used in our favor.

"Okay, maybe we're looking at this the wrong way. Instead of inside out, what about outside in?" My gaze darted between Hanna and Tracker. "You two were the last to be on the outside. To be in HDF or around Istvan. Can you remember anything that might help?"

"As soon as Istvan debriefed me about my time at Sarkis, and I asked to go see my parents, he had me hauled into a holding cell then brought here." Hanna scooped some gruel into her mouth, her face not able to fight the flinch of disgust.

"He said nothing to you?"

"Just that my whole family had turned out to be grave disappointments and traitors." Her blue eyes went from her mom to me, her voice lowering. "He asked me about the nectar." Her tone was poignant, hinting back to the conversation we had at the canteen that day, reminding me she knew I had it.

"Nectar?" Tracker's spine went straight, his voice peaking slightly louder than it should have. He instantly bowed his head, our whole table going still, waiting for a reaction from the guards. Fortunately, most of them were away from our table, unfortunately poking at Killian.

"You didn't tell him anything, did you?" I finally spoke again.

"No," she refuted strongly.

"Do you know if Caden did?"

Hanna wagged her head. "I don't know. I never saw him after we left the square. But General Markos would debrief him first." The highest-ranking officer was always interrogated first. It was how it was done. Caden far outranked Hanna. "When the General spoke to me, he didn't seem to have any idea where it was."

My shoulders eased. "Good. I can't have him finding it."

"Wait. Are you talking about the same nectar we were looking for in Killian's tunnels?" Tracker addressed me. "Did you find it?"

I let out a scoff. "You could say that." *And part of it is sitting right across from you, buddy.*

Tracker's eyes widened more. "You have it." He stated with awe, then his gaze went over me. "Where is it? How did they not find it on you if you had it? Do you have it now?"

"No. But I know where it is. Sort of."

My only hope was whoever went through the pile of jackets and bags didn't have a clue what it was. It was far better off staying in innocent hands until I could get to it. I felt confident I would be able to find it the moment I got out of here, as the pull to it would lead me like a compass. It was part of me.

"Where is it?" Tracker responded automatically.

My mouth pinned together in a flat smile, letting him understand no one at this table would know except me.

"I can't believe you actually found it." He shook his head in disbelief. "That it's real."

"Oh, it's real."

"The power it's supposed to have is immeasurable. Why didn't you use it if you had it?"

"I did," I muttered without thinking. "Brought Andris back to life after his base was bombed."

"Wait." Tracker blinked at me, his shoulders pushing back. "It can bring people back from the dead?" I knew that tone, his look. The hope.

"It doesn't work lik—"

"Chow time is over! Let's move!" Joska yelled, strolling past our table, shutting me up. "Now!"

Our group got up quietly from the table, walking to the stairs to the level leading to the factory. Tracker got lost in the crowd, and I lost my chance to tell him I could never bring Ava back. The nectar didn't bring people back from the dead. It was only in the first moments of death, when life still clung to the body.

I searched for him by Lukas when we got up to the factory, but he wasn't there, and with the growing numbers of inmates coming in daily, he was lost in the throng, men outnumbering the women prisoners by more than double.

Most of the day had gone by when I suddenly found him next to Lukas, his shirt not yet sticking to his body, as if he decided to finally come to work, though I knew that couldn't be the case. Every single inmate worked, no matter age, sickness, or capability. If you collapsed or died, they would drag you off as though you were rubbish.

Joska and Kristof were in rare form, strutting around the women, poking at Rosie and me the most. I tried not to react, but their aggression increased instead of diminishing at our lack of response.

"You think I can't kill you right here?" Kristof rammed his baton into my back, slamming me against the sewing machine. His fingers wrapped in my hair, ripping out strands as he yanked it back. His fragile male human ego was bruised because I took him and all his buddies out in the shower room by myself. "What you did? I'm gonna fucking slice you into pieces slowly and fuck your corpse. You will pay, bitch."

"Kristof," Boyd warned from across the room. "Leave that one *for now*."

Kristof snarled in my ear. "The moment he's not looking, I'm gonna fuck you up so bad. Find a place to put this." He tapped the spiked club on the table next to me, the threat very clear.

"Yeah, this whore needs to pay." Joska twitched and paced behind us, feeding off Kristof's energy as though he could no longer control his actions.

"Oh, what's wrong, *Kurva*?" Kristof sneered at Rosie across the table. "You getting jealous? Don't worry, I know how much you love to choke on my dick. I'll be fucking you after her." His nails dug so deep into my scalp; I could feel blood leaking down the back of my head. Pain filled my eyes, and I bit on my lip, trying to keep my cries from escaping. His baton whacked me again across the back.

"Stop!" Rosie choked out. "Please!"

Kristof went deadly still.

Fuck. Fuck. Fuck.

"What did you say?" He let go of me, standing fully upright. Tension slathered every inch of the air, a bomb ticking under my feet, and I had no real way of defusing the situation. "You telling me what to do, you fucking *picsa*?" *Cunt*. "You think you have a right to even speak?" Fury lashed out from him, his body moving with a speed no human should possess. He fisted her head, yanking her so violently to the floor Rosie's skull cracked on the surface, a scream gurgling in her throat as he dragged her over the rough floor.

"No!" I tried to yell out before Joska's hand grabbed me by the throat. Sounds I never heard a human make came from him, like hooting noises of an angry gorilla.

Gods, what if they took on the qualities of the fae essence? If his pills were from a gorilla shifter, would they give him the same primal qualities?

My gaze darted around the room, suddenly noticing the characteristics of wild animals instead of soldiers. A mass of them acting similar to hyenas or chimpanzees were riled up and squawking at the prospect of blood and death. Some others prowled similar to lions, ready to jump in and tear into flesh.

What if these pills made them the worst of man and shifter combined?

"Markos said not to kill Kovacs yet," I heard a fae guard yell, but neither Kristof nor any HDF men listened, their cries for blood snarling louder.

Kristof slammed Rosie's head onto the ground again, her body going limp. He tore at her clothes, causing all the artificial fae to go berserk.

*Feral.*

"No!" I screamed, feeling energy bubbling up inside me, sparking within my body. When Joska's boot kicked me hard, I heard my ribs crack, freezing my muscles in place.

A bellow roared in my ears, a form cutting through the savage guards, capturing my attention. Killian stood there; his expression cold. Furious. Even with his collar, I could feel his rage, his magic trying to break through. He swiped a baton off a guard and darted to us, cracking it across Kristof's temple with a wet thwack.

Blood, brains, and matter sprayed over the floor and across my face.

Killian moved and spun like a samurai, a brutal and beautiful dance, making me see another man under the noble title. One who was trained to kill and fought with skill, which came from a past not of aristocratic blood.

Killian struck Kristof again on the other side of his head with a force that reverberated against my skin. Like a falling watermelon, Kristof's head burst into bits and chunks, drenched with red juices, meat, and black seeds of his brain.

His body dropped.

Killian heaved with fury, standing over Rosie, covered in Kristof's blood. He didn't look like a nobleman. He looked like a warrior. Fierce and deadly.

A king.

There was a hush of disbelief, of awe, all eyes on him as if he were a god.

Then the truth sunk in. A prisoner had just killed a guard. HDF considered that a declaration of war, but before they could react, a man in yellow screamed, pointing at HDF. "Revolt! Kill them!"

Commotion and chaos imploded in the room.

Gunfire, yells, and moving bodies streamed through, instantly absorbing Killian and Rosie from my view.

I struggled to get up, feet stomping on me as hundreds of people darted away and toward the chaos.

"Brexley!" Scorpion's voice cut through the throng, scrambling over to me. "Come on!" He yanked me to my feet out of the way of the horde, his eyes meeting mine as we saw the entire room clash together.

The revolt had started. Killian sparked the flame into a full fire.

"We have to do this now," Scorpion yelled.

"But…" I gaped, peering around.

*"No buts! We have to try now!"* His shade barked into my ear, shoving me for the gate as he whirled on a guard, engaging in a fight. *"Go!"*

"I can't leave Warwick," I screamed, trying to turn back toward the prison. I wasn't ready. I was sure they'd bring Warwick up for the Games.

"Brexley!" Ash came from the mass of people, grabbing me, ending my connection with Scorpion. "We have to try to escape." Lukas, Maddox, and Wesley were with him, holding shovels and tools they worked with as weapons, ready to defend. The room drummed with bangs and loud noises, people already running for the gate, their bodies getting electrocuted when they touched them, falling lifeless to the ground.

"I won't leave Warwick."

"We can't wait," Maddox bellowed. "It's now or we die."

This wasn't supposed to happen now. But that's not how life worked. You took the opportunities you could. We had no do-over or practice runs. Our escape had to be now.

Locking down my jaw, I turned back to the gate, seeing prisoners already trying to get through it in panic. The gate was electrified and killed each one who tried, but it didn't seem to stop the next one from trying as well.

"While I try to bring it down, get them fighting and defending, not throwing themselves at it." I ordered the boys as another person flung themselves at our only exit with irrational desperation. They were so scared to die here, but might end up killing themselves in their own terror.

The boys fanned out while I faced the gate. "Fuck, please work." My body and voice shook, my ribs aching with every breath from Joska's boot. Closing my eyes, I tried to center myself, cut out the noise, though the screams and gunshots zigged up my spine, rattling me. Did one of my friends just get shot? Was Rosie alive? How would I get Warwick out?

"Focus." I breathed out. Though I had no idea what I was supposed to focus on. There was no manual on my powers. I didn't even know if this would work, though something deep in me knew my magic was immense. It could cheat death of its victims, control ghosts, bring down a wall between worlds. What else was I capable of? I wasn't only made from a witch, necromancer, and Druid, but also Aneira, a Seelie Queen of the Otherworld.

"If you are part of me, a good time to show yourself would be now." I rolled my fists and dug in deep, reaching for the power embedded inside me, screaming for it to take over and demolish this cage. A guttural cry parted my lips, and I flung everything out at the gate.

Nothing, I mean nothing, happened. Not a zap of electricity or whirl of wind threaded through my body.

"Brexley! Now!" Ash yelled, jolting my eyes open.

The thunder of screams, gunfire, and cries roared back at top volume, stabbing up my spine, pushing more fear and panic down my throat.

"I'm trying!" I shook out my hands.

"Try faster," he barked.

Sucking in shaky breaths, I closed my eyes again, pushing out the sounds of death pinging around me. All these lives depended on me. I was so stupid to suggest this. Arrogant. Cocky. To think I could possibly have the power to do anything more than chat with ghosts. How could I neutralize extensive spells from one of the most powerful Druids in the world?

Burrowing in deeper, I could feel the broken pieces inside me, the fire and heat of my rage building them back together, but it felt like it was on the other side of thin glass, just out of reach.

"No!" I growled, forcing myself deeper, pushing through.

It took me a moment to register the ground vibrating under my feet. The sharp squeal of the gates moving, metal locks opening. My lids flew open.

The gates started to part.

"You did it!" I heard one of the guys yelled over my shoulder, the mass of inmates cheering and running into the tunnel.

No. I didn't. I knew I hadn't.

The ground under my feet vibrated harder.

This wasn't me.

"Wait!" I shouted at the people fleeing, running into the dark channel, but it was too late.

Their shrieks echoed as they hit the spell, flying back, their bones crunching to the ground.

Headlights came into view, blinding me.

*Holy shit.*

Heavily reinforced, iron-clad SUVs, with guards running along the side, came down the passage, extending back at least six or seven cars. The top of each was armed with a long gun and another soldier, pointing it at us, the symbol HDF on the front.

Instead of freeing these people, I realized I had led them straight into a trap.

We had nowhere to run. Nowhere to go.

I had failed everyone.

Blood and gore covered the floors as dozens were shot dead until the soldiers regained control, rounding us up like cattle.

More than eighty new HDF guards descended on us, guns pointed at our heads, and anyone who didn't comply was killed or pistol-whipped into submission.

A guard primed a handgun at my temple as I watched a soldier open the door of a hummer, saluting the man inside. The familiar figure climbed out, his eyes latching on to mine instantly, a dainty woman accompanied him.

"Well, well…" Istvan's voice iced my spinal column. "Why am I not surprised you are at the center of this." Istvan strolled to me, surrounded by armed guards. The new soldiers were clean, meticulous, and robotic in their movement, reminding me of the night in the square. Their demeanor only highlighted the difference between them and the guards down here, and the change that was happening and would happen to these fresh faces as well.

Markos stopped right in front of me, his eyes glinting as they rolled over me. "I feel a strange pride in knowing you don't give up. That I raised you to be a fighter."

"You didn't raise me," I snarled, the soldier behind me pressing the barrel of his rifle harder to the back of my head. "My father raised me. Everything I am is because of him."

We both knew it was a lie. As much as I despised Istvan, he made sure Caden and I weren't just trained and educated, but could scheme, strategize, and play the game of the cutthroat elite.

He probably never considered his teachings would turn against him.

Istvan gazed down at me with a snarl. "Truer than you even know," he mumbled, tugging at the cuffs of his new uniform trimmed in gold, similar to the ones we had been sewing. Even more medals decorated his chest and arms, like he was awarding himself more every day. He used them to intimidate and make people believe he was beyond reproach.

He was right; he had taught me a lot. The tricks to influence and change perceptions. Propaganda.

Most people could easily be swayed and not even know they were, instantly bowing, letting you take over. Letting you control their lives, their minds, because of a perceived idea that you knew more and could "save them."

All smokescreen, lies, and theater.

"Shrewd. Resourceful. Strong. If only you had been born as my son." He peered down his nose at me. "What a general you would have made."

"You speak as if those things are coveted. That I would desire them." A derisive laugh came up my throat. "Males think they are the greatest beings, the highest level achievable. The strongest and the most powerful. Even more so with shiny awards they give themselves on their puffed-up chest. When those things would *just limit* me."

*You have no idea what I'm capable of.* I glared at him. Hell, I didn't even know what I was capable of.

Istvan's back straightened, his chin rising at my statement. "We'll see, my dear." His lip lifted. "Good thing I changed the Games to tonight."

Acid sunk my stomach. Tonight?

A tick in the back of my head made me wonder how he was even able to get here so fast if they were called because of our revolt. HDF was over forty-five minutes away on these roads. There was no way unless they happened to be coming here anyway. And if they were coming here anyway, why would he have so many soldiers with him?

"You will see, you and your insurgents here, exactly what happens to those who go against me." He leaned in closer. "Show me how far you can push those limits, Brexley. How far *you* will go to survive."

# Chapter 8

Fire crackled and sputtered from the pits, taunting and beckoning us closer. Energy clashed and struck the walls like cymbals. Lights shone down on the arena, the stage. Seats filled up for tonight's performance.

*"All the world's a stage, and all the men and women merely players."*

Shakespeare was a little too on the nose for me right now. But it's all we were to Istvan. Chess pieces and bit actors. A game in life, entertainment in death.

My gaze shot to Rosie, imagining this was not how she saw her last performance going. She stood only a few spots down, her eyes glazed, her head still bleeding. She struggled to stay on her feet, but she was alive.

For now.

I knew someone was going to die tonight. Glowering up at Istvan, his arms behind his back, smugness over his features. I realized how well he had done his research. He knew every player he wanted in the arena to be pitted against each other.

Scorpion, Ash, Killian, Kek, Maddox, Birdie, Wesley, Kitty, Hanna, Rosie, and Lukas.

Istvan didn't pick them by accident. Every one of them was personal, meant to hurt and punish me. This was the ultimate game of survival, showing the truth of people's character. Who you really were when it came down to life and death?

*"How far, Brexley, are you willing to go to survive?"*

The stadium was filled with inmates and all the HDF soldiers, the energy a strange mix of hunger, fear, excitement, and horror. There were no songs for blood, no chants for death, but the prisoners up in the stands knew how easy it would be for them to be thrown in with us if they fought back, if they vocally retaliated.

They happily made us the sacrifice to appease the god before them and so played along.

Figures moved from the doorway behind Istvan's private balcony. Olena and four others came from the shadows up to the railing, gazing down at us, covered in their finery and entitlement.

As if I ran into a wall, everything stopped. My head spun, and it took me longer than usual to understand. To grasp the people near Istvan. To make the connection.

Olena was next to Istvan, looping her arm in his, with a conceited smile painting her red lips. Caden moved in on the other side of her, his arms behind him, his face expressionless. The jolt of seeing my old best friend wearing the new HDF uniform, the marker on his breast and arm declaring he was only a rank below Istvan, should have been enough to tip everything sideways.

He wasn't. It was the three on the other side of Istvan, two men and a woman.

*"Ty vole!"* Fuck! Shit! No way! Lukas's entire body jerked, stumbling back, a hiss sliding through his teeth. His green eyes filled with shock and confusion. His gaze locked on the stunning blonde woman up on the balcony.

The same bright green eyes looked back at him.

The lover of Prague's leader.

Sonya.

Lukas's mother.

And standing next to her was the Prime Minister Leon. My brain couldn't even connect the dots before the fourth person stepped up into view, arrogance perfuming off him, almost knocking me off my feet.

"Iain." Killian breathed out his name, his expression a mix of shock, disgust, and bewilderment.

The cute young guard I taunted and teased when Killian first had me locked up in the palace stood at the railing, peering down with smugness. The one I so easily brushed off as naïve and sweet. The way he looked at me now, I realized it had all been an act.

73

The boy who blushed around me was a lie.

"It was *you*." Killian snarled. "You were the spy. You blew up my palace."

Iain smirked, his head dipping with pride and affirmation.

My jaw dropped. Iain was the one who planted the bombs?

It made sense. He was close enough no one questioned his motives or presence. Someone who almost wasn't seen or thought about because of his rank and shy demeanor. He purposely made himself part of the background, unnoticed and unquestioned.

Iain's mouth curled into a cruel smile. "Your arrogance made you blind, *lord*." He spit on the title. "You thought yourself *so* smart, *so* above the rest. Always ten steps ahead of everyone else, dismissing anyone you deemed below you. Well, look who is beneath *me* now."

Killian's jaw tightened. "Why? You throw your lot in with humans? You really think the fae are going to be all right with a human taking over?"

"No. That's why they have me." Sonya spoke. She didn't look much over thirty, with creamy skin and caramel blonde hair. Her bright green eyes popped like emeralds. The more I looked at her, the more I saw Lukas.

"They might not take a human, but they will take another noble fae, descended from Queen Aneira's court, sitting on your throne." She touched Leon's arm.

Pieces started to snap into a picture.

Killian huffed, his head shaking. "The worst foes are those who have no side but their own."

Sonya let out a peal of laughter.

"That's rich coming from you." She leveled her attention on Killian. "The one who murdered the rightful successor to get where he is. The one who came from nothing to become leader of the fae. I know who you are, Killian, and what kind of low-grade thieves you arise from."

Killian's chest expanded, the lock on his jaw tightening.

It was all beginning to make sense, though everything about it scared the hell out of me. Istvan and Leon were working together, putting Sonya, Leon's fae lover, in Killian's place. It gave them all the power with none of the fight from the fae in Budapest, while they continued to advance and strengthen their army.

It was why I didn't recognize so many soldiers in here. They were Leon's men. We all thought their egos were too big, and maybe they might clash down the road, but they decided to work together for this. And with Olena, they had Ukraine.

We were fucked.

"I should have seen this coming. From both of you." Lukas curled his hands into balls, his glare darting from his mother to Iain. "Can't stop wanting Mommy's approval, can you, Iain? You're so fucking pathetic," he scoffed.

"Look around, *little brother*, at who's the one up here and who's the one about to die?" Iain snapped back.

My head jerked between them, shock widening my eyes. "Brother?"

"Half." Lukas scoffed, his head shaking. "Way before she met my father, before she used my dad, crushed his heart, and walked out on us when I was a child." Sonya flicked her eyes with annoyance, as if the topic of Lukas's father bored her. She seemed little phased at having one of her sons in the pit about to fight for his life. "She was whoring herself to a married noble fae, got pregnant with this bastard." Lukas motioned to Iain. Now I noticed they had the same coloring and blond hair.

Every piece had been meticulously planned and perfectly executed— who Iain was to Sonya and how they were moving her in to take over Killian's role.

Game. Set. Match.

I had to hand it to Istvan. He played this out faultlessly.

My gaze slid toward the general but paused on Caden. You could see nothing in Caden's expression. At one time, I could read him like a book, now I saw nothing but a wall. How did he feel about Istvan marrying his fiancée? What about his mother being missing? I know Caden loved her dearly, but could Istvan's power over his son sway that?

My gaze bounced back to Istvan, his focus on me, as if he were watching for every revelation to unfold on my face. Our eyes locked, his superiority inching his frame taller, his eyes brighter.

"My friends, I know you came to see some entertainment." He spoke to Leon and Sonya but stared at me. "Let me not keep it from you any longer."

The gate squealed behind me, the sound of a heavy object hitting the dirt, spinning me around.

At Boyd's feet, a huge, bloody, dirty mass lay on the ground. It took nine of them to carry the beast in. Boyd winked at me before they all retreated behind the gate.

"Warwick!" I screamed, my legs already running. My knees scraped the ground as I fell next to him, rolling him onto his back. "Warwick?" I brushed the knotted hair from his face, my hands on either side of his head.

A sob stuck in my throat, seeing how much worse he was in the light. His face was so puffy from the trauma I could hardly recognize him. "Farkas…" I leaned closer, trying to put as much energy as I could into him, taking on a heavy dose of his pain, attempting to heal him.

His lids parted, letting me see the strip of aqua in his eyes. I didn't realize until he was here how much I missed him, how off I felt without him. We balanced each other, keeping the other from falling over either side.

"Princess…" he croaked, his voice barely making it out. His hand covered mine, taking several beats to gather the energy to talk again. "I think you owe me a lot of blowjobs for that."

I coughed up a mix of laughter and relief, and a smile prodded my lips, I didn't think myself capable of, given the circumstances. "Deal."

My mouth covered his, claiming the Legend with every ounce of my soul. A low, pained grunt huffed from him as I wrapped my tongue around his, sucking and licking, giving him what he needed. Our connection was better than any healing remedy out there. His starvation switched quickly, gorging on my power, slinking through my soul, forcing a moan out of my lips. I could feel him everywhere. Taking without apology and demanding more. A growl crawled up his chest, his fingers threading through my hair, grabbing the back of my head, yanking me closer, deepening the kiss into crude desire.

The man had the power to make me forget everything and everyone around me, crumble my walls, and seize my soul and make me beg for more.

*"Kovacs…"* I could feel his lust, his need for me sliding over my skin, through my pussy.

*Clank.* The arena filled with the sounds of hydraulics, breaking me away from Warwick. A dozen massive metal cages rose from the ground we were standing on. Trapdoors strategically placed around the pit were nearly undetectable to the eye.

"What the hell?" I muttered, climbing to my feet.

Instantly roars, snarls, and howls echoed from inside the barred cages, animals frantically pacing back and forth.

Holy. Fucking. Shit.

Istvan had taken another note from the Roman games.

Dozens of wild animals filled the cages, bursting with rage and fear, ready to kill.

"They haven't been fed in a while." Istvan grabbed two drinks from a table set out for him and his party. "This should be exciting. Anyone want to take bets?"

Olena giggled with delight as Istvan handed her a glass of Pálinka. Caden still didn't move, watching every move between his father, new stepmother, and us. For one second, his gaze found mine like he needed me. A flare of the connection burrowed into our DNA, an instinct to seek each other out. For one second, I could feel my old friend there.

A roar from a lion snapped my attention back to the cages. Multiple tigers, boars, lions, and bears occupied the pens.

Istvan realized we wouldn't battle each other and changed the battlefield to one we couldn't protest by bringing in an opponent we had no choice but to fight.

The animals didn't need to strip away the layers and find their primal instincts to survive. We did.

Kill or be killed.

The crowd of soldiers cheered as the metal doors unlocked with a clank, freeing the hungry, wild beasts.

My spine went ramrod straight, fear flushing through me, oxygen barely skimming my lungs. Warwick struggled to his feet next to me, stronger than he had been when he first came in, but still frail. We both observed the dozens of predators prowling out of their cages.

We were wounded, drained, and defenseless. Easy prey.

My attention went to my friends, all of them instinctively clumping together. Safety in numbers. It was true in some cases, building a wall of defense together, but there were times it made you more vulnerable, easy for them to circle and attack. Istvan once demonstrated this to Caden and me through a game of billiards. Grouped together, you could hit a lot at once, but once they were divided, you had to go after each singularly. Right now, the beasts had their kills all in one lump.

Warwick rumbled next to me, and without a word or look, I could sense he understood the same thing. We were the only two still alive who had fought in the Games, who understood the strategy of survival.

*The art of war.*

"Split up in pairs," I bellowed, my arms waving. "Find anything you can to use as a weapon or shield."

No one hesitated at my order. They accepted my strategy, darting in different directions, already confusing the animals, who cranked their heads in different ways, trying to pick out the weakest link.

I assessed everything in the stadium which could be used as a weapon. Roars thundered the massive room, echoing the heartbeat thumping painfully against my ribs. The tigers reacted first, swiping their claws at the closest victims.

"There." Warwick huffed through his swollen mouth, pointing, his legs already moving for a torch on the outside of a gate. It was something we had once used to fight against each other in Halálház Games.

In Věrhăza, we stood together.

"Get up on a cage," he yelled back at me, yanking the torch from its holder.

Right as I turned, my brain registered something leaping for me, a large orange and black mass, before the weight crashed into me, the claws sinking into my skin. The tiger and I hit the ground, the weight crushing me.

People always assume lions were stronger, when in actuality tigers were. With their condensed muscle mass and agility, they were a far more aggressive and faster breed.

My mind blocked the excruciating pain shredding through me, adrenaline and terror taking over as teeth snapped for my face, claws digging into my flesh.

*"Brexley!"* I could feel Warwick's voice bellow within me, his fear and rage pushing out all his own agony and thrusting his energy into me.

A cry broke from my mouth, my fist cracking into the tiger's throat, then its eye. The beast bellowed as Warwick singed its body with the flame from the torch.

Roaring, it bucked back in defense, retreating off me. Warwick's palm fisted my collar, yanking me up. "Come on!"

Feeling wobbly, I got to my feet with no time to reflect on wounds or broken bones. I was alive, and that was the baseline to keep moving.

"Get up there!" He shoved me up on top of a cage before climbing up beside me. Blood soaked my uniform from the cat's nails, turning the gray into a muddy brown, my limbs shivering with adrenaline, pain, and fear. The arena was a sea of movement, filled with screams and roars, chilling me to the bone. My attention swept over the pit.

Scorpion, Hanna, and Maddox had climbed onto a cage across from ours, their backs together, fighting off beasts from all sides. Kek and Lukas were on one farther away, while Killian, Sloane, and Rosie scaled one next to us.

Birdie, Wesley, Ash, and Kitty grabbed other torches and fought near the fire pits. Birdie and Wesley were amazing fighters and worked together well, but Ash and Kitty surprised me. Enthralled me with their movements as if it were a performance.

Whatever issues they had disappeared when they had to work together. Their unity was ingrained in their very beings. They knew each other so well; it was as though you were watching one person. They moved and fought like a dance; a rhythm so deeply-rooted they didn't have to think. They just were. And through all the chaos and fear, the tiny little moment gave me hope. That no matter what, they were family, along with Warwick. And they would fight and die next to each other without question.

"We need more weapons." Killian's voice yanked me back. Puffing himself up, he struck his boot and swung at the lion trying to jump up on the cage with them. Rosie kicked at it as well. "We can't sustain this."

We couldn't. They would wear us down and leap the moment our walls started to deteriorate.

Once again, my gaze shot around the space, trying to find anything we could use; otherwise, this was a lost cause. Even the gladiators got shields and swords. My attention darted up to the points board. This time, I noticed several HDF and Hungarian flags sticking out from the top of it. They were on wood poles.

It would take a nimble person to get up there, but we had to at least try. I turned to the only person I knew here who could scale things like a monkey.

"Birdie!" I screamed at her, pointing up at the flags.

Her head went from me to the potential weapons high up. She didn't bother responding, her tiny figure beelining in that direction, probably quickly mapping out her course as she went. Hopping up on a cage, she leaped to the wall surrounding us, using the frame of the gate to pull herself up onto the ledge where the stands started. There were hollers from the crowd—some seemed to be cheering her on, while others hissed, trying to grab for her, and push her back into the pit. Birdie dodged and weaved past them, climbing higher up the stands. Springing, her tiny frame flew like a bird, jumping onto the points board, clamping onto it with everything she had while she scooted and slinked up the side, reaching the top.

"Damn." I heard Warwick breathe out next to me in reverence.

Birdie ascended to the top, yanking out the flags. They waved in the air as if she had just won the quest, then she tossed them to us.

Wesley darted over, grabbing the first one and passing the rest to any group who had no weapon at all. Killian, Scorpion, and Kek each got one, while Warwick, Kitty, and Ash had the torches.

It still wasn't enough. We needed a plan, or we would not survive.

Birdie started to descend, but this time the crowd was ready, knowing the only route she had accessible to her. Running along the ledge of the seating area, soldiers rushed for her, one pulling out a knife. My mouth opened, primed to scream at her.

"Birdie!" A male voice stole my cry of warning. Birdie jerked to the sound, the movement shifting her slightly out of the trajectory of the weapon.

A grunt came from her mouth as the blade grazed her hip, her body falling from the ledge.

"No!" I cried out, her form hitting the dirt with a thud. Wesley zipped to her, getting her to her feet and back toward the fire. Her features seized in pain, and she was limping, but otherwise, she seemed okay.

Her gaze lifted to the stands, to the one who called her name, who warned her.

Caden stood at the rail, his hands gripping the bar, his jaw locked down, eyes on her, but his face held no emotion as if he had never opened his mouth. Istvan stared at his son, his cheek twitching with fury, shock, and embarrassment. Caden had warned her. *He helped a fae.*

My thoughts were quickly dashed as a bear vaulted for Ash and Kitty with a roar. Its claws sliced across Kitty's shoulder, flinging her to the ground, ramming straight into Ash, almost throwing him into the firepit.

"Noooo!" Warwick belted. His instinct to protect them already had him jumping off the cage, running like a madman toward any foe wanting to hurt his family. He darted right up to the beast, thrusting out his arm, burning the back of the bear with the flames of the torch.

It reared up, veering around, its paw swinging around in defense. Its mouth opened in a feral snarl, showing off long, pointed teeth. Standing on its hind legs, the bear eclipsed Warwick, stretching over fourteen feet tall.

When the wall came down and flooded Earth with magic, it altered the wild animals' DNA. They were bigger, deadlier, and more prehistoric-looking than the ones I saw in pictures of zoos from the time before Earth and the Otherworld meshed.

"Warwick!" My throat shredded in my horror. The bear came down on him with all its weight, slamming Warwick to the ground, nails digging into his chest. Before I could move, Maddox leaped from his position on top of a cage near them, flinging himself onto the back of the bear. His arms wrapped around its neck, digging one of his hands into its eye.

The bear's pained roar shuddered throughout the entire place, vibrating the ground. In a blink, it shook Maddox off, casting him to the dirt with a thud, stealing the air from his lungs.

"Maddox!" Scorpion shouted. The animal's massive paw slashed across Maddox's body, the claws gutting him, dumping blood and his insides out onto the dirt. Warwick punched at the bear, trying to stop him as Maddox screamed, his back arching and thrashing while the bear ripped him apart.

The bear reared back on Warwick, its talons slashing for The Wolf.

My mouth opened in horror; tears and grief plunged through my lungs. "Noooooooooooo!" The cry erupted deep from me, burning and sizzling through my soul and up my spine. Time seemed to stop and speed up all at the same time. My universe crashed at my feet.

Fury. Grief. Hate.

My broken pieces forged in wrath, assembled with rage.

I warned the world if it took him from me…

I'd burn it to the ground.

# Chapter 9

Power scorched my veins and seared my vision. Lightning crackled and popped overhead, blowing out all the lights except the one illuminating from me. I could taste the strands of all my magic. Sweet with life, bitter with death. The energy of the air, which was Aneira's dominant force, whipped and snapped through my hair. I could sense the ghosts haunting this land, from wars past to the newly deceased, all coming to me like a beacon. Their light. Their Queen.

I was life. I was death. I was the in-between.

I was *The Grey*.

I could feel it in my bones, etched within my DNA. There was nothing the same as me. No group or classification to define me. A fluke of circumstance and timing. Tad once told me I had the magic from Aneira's family line. One side the power of air, the other the power of fire. I contained them both.

I was my own to define. To take life and to give it back.

To control it.

Spirits zinged around me, death at my beck and call. My own soldiers. They needed no direct order; they could feel what I wanted.

To take out all threats to my family.

"Mine…" I growled, my gaze on Warwick, my energy commanding the ghosts which came in by the dozens, this land a graveyard of wars past and present.

*Crack!*

Multiple bolts of lightning zapped down on the pit, and thunder boomed, tossing me back on my ass into the dirt. As if a switch turned off, everything went quiet. Still.

The fire from the pits lit the room until the backup generators kicked on, lighting the stadium in dim light.

My head spun as I pushed myself to sit up, feeling energy still crackle under my skin. Warwick was a few feet away, the bear lying motionless next to him.

Blinking, my gaze wandered over the quiet space. No roars of animals, no screams of fear and death. Not a whisper. They were all scattered across the arena. I could see some of my friends moving, stirring from their haze.

But not one animal twitched.

They were *all* dead.

My invisible soldiers had killed for their queen.

Tension hung in the room like daggers. Shock. Confusion.

"Warwick..." I crawled over to him, my hands and eyes scouring his body in the dim light, noticing he was still in one piece and breathing.

"*Sotet démonom.*" His lids lifted with a groan, his mouth barely moving, his eyes darting around seeing the lifeless animals around us. "Saved my ass again..." He coughed, his breath wheezing in his lungs. He yanked my face a breath from his. "Still doesn't get you out of giving me blowjobs."

A chuckled curled me over him, my lips grazing his. "Tit for tat, Farkas."

"Gladly, Kovacs," he rumbled against my mouth.

Movement around me jerked my head to see my friends sitting up, their expressions struck with bewilderment and touches of fear.

They all roused except one.

"Maddox..." I whispered out, scrambling over Warwick to the gutted body covered in blood, his eyes staring absently into the void. "Oh, please, no." I skirted up next to him, my hands on his body.

"Noooo!" Scorpion bellowed, racing over, falling down on the other side of him. "Maddox, you asshole, you can't die." Scorpion turned to me with wild terror. "Do something! Help him!"

I had nothing left. I had used it all up. I couldn't even feel Warwick or Scorpion, our link dulled, but I still tried to dig deep. "Come on..." I grunted, trying to force energy up. But it was like twisting a dry rag, hoping for a drip of water. Panic and grief spiraled tears down my face. "Please," I begged, trying again, but nothing was there. I could sense he was already gone.

83

I was too late. Maddox was past my help.

"No, no, no!" Scorpion barked, his anger flashing over his face seeing my grief-stricken expression. "Try again!"

"I'm sorry..." I croaked, my shoulders sagging. Scorpion's anger turned to utter pain, his attention going down to his friend. The agony at seeing his comrade—a brother—dead shattered through him, causing my own. "I'm so sorry." I felt useless, guilty I couldn't save him and even more so because they were all here because of me. From the day I walked onto their base, all they knew was death, loss, and pain.

Scorpion leaned over Maddox, his grief silent, which made it even more palpable to me. Birdie and Wesley, the remaining two of their group, came around Scorpion, mourning another loss. Another fallen comrade.

The cold prickles of eyes scratched at the back of my neck, popping the little bubble I was in. A wave of fear rushed in, awareness that every single thing I had done had been observed.

Twisting my head back, my attention landed on Istvan. The general's penetrating gaze burned into me, his jaw locked, his shoulders tight.

Fuck.

Slowly, I stood up, facing the party up on the balcony. They had seen and experienced everything. And there was no explanation for why all the animals were dead while most of my friends dusted themselves off, getting to their feet. Battle worn, but alive and unhurt.

Leon, Sonya, Iain, and Olena's expressions were struck with terror.

Caden looked confused, almost hurt, as if I betrayed him.

Istvan stared at me, no emotion telling me either way how he felt, which was worse than the others' fear. Fear was a normal response. But he examined, studied, and assessed me like an experiment.

I could see his mind whirling as he took in the information of what he observed, putting it together. Then he did something which iced every bone in my body. He *laughed.* Istvan's head fell back, though you could hear no real joy in the sound. It was calculated—controlled.

His blue eyes found mine, his face suddenly serious. "My dear, you keep surprising me at every turn." He studied me for a few beats, showing no hint as to what he was really thinking. "Maybe I should have listened more when Dr. Karl said you were different, that you changed when you returned home, and you were no longer *human.*"

The memory of Dr. Karl's note attached to the files left for Istvan I found in his office months ago came back to me. *"No human can sustain even half of these levels. Ms. Kovacs should be dead. She is not even showing signs of organ failure. If anything, she seems stronger and healthier. We must discuss these results in private. There seems to be just one explanation."*

Peering at Istvan, I realized he was neither shocked nor fearful of what he saw. It was almost as if he were waiting. Wondering.

Dread dropped my stomach into the earth.

"I was told recently you were given the fae pills daily under Killian's watch." Istvan lifted his graying eyebrow, glancing at Killian, then back at me. "And they did not affect you."

*How did he know?* Before I could even finish the sentence, my attention darted to Iain. A slow, smug smile twitched on his mouth, happily taking the credit. *Of course.* He was the only one who could have said anything to Istvan. He was there the whole time, seeing and hearing everything about the tests.

"I looked back at the timing when you *robbed* them from me." Istvan shot a look at his son and me, telling us he knew I wasn't alone. "Did you know the whole batch was heading for Leon." Istvan motioned to the prime minister. "Every one of those soldiers died. Painful, brutal deaths. And all of Killian's test subjects died in the same fashion. *Except you.*" He let his accusation ring in the air. "Out of all the test subjects, you are the one it worked on. Why is that? Why didn't you die as the rest did? Simply luck?"

He tilted his head, studying me.

Staying silent, my chest pumped up and down. Istvan was figuring it was the pills that turned me into this and gave me fae-like powers. In reality, I was always this way, which is why the pills didn't kill me too.

His lips pressed together. Pushing his shoulders back, he motioned to the guards behind the gates down in the pit. "Grab her."

"What?" Caden jerked to his father.

The guards reacted instantly. The gates squeaked open, and dozens of armed guards filed out of the tunnels, coming from opposite directions.

Warwick shoved me behind him, growling at the sentries. Ash and Scorpion clustered around me in defense, everyone else following behind.

I could see how this would play out. The newly fae guards were strong, energized, and armed to the teeth. We were weak, bleeding, and some barely standing.

They would join Maddox in a matter of seconds because they were trying to defend me from something they couldn't stop, no matter what they did. I wouldn't let them risk their lives. We had lost too many already.

"No!" I pushed around Warwick, stepping in front of them all, my head shaking. "Don't."

"What the fuck are you doing, Kovacs?" Warwick gritted, glaring at me. I hoped my expression conveyed everything I wanted to say. The connection between us wasn't even humming yet. I knew it would; I felt the binds there, but using so much of my power blew out the fuse, and it needed more time to build up again.

"The only thing I can," I responded, feeling the pounding of feet coming up behind me.

"No," Ash barked, stepping forward, a burnt-out torch still in his hands.

"Please." I put up my palm. "This will just end badly. I can't lose any more of you... I just can't."

My friends shifted on their feet, not liking my choice. They glanced at Warwick, ready to respond if he gave them the word to fight.

"Don't." I pleaded with him. "Please let me go. There is no other option."

The guards came up from behind, clutching my arms and binding them with cuffs, pulling me away from my family.

"Wait!" Warwick's voice boomed through the arena, turning all our heads to him. He pointed his gaze at Istvan. "Take me too."

Istvan's brows hitched up high on his forehead in surprise at Warwick's words. It only lasted for a moment before I saw it shift into interest.

"No!" I shook my head violently, yanking against the sentries' hold. "Just me! You don't need him. You just want me."

"No!" Warwick half spat at me, signifying where I went, he went. "If she goes, I go too." He motioned between us. "You know you've dreamed about possessing me. The *great legend*, Warwick Farkas. The infamous Wolf. Come on. Take me." He hit his chest in a challenge. "Just think what you could do with *my* blood."

Istvan's curiosity flamed instantly into desire. Not sexual desire, but desire for more power, more dominance. To own and control *The Legend*, Istvan would become lore in his own right. The man who caught *The Wolf*.

Greed and ego perfumed off Markos, and he gave his guards on one side a slight nod.

A cry bellowed from my lips as they swarmed around Warwick, my body curving forward.

Istvan smirked. "Take them both."

A gun was primed at my head, my teeth crunching together at every pothole or bit of rough terrain the armored car rolled over, thinking this would be the time the guard's finger would slip, and he'd blow my brains all over the seat.

My muscles were locked tight. I hadn't moved a hair as the caravan headed back to the city, afraid of any notice from the soldiers I was jammed in with. They were high off their catch and buzzing with toxic male adrenaline, which was never good for a lone female.

There were no windows in the back of the armored truck, and with my slight view of the front windshield, all I could see was darkness.

Istvan, Olena, and Caden were in the car in front of ours. Iain, Sonya, and Leon were behind us, and somewhere after them, they had Warwick. Purposely keeping us separate. And of course, I couldn't contact him or see if he was all right. The worst time to have our link burned out.

The car finally slowed, and through the front windshield, I could see us slip out of the night and into another dark tunnel, following down a passage adorned with fire bulbs every few yards.

My heart started to race when we pulled into a wider area, the caravan of armored cars parking together. Some stayed back in Věrhăza as Istvan ordered more guards on the gate we had tried to break out of earlier.

The heavy car door unlocked and opened, my stomach twisting as he shoved the gun into my head.

"Move."

Climbing out of the car, I immediately searched for Warwick. He was brought out of the car next to ours, his eyes already on me. To others, he'd appear cold, callous, and even bored, but I could sense all the colors of him. His rage, apprehension, and exhaustion. His love, life, and determination. He bristled with carnage and violence, and I knew I was the only thing keeping it from spilling out.

"Take them to the cells." Istvan directed the men around us, already turning his back on me as if I were nothing—worse than a stranger. One he had never spent hours teaching, never sat across from dinner, on holidays. I lived with them for years, but all those memories were gone.

Several guards walked me toward our prison.

Istvan, with Olena on his arm, spoke to Leon. "I'm sure the ladies would prefer to head back to HDF where they can talk dresses and plan for the gala." So many human males were sexists. Istvan's misogyny was legendary. "But I want to show you what I'm doing down in the labs."

Labs. I figured he'd bring us here, but now I knew for sure exactly where I was—under the factory in the industrial area in the 9th district.

Olena grinned with delight at the idea, her face a pretty picture of vapid emptiness, while I physically saw Sonya stiffen at his words, the muscles in her face twitching and tightening.

Fae did not think of women as less than men. They were warriors. Leaders. Generals. But many human males thought females were just interested in pretty things, to be patted on the head and protected.

"Actually, I would be interested in seeing the labs," Sonya replied rigidly. "I need to understand what is going on and am quite interested in the process."

I watched Istvan shift on his feet, his lips pinching.

"Of course." He nodded, tension running through his tone as well, his gaze darting to Leon as if he should put his woman in place. Leon stood there with a blank expression, but I could sense the threads of his own self-importance and resentment billowing off him. The prime minister might appear to be accepting his alliance with Markos, but he didn't like it one bit. Two huge wannabe alphas in the room puffing up their chests at each other when the real one was behind me, being propelled down a hallway to another prison—all for me.

Glancing over my shoulder, trying to spot Warwick, my eyes landed on Caden. He stood there watching me intently, his features hiding his feelings, but for one second, I thought I saw the boy I knew in his eyes. The softness and love that had looked upon me so many times. A friendship that was supposed to stand the test of time.

"Move it!" A guard shoved me harder, breaking the connection, and taking me further away from freedom.

We were escorted through a long, dim corridor and down another flight of stairs. My skin prickled with a chill you only experienced far underground. I bit down on my lip. The smell of damp earth and stagnant air doubled my pulse.

The guards herded us through several security doors and guard posts, walking us into a room lined with small cells. The blueprint reminded me of the brig at HDF. The holding cells were similar, little more than cement and iron bars. Cold and harsh. Except in HDF, they were modern, sterile, and brighter.

Just a few bulbs lit up these underground cells, and prisoners were only given a bucket to relieve themselves. Even Věrhăza gave you a blanket and a hole to piss in.

Figures moved up close to the bars, peering out at the new arrivals. Adult women and men looking to be of various ages and races.

All fae.

"Put them in the back two cells." One guard took lead, pointing to the furthest ones. "They can't escape those." If this was similar to HDF, the back lockups were built with multiple heavy-duty locks and thicker iron bars to contain the stronger and more dangerous fae criminals.

A pair of soldiers pushed me roughly into a cell while a group shoved Warwick in the one beside mine, the wall between us over two feet thick.

Our eyes caught right before we were pushed inside.

The link wasn't there yet, but I could feel it thrum through me, hinting on the horizon. Although it didn't feel necessary at this time, I knew he could read everything in my eyes without it, feel my emotions from afar. And know that once again, we would get through this.

We would fight.

We would kill.

We would survive.

My lids fluttered when murmuring reached my ears. My eyes burned, and my head pounded with exhaustion, only drifting in moments of surface sleep. My body ached, and my muscles were locked up from the cold concrete floor.

Sensing a figure on the other side of my cage, my eyes bolted wide open. I spotted a familiar man peering through his glasses down at me. The lights were very dim here, but I would recognize the pudgy, short stature of Dr. Karl anywhere. Two guards were on either side of him.

Not reacting, I watched him write notes on his clipboard before he tucked it under his arm, reaching for an object in his white coat pocket.

"I will need to run a primary test on her blood first," he spoke to the men. "Restrain her."

I didn't fight as the men banged into my cell, grabbing me by the arms and pinning me against the wall. I could feel the hum of Warwick jolting in the cage over, a breeze of him brushing over my skin.

"Kovacs?" he growled through the bars to me.

"I'm fine," I replied to him, my voice steady. The guards were of no consequence to me. The only focus I had was on the doctor I had grown up with. He had been there for all my vaccinations, my wounds, and broken bones, giving me lollipops and smiles. At one time, I thought he was a kind man.

"What happened to you?" I sneered as he moved closer to me, a syringe in his hand. "I thought doctors wanted to help people?"

"That's what I'm doing." He wrapped a rubber band around my arm, popping out my veins. "I am helping people. *Humans*. How do you know fae essence isn't the future of vaccinations for human diseases? The cure for cancer?"

"For erectile dysfunction?" I arched my brow at him.

He huffed like I was a silly girl. "Science is ever-evolving. Sacrifices have to be made along the way."

I tried not to flinch when he jabbed my arm with the needle.

"You can make it sound as sensible and pretty as you want, but there is a fine line between true science and a quack. You sound exactly like Dr. Rapava. Whatever he started out to do, he went off the deep end, pushing his experiments further and further. Where is your line, *doctor*? Do you have one anymore? When does killing innocent children and sucking the essence out of beings, killing an entire species to enhance another, too far for *science*?"

"They aren't innocent. They shouldn't even exist. They go against science and nature."

"Says who? *You?* Other humans? Weren't they technically on the earth first? Who gives you the right to say they don't deserve to exist?" I sneered. "They were here before us. Maybe it's the humans who go against nature." I thought of someone like Ash—he was nature, beauty, and kindness. One with the earth. He could never be against nature. Fae believed in harmony with other living things, to give back to the environment as much as they took.

Humans were the selfish, arrogant, greedy ones who robbed the earth of its resources and splendor for their own personal gain, believing it was *owed* to them.

"Of course, you would be on *their* side now. You are one of *them*." Dr. Karl's lip rose, yanking out the syringe from my arm, the barrel full of my blood. "I knew the moment you came back to HDF something was amiss with you. That you weren't right. All the tests I did were correct from the beginning. You came back *wrong*."

"It's sad someone such as you, sworn to help and heal, is so closed-minded and unaccepting. You are a fraud, *doctor*." I spat out the title with disgust, leaning in closer, my emotions getting the better of me. "And guess what? I didn't come *back* wrong... I was always this way." The moment the words came out, dread dropped in my stomach.

Slamming my mouth shut, I kept any emotion from my face. I hadn't meant to let it slip. I didn't want Istvan or Dr. Karl to know I had always been different, that the very thing they were hunting for was me. Let them believe it was the pills that changed me, because if they found out the truth and tapped into it, somehow used me... I couldn't even contemplate it.

Karl's lids narrowed, trying to work out my meaning. After a few beats, he shook his head and retreated from my cell, the sentries following, locking the door behind. They'd rather believe I was corrupted now than consider I had been fae all along. They watched me grow up, cared for me, and witnessed I was no different from human children. If they were wrong about me, that meant they were wrong about fae.

He turned and faced me. "General Markos thinks you are the key to what we've been looking for. The perfect formula resides in your veins." He lifted the syringe, examining it as if it would give him the answers. "If he's right, you will never leave this building again." He paused. "And if he's wrong, you will end up like your father." He stepped away, leaving me staring at the empty spot.

# Chapter 10

"Warwick?" I whispered hoarsely, standing in the corner closest to him. Dr. Karl and his little gang had just left his cage. By the speed they were in and out, Warwick gave them no fight. "Warwick?" I called again. He was pulling back. The link was coming back, but slowly. A hint of his shadow, a buzz of energy, but something I could still chalk up to my imagination if I didn't know it was real.

"I'm here." His deep voice was low and gravelly, climbing up my legs, throbbing at my core. I could tell he was sitting on the ground against the adjacent wall we shared.

"You okay?" I lowered myself, flattening my spine against the same concrete, wanting to feel him through it.

"You're worried because they took some blood?" He snorted. "Princess, I've bled enough to fill oceans. Mosquitos have taken more from me."

"I was talking about the other stuff." The torture. The hole. The Games. We had yet to have a moment to connect since he was taken from me in the shower room.

He scoffed. "Been through worse."

I turned to peer out the bars. Even if I couldn't see him, I knew we were only feet apart.

Warwick didn't expand on his response, and I didn't really need him to. We weren't the type to speak our feelings out loud. We didn't have to. Our connection was deeper and stronger than any words spoken.

"I felt them in the pit—they killed for you," he finally said after several moments, meaning the ghosts.

Sighing, I tipped my head back on the cement, pulling my legs to my chest. "They came for…"

"*The Grey.*" He rumbled back to me, forcing a wheeze from my lungs. The power of the title skating over my bones was terrifying and familiar at the same time.

"How… how did you know that name?" I jerked my head toward his cell.

"I don't know," he replied, his voice displaying no real emotion. "I could feel it wrapping around me, feeding off and strengthening me. Like we're each other's fuckin' charging station."

I twisted toward the corner, taking in his meaning. I had felt it too. Each time we shared energy or helped the other heal, we took and gave. My power was tied to him from the very beginning, as he was to mine. And it only strengthened and bound us closer together.

"I don't know what's going to happen to us here," I said quietly, not speaking my true fears of what was ahead. "The hole might be a holiday in comparison."

He exhaled, and I could gather he was thinking the same thing. Without our link to help each other through, one of us might not survive.

"You know what seems to spark that connection back to life…" he tapered off; his voice filled with innuendo.

I let out a small chuckle. "Kinda hard from this distance, Farkas."

"You underestimate my hardness and size once again, Kovacs."

I groaned out a laugh, my hand rubbing my face, though heat danced down my thighs, making my nipples tighten. He could turn me on in the most demented and terrifying conditions.

The man was gifted. In more ways than one.

"Am I wrong?" I heard something slide over the ground, my gaze catching his hand trying to reach me through the bars. "We fuck, princess, and the world thanks us."

Another snort vaulted from my mouth and nose, my head shaking. "Can't disagree with you." I pulled myself closer to the corner, pushing my hand through the bars as far as I could.

The tips of our fingers grazed, and I felt the electricity spark down my arm, going straight to my pussy, forcing my breath to hitch. Our skin was barely in contact, but feeling him, touching him, gave me life. It filled my lungs with more than air.

*"You feel like fucking life. Air in my lungs."* Warwick's sentiment rushed back to me, filling me up and forcing me to chew each syllable like it was food.

Warwick grunted, straining until he wrapped two fingers around mine. The simple act heaved emotion from my gut. My eyes watered, a little whimper escaping from my lips as I held on for dear life, not caring the bars were cutting into my arm.

I had no doubt what I felt for him, what I always had but had been too scared to face. I still was. He wasn't someone you just loved, simple, sweet, as I had Caden. Warwick demolished and consumed. A love that razed you to the ground, taking the world with you.

His fingers squeezed firmer around mine. And I knew in my gut he felt the same in return. We might not speak it out loud yet, but it was there, sparking between us, tying a firm knot on our survival together or our death.

*"Kovacs..."* I heard a whisper of breath in my ear.

I let out a quiet cry. Relief. Happiness. It was barely there, but it was enough to know it was coming back. I pushed my shadow toward him with all my strength. It was only a second, but I was with him.

He leaned against the wall, his head tipped back exactly like mine, his eyes shut, a hint of a smile shadowing his mouth.

His eyes popped open as if he could sense me.

"Anytime you want to start on those I.O.U. blowjobs." He lifted his brow.

A blink and I was back in my cell, the link not strong enough to hold for long yet.

"Or are you hoping for a threesome?" he rasped out, his finger stroking mine.

"So, you're open to me bringing Scorpion in then?" I pushed up my voice with a hopeful glee, a grin riding over my mouth.

He pinched my hand painfully.

I laughed.

He held onto my fingers before I could jerk them out of his grip. "Think you're funny, Kovacs?"

"No, I was being perfectly serious. The man is really hot."

A growl came from the legend, his hand clamping down harder. It was all bullshit. We both knew there would be no one else.

"All your boyfriends combined couldn't even come close to me."

Wasn't that the truth.

"And all the tree fairies, sirens, and snake shifters in the world couldn't even *try* to compete with me."

"Don't I know it," he huffed. "You have a fucking leash around my neck, and I not only want it and like it... I need it."

I frowned. "You don't have a leash. You freely walk by my side, *Wolf.*"

The moment the final word came out of my mouth, I felt my body seize, a flash in my head of us together, blood and carnage around us.

The Grey.

The Wolf.

His fingers strangled mine as if he experienced the same thing.

*"Kovacs."* A tingle started up my thigh, the lightest touch sliding through my folds.

"Fuck." My back arched, oxygen catching, my hands rolling into balls, my nails digging into his knuckles.

A noise came from Warwick, filled with dark desire. Carnal.

The invisible ghost of his hands palmed my thighs ever so lightly, pushing them apart, his mouth skimming lightly through me. Even the hint of his touch and my body reacted, pulsing hotly, feeling it spread through my veins. I held onto his actual hand, my lids slamming shut, my nipples hardening, my skin crackling with energy.

"Warwick." I bit down on my lip, feeling him more prominently with each beat of my heart. His tongue slid in deeper, lips sucking and nipping.

"Oh, gods..." I croaked, my body responding, my hips lifting, pushing against his presence.

My lashes fluttered open, my gaze landing on blurred aqua eyes, glinting with hunger, his fingers teasing my entrance.

Lights abruptly flicked on through the room, like morning had just been turned on by a switch. The air was filled with the sounds of men yelling and metal clanking. I jolted with the sudden harshness, my hand letting go of Warwick's, slicing through our link with a cleaver. My body screamed with anger, being torn from bliss and plunged into fear in a second, pounding my pulse in my ears.

Scrambling up to my feet, I stood against the far wall. Armed guards came straight down the row for us, the soles of their shoes pounding across the cement in a steady rhythm. A sound that screamed pain and danger. Dread sunk in my stomach, knowing my reprieve was over.

Unlocking my cell, they ripped open the door, barking orders at me.

Hands grabbed me. Cuffs circled my wrists. They heaved me out, practically dragging me down the passage.

"Kovacs!"

My head whirled around, catching Warwick's eyes. His hands circled the bars.

"Whatever it takes."

It was not a request.

The cluster of guards hauled me a different way than we came yesterday, the underground passage growing brighter with lights the farther we went, reminding me of the passages Ash and I went down to get here.

My head jerked to the side as we passed another set of cells. This one was filled with children, crammed together, all various ages and races, but all fae. The older ones seemed to take on a parental role, holding the younger fae, who could only express their terror through wails. They were all still children, but they looked far past their years. Their eyes were devoid of hope; they were only surviving because that's what we did. The will to live was built into our DNA.

My gaze searched the single cage, hoping to see the little girl I had seen on the table when Ash and I came in. The one I promised myself I would help.

She wasn't there.

I knew it already; there was no way she would have survived, but it didn't stop the wretched sickness from charring the back of my throat and watering my eyes.

A young boy of barely six stretched his skinny arm through the bars, trying to grab one of the guards, whimpering, "Hungry…"

"Get the fuck back—disgusting, dirty fae." A guard tugged his baton from his belt, banging against the bars. An older girl with feather-like hair yanked the young boy back quick enough; the club missed hitting him. She pulled him to her, glaring at the guard.

Then the little girl's eyes met mine, her walls still up, but she watched me with curiosity before I was dragged away from them. Acid gurgled in my stomach with heartache and anger, rage sparking adrenaline into my vessels. The feel of energy pumped off my skin.

We turned down another hallway, a set of doors with a card-only entry next to it.

My throat tightened, struggling to swallow, anticipation grinding down my esophagus. A guard swiped his card, the door opening. I knew in my gut what was on the other side, but I still wasn't prepared for it.

A wheeze cut up my throat, the sensory overload like a gut punch. The loud beeps, machines humming, and pained cries rammed into my ears. My nose picked up on cleaning products, piss, and body odor, while my sight felt overwhelmed by activity, trying to take everything in.

The dome ceiling above, from which Ash and I had peered down, gave the room a vastness, which echoed all the pain and horrors in the space. It was so different to see it from above, peering down through the glass, than being right in it.

They had twice the tables I recalled from last time, each one filled with fae. Small to tall, skinny to fat, young to old. They were hooked up to those machines, being forced to shift while being drained of their essence. Some fought and cried while the rest lay there, with no life left to give, waiting for the end to come.

The back of the room had even more water tanks, going down another wall in an L-shape. Most were filled with young men, in boxer briefs, floating inside. They were unconscious, covered in monitors and tubes, breathing through a respirator. Fae essence was being pumped into their system.

"What do you think?" Istvan stepped into my eye line, and it took everything in me not to shudder. I was so distracted that I hadn't noticed him. He flicked his head over his shoulder. "The new and improved way. Only the privileged and exclusive are selected or can afford it. Our waiting list is already a year long."

I tried to keep my breath steady, my jaw locked shut, not looking at him.

"Come, Brexley, let me show you. Maybe you will see what I am trying to do. What I am creating here." He motioned me to step forward as he spoke to the guards. "You are dismissed."

The guards bowed, retreating at his order.

He walked up closer to the tanks, stopping in front of one. My chest squeezed out a noise, my eyes locked on the mostly naked man inside. I knew him. Grew up with him. He was the son of Istvan's right-hand man, Lieutenant Andor.

Reaching out to a clipboard hanging next to the tank, Istvan read. "David Andor. Age twenty-seven. Diagnosed with stage four lymphoma last year."

97

I remembered that. He had to quit the HDF force. It was said he only had months left to live.

"Completely cured now." Istvan's attention sat heavily on me, waiting for my reaction. His ego needed me to be awed and enamored. "He is cured of his fatal disease *because of me*. Living *because of me*."

"Is he living, though?" My gaze shot to him. "Even alive, won't he be under your thrall? Duty-bound to you for his remaining days. And those might be shorter than he thinks."

"Not so, but isn't it still such a small price to pay for your life." Istvan almost shrugged, his tone becoming businesslike. "But this way, we have found they are not *thralled,* as you put it. They don't have any of the side effects of the pills, except one." He shifted on his feet. "The finding of Dr. Rapava's fundamental theories and experiments on this type of fae to human transfer was good. It has a much higher success rate. Very nearly faultless."

"Nearly faultless? What does that mean?" I retorted, wiggling my arms still cuffed behind my back. "And I'd think you'd want them obedient dogs to do your bidding."

"Most people are meant to be footmen. There are merely a select few who are meant to lead through history." He nodded to the tanks. "And even less who change it."

"You mean yourself." I wrinkled my nose. "The rich can afford to save their sons, while the less wealthy become your minions."

A smile took over his features, making the hair on my arms stand up. "You really would have been a great ruler of Romania. A great asset to me." He shifted to fully face me. "Andor and his entire family, whatever happens to Daniel down the road, will forever be in my debt. Emotionally as well as financially."

"Ah, yes, I remember. Better to have those owe you than have friendship," I repeated a phrase Istvan had said to Caden and me many times. "Friends are never as faithful as a person whose whole world is in your hands."

A smugness lit up his eyes at me recalling his teachings.

"If only you and Caden had actually listened to my words of advice. Things could have been quite different."

My lids narrowed on Markos, my intuition sensing a deeper underlying meaning.

"So why do you need me if you have it all figured out?" I nodded to David.

"Because as much as we are advancing, the one weakness in this… they are still dying. David is not the first person we cured of disease to have them die later on. All from a pulmonary embolism."

"All? Do the Andors know?" I narrowed my view on Istvan. "That he will die anyway?"

"If he dies, it will not be from cancer."

My teeth locked together. The hatred and loathing I felt for Istvan almost choked me. Lieutenant Andor was an asshole. I hated the man, but what Markos was doing was beyond cruel. He gave them hope—their son back. Only he would be ripped from them anyway, and all they would get was endless debt and forced loyalty.

"It's why you are so fascinating to me." Istvan studied me as he would a bug. "I should have taken more notice of Dr. Karl's tests when you first returned after your *stay* with the fae lord. I'm paying attention now, especially after what you did in Věrhăza. Oddly, I feel I need to thank the fae lord for giving me such a gift. You might be my miracle."

"Glad we are cutting the bullshit. You knew I was with Killian before I even returned to HDF. Spied on me. Tried to play me. You even had my death planned out, blaming it on the fae to manipulate Caden."

"And you finally admit you were in my office that night. Eavesdropping. And stealing from me."

I didn't respond. It wasn't a question.

"Well, lucky for me, I didn't kill you, because you have become far more useful to me." He lifted a brow. "And what I saw in Věrhăza… I don't know why you are special. Why the pills worked on you and no one else. Why you live and thrive. How you have magic." He tipped his head. "I feel you were meant to survive, to be brought here and now, so I can achieve my objective—to save the human species."

"Of course." A dry laugh erupted out of me. "This is all about you. That you are some king or God and not some narcissistic psychopath."

His mouth shut, a nerve along his jaw jumping. The hisses from the machines and cries of pain felt far away as Istvan and I stared each other down. He took a step, getting close to me, his icy blue eyes filled with ire.

"Watch yourself. I have been very lenient with you over the years. Treating you the same as family and far better than you deserved, especially after what your father and Andris did."

The rage and grief at what happened to Andris burned up my esophagus, rumbling the fire in my gut. Istvan shot Ling straight in the head in front of him, then pitted him and me in the ring together, all because Andris fell in love and found out the world wasn't so black and white.

"The only reason you are even alive is because of the blood in your veins." He leaned in closer. "The moment we have a replica of it, you are dead. And I will make sure you *stay* dead." He stressed. "Then I will forget all about you. As my son will do after I've cured him."

"Cured him?" I jerked back, my forehead wrinkling.

Istvan stood straighter, his shoulders pushing back.

"You don't think I noticed he came back from Andris's fae group different as well. Maybe not in blood, but in mind. He's always been weak when it came to you, but even more so now and for *fae* too. I could see it before, but last night showed he's developed feelings for them. He needs to see the bigger picture." A bitterness snarled his nose. To Istvan, empathy and caring were a weakness.

"I hope to make him stronger. Powerful. Impervious to weakness and sentimentally. The leader I know he can be." Istvan turned, striding past the tanks, going down the new row against an adjacent wall.

"What are you talking about?" I followed behind, stopping beside the man I had spent the last five years living with. His gaze was on the newest water tank at the end.

Slowly, my gaze followed his.

Oh. My. Gods.

A harsh noise shot from my lips, and I stumbled back, my eyes wide in horrific shock.

Holy. Fuck.

A figure floated inside the tank in only his briefs, equipment and monitors attached all over his body, his eyes closed.

"Caden." His name came out more of a squeak, my lungs contracting, not able to take in air. I couldn't speak or move; my shock at seeing Istvan's only son, the boy I loved at one time, and still cared for, being used as a lab experiment rendered me frozen. I just saw him last night, standing next to his father. What happened since then? Was this Caden's choice?

"Don't worry, he's fine." Istvan peered at an electronic pad on the side of his tank, showing vitals and blood pressure. "I would do nothing to hurt my son. Not if I can make him better. Stronger. Invincible. A *legend* in his own right."

Dread dropped like rocks in my stomach at his words. What did that mean?

"He's being prepped for his procedure later." Istvan slapped the glass as if he were patting his son's shoulder with pride. His gaze went behind me, toward the doors, excitement dancing in his eyes. "Speaking of…"

I felt it. My body ignited with familiarity, knowing who was there before I could even look. Istvan's plan was suddenly clear. He was sicker and more twisted than I even thought, but now it seemed like something I should have seen coming.

"Here comes the donor," Istvan relayed.

I whirled around, my gaze landing on aqua eyes.

Warwick.

# Chapter 11

"No!" A cry broke from my lips. In an instant, guards were on me, holding me back from reaching Warwick. I didn't even realize I had been moving to him.

*"Te geci!" You son of a bitch!* Whipping my head to see Istvan with a haughty smirk on his face. Thrashing against my wardens, I pitched myself toward him. *"Mi a fasz van veled?" Why the fuck are you doing this?*

"Because I can," Istvan replied honestly. "If this man is what all the stories claim him to be—deadly, powerful, can escape even death—what father wouldn't want that for their son? I would think you'd want it for the boy you claimed to love so deeply." He peered at Caden, then to Warwick, his tone mocking. Challenging. "Oh, how fleeting young love is. So ardent in the moment, so flimsy to time."

"You should talk," I spat. "Where's Rebeka? How fast did you toss her over for some young girl for political reasons?"

"The only reason marriage is even worth anything is to strengthen holds between countries and claim more land. Rebeka was no longer of use to me."

I blanched at his words.

"Don't give me that look. You are not so naïve. Rebeka used me as well to achieve a higher position in life. But before you think me so heartless, I did love her. I will always love her, but my country, my people, come first."

"You mean your ego comes first," I seethed. "Look around, this has nothing to do with humans or helping anyone." I motioned to the test subjects in the tanks, the people being tortured on the tables. "This is solely about you. About your hunger for power."

His chin lifted. "I don't expect you to be wise enough to see the bigger picture. To understand the cruelty of life and know sacrifices always have to be made to advance."

"I. Don't. Know. Sacrifices?" I spit out each word with venom. All the people I'd lost, what I had been through, forced to do, to survive.

"You are young. You have no idea how cruel life can be."

I rejected his implication that arrogance and misogyny in youth meant you were impervious to pain, and being a woman meant I never experienced hardship. What was sick was he *did* know the torture, assaults, and heartbreak I had been through, and yet I was still naïve and foolish to him. He was the one who had no idea.

"I don't get you." I wagged my head. "You claim to hate fae, but all you want is to be one of them."

"I don't want to be *one* of them." His lip curled in disgust. "I want to be *better* than them." he replied, as if it was the most obvious thing in the world. "The best of human and fae together."

"Isn't that just a half-breed?" I blinked in confusion. "The people you called an abomination?"

"Not a half-breed, but our *own* species. A super-soldier." He peered purposely at me. "Neither fae *nor* human."

*Neither fae nor human.* Ice slid down my vertebrae, my pulse pounding in my ears.

"What do you mean?" I licked at my dry lips, sensing the answer but hoping I was wrong.

"Dr. Karl ran your blood work this morning." Istvan turned to me. "Do you know what he found?"

No sound made it out of my throat.

"Your Immunoglobulin M levels are even higher than last time, which were already past any level of survival." He tucked his arms behind his back, strolling closer. "I know you are not human anymore after taking the pills. However, your levels even eclipsed the fae we tested here."

*Pills have nothing to do with it. I've never been human.* I could hear the gulp I swallowed down resonate in my ears.

"You know what we found when we tested his blood?" Istvan flicked his head at Warwick, my gaze following. Something about him made an alarm go off in my head, but Istvan's voice drew me back before I could analyze it. "The same thing… not just close to your level, but the *exact same*."

Not a muscle moved; no expression passed over my face.

"You know what else we found?"

Silence.

"Neither of you fell under human or fae."

*Fuckfuckfuckfuck.*

"I no longer need this nectar to make my army. I have it right here." He nodded at us. "You and Warwick are ground zero. The start of a new race."

My mouth opened to rebut his claims when movement from Warwick shot my attention to him. His legs dipped, and he stumbled back into the guards.

Blinking, my regard went over him—limp, eyes glazed, unsteady. I realized this whole time he hadn't said a word or even tried to fight against the guards.

"What the hell did you give him?" Alarm ticked at the back of my throat.

"Come now, Brexley. I taught you better. Do you really think I wouldn't sedate the man known to be a legend? The one called *The Wolf*?" Istvan strolled closer to Warwick, examining the beast of a man. Greed blossomed in his eyes, excitement at what Warwick could provide him. What he could create.

"Please…" I wrestled the group of guards, getting a few steps closer. "Don't hurt him."

Istvan's head snapped back at me, understanding creeping over his face. "You *love* him."

The claim made me suck in. I didn't respond. Istvan wasn't allowed to know my heart. To have access to my thoughts and emotions. Though, even as I locked my expression down, I knew it was still written all over me.

The word seemed so tiny. Four letters couldn't contain what I felt for Warwick. What we had together. Time and space couldn't even hold us. Only to each other were we bound.

We bled in bed. We loved in battle.

We defied nature and eluded death.

Love was insignificant compared to what I felt—what I would sacrifice for him.

"Use me instead." The proposal shot from my lips. "Take my blood. Use it on Caden or whomever you want. Just leave him out of this."

The thought of Istvan ripping his essence, taking away everything

Warwick was, the part of me inside him, the link we shared. It was the worst of violations. I'd rather be skinned alive than feel Warwick being shredded, the bond between us snapping forever.

"I'm taking it all—from both of you." Istvan's arrogance was mocking and cruel.

His claim kicked me in the chest, my lungs wheezing. He would drain Warwick of his essence and blood.

Anger sizzled my veins, forging and building back my broken pieces. "Don't. Fucking. Touch. Him."

Scarlet burned over Istvan's cheeks, his boots stomping to me until he was an inch away. "You have the audacity to tell me what to do?" Ire strained the muscles in his cheek. "I will take what I want, when I want." He stepped back, spinning for Warwick.

*Wanna bet?* I heard a voice inside me. A power living between life and death—a potency which rattled my bones. The cuffs around my wrist whined as I pulled on them, a sweep of wind whipping through the underground room, flicking my hair. I leveled my gaze on Istvan. I could feel my connection to Warwick like a hot wire running between us, though instead of more power accelerating my magic, a slight sluggishness tapped at our connection.

Istvan turned back to me. Instead of fear in his eyes, I saw smugness.

Pain shot into my arm, and my head snapped over my shoulder.

Dr. Karl stood there, a syringe in hand, pushing liquid into my arm.

The wave of drowsiness kicked in almost instantly, swaying me forward, forcing the guards to stumble with me, trying to keep me up, the fire dampening inside me like a bucket of water.

My lids batted to stay open but muscles going lax, as a haziness crept into my vision.

"I am always ten steps ahead, Brexley." Istvan tugged on his cuffs. "Always."

Whatever Dr. Karl injected me with kept me awake, but left me fuzzy, barely clinging to anything substantial. I had no understanding of anything. My mind couldn't hold on to thoughts for long; they floated away into the ether like dust. Forgotten.

A vague memory of being removed from the main room and brought to a smaller lab filled with medical equipment still hovered somewhere in my brain. I recalled them strapping me down, cuffing my wrists and ankles to a gurney before poking me with needles.

I could have been here minutes or days; I didn't know. I was tranced by the red liquid coming from my arm, coiling in the tube and filling a blood bag. Dr. Karl had changed the bag a handful of times so far. There was a fleeting thought telling me this was abnormal that so much blood shouldn't be taken from me at one time. No one would survive with so much blood loss. It made me sad. I wanted to keep my blood. It was mine.

"How is it going?" A familiar voice stirred me from my trance. Istvan strolled into the room, his question directed at the doctor.

Dr. Karl's head jerked up from the microscope he was peering into, his gray brows furrowing. "It is remarkable. Completely impossible." He shook his head. "But I've tested both of theirs several times to make sure."

"What?"

"The more I take, the more her system protects itself, replacing itself faster than I can drain her of. Her antibodies are so off the charts, but each time they rise, she seems to get stronger." He threw an arm out at me. "I've had to secretly sedate her four times already. Her body is healing itself, burning through the drug."

Istvan blew out his nose. "We've had to re-sedate him over a dozen times."

Him.

Warwick.

"The blood you brought me of his last time… It was the same as hers… *again.*" A slight hysteria upped Dr. Karl's voice. "*Every time,* no matter how little or how much I take, they are *always* the same level. Exactly. It's so strange." He rubbed a hand over his sweaty forehead. "It's as if they are linked. Some telepathic connection or something."

*"Life connects you, but death binds you."* Tad's sentiment flickered into my head. There was no science to what was between us. It was in our DNA, made up of our bones, of our blood. Our lives twined and twisted around each other. Protective and defensive.

*"Warwick?"* I called to him in my mind.

The buzz was there, but through the drugs and exhaustion, I could barely feel him tug back. *"Princess…"*

"I thought you didn't believe in that kind of science," Istvan spoke, swaying my attention back to them.

"I might be changing my mind." Dr. Karl patted his head again. "None of this makes sense otherwise. These two are connected; I have no doubt. But how, why, or what does it mean is the question?"

"That's what I'm expecting you to figure out," Istvan replied, taking a step away from the doctor toward the door. "I need to go. Those *bandits* are getting out of line. Once their use to me is gone, they will be a thorn I can finally pluck for good."

Bandits?

"I thought you've had a deal with the Hounds for years now?" Dr. Karl's head lifted. *What? The Hounds? Vincent's gang? A deal for years?* "They'd do your bidding when you needed, and you'd leave them alone, let them raid the Savage Lands unrestricted."

"Except for my businesses. They seemed to have forgotten that part of our agreement. The rats need to be reminded who is actually in charge— who rules this city and *them*." Istvan tugged on his cuffs, billowing with arrogance.

The Hounds have been working for Istvan?

Vincent seemed like the last man who would make a deal with Istvan. But at the same time, if he got what he wanted from it—free rein to rob and murder, growing his business, profits, and gang—it seemed exactly what the Hounds would do.

I should have gutted Vincent when I had the chance.

The door opened behind me, and then a woman's voice followed. "Sir, what do you want me to do with her?"

The voice. Why did it sound familiar?

My neck craned up and back to peer back at the door, hoping against hope I was wrong.

I wasn't.

Lena, the woman who helped me break into this place, Maja's daughter, stood in the doorway, a young, scrawny, and filthy human girl of eighteen or so standing next to her.

For one brief moment, Lena's gaze met mine. My heart pounded. Terror gripped my stomach, wrenching me from my drug-induced stupor. Lena's eyes widened, but she quickly covered up her surprise, shifting her head firmly to Istvan, like I was nothing but a lump on the table.

"Sir?" She cleared her throat.

"Yes. Leave her here." Istvan ordered. "Then go finish prepping my son's tank for tonight. I want him ready when I return."

"Yes, sir." She dipped into a low curtsy, her head bowing, but her attention slid back to me again. Brief, but it was filled with something my brain couldn't decipher. A warning? A threat? Did I really know or trust her?

Before I could even blink, Lena was gone, leaving the girl shaking and alone near the door. She didn't even try to run. She was painfully thin, with stringy hair and scarred face from pox, which had swept through this country several years ago, killing thousands of people in the Savage Lands.

"I wish I could be here, but I must go. Deal with this problem." Istvan didn't even acknowledge the girl, striding around her. "Document everything and send someone for me if anything goes wrong." Istvan went through the doors, set on his latest crisis.

"Come here, girl." Dr. Karl ordered, waving the emaciated girl to sit on the gurney next to mine.

Dread prickled in my chest, clearing up my vision and mind more, watching her silently climb on the gurney. Trembling. Defeated.

"What are you doing?" I hissed, my gaze darting between her and Dr. Karl.

"We are testing blood transfusions. Changing their blood type to match yours." He bound her wrists and ankles, moving the rolling blood bag closer to her, attaching a syringe into her wrist, a tube connecting her to a bag of my blood.

"No." I yanked against the cuffs, the beeps on my heart monitor getting louder and faster. "You can't do this." Though I knew they could and would. My words were pointless and wasteful.

"This girl is riddled with sexual disease and suffers from malnutrition from living in squalor. This is a wonderful opportunity we are giving her." Dr. Karl spoke as though she should be bowing down at his feet, an honor that he took a moment of his time to help a piece of trash like her. "A chance to do something good with her life."

"You don't know what this will do." I wrenched harder at the restraints.

"Someone needs to calm down." Dr. Karl turned to me. Before I could even react, he jabbed me with another sedative, my insides warming and melting instantly, though my mind struggled going down. I shook my head, my refusal falling dead on my tongue, my eyes watering.

I had no choice but to comply. The lethargy took over, along with the sensation of being violated. My very essence was being pried from me and shoved into a stranger. A cry only gurgled in my throat before everything became a hazy trance.

"This should take an hour or so. Then I'll want to test where you are." Dr. Karl turned on the machine, pumping my blood into her arm.

Exhaustion fluttered my lids. My body was working so hard to defend itself, and I could do nothing to protect it, to stop the machines from raping more of my essence. Taking, violating, robbing.

After twenty minutes of the red liquid continuously slipping into her veins, lost to me forever, she started to stir as if she had been zapped with electricity.

"How are you feeling?" Dr. Karl didn't even look at her, checking her monitor and writing notes on his clipboard. "Dizziness? Nausea?"

"Actually…" She licked her lips. "I feel amazing." Her voice was soft and light, though it held strength and the knowledge of the pain and suffering life can deliver.

"Describe everything you are feeling." Dr. Karl pulled out an otoscope, peering into her eyes.

"As though I could run for days. I feel energy I haven't felt… ever." She gushed with a giggle.

Cranking my head to look at her, I noticed her hazel eyes were bright, her cheeks flushing more and more rosy with every minute passing, the pockmarks lightening. Her hair even had a shine to it.

Robbing me of mine.

"Like I can barely sit still. Lighter and healthy. Is that strange to say? But it's true. I feel strong. Powerful."

He wrote everything down. The hiss and beeps chirped like an alarm, burning through my veins.

Attacked. Ravaged. Desecrated.

*"Warwick…"* I reached out, feeling our connection diluting, a single drop of ink in an ocean. I could barely feel the buzz anymore. To know he was all right.

*"Farkas?"*

Nothing.

*No. He's fucking mine!* Anger burned through what was left of the drugs, fear swirling in my stomach, boiling down the back of my throat.

The sound of thrashing snapped my attention to the girl with a sudden movement. Her cuffed legs and arms knocked violently against the gurney as she started to cough and wheeze.

My mouth parted as she convulsed, her mouth open, gasping for air but not seeming to get any.

What the fuck happened? She was fine a moment ago.

"What the hell?" Dr. Karl moved to her. It seemed he had no idea what to do as her body seized and jerked on the table, and he rushed to find his sedative.

"Help her!" I screamed.

Sounds ripped up her throat, tearing through her esophagus. Blood spurted up like a fountain, forcing her to choke on it. Her head turned toward me, and I froze in terror as I watched blood pour from her eyes and mouth, flashing me back to the day in Killian's lab, watching that woman die in front of me. The horrific scene which had stained my soul was now repeating itself.

Panic and terror also bled from her eyes, her gaze directly on me as if she were begging me to do something.

I couldn't move or speak. Petrified.

Her body jolted again, her mouth moving. "Help me..." The words barely left her lips before she went still.

Dead. I knew because I could feel her life slip away, not even lingering for a moment, her soul taking flight, free of her body's limitations.

Dr. Karl danced around her, pumping her chest and pulling out the defibrillator, panic soaking his clothes with sweat. "No, no! You can't do this. You were fine! It was working."

Swallowing, I stared up at the ceiling, numb, blank.

The girl was alive just five minutes ago. Now, she was dead.

Istvan was to blame, but I knew I would carry the burden of her death.

"Take her back to her cell." Dr. Karl pointed to me from his lab table when two officers entered. Karl had long since given up trying to save the girl, but his nervous energy sprang up around him. Not because of her death, but because he was scared to tell Istvan the test had been unsuccessful.

Istvan didn't tolerate failure.

"And remove that as well. It will contaminate all my experiments." He pointed his finger to the dead girl next to me. She was no more than garbage soiling his lab now. "Also, while you are at it, get someone to come in here and clean this mess up right away."

The guards nodded, one heading quickly for me, the other frowning as he was left with the dead body. "Bastard," he muttered. The guard unlatching my binds smirked with a quiet chuckle.

"You owe me." The other one with curly brown hair glared over at him, unbuckling the girl.

Her mouth was

still parted in her final words. Her vacant eyes scraped into my soul as if it were my fault.

I didn't even know her name.

"Come on." The young guard yanked me up, my legs unsteady, my head spinning at the sudden movement. I was drained, physically and mentally, but followed the man without a word.

The other officer wrapped up the girl in the cloth from the gurney and threw her over his shoulder like a sack.

"Don't forget to get someone in here. Pronto!" Dr. Karl yelled after the men when we exited the lab.

"Yeah, yeah... we hear you, fat pig." The one holding me, with short blond hair, muttered under his breath. "Thinks he can order us around like he's the general."

"Right?" Brown Curls huffed, hitching the dead girl higher on his shoulder. "We're not those pill-poppin' mindless drones the general has at HDF and Věrhăza."

My ears pricked at their chatter. They didn't consider me anything more than a walking lab rat.

"Fuck, I've heard things about the ones in Věrhăza... like feral and shit." Brown Curls shook his head, his grip on my arm tight.

"Guess you get what you pay for."

They both laughed, and I ground my teeth together. Entitled bastards.

"My father is still bitching about how expensive the tank treatment was." Blondie shook his head.

The other guy nodded in agreement. "But so fucking worth it."

These two were part of the tank experiments?

Now that I was aware, I could see the huge difference between those in the prison and these guys. The guards at Věrhăza were aggressive, mindless, and feral. These guys seemed "normal" besides the fact they had been turned into fae. Machine-made. Did they know at any moment they could die? Was it weeks? Years? Would it be worth it to them?

"Help me dump this one, find the servant girl, then we can head out for a beer after we return her." We moved down the hall.

"How about you find the servant and discard the body, and I'll take her back?" Blondie grinned, tugging on my arm.

"You owe me, asshole."

"Fine." Blondie sighed, turning us down a new passage. This place was much bigger than I first thought.

"Hey! Girl." Brown Curls yelled out at a woman down the hall.

Lena stopped, her gaze quickly jumping over me, her throat bobbing.

"This needs to be dumped, and Dr. Karl needs you to clean up the mess in the lab." Brown Curls continued as we strolled right up to her. "

"Of course. I'll go get the trolley. Wait here."

*"Lena and I work at the factory they are using for their fae experiments... we were promoted one day out of the blue about a year ago. To do cleanup."* The words of her brother, Emil, flung back into my head. Is this what they meant by cleanup?

As if she could hear my thoughts, her eyes shot to me. Something in them tugged at my subconscious, as if she was trying to tell me something. But before I could understand, she turned for a door next to us, opening it slowly.

I pinned my lips together to keep from making a noise. My eyes gobbled up what was on the other side of the door. Rows and rows of jail cells. The ones I could see were more like the HDF prisons. Sterile, clean, and even had seatless toilets, unlike the fae cages.

Men, women. Young and old. Sickly, thin, and haggard.

Humans.

They all looked as if they had been plucked right off the streets of Savage Lands. Those who had no shelter, no job, and no food. Living from moment to moment, hoping for someone to actually see them. To care and help.

Lena grabbed a tilt truck, wheeling it through the door.

As the door started to shut, someone moved in the farthest cell against the wall, the same double secured type of lockup Warwick and I were in on the fae side.

I caught a flash of brown eyes, dry, tangled reddish-brown hair, and a boney figure huddled against the bars.

I blinked, and the door closed, but my chest heaved as if it understood something my brain hadn't picked up on. Prickles danced down my vertebrae, my head dizzy, stumbling me to the side.

"Whoa..." Blondie grabbed for me. "Let's get this one back to her cell before she passes out on me."

Brown Curls tossed the girl's body into the bin, brushing off his hands.

"Dump her and get to the lab," he ordered Lena.

"Yes, sir." She bowed her head.

I didn't even glance at Lena as they pulled me away, heading back for the fae side, my mind still reeling.

*You're delirious.*

I was exhausted. Weak. Traumatized. Hallucinating from blood loss and hunger.

There was no way I saw who I thought I saw.

Chapter 12

"Guess you missed chow time." Blondie mocked in my ear while he hauled me down the row of fae cells. Numbly, I turned to peer in the string of cages. Some people were licking their tray, trying to get any morsel of food from it, while a few trays sat untouched on the floor next to them. Other prisoners were tucked in a ball in a corner, either too weak to move or no longer cared to preserve their lives.

My lungs squeezed when I looked into one cage. The man stared blankly back, empty of life. He was one I noticed on the extraction table in the main lab today. Even though he was skin and bones, he actually appeared to be wrinkling, his hair graying. It made sense, though. Ripping out fae essence took the magic which kept them young and eternal.

On the way back to my cell, seeing the starving, tortured, innocent children in the cages, reaching their boney arms out to me, pleading for help, snapped something in me. I was barely holding on anyway. The sound of the guard dumping the girl's body in the trolley like a hunk of meat, the thump of human flesh and bones, echoed in my ears. Her bloody, terrified eyes staring at me on the gurney, begging me for help, replayed over and over in my mind. The children's cries. The vision of Caden in the tank. Warwick being part of this. And only yesterday, we had lost Maddox.

I never had time to mourn one before more devastation rained down.

It all came at me like a tsunami, overwhelming and drowning me in grief, pain, and guilt. It was too much, stealing the air from my lungs and making me sag under the weight. All I could do was shut down. Switch everything off and compartmentalize, otherwise I would never get up again.

"Pick it up." Blondie rammed his legs into mine, trying to speed me up. Movement caught my eye in the cage next to the one I called home. An enormous figure stepped up to the bars, wrapping his hands around the metal barriers. Warwick's face peered through, his knuckles white, his eyes pinned on mine, his nostrils flaring when our eyes met.

My touchstone.

Relief burned the back of my lids, seeing him bulldozed into the walls I was trying to keep up, tearing at my foundation. But I couldn't afford to let go because if I did, I might not come back from it.

Pinching my lips together, I slid my gaze away from his. I concentrated on the officers returning me to my pen, the vibration of the metal slamming, the locks clicking, their boots strolling away.

"Kovacs?" he rumbled. At the sound of his gravelly voice, my lids slammed together, squeezing back the tears I could feel trying to break through.

My mouth wouldn't open. I leaned against the wall, sliding down until my butt hit the ground. Tucking my knees in tighter, I leaned my forehead on them, trying to breathe in and out.

Still in the prison outfit from Věrhǎza, I stared vacantly at the dried blood dyeing my gray pants a murky brown. Mine. Maddox's. The remains of his life were painted on my clothes like a tribute. Although he was no longer a lone tribute. Specks of fresh red from the young girl were also sprinkled over my entire frame. Soaking into my skin and fabric, marking both, though only one could be washed out. Another ghost that would haunt me.

"Kovacs?" he tried again. I felt the tug of our bond, but it was barely there, a whisper. They did this to us, unraveling our bond, separating us not just physically but mentally as well.

My nails cut through my clothes into my skin. The breath of his touch was too much, leaving me flayed open. Slamming against the link, I tucked in tighter into a ball.

*"Az istenit!"* he hissed, a touch of anger hinting in his timbre. He went silent for a long time, but I could feel his tension. Frustration. Worry.

He took a few breaths. A deep sigh, then the sound of him sliding down the same wall we shared. I swear I could feel the heat of him seeping through the stone and into my back. My spine flattened against the wall, craving his warmth and touch like a drug. I didn't want words; I didn't need platitudes. I just needed him. His arms around me, engulfing me, blanketing me, where I could no longer feel pain.

We sat in silence together for a while before I heard something slide over the ground, lifting my head to see a plate of food being pushed over to me. The tears I thought I had reined in threatened to appear, glazing my eyes.

He saved half his rations for me. Wiping my eyes with the heel of my hands, I felt my throat close even tighter.

"You have to eat, no matter what you feel. If we're gonna get out of here…" His voice tapered off to the point it was barely a whisper, but I still heard him say. "I need you."

A choked sob silently opened my mouth, a tear escaping.

He pushed the plate a little farther.

"Brex." An order. A plea. So much packed into those four letters.

My stomach coiled and burned at the thought of food, but eventually I reached out, dragging the tray to me.

More than hearing it, I could feel his exhale slither over my skin. For a second, I could see him lean his head against the wall, his eyes closed, relief lowering his shoulders.

He had not lost me yet.

Whatever was on the plate tasted bland, dry, and old; my throat tried to gag it back up, but I forced down each swallow. I needed whatever fuel I could get to keep me physically going. I had so much blood drawn from me, I shouldn't even be alive.

When I finished, I propped myself back up against the wall, shifting as close to the bars as I could, needing him to feel my gratitude. Not just for the food, but for being there… for always being there. Before I even knew him. Although, in some ways, I had known him my whole life.

Skating my hand through the bars, I reached as far as I could go. There was a beat, which seemed to last forever before his huge hand engulfed mine. It was warmth, comfort—home.

My entire body went lax from his touch. A whimper caught in my throat, my fingers wrapping hard around his like he was my only lifeline. It was the only thing keeping me from going under. From slipping into the complete darkness.

He kept me in the gray.

No words were necessary to explain what either of us had gone through. Although our link was depleted, I somehow still understood and sensed him, as I knew he could me. We just were. We had no doubts, no clarification, no fear of what was between us anymore. It was a safe place we could just be.

Threading his fingers through mine, another long exhale escaped my lungs as I slumped into the wall as if he were my own personal sedative and charging station at the same time.

*"I love you."* I only said in my mind, not even trying to push through the bond. But I felt Warwick go still, his muscles locking up.

Fuck.

Did he hear me? Was it too soon? Did he not feel the same way? Hurt and rejection weeded through me as he yanked his hand away.

But it quickly flipped to alarm when he leaped to his feet, his energy throbbing with defensive energy.

With the padding of slipper shoes on the cement, a shadowy figure moved quickly down the corridor for us, causing me to scramble up as well, preparing for our visitor.

The figure of a woman came into view.

"Lena?" My brows wrinkled, not expecting to see her.

She put a finger to her mouth, peering over her shoulder nervously.

"I don't have a lot of time." Nerves rushed her voice, her tongue swiping over her lip. "I am taking a huge risk."

"What are you doing here?" I moved closer to the bars.

"Better question. Who the fuck are you?" Warwick's grumble could be felt under my feet, making her suck in a gulp of air, her eyes widening at his penetrating voice and massive frame. Even behind bars, he made men who could turn into monsters piss their pants. But Lena gulped down her fear, swiping it from her features, though I could see her hands trembling.

I had forgotten he wasn't with us when we met Lena and Emil in the pub, and we didn't have time to get into all the details now.

"She's a *friend*," I stressed. It was a question, a challenge. Lifting my eyebrows, I waited for her response.

"I wouldn't have risked coming here if I wasn't." She swallowed, glancing again over her shoulder, nervous energy twitching her feet and hands. "But I can't stand aside; they wouldn't want me to." Her voice broke at the end.

"Who wouldn't?"

Her eyes lifted to mine, watery and grieved. "Emil is gone."

"Gone?" Dread sunk my stomach.

"His wife told me he was ordered to do something for General Markos a week ago. He never came back."

"Do you know for what?"

She shook her head. "No, and I know not to even ask." She brushed at her eyes, trying to hold back the tears. "I think he's dead."

116

Sorrow bowed my head; I wasn't sure how to respond. Comforting people wasn't something I was used to. "You don't know that."

She scoffed, using her long skirt to pat at her eyes again.

"Let's not bullshit each other." She cleared her throat. Stern. To the point. "The land of hopes and dreams is for people who can *afford* the luxury of wishing. My brother is most likely dead. My children have been threatened, and if I don't do everything Markos wants…" Her steady gaze met mine. There were no longer tears or grief. "He will kill my mother."

I jerked back. "What?" The image of a short, sweet woman with kind yet stern eyes, a mini version of the woman I considered a grandmother, stood before me.

My lids closed briefly, my head shaking, realizing I underestimated Istvan's conniving ways again.

*"I am always ten steps ahead, Brexley. Always."*

"I can't believe I didn't see it earlier."

"What?" Lena asked me.

"It's why you and Emil were even picked for this job in the first place. He had you marked from the beginning." I ran my hands through my snarls, pinching my scalp in frustration. I felt so stupid. "Istvan doesn't do anything without a reason. With Maja living under his roof, he had knowledge of your family, and he knew all he had to do was push down on a pressure point, and you would have to do everything he asked."

She glanced down with a dip of her head, as if she felt the burden of all of this.

"I owe you a lot, Brexley. However, my family comes first. Whatever I have to do, I *will* do." It was a warning.

"What is happening?" Warwick snarled, his hands wrapping tighter around the bars. "Do you know?"

Her mouth tightened, a slight tremor in her jaw at his violent energy. "In my debt to *you*." She faced me. "I came here to warn you, warn both of you. Tomorrow evening, the leaders from Bucharest, Prague, and I think Ukraine will be coming here."

"Why?" My voice strangled out, trepidation souring the food lumping in my stomach.

"Because." She inhaled, her hands twisting together. "Tomorrow night is a presentation. A show…" She gulped. "It isn't just Caden he plans to show as proof, changing him to fae with your essence and blood." Her gaze darted to Warwick and back to me. "Istvan plans to do the experiment on himself, live in front of them."

Cold ice poured down my lungs.

Fuck.

Of course, Istvan hadn't taken the pills or done the essence exchange yet. He would let others be the guinea pigs. Let them die. But now he thought he had the perfect formula in Warwick and me.

But that girl had died today.

"When—when did he plan this?" I gripped onto the bars.

Lena frowned, perplexed by my question.

"As far as I know, the night you were brought in."

*Before* the testing was done on the girl. Was that why Dr. Karl had freaked out so much? If he didn't provide the perfect results, his life was on the line too.

Istvan was too narcissistic. He had already declared this event, had spoken with cockiness instead of waiting for results.

"That's not all. There's something else you should know. He has someone locked up—" A bang echoed down the hall, making her jump, her head darting back at a sound. She pushed away from the cells. "I have to go."

"No. Wait!"

"You can't tell us anything else?"

Warwick and I spoke at the same time, and she looked between us, sorrow in her eyes.

"I'm so sorry. I wish I could do more," she uttered before darting away, vanishing into the dark shadows.

"Fuck." Warwick grunted under his breath, tension infusing the stuffy air.

Leaning my head on the bars, I ground my teeth so tight together my jaw cracked.

"The girl today," I started, coming out in barely a whisper. "She died. My blood killed her." I squeezed my lashes together. "Violently."

"Then it might do the same to Istvan." The bars on his cell rattled as he leaned against them. "Problem solved."

"And Caden?" My voice shot up with anger, terror, and helplessness. "What about him? He'd be worth sacrificing for Istvan, am I right? You're probably happy to get him out of the way."

He stayed quiet, not taking the bait, which only made me lose it more.

There was no winning. At every turn, we were pounded with more grief, pain, and loss. The moment we thought we climbed out of one pit; we were tossed into another.

"Well, I'm sorry. I won't kill my best friend because of your ego. Do you care about anything other than yourself?" I spat. I was lashing out, saying things I didn't mean. I didn't care. Pain was a ticking bomb inside me, ready to collide and knock down everything in its path.

*"What do you think, princess?"* His shade growled angrily in my ear, stronger than before. The feel of his breath, the heat of his form, sent shivers down my body. Desire clenched my thighs. I was vulnerable *to* him. Needy *for* him. Dependent *on* him.

The bomb detonated inside.

"Fuck off!" I batted away at his shade, striking a firmer physique than I was thinking would be there. Whipping around, my gaze fell on his enormous frame behind me, aqua eyes blazing into me. He was far from completely solid, but it was a lot stronger than it had been earlier.

I was noticing when my emotions pitched—in terror, fury, or desire—it shot energy through me, bubbling the magic between us to the surface and knocking it out of its slumber.

Fight or fuck.

Love or hate.

We walked the line between.

*"You think I'd even be here if I only cared about myself?"* His shoulders expanded, anger flaring his nose. *"You're right, I might not give a shit about Caden, but* you *do. If I didn't give a shit about anybody, I'd be with a dozen women right now, letting them fuck my brains out instead of being tortured and used as a science experiment."*

"Then go! I'm sure the mighty *Legend* could rip the hinges off the wall and walk right out." I waved my arms to the doors. "I wouldn't dare try to keep you away from your thirsty harem."

*"My harem? That's rich."* He scoffed, his head dipping, prowling for me. *"You're the one with a fucking harem, princess. How many boyfriends are you up to now?"*

"Jealous?" I sneered, my feet retreating as he strode for me, my spine slamming into the wall.

His boots tapped mine, his frame looming over me, glaring down with fire and fury.

*"No."* He gripped my jaw, leaning closer, growling in my ear. *"Because I know who your pussy belongs to."*

The power of his words never ceased to rip the air from my lungs. My body reacted as though he owned the rest of me as well. My nipples hardened, skin flushing with need, my core pulsing. How easily he had me panting. An obedient puppy. It was me on the leash. He tugged, and I came running.

"*Stop.*" He tugged on my chin, forcing me to look up. "*Mad at the world, take it out on me. You're hurting, hit me. Want to cry and scream? I will be here through it all. I can take whatever you dish out, princess.*" He pressed in closer, making me feel the outline of his hardness, which I knew still couldn't compete with the real thing. "*But don't for one moment say I don't care. I can see through your bullshit. There are no walls between us. We're done with that.*" He slid a hand up my jaw, cupping the back of my head with a tug. "*Though we can fight like hell in the bed and outside.*" He yanked my head back, forcing my mouth to open as his crashed down on mine, devouring me with hunger, feeling much more solid than I expected.

Flames scorched my skin, burning me alive. His tongue flicked and tangled around mine, sucking until a low groan pushed from my lungs. With every lick, bite, and attack of his mouth, he felt more and more concrete. Weaving inside me, scraping through my soul, forcing a gasp from my lips as my nerves trembled under the intense sensation.

"Oh, gods," I groaned, an orgasm hinting just from that.

"*Been called worse.*" Warwick slid his mouth down my neck, tugging my prison uniform top and sports bra over my head and tossing them on the ground, his mouth claiming my breast, flicking the nipple with his tongue.

"Warwick…" My back arched.

His hands dragged down the curves of my body as he went to his knees, tugging at my stained pants.

"No." I grabbed his hand with a whisper. "I feel so disgusting and dirty. I'm covered in sweat, dirt, and blood."

"*I don't care.*" His penetrating gaze lifted to mine with a feral lift of his lip. "*I need to fucking taste you now.*" He yanked down my pants, along with my underwear. He didn't need to, but it made him feel even more real as he blew against my folds. A low growl vibrated against my inner thigh as he tugged my leg over his shoulder.

"*Fuck, Brexley…*"

My lungs faltered, my body sparking and tingling as I felt his mouth slide up my inner thigh. My nails dug into the wall, my breath shallow, my hips already pushing toward him, begging for him.

His tongue sliced through me, my body practically convulsing at the onslaught, a cry tearing from my chest. I no longer cared where we were or who could hear us. Pleasure was so fleeting and rare; you took it where you could in this world.

Plus, the more we "bonded," the stronger it became.

*"Fuuucck."* He groaned loudly against me, only making me whimper and claw at the back of his head, pushing him harder into me. *"Fuck, I forgot how good you taste."* He spread me wider, his fingers rubbing through me.

Energy danced around us, the flutter of ghosts, the shifting of people, soft groans of pleasure, the bulbs flickering down the passage.

Heat was already racing through my veins, my hips rocking against him while his lips, teeth, and tongue devoured me.

"Fuckfuckfuck." I was already hurtling toward the ledge. Maybe I was strung so tight, it wouldn't have taken much to get me off.

Nope. It was all Warwick.

He didn't kiss; he consumed.

He didn't fuck; he claimed like a mythological warrior.

He fought, killed, pillaged, and declared ownership of anything he desired.

"Warwick." I threaded my fingers through his hair, yanking his head back. He growled, looking up at me, his mouth glistening and puffy.

"Now." I dug my nails deeper into his head, making his eyes spark. He rose to his feet, yanking down his pants.

Fuck.

Seeing his massive cock, pulsing and hard, had me dripping. He grabbed my leg, propping it up on the bars and opening my hips. Clutching my thigh, he dragged himself through me, hinting at my opening.

Whimpering, I bit down on my lip until I tasted blood.

Warwick's chest vibrated, one hand grabbing my head, his mouth taking mine as he thrust inside me.

I moaned so loudly it echoed down the hall, feeling myself stretching, trying to adjust to his size.

A string of curse words came from Warwick's cell, reminding me this wasn't even the real thing. I seemed to always forget how authentic this felt. To an outsider, we were alone, in two different cells. But the man in front of me was becoming more vivid. I could feel the vein in his cock rubbing against my walls, causing my toes to curl and my head to spin.

Warwick's shade drove in again, rough and needy. His hand grabbed mine, threading it through the bars until I felt Warwick's real hand grasp mine.

"Oh, shit!" I cried. His touch multiplied everything until my body was trembling.

121

I was suddenly in his cell, my spine grating against the stone as he fucked me deeper.

"Fucking hell, Brexley…" Warwick grunted, his hips crashing against me, pounding and unrelenting, the grip between our hands so tight the bones in my fingers popped. But nothing mattered.

Gasps and moans filled the cells, everyone feeling our energy, taking away all pain and trauma for a moment.

A spark of white light.

A gust of wind.

A rumble of thunder.

His thumb rolled over my core, hurling me completely over, ripping my vision from me.

"Warwick!" I heard myself scream.

*"Sotet démonom,"* he hissed, pounding harder, as I felt his hot cum explode inside me, tearing me from the present.

Fire crackled; wind howled. I was hit with a vision of us at night on a field of bodies, our boots saturated with blood, gore and wounds covering us as we walked together, like we were death itself.

*The Grey.*

*The Wolf.*

The flash was only for a moment before I was flung back to earth, gasping and wheezing for air, my bones shaking vehemently.

Our fingers still locked together, we both took a while to speak or move. His shadow kissed me deep, then he was gone. The bond between us was now strong, and the energy we created together thrummed in my ears and wound around me like a web.

I heard someone sigh dreamily from a few cells down. "What the hell was that?"

"Yeah, you're welcome," Warwick mumbled, causing me to laugh.

We let go of each other, my fingers aching and bruised, but damn, it was worth it.

"Did it help, Kovacs?" He exhaled deeply, sliding down the wall.

"Is that how you keep me from flipping out?" I frowned at the disgusting clothes I had to pull back on again.

"Whatever I have to do. Just keeping the world safe."

"Aren't you the hero."

I heard him chuckle darkly. Warwick was anything but.

He was no hero. He was a terrifying, deadly legend.

One who fucked like one too.

"And that was without even touching you, Kovacs."

# Chapter 13

It only felt like a moment after I closed my eyes that the guards came tramping in, lights flipping on, my lids bursting open at the intrusion.

Clambering to my feet, I could feel Warwick's presence bolt up in the cage over. Protective. Wary.

"General is in rare form this morning." Blondie sneered at me, hitting his baton against the metal bars while Brown Curls swung my cell door open, coming for me with manacles. "You ready, lab rat?"

Snorting, I leaned closer to Blondie through the bars. "And what the fuck do you think *you* are?" I smirked as Brown Curls cuffed me. "I am the very thing your daddy had to fork over thousands for. And guess what, junior? You still aren't even close to what I am."

"Shut the fuck up." Blondie's shoulders rose, the bat thwacking the bar at my face.

I laughed while Brown Curls yanked me with him, hustling me out of the cell and down the corridor.

*"Kovacs..."* A growl nipped at the back of my neck.

My neck craned back to see Warwick, his body pressed up to the bars, appearing as if he were ready to rip through them.

There were no words I could give him, no assurances everything would be okay.

My shadow slipped back to him, and without a word, I went up on my

123

toes, pulling his mouth to mine kissing him deeply. The feel of his anger and fear vibrated through me, coiling around my bones, giving me strength.

But it was the other emotion I felt from him that had me gripping onto him for dear life.

*"I heard you last night."* His spirit grazed my body as I walked down the hallway while I also stood in front of him in his cell.

His aqua eyes peered down at mine, his hand brushing my dirty hair out of my face. His Adam's apple bobbed as he tried to swallow back his emotion.

*"Same, Kovacs."*

I didn't need to ask what he heard. I could see it in his eyes, feel it in his soul.

His version of saying *I love you* back.

A smile lighted my face as his hand clasped the back of my head, pulling me hard against his mouth. Breathing me in so deeply, he couldn't possess more of me, but I still wasn't close enough.

With Warwick, it's never enough.

"Brexley." The voice plucked the string between Warwick and me, cutting it off with a snap.

Istvan stood in front of me. His icy blue eyes stared at me, his expression unreadable, his frame tense.

The guards moved me all the way into the lab room to him, my gaze catching Dr. Karl next to a gurney—the one the girl died on yesterday. Today, a man of barely twenty was strapped to it. He looked to be slightly drugged, though I could still see fear in his features.

"No." I shook my head, my body instantly backpedaling, ramming into the two soldiers, who shoved me forward. "Don't do this."

Istvan motioned for the officers to take me to the gurney.

Struggling, I tried to dig deep, to find that thing inside of me, the forging fire building back brick by brick. The magic of a fae queen. It bubbled, but I felt no explosion of power, no electricity or wind striking the air at my command. I had no way of controlling it, like a genie who had enormous power but couldn't do a thing until someone else rubbed me the wrong or right way.

Dr. Karl sauntered over to me after I was restrained. Wiping down my arm with rubbing alcohol, he slid the needle into my arm, my body instantly going limp, the fight leaving me.

"I think this time will be better, sir." Dr. Karl spoke to Istvan, his speech pattern quick and nervous. He put another needle in my vein, taping it down and turning to the other victim. "He is much stronger than the last.

124

She was riddled with disease. Clearly too weak to handle it. He is perfectly fine, except for Byssinosis, a Mill Lung disease. I feel positive this will work this time."

"It. Better." Istvan's words were controlled, but I could hear the threat. The demand for a positive outcome or else.

Sweat dripped down Dr. Karl's forehead, and he swallowed, understanding the same thing.

Curving my head, I allowed myself to look at the form next to me as Dr. Karl hooked him up to the blood bag we'd be sharing.

He had dark eyes and hair and was skinny but all muscle, the kind you got from doing physical labor, day in and out. Young, but already held the burden of a hard life on his face. His head turned to me, his eyes meeting mine; they were filled with a fear—a plea—as if I could help him.

My head jerked, my eyes going to the ceiling, not able to look at him.

*Maybe this time it will be fine. What if this does help him? Can I help others?*

I clung to that hope, my heart racing through the sedative when Dr. Karl turned on the machine, yanking my blood from my veins.

The knee-jerk reaction to defend, to protect myself, trickled sweat down my spine. Today it hurt more. I could feel every molecule of myself being ripped away this time. The sedative was gone, and my body struggled against the binds, noises huffing from my nose.

"What is wrong with her?" Istvan barked.

"I-I don't know…" Karl was right there, checking vitals and my drip, fiddling uselessly around me.

"Did she already go through the sedative?" Istvan stomped closer.

"She shouldn't have." Dr. Karl's voice pitched up. "I gave her double the dosage, and it took her much longer yesterday to burn through it. It's only been ten minutes."

Istvan waved in my direction. "Well, something is wrong."

*"Kovacs."* Warwick stood over me. The grip of his fingers on my face instantly stilled me. His presence was calming, but the pain did not relent. If anything, it amplified. Slicing the connection between us. Shredding my power from me.

It was why I was burning through the sedative faster, why it felt something was ripping me from the inside out. After last night, the bond between us had become stronger. There was more to cut, to shred from me, our link layered like generations of wallpaper glued to a wall. It felt as if someone was trying to rip it away with their fingers, coming off in strips and pieces.

125

Warwick's adrenaline pumped through my system, fighting with me, but I could feel him waning, being shredded away from me, like peeling my skin right off my body.

*"Hold the fuck on, princess,"* Warwick growled, his shadow flickering, before the tie between us was snuffed out.

"Noooo!" I belted, my back arching off the gurney, thudding back down in a crash of metal and cries.

I would not lose Warwick. Nothing would survive if it got in my way.

A guttural scream bellowed from the man next to me, instantly stopping my flailing as he thrashed. His body jackknifed with horrendous wails, blood spewing from his lips.

"What the fuck is going on? What is happening?" Istvan snapped. His default when he got scared was anger.

Red liquid pooled from the young man's eyes, his body convulsing.

Oh, gods, no. It was happening again.

Dr. Karl pranced between us.

"Do something!" Istvan yelled.

Dr. Karl ripped the tube from his arm, my blood splashing onto the floor in a sea of red. I knew in my gut it was too late.

Crimson gurgled and foamed from his mouth, and the man's eyes widened, a guttural, terrified noise building inside his chest. It was the sound of someone who knew he was going to die. He let out a howl then stopped, his body going limp. Motionless. His eyes staring blankly above.

His spirit slipped away, just as the girl did yesterday, leaving his shell vacant.

Dr. Karl pumped at his chest, pressing defibrillators above his ribs. It all was for show. He knew it too, but I could see the palpable terror he had of admitting another fail to Istvan.

"I'm sorry, sir," he fumbled, talking quickly. "I am so sorry. I don't know what happened. It should have worked."

Istvan's jaw tightened to the point that veins popped in his neck.

"Get another one," Istvan commanded the guards at the door. "And take this one away."

"What?" Dr. Karl swung to him, eyes wide, while Blondie unlatched the dead body, dragging it off the table.

"We do this again until we get it right. This time no sedative. I don't want anything affecting the results."

"But—"

"I don't care if you go through the entire Savage Lands population. We don't stop until it works. Everything is riding on this," Istvan shouted, stomping up to Karl. "Get this right. *Today*. Do you understand me?"

"Ye-ye-yes, sir." Dr. Karl nodded, his skin sweaty and pallid.

The door burst open, Brown Curls bringing in the next test subject. My attention went to him and then to the figure next to him—terror carved through my gut, my chest cracking.

He had a girl of maybe ten.

"Noooooooo!" I screamed, writhing against the manacles holding me down.

"Put her here." Istvan pointed at the now empty gurney. Blood still pooled on the floor around it. The little girl started to cry, wanting her mommy.

"You sick fucking monster!" I seethed, my nails curling into my palms at my sides. "What the hell is wrong with you? Do you have any soul left?"

Istvan's chin flicked up, his mouth pressed. "I don't expect you to understand."

"Understand? She's a child!"

"Research has shown they are a lot more resilient. Their bodies bounce back." He defended his actions. "It's how we evolve, Brexley. Learn. Grow. Wouldn't you rather know you helped save thousands of lives? Helped cure diseases, take away suffering? I do… so who's the one here with no soul?"

A strangled noise scratched my throat, my arms and legs kicking and knocking against the restraints. The little girl cried harder, running to Istvan as though he was the one who would protect her from *me*. I was the monster.

I tried to calm down but then Istvan pushed her back to the officer. He put her on the bed, strapping her tiny ankles and arms down.

"It's okay." *Lie*. "It's going to be okay." I forced my tone into a calm, soothing timbre. Her whimpers were knife cuts to my gut. "Hey… look at me."

It took more coaxing before she lifted her brown eyes to me. She was the same age as the little fae girl I promised I would get out of here. I failed my promise to her.

"What's your name?" I tried to distract her from what Dr. Karl was doing, the large syringe in his hand.

Sniffing, her small voice barely made it to me. "Mischa."

"Mischa, I'm Brexley." I tried to keep my voice even, pretending this

127

was all going to be fine. Dr. Karl hooked her to the machine, her eyes watering again, her chest moving up and down frantically. Her fear was palpable, only upping mine.

"No diseases, no drugs, no sickness. She is the purest specimen we have to test on."

*Purest specimen.* They did not see the scared little girl. The one who had a family and a whole life to live. All they cared about was themselves. Their power. Their rights. Their own egos.

My narrowed eyes shot to Markos. "You may be a human, but you have no humanity. Rotten from the inside out."

"Shut up," Istvan snarled.

"You claim fae are soulless murderers? Look at yourself, Istvan. How can you do this to a *child*? How about your own child out there?" I flicked my head toward the main room. "What about the woman you spent the last twenty-three years with? *Where is* Rebeka?" Istvan's blue eyes shot to me, his jaw working. "Did you kill her?"

Istvan's cheek twitched.

"Where is she?"

He ignored me, nose flaring, his eyes blazing. "Do it now," he ordered Dr. Karl.

Dr. Karl jumped, turning on the pump.

A guttural shriek jolted up my esophagus. Without sedation, I could feel every molecule of my blood being seized from my veins. Taking Warwick away from me.

Out of the corner of my eye, I watched my plasma fill the bag and start down the tube to her arm. With every centimeter it moved, panic trounced my limbs.

I was going to kill this little girl.

"No!" I screamed out. *"Warwick!"*

I could hear a roar echo from the room over, the walls vibrating, jolting all the heads toward it.

His other self was over me again, his lip curled, his breathing heavy.

Fury and violence.

*"Use me, Kovacs."*

The little girl started to scream in agony, her tiny body shuddering.

And I shut my eyes, giving over to whatever power we had together, allowing his energy to slip into me, filling my muscles with strength.

Adrenaline flooded into my body, and I yanked on the restraints, hearing them tear apart.

"Sedate her!" I heard Istvan bellow.

"You told me not to!" Dr. Karl exclaimed.

"Do it now!"

I couldn't let them drug me. Digging deeper, taking more from Warwick, I felt the high of his magic, the greed of wanting it all. A bellow heaved from my mouth, the clasps breaking away with a snap. I scrambled off the gurney.

"Guards!"

Screams bounced around me, officers moving for me, but my only focus turned on the girl. Blood was already dripping from the corner of her mouth, sheer panic in her eyes.

I ripped the IV from her arm, and she let out a shriek, her body going limp, silencing her cries. I could see her chest still moving up and down. Her body was probably traumatized, needing to shut down.

But she was alive.

A prick of pain went into my bicep, warmth and dizziness instantly dipping my knees. My gaze shot over to see Dr. Karl, once again retracting a needle from my arm, dousing me with a sedative.

Istvan came for me, his fury wrinkling his face. "You little bi—"

Commotion came from next door, stopping his descent on me.

"General!" I heard a man yell. "Help!"

Istvan didn't even hesitate. His hand wrapped around the back of my neck, dragging me with him, my legs struggling to keep up.

We entered the room as Warwick slid off the table, his broken cuffs dangling from his wrists, guns pointing at him from every direction.

"Is this what you are looking for, Farkas?" Istvan gripped me harder, pushing me slightly in front of him.

Warwick stopped short, his lids narrowing on me, then going to Istvan.

"You be a good boy, and I won't snap her neck right here."

A snarl rose from the Wolf's chest, but he didn't move.

The drugs in my system softened my muscles, my attention, and the link between us, making me effectively useless.

"Since Brexley has been nothing but a disappointment, how about we try you instead?"

Warwick lurched just a hair, and Istvan whipped out his gun, pressing it into my head. I could feel Markos's nervous energy.

He feared Warwick.

"You move an inch, and she's dead." Istvan's hand tightened on my neck. "She is utterly useless to me now since transferring her blood is only killing people. I have enough of her blood to study and duplicate. But you, Farkas, you will be an excellent substitute until I can locate the nectar."

My head lifted at the last words, my loopy gaze landing on Warwick. He kept his feral gaze on Istvan, but I could feel he was aware of me. A tick in his eyes seemed to be telling me, *don't you dare utter a word, princess.*

"Karl, hook him straight up to Caden."

"What?" Dr. Karl's mouth fell, his skin the color of his coat. "Sir, we've never done it this way before."

"Do it!" Istvan demanded, his hold on my neck pinching a nerve. He was starting to lose control.

All the important leaders were coming this evening to watch this big production so Istvan could solidify his place as *their* leader. He had everything to lose if this didn't work out. They wouldn't take him seriously anymore. To Istvan, that was his goal. Nothing else mattered. Logic and safety disappeared when you had everything riding on one thing.

"Go!" Istvan ordered Warwick, pressing the gun into my head harder. "Don't think for a moment I won't do it." Everything in Istvan screamed he would indeed kill me if it came down to it.

Warwick's shoulders rose and fell, his expression a deadly mask portraying the underlying threat—someday he would gut him like a pig if he had the chance. But he took in another breath and turned for the table Dr. Karl had moved to Caden's tank.

The doctor was locked in on doing his duties as sweat dripped off him, his nerves bouncing off the walls, probably feeling it was *his* life on the line too.

Warwick's eyes met mine while getting up on the table. I wanted to scream, to cry, to destroy this whole room, to stop this from happening, but my mouth wouldn't even open. He was only here because of me. Volunteering himself to Istvan to be by my side. Subjecting himself to torture and going to the hole... for me.

He laid down, his muscles flexing, his jaw rolling when the guards cuffed him down again. This went against his nature. His very being. He didn't submit. He didn't lie down. The Wolf wanted to fight. To kill. To rip everyone apart. His darkness wanted to take... to feel blood under his nails.

But I was the one who kept him from falling in.

Staying in the gray.

"Sir, once again, let me say we have never tried it this way. Taking fae essence straight from the donor into the patient directly. I don't know what the outcome will be."

"Wouldn't it be better if the essence came straight from the source instead of a machine?" Istvan moved us closer.

"Possibly…"

"So, shut up and do it."

Dr. Karl nodded, licking his lip, his Adam's apple bobbing. He stuck monitors to Warrick's temples and inserted strange-looking IV pumps into his body and up his nose. I recalled seeing them on all those fae victims they were sucking life from. That little girl forced to shift over and over.

This was how they took a fae's essence. Anger flicked in my stomach, my chest clenching, my hand slowly rolling into a ball.

Dr. Karl rechecked everything, then turned to Istvan with a nod.

Istvan peered up at his son, my gaze following. Caden floated in the thick substance, air going in and out of his mouthpiece. Unconscious, but his eyes fluttered under his lids like he was trying to wake up, as if he knew something was about to happen.

A shot of fear sizzled up my spine at the notion of anything happening to him. I couldn't watch my best friend or the man I loved die right in front of me.

"Turn it on." Istvan nodded his head at Karl.

Taking a deep breath, Karl's hand hovered over the button.

In a blink, he flicked the machine on.

# Chapter 14

Warwick's body would have jackknifed off the table if he wasn't strapped down. His teeth cracked together, keeping the grunt trapped inside his chest, though it still hummed over the sound of the machine.

It was only a moment before Caden's body convulsed inside the tank. The horror of what I was seeing, what Istvan was willing to do to his own son, almost paralyzed me more than any sedative could.

This was a trial for Istvan. If this worked out for Caden, he would do it too. At least then he'd have the power of a legend until he could find the nectar.

He would take all of Warwick.

We were both dead.

*Hiss, pump, hiss, pump.*

Warwick jolted, spit flinging from his mouth, trying to lock down his reflex to pain. His nose flaring, each breath was a struggle as they ripped his soul from him.

From me.

Fury whipped through my lungs. The sensation of him being sliced from my own soul seared venom down into the pit in my stomach.

Forging. Building.

It burned through the drug clouding my mind like a war party, set to burn down everything it crossed.

A snarl was torn from Warwick, his head going back, knocking brutally against the hard surface he was on before a long bellow howled from him.

Suddenly, Caden's eyes burst open, forcing Istvan to gasp. "It's working, isn't it?" he shouted at Dr. Karl. "It's really working!"

I loved two men, but only for one I would obliterate the world.

I could feel the power inside me. The source that hid under the surface, simmering deep at the edges of my soul. My fear of it, of what the power could do, what a light Seelie queen and a dark Druid were capable of when mixed together.

The Grey.

All I understood was they were taking what was mine. Hurting him. Destroying the bind linking us. Bringing him back to life weaved our lives together forever. I gave him life on that field, a part of me. They were not going to take it away.

"Nooooo!" A current of wind gushed through the room similar to a squall, twisting and coiling my hair up into the air. Istvan let go, his head darting around, then landing on me, realizing it was me who was doing it. Fear danced in his eyes. Lightning cracked, the pop of electricity zapping across the room.

"Stop!" Istvan's voice was lost as my rage kept climbing, a boiling pot of water hitting the rim and bubbling over.

The lights burst, spraying glass across the room, forcing everyone to duck, trying to cover from the shards, leaving us in mostly darkness.

I could feel the souls of the dead coming to me. Their energy zipped around the room, ready to do my bidding.

"Brexley!" I heard Istvan bark from his hiding spot. "Stop this!"

*No.* I snarled in my head, the energy vibrating through me. I didn't want to stop. The power was addicting. Thrilling. Like being free. I wanted more.

The spirits whizzed near me in excitement. Another bolt of lightning speared the room, slicing down a row of water tanks, followed by another.

*CRAAAAACK!*

Every tank shattered. Thousands of gallons of liquid burst out, crashing into the room, a tsunami knocking people off their feet, burning out the equipment, and slamming anything loose into the walls and guards.

Screams and cries bounced around me, but nothing sounded close.

"Kovacs!"

133

It was the only sound that penetrated. Turning my head, my gaze latched on aqua eyes. He was still strapped to the table, soaking wet, blood tricking out of his nostrils. I was snapped out of my trance in an instant, darting over to him. My fingers unlatched his binds, helping him sit up. I felt no buzz between us. The link burned out. But I no longer feared it wouldn't come back.

"You okay?" Lights spurted and fizzed overhead; just a few on the far wall still lit the room enough to see. The place was quiet of voices, which twisted my gut, but I didn't have time to think about it.

"Had better days," he grunted, sliding off the table, his arm around me, legs dipping when he tried to put his weight on them. "We've got to get out of here."

"Yeah…" I took one step, my focus taking in the object only feet away, laying in the debris, the water retreating down a drain.

"Caden!" I ran for the body, falling down next to him, water going up to my hips, panic thundering my pulse in my ears. "Oh, gods. Be okay… be okay." I pressed my fingers into his neck.

Did I do this? Did I kill him?

"Caden, come on." My arms shook as I leaned over him, trying to feel any breath. I didn't hesitate, starting CPR, my hands pressing into his chest, my mouth covering his, blowing air into his lungs.

"Please…" Panic quaked my voice and tears burning my lids before slipping down my face. I recalled so many key memories with my best friend. "You can't leave me." I pumped harder, trying to give him life. Once again, my magic was gone when I needed it the most—to save someone I cared about.

"Brex…" Warwick's tone said everything, his hand reaching out for mine over Caden's chest. The moment Warwick's hand touched him, a wheezing gasp heaved Caden upright, his eyes bursting open wide. And I swear I saw his eyes glow, as if fire was burning behind the brown, before he blinked, and they were normal again.

"Oh my gods, Caden!" A cry broke free, my arms wrapping around him. Pulling back, I peered at him. He looked confused and disoriented.

"What the fuck happened? How…?" He looked around.

The shouts of soldiers heading our way from other parts of the underground building volleyed into the room.

"Come on!" Warwick got to his feet as I helped Caden up. "We've got to go now."

Caden was weak, dazed, but alive.

"Do you think you can make it?" I held on to my friend as he swayed on his feet, barely keeping upright.

"No, I don't think I can." Caden whispered, his voice rough and scratchy.

A hacking cough and groan came from behind us, spinning me to the noise.

Istvan was stirring awake.

"Go, Brex." Caden's gaze went from him to me. In that moment, I saw the love he still had for me. The part of him that would always choose me over his father.

"I won't leave you."

"You have to." He touched my face. "Just know, the moment I went back to HDF—I *had* to act as though I was with him."

"Act?"

"I was never against you." He dropped his hand away. "Now go!" His attention went to Warwick; a pointed expression passed between them. Warwick dipped his chin, answering Caden's unspoken words.

Warwick moved to me, grabbing my arms.

"No!" I tried to fight him.

"Brexley, go." Caden helped push me. "I can't leave her."

"Leave who?" I asked, while Warwick was leading me toward the exit. "I don't understand. Come with us!"

"I can't." Sorrow flickered over Caden's face. "I won't leave my mother."

*My mother.*

"Wha-what?" I sputtered in shock. "Your mother?" The pieces were clicking into place—the woman in the back cage before the door shut. The image of her huddled on the floor, her eyes meeting mine briefly. Nothing about her would be recognizable as the elegant, graceful perfection of the woman I grew up with—the one who could be a queen. This woman was dirty, gaunt, beaten, scared, and in filthy rags.

Except for the eyes. Her son's eyes.

"Oh, my gods..." My hand went to my mouth, the realization knocking like a drum. "Rebeka." She was here. This is where Istvan had hidden his wife. Was he using her as a lab experiment?

Yells from guards, followed by a groan from Istvan, captured Caden's attention.

"Go," he ordered again.

"No, I won't leave either of you."

135

"You don't have time, Brex." Caden wheezed, his throat raw, his legs still unstable. "He will kill you. He'll kill both of you."

Warwick gripped me tighter, trying to get me to move as pounding steps came for us. Time was running out.

"What about you?" My feet shifted with Warwick, but I still leaned toward Caden.

"I'll be fine," Caden said to me, but his gaze went to Warwick. It was odd, but I felt them understand each other. A nod of the head.

*"Állj!" Stop!* A bark came from the main doorway.

We whirled for the only other exit out of here, the one leading back to the cells.

"Get them!" I heard Istvan's voice strain, climbing up to his feet. "Shoot to kill!"

"Fuck!" Warwick hissed, both of us ducking as shots rang out over our heads, spraying sparks down on us. Ankle-deep in water, the equipment floated around like a minefield, slowing our retreat. I paused, swiping up a piece of debris I could use as a weapon—a broken piece of thin pipe with a jagged edge. It wasn't a gun, but anything was better than nothing when guards and bullets were heading straight for us.

"Come on!" Warwick yanked me through deeper sludgy water, things bumping my leg. Peering down, a scream caught in my chest. A dozen dead bodies floated on the surface, some face down, some staring blankly above, but it was the one knocking into me that held my attention.

David Andor.

Seeing his lifeless carcass and empty eyes slithered around my ribs, tightening in and choking the air from my lungs. He was dead. *All* of them were dead. Not one person had survived in the tanks. I had killed them, whether with my magic or by cutting off their air. They had all perished.

Except Caden.

*Bang! Bang!*

A squeak lobbed up my throat as we ducked and weaved to avoid bullets. Warwick shoved the door, breaking us through to the familiar passage which led to our prison.

"Don't let them escape." Istvan's voice boomed from behind.

"Where the fuck do we go?" Warwick yelled back at me, our feet pounding across the cement, our wet clothes weighing us down. "This leads us right back to our cells."

*Shit. Shit. Shit!* My brain whirled, trying to figure a way out of here.

*"There are three levels under the factory. Not only do they all join to*

136

*each other, but the middle level leads straight to the Ferencvárosi railway station.*" My conversation with Nora came back to me.

Another memory popped into my head when Ash and I were hiding behind the viewing dome a level above us.

"*Tell Dr. Karl more shipment is coming in. I'll prepare the side bay for their arrival.*"

A shipment from the railway station.

The prisons and labs were the bottom level. The viewing bay was the second, and where Ash and I got into the fight with those soldiers had to be the first.

That meant…

"We need to go up," I screamed as we continued running, the sound of guards gaining on us from behind. Tension sprang down my arms and legs, my heartbeat pounding in my ears. If there wasn't a way out, we were just herding ourselves into a pen for Markos.

Trapped.

Dead.

Warwick's boots pounded the ground, searching for any doors or way out, while we took the same route we had taken several times in the last few days.

"There are stairs behind that door." A small voice brought me to a complete stop, whipping my head to a cage full of emaciated bodies and sorrow-filled faces of the fae children.

An older boy pointed his arm through the bars at what resembled a tiny closet, almost hidden in the wall. "Behind the door are stairs. I've seen them come in and out."

Warwick started to run for the doorway.

I didn't move a muscle.

"What are you doing?" Warwick growled, motioning me to hurry. "Come on, we don't have time."

"No." I shook my head. "Not without them."

"Kovacs…" He gritted his teeth, his gaze darting from the corridor soon to be filled with soldiers to the kids. "It's impossible. We can't save them right now."

"I'm. Not. Leaving." I shot every word to him. I hadn't been able to save the little girl. And probably a hundred others similar to her. Like Rodriguez's little sister. I still felt I owed it to him. To save someone's sister, daughter, son.

Warwick growled. We stared each other down. I would not relent.

*"Az istenit!"* Warwick dug his hands in his hair, frustration bellowing from him, swinging around for the cages. I was right by his side, searching for a way to break into them. "There are no fucking keys, Kovacs. How the hell are we supposed to get them out before the guards shoot us down?" He motioned back down the tunnel, filled with the sounds of yells and boots hitting the ground. Every second was counting down to our last.

Did I just hang the noose around our necks? Was my need to help them only ending our lives and saving none?

"Don't happen to have a spare brownie and imp on you?" He shook the bars, trying to find the hinge's weak spot.

Damn! Opie and Bitzy would be very handy right now. I missed them so much.

"No, but you have me." I pinched the rod I picked between my fingers, going down on my knees to work the lock, the kids gathering close, their faces hopeful and pleading. From my years of being a thief, breaking locks was second nature. I just hoped these weren't spell-locked or goblin made.

"Fucking hell, woman." Warwick shook his head with a grunt. "You really want to challenge death, don't you?" Whirling around as guards closed in, Warwick roared, bulldozing straight for the first string of officers in the tunnel. In the tight corridors, they couldn't spread out, allowing him to slip right up.

Gunshots fired, then bellows and the sound of flesh being hit.

Biting my lip, I fought back the urge to look behind me, keeping my concentration on the lock, not wanting to waste even a second Warwick was trying to give me.

The thud of a body hit the ground next to my leg, an HDF uniform patch in my peripheral. A large hand swiped down and grabbed the gun from the victim, shooting down others of his troop.

*Brexley, focus!* Adrenaline discharged, my arms were quaking as I worked the lock, the kids cheering and screaming on Warwick and me as the fight continued behind me.

At any moment, Warwick could be killed.

At any moment, I could be shot in the head.

And I had no magic to help us. The link to give him strength was dead. The power in my DNA was in hibernation.

The pipe slipped from my sweaty hands, clanking on the floor, pushing up my fear and speeding my heart rate.

"Hurry the fuck up, Kovacs!" Warwick's voice strained as he kicked another guard to the ground.

A whimper came out of my mouth, and I tightened my grip on the weapon. It was too big, the point not slipping into the lock. It wasn't going to work.

*Fuckfuckfuck.*

My eyes lifted to a little boy standing before me. His bottom lip trembled, his eyes wide, pleading with me to not give up. To not leave them here.

*"A kurva életbe!" Fucking hell!* I stood up, desperation and rage exploding through me. I lifted my arms, and with all my might, dropped the spear like an ax.

*Clang!*

The metal vibrated, squealed, and pierced the air as I struck it again and again. My anger took over. There had been so much loss. So much death. So much pain.

All I wanted to do was save these kids from any more of it.

Grunts, yells, gunshots, and bones crunching mixed in with the piercing bangs of metal, like a song of agony. Of heartache and pain, a melody for the words we could not express.

If I died here, at least I went out trying to save them.

I drove the pipe into the lock resembling a madwoman, shrieking with effort, epinephrine roaring through my muscles.

*Clank!*

The lock snapped, and I stood for a second in shock as the door fell open.

*Holy shit.*

I reacted in the next breath, flinging open the gate, motioning the kids to move. "Go! Go! Go!"

The oldest boy and girl took control, moving the children to the doorway like a gaggle of baby geese.

Not hesitating, I grabbed two guns off the ground from fallen officers, shooting at anything around Warwick, their bodies dropping to the ground at his feet.

He twisted his head, his gaze catching mine, blood gushing down his nose and mouth. His eyes lit up in flames of violence and carnal hunger, sending shivers through me. *Lust.*

Fuck that man.

"Come on!" I belted, forcing myself to not rip his clothes off right there. Heading to the door, I wanted to be the front line to what we might come against once we reached the top.

Warwick shot four more guards before darting after us, taking up the rear. The pounding of all our feet going up the skinny stairway matched my pulse as we made our way to the next level.

Pushing through the door, I peered out. No guards yet, but I could hear them coming for us, their yells telling me they were very close.

"Hurry!" I pulled the door open wide, motioning for the kids to head down the tunnel. Only a few got out before a group of officers came around the corner.

"Run!" I ordered them as I fired at HDF, forcing the soldiers to duck behind the wall.

The children filed out, the older ones holding toddlers on their hips or backs, getting the group down the long dim tunnel.

Warwick came up the stairs, barking at me. "Go! I'll hold them off."

"We do this together, Farkas." I shot at a few HDF sticking their heads around, trying to shoot us. "Always."

He peered at me for a moment, his jaw moving as if he wanted to speak, but he clamped back down, his head dipping in agreement.

We worked as a team. Equals. Whatever lay ahead, we went in together, and we came out together.

Or we didn't at all.

In sync, we both trotted backward, firing at anything that moved, until we got deep enough in the tunnel they started to venture out, coming for us.

"Run." Warwick roared, whipping around and taking off. Our legs pumped together while shells struck the ground and walls near us, our forms zig-zagging to stay out of the line of fire.

"Shit!" Warwick hissed under his breath while his attention locked ahead. Squinting, I realized what he was looking at. A gate blocked off the tunnel ahead. A checkpoint. But of course, it wasn't the worst thing.

There were guards stationed there, and all five officers had the kids at gunpoint. Soldiers were coming from behind, and a blockade was in front.

*Ó, hogy baszd meg egy talicska apró majom!* Oh, may a wheelbarrow of small monkeys fuck it.

We were screwed.

"Remember when we had to cross the bridge when I took you from Killian's?" Warwick peered sideways at me.

"You mean the one we got shot and almost died on?

"But we *didn't*." His voice was low and growly. "I'm not going back, Kovacs. Just like that day. It's forward or nothing."

Inhaling, I nodded my head. "You know this is suicide, right?"

A cheeky grin hitched the side of his mouth.

"Only way we seem to like it."

There was no turning back. Death was a possibility this way, but if we went back, it was a certainty.

"Stay back, or I will shoot." A guard jabbed his gun into the temple of the oldest girl, with a toddler on her hip. "It will be your fault these kids die."

A low, vicious snarl rose from Warwick, crashing goosebumps down my flesh. The Wolf, the Legend who thrived off killing, who could murder someone with one hand, inched closer to the soldiers.

The calls from the ones behind were creeping up fast. We only had moments before they would catch us, and the game would be over. This was our only chance.

We needed a distraction.

In a blink, my hand lifted, pointing to the guard on the end, and fired. Right between the eyes. His frame jolted before it crumbled to the floor, before he had time to realize he was dead.

Screams erupted from the kids, and the guards stood shell-shocked for a moment—it was enough.

Warwick and I pounced.

Slipping in, I knocked the arm holding the gun to the girl's head, before elbowing his face. He stumbled back with a cry while I whirled around, discharging my gun into the man sneaking up behind me.

Blood sprayed over my face, his frame hitting the ground. My lashes dripping with blood, I peered over at Warwick. The two he'd been fighting were already on the ground.

Feeling my eyes on him, he turned with a wicked half-grin.

"Keys?" I turned away, needing to focus on getting out of here. "Check the guards."

The kids started to pat down each one with precision, going through pockets and taking everything they could find. Scavengers. Shown at a young age how to live in the Savage Lands.

*Bang! Bang!* Gunshots rang out behind us.

A little boy screamed next to me, his body tumbling to the pavement, curling into a ball, his hand gripping the hole in his stomach.

"Petr!" another boy cried out his name, scrambling to him.

My head bolted up to see dozens of HDF jogging toward us, guns raised, ready to assassinate us all.

"Keep looking for the gate keys," I ordered the younger ones, tossing guns from the dead guards to the older kids. "Just shoot at them! Don't stop!"

I didn't know if they even knew how, but it was the fight to the death right now, and Warwick and I couldn't cover them all.

The eldest girl took to it without hesitation, lifting her arms and firing at HDF, baring her teeth at them in rage and fury.

The soldiers marched for us, getting so close they wouldn't miss hitting their target. The sound of heavy cars crunched over the pavement, silhouettes of a tank behind them, the cannon pointed at us. My stomach dropped.

We were going to die.

"Found them!" A little blonde girl, no more than five, sang out, running to the gate. All of them seemed so much older than their years.

"Fucking hurry!" Warwick gritted, his gun clicking, the chamber empty. He tossed it to the side, snatching another from a guard he killed, shooting at the parade edging closer.

Pain suddenly exploded across my chest. My arm went limp, and I dropped my weapon, a cry howling from my throat. Red liquid soaked through my top, a bullet wedging just below my collarbone.

*Bang!*

The older girl shot at the soldier advancing on us, killing the one who shot me without hesitation. I gaped at the mini badass. I could feel her anger and pain, everything she suffered coming to the surface.

"I did it! It's open!" The little blonde girl shouted, the gate squealing wide, giving me a breath of hope.

"Go!" Warwick yelled, rushing the kids to move while he and the older girl covered us.

Rushing them out, I stopped at the little boy bent and wailing over the boy who got shot.

"Get up, Petr! Please wake up!"

"Come on, we have to go." I reached for the kid.

"No!" He clung to Petr. "He needs to wake up! Petr! Petr! Please wake up." The howls tore at my heart, bile heaving up my throat because I knew Petr was never going to wake up.

There was no time to console or try to explain his friend was dead.

I snatched him up with my good arm, adrenaline dulling any pain. The boy kicked and screamed against me, reaching for his friend. "No, I can't leave him!"

I knew we couldn't take him.

This was life or death. And the one in my arms was still alive.

Warwick picked up the older girl like a football, following me through the gate, slamming it on the group scurrying for us now. "Run!"

And we did.
Through the volley of bullets, darkness, and death.
We ran for our lives.

# Chapter 15

Feet pounding.

Hearts beating.

The tunnel seemed to go on forever, terror strung like cobwebs as we rushed forward, guards screaming and shooting at us from far behind.

The locked gate had only held them for a minute or two before they broke through, coming after us. There was no way they didn't already have soldiers heading to head us off down the path. Our escape or capture could be down to seconds.

The route under our feet inclined, bringing us up to the surface. A breeze brushed against my face, and I could smell a hint of diesel fuel and coal, the odor I connected to trains. While Unified Nations went solar, electrical, and eco-friendly, the East went backward, losing the power lines they used to run on and falling back on fossil fuels.

My ears filled with the resonance of tracks clinking, the hum of engines, the echo of a whistle, and steam releasing. Hope beat inside my chest, like light really beckoned at the end of the tunnel.

The Ferencvárosi train station. If we got there, we had a chance of escaping.

"Hurry!" I croaked. Blood trailed down my arm, pain throbbing through my shoulder, dizziness spinning my vision. Adrenaline was the only thing pushing me forward.

The kids with thin, boney legs sprinted faster, helping those who couldn't run as quickly, understanding freedom was not too far away.

Dread soaked into my legs when I spotted another large gate at the end of the passage. Guards shouted from the other side as well as behind us. The silhouettes of figures rushing for the gate in front of us, weapons in their hands.

Fuck. I knew it wouldn't be so easy, but it felt wrong to get this close and fail now.

"Do or die," I muttered to Warwick.

"Seems to be our motto."

Warwick and I barreled forward, lining up with the gate, our arms through the bars, firing at the oncoming guards, while the little blonde girl tried the dozen keys in her hand on the lock.

Bullets pinged off the metal, volleying for us, the older kids next to us returning fire.

A shell knocked Warwick backward, pain growling from him, but he didn't stop firing. I knew he was hit, but neither of us could stop or help each other now.

We just had to survive.

A cry came from the other side of Warwick; a little boy hit the ground. Another scream.

The little blonde girl dropped the keyring to the floor, her butt hitting the ground as blood spilled out of her hand where she'd been shot.

"No!" I shrilled, anger and terror driving a wail through me. I no longer felt pain. I pulled the triggers on both guns I held, belting out a cry of death, slaughtering anything in my range.

My magic was gone, but fury can be a powerful force.

Another girl snatched up the keys, picking up where the first girl left off, understanding survival was the only priority… everything else came later.

Compartmentalizing was the only way to live in this world, endure and continue on.

Gunshots discharged from behind us, the other group of soldiers catching up with us.

Time was running out. I could feel the tick of the clock. The anticipation of a bullet hitting my spine.

*Clank.*

The last gate released. The clatter was a freedom song, squealing with glee as it opened.

"Go!" Warwick belted at the kids, jumping in front of them, getting behind a small barrier, covering them so they could slip out either side. "Run and don't look back!"

The kids did as he said, scrambling out of the tunnel and heading for the tracks in various directions. Shadows and fog crept in around the trains, gobbling them up in darkness and allowing them to slip away into the freedom of the night.

"Go! Go!" I waved the rest to retreat.

The older girl picked up the little blonde who had been shot in the hand, and without a second glance, sprinted away, the last two kids alive slipping out of HDF's reach.

I didn't even let out a sigh of relief when I heard the squeal of car tires in the distance.

My instinct knew who it was. I knew who was coming for me.

Istvan.

"Warwick." I hid behind another small barrier next to him, the sentries steadily moving in.

"Yeah, we should go," he replied dryly as his gun clicked empty.

Only a few shots left, I covered him as he leaped behind my barrier with me, emptying my gun.

We had no more weapons. No more protection.

"Remember what you said, Kovacs? Better to die free than live a life in a cage." His aqua eyes pierced mine. "On three… and as I told the kids, run and don't look back. Whatever happens." His meaning—if I get shot, don't stop for me. Keep running.

Panic clogged my throat, knowing this could be it.

"One…"

I took a deep breath.

"Two…"

I pushed my shoulders back, rolling on my toes.

"Three!"

Warwick and I bounded up. My arms and legs moved as fast as they could as I sprinted for the train tracks.

Shouts and bullets volleyed our way. Pain sliced into the side of my thigh, my leg stumbling at the impact.

"Kovacs!" Warwick grabbed for my hand, yanking me forward, trying to keep me going as soldiers descended on us. Weaving past the train carriages, we broke out onto the tracks.

Headlights assaulted my eyes as several armored trucks drove out onto the rails, spotlights on top of the roof shining on us like a target, guns sticking out of windows pointed at us.

"Fuck!" Warwick whirled us in a different direction as the three cars bounced over the rails, shooting at us.

My legs struggled to keep up. Locking my teeth together, I pushed myself to keep going.

"There!" I pointed, seeing a gap through a fence not far from us.

Warwick pulled me harder, jumping over tracks as volleys pinged off the ground and fence around us. One struck the spot right before we slipped through.

"Brexley!" I heard Istvan's voice boom out. "Hear this! Every day you stay away, your friends at Věrhăza suffer for it. This is on you! If you come with me now…"

I paused.

"No," Warwick growled at me, his grip on me tightening.

My gaze lifted to his in doubt.

"No." Final. No question. "Don't fall for it. They will not be any better off if you give yourself over to Istvan. He will kill you after he kills them in front of you." Giving me no time to respond, Warwick threaded his hand in mine and yanked me to follow.

Covered in blood, wounded, and weak, we slipped into the night and ran straight from Istvan's evil lab to the seedy world of the Savage Lands.

We cut through the seediest section of the Savage Lands, using the darkness as protection. It wasn't Istvan I feared hunting us through these parts; it was the trouble walking these streets waiting for an opportunity. I worried Markos would have spies through here. Webs of people working and living among the destitute, relaying any information back to him for a coin.

"This way," Warwick said quietly, his hand still in mine, leading us down an alley past a butcher shop. One that probably stuffed the sausage with things other than animal meat.

Stopping at a back door, he peered over his shoulder, glancing around before he did a double knock and three taps on the alley door.

"A butcher shop?"

"During the day, it is," Warwick replied, hinting at something more.

After a few moments, a slot opened up by the peephole, two eyes peering out. "Fuck." A growly voice snarled on the other side, the view hole slamming shut as quickly as it opened.

Bolts unlocked before a massive bald man wearing a blood-stained apron opened the door.

"Get the fuck in here," he snapped, waving us in. He peered out the door before he slammed and locked it behind us.

*"Te geci."* You bastard. "What the fuck, Warwick. You just show up here?" the guy huffed out in a Polish accent. He wasn't as tall or as big as Warwick, but he still held his own. His bearded face, heavy frame, and severe attitude made him quite intimidating. By his looks, he wasn't full fae, but something about him told me he wasn't full human either. A half-breed like Warwick.

"Good to see you too, Gawel."

The guy crossed his arms, narrowing his eyes at Warwick.

"Where the fuck have you been? I thought you were dead." He narrowed his gaze at the blue prison uniform Warwick still wore, though it was ripped, worn, and covered in blood.

"Probably should be," Warwick replied, nodding to me. "Need your help."

Gawel blinked, his jaw rolling, his gaze going over both of us, taking in our injuries.

"Nothing's changed, I see." He huffed. "Come on." Turning away, he lumbered down a dark hallway full of meat hooks crusted in blood and gore.

I swallowed. "What are we doing here?"

"Told you, Kovacs. I know more than one place that takes in vagabonds and the depraved." His hand pressed into my back, urging me forward. "Gawel is an asshole, but I've known him a long time. I trust him."

"You?" I peered up at him. "Trust?"

A slight reflex twitched his mouth.

With every step I took, I could feel energy leaking from me. My arm and leg throbbed, my stomach rolling with bile. You'd think my body would be used to being shot by now.

Gawel stepped into a room, flicking on a light. A gasp bubbled in my throat, my legs automatically stepping back, knocking into Warwick.

The room was cold, with white tile walls and floor. A large drain was in the middle, collecting blood that dripped from the tables. Slabs of indescribable meat, bones, intestines, and other animal parts were strewn across butcher tables or hung from hooks. Cleavers, knives, and saws hung from racks spread around the room, while one table held a giant meat grinder. The smell of it caused my stomach to churn.

Gawel turned back, noticing I hesitated at the door. "Don't worry, girl. I'd gut him first… giving you time to run before I came after you."

*"Gennyla'da."* *Shitbag.* Warwick huffed with humor, his hands clasping my arms and walking me farther into the room.

I grew up privileged; I never had to see where my food came from, how the meat on my plate had to be slaughtered and diced before it was beautifully presented with sauces and garnish.

"Hop up, girl." Gawel tapped on the only clean table, nodding at me.

I looked at Warwick.

"Can't find a doctor, you go to a butcher." Warwick led me over. Twisting me around, his hands grabbed my hips, and I hissed in pain as he set me on the table. His body was between my legs, his hands brushing dirty strands of hair away from my face. "They know how to dig out bullets, sew up flesh, and marinate the meat."

"Marinate the meat?"

Gawel let out a short chortle, pulling a flask from his apron and handing it to Warwick. Warwick took a long pull, his eyes watering. "Damn, I always forget you Polish fuckers know how to drink."

Gawel almost looked as if he might smile. Then it was gone.

"You have to undress," Gawel ordered, grabbing a pair of pliers and wiping them off with rubbing alcohol. "I need to check out and clean the wounds."

Warwick's eyes were heavy on me as he set down the flask, his fingers gliding down to my hips. "Take a deep breath."

I did as he carefully tugged at my gray pants, crusted with dirt and fluids. Biting my lip, I lifted my hips, the pain in my thigh causing sweat to trail down my temple. He pulled the disgusting prison pants down my legs, dropping them to the floor. His eyes held mine for a moment before stripping off the filthy, blood-soaked top, leaving me in my underwear and sports bra.

"That too," Gawel grunted, motioning at the bra. The bullet had gone through it, probably infecting the wound with sweat and dirt.

A rumble came from Warwick. His face was impassive, but a nerve in his eye twitched.

Sucking in, his fingers slid underneath the elastic band, tugging it up over my bullet wound. I cried out in pain as he drew it over my head, ripping it off like a bandage and tossing the material next to the pants. His gaze moved down to my bare breasts, his eyes flaring, jaw clenching.

In utter pain, my nipples still hardened, my skin still tingled as his gaze trailed over me. The link was burnt out, but we still had a connection that hummed in my body. A bond that went past magic.

It was just us.

"I could try to heal you right now." His voice was so low, it dragged over the ground, sending shivers up my spine. His fingers glided down the sides of my ribs. "Fuck you on this table."

"Fae bullet." I breathed out heavily. "We both need to get them out before they poison us." Goblin metal was poison if it got into the bloodstream.

"If I wanted to watch people fuck, I'd go downstairs. Want my help or not?" Gawel snapped.

Warwick nodded, grabbing the flask off the table and unscrewing the lid, taking a gulp before handing it to me. "Drink up, princess. There's no sedatives here."

Blowing out, I tipped the flask into my mouth. The burn had my eyes watering, but I swallowed down as much as I could, coughing between sips.

"Damn. I'm impressed, girl." Gawel said, though his voice sounded indifferent. "You chugged Bimber."

My forehead furrowed.

"Basically, Polish moonshine, princess." Warwick smirked, his hands flattening on either side of my hips. "Very potent and *very* illegal." Leaning in close, he slowly slid his lips over mine, letting me taste the potency of the alcohol on his before backing away. Taking a swig, his gaze was on me, but he spoke to his friend. "You'd be awed by what this girl can take."

Gawel's gaze darted from Warwick to me, an eyebrow raised in surprise, but he didn't say anything. He leaned in, inspecting my two gunshot wounds.

"Not gonna lie; this is going to hurt," Gawel said bluntly. "Are you a screamer?"

Warwick snorted, his eyes dancing with heat. "Fuck yeah, she is." He leaned into my ear. "I can't take away your pain right now." Warwick handed me back the flask. "So, drink until you can't feel your legs."

I tipped the flagon back, pouring the burning liquid down my throat, gulping and swallowing almost the whole thing.

"Whoa, whoa! This isn't water, girl. This shit is hard to get, and it ain't fuckin' cheap." Gawel growled, swiping back the bottle.

My chest and throat burned, the room already spinning, their voices a little more distant.

"You have to keep her quiet. I can't have anyone hearing her." Gawel primed the pliers between his fingers. "Here." He handed Warwick an object.

"Kovacs?"

I blinked, looking up at Warwick, and swaying from the alcohol and blood loss.

"Bite down." He pressed something leathery against my lips right as Gawel dug the pliers into my shoulder.

My mouth opened in a guttural scream, and Warwick shoved the leather strap into my mouth.

"Bite down like it's me you want to tear into, princess." He breathed in my ear. "Just focus on me."

My teeth dug into the strap, my eyes on him, tears rolling down my face. Screams rolled around in my chest and clawed at my throat, but I didn't stop looking at Warwick, his gaze trapping me, holding me as pain tore through my nerves.

Gawel dug in again, and my body reached its limit, exhausted, tortured, and drained of so much blood over the last few days, it broke down and let the darkness pull me under.

"Do I dare ask?" A man's deep voice spoke, stirring me to consciousness.

"No questions, you know that." Warwick's resonance thrummed through me, yanking me further from my peaceful slumber.

"You show up here after years… *with her*," Gawel replied. "I know who she is, Farkas. She's in every Leopold paper." A pause. "What the fuck are you doing?"

"You don't understand," Warwick rumbled. My lashes flicked open. I was still on the butcher table, but a cloth was now wrapped around my chest, covering me, my wounds stitched up. It wasn't the injuries hurting as much as my head did. The grain alcohol pounded so hard through my veins I could hear it echo in my ears. I flinched at the pain, and the slight movement had every muscle screaming in protest. As much as I wanted to close my eyes again and disappear from the pain, his presence commanded me to stay with him.

The man was breathtaking, wearing only pants, his arm bandaged up now, his tan chest a blanket of tattoos, scars, and muscle.

Gawel scoffed. "You think you're the first to get into a mess over some pussy."

In a blink, Warwick slammed Gawel against the wall, his face only an inch from his, his hand knotting into the butcher's apron.

151

Stacey Marie Brown

"You say one more thing about her like that, and you will be the gutted pig."

Gawel blinked.

*"Jasna cholera." Holy shit.* Gawel muttered in Polish, staring at Warwick. It wasn't fear which flickered over his expression but shock. "Are you in love with that girl?"

Warwick snarled but let him go, strolling away, his head shaking as if he was trying to shake off the claim.

"I've known you for centuries. The reason this place even exists is because of *you.* But not once in all that time have you ever let a woman close. No more than a steady fuck every once in a while."

"Shut the fuck up, Gaw." Warwick ran his hand over his head, squeezing the back of his neck.

"Warwick." Gawel pushed off the wall. "What the fuck are you thinking? *Her,* of all people? The princess of HDF? She's a fucking human! And one of *them.*"

"You have no idea what you are talking about." Warwick snapped, his teeth showing. "She is not one of them. Just stay the fuck out of it."

Gawel exhaled, tugging on his beard. "I knew you were a crazy son of a bitch, but I didn't think you were masochistic."

Warwick scowled at him.

"Yeah, actually I knew you were into that shit too, but fuck…" He started ambling for the door, his head wagging in disbelief. "You can stay for only *one* night."

"It's all we need."

"You remember where everything is?"

"Yeah."

"Okay." Gawel snipped with annoyance. "Just stay out of trouble down there and maybe keep a low profile. I don't need this place being busted up because of the bounty on your head."

"What's it up to now?" Warwick smirked.

*"Almost* enough to turn your ass in myself," Gawel spouted from the door, swinging around and stomping out.

"He doesn't seem to care for you very much." My voice cracked on a hoarse whisper.

Warwick turned to me. A slight twitch tugged up the side of his mouth. "He doesn't like anyone."

Pushing myself up, my body revolted at the idea. I grit my teeth in a groan.

152

"Go slow." Warwick was right there, his palm cupping my neck and face, helping me up.

"I can't believe I passed out. How embarrassing. You'd think my body would find getting shot to be old habit by now."

Warwick's other hand gripped my other cheek, centering me in a sitting position, his gaze meeting mine.

"I'm pissed your tally is one higher than mine now." He moved in, his lips brushing mine, taunting me.

"I didn't know this was a competition."

"*Everything...*" he growled in my ear, "is a battle with us, Kovacs. Constantly challenging and pushing each other. But we both know I will always win."

"Oh, really?" I lifted a brow.

He drew back; a smile of mischief hinted on his lips.

"Then I challenge you to get rid of this headache. Actually, all my aches."

"Done and done." He curled his hand around mine, helping me off the table. "Follow me."

"Think I need some clothes." I wobbled when I slid off the table, tucking the thin towel around me tighter, the fabric barely hitting my upper thighs.

"Don't worry, where we're going, no one will notice... and you might be overdressed."

That didn't ease my tension at all.

# Chapter 16

Trailing after Warwick, we went through a storage closet with a false panel in the back, opening up to another room. We continued downstairs, through another secret door with a large troll-looking guard, and proceeded down more steps, which hurt like hell. The fact I was walking at all, I took as a plus.

We came to another small door, which almost blended in with the wall. Grabbing the knob, he turned to me. "Be prepared."

I started to ask him why as he opened the door, flooding music, a strong ammonia-like smell, and voices at me, pummeling my senses. Shocked, my eyes gobbled up what was behind the hidden door—a world you could never imagine under a butcher shop.

At least a hundred people milled around, laying, dancing, and lounging throughout the space. My jaw stayed open as I stepped into the large, hazy room with him.

Through the puffs of smoke, I could see couches, lounges, and beds—the place a sea of different types, from a four-poster canopy bed to mattresses on the floor. Colorful fabrics draped the wooden furniture and walls. Dozens of low-burning lamps hung from the ceiling, giving it a dim, seductive glow. Sensual music came from speakers as men and women, fae and human, lay in various stages of undress, smoking on pipes, passed out, or fucking right out in the open.

"An opium den?" I blurted out. As ruthless and feral as this country was now, most drugs were still illegal. That's why the black market did so well. Opium was one of those even the fae succumbed to. Producers of the drug were making it magic-laced now, adding to the high and, therefore, the addictiveness.

Opium dens were highly illegal, but hardly patrolled in the Savage Lands and even rarely controlled. Istvan would only act, sending out troops, when the elite in Leopold started to hear of things on the other side of the wall and get righteous.

"Told you this place was only a butcher shop by day." Warwick winked down at me.

"I heard him say you were the reason it even existed." I peered back up at him.

He exhaled, his head bobbing. "I've known Gawel since my days of running this town. Let's just say it was one of the numerous business ventures I got into during that time."

"Is there anything you don't control in some way?"

His expression lost all humor, his focus pinning me to the floor.

"You."

The air in my lungs caught in my chest, feeling the power of his claim.

He turned to me, his enormous frame looming over mine, his fingers trailing over the top of my towel.

"The secondhand opium should help with the headache." His hands grabbed my hips, flattening me against him. "The rest I'll have to take care of myself."

I already felt high, but it was all him. My drug of choice.

Taking my hand, he pulled me to an empty bed toward the back. The see-through silk drapery hanging off the teak bed didn't give any of us privacy.

I didn't care.

Not only did no one around us care or even understand reality anymore, but Warwick and I were past decorum. We ate propriety for breakfast with our hands.

Hunger darkened his eyes, his fingers tugging at the towel, dropping it to the ground. Shivers ran over my skin as his regard went to my breasts, his tongue sliding over his lip. Bending over, his mouth covered my nipple, flicking and sucking.

My back arched, a moan shuddering through me. My nails raked up the back of his head while his tongue flicked at the other nipple.

"Warwick…" I breathed, his name a demand for more.

A noise vibrated in his chest, his grip tightening on my jaw while his entire body pressed into mine. His heavy erection was hot against my naked skin; he pushed against me as his mouth collided with mine with a growl.

The man could destroy me with just a kiss, marking me with more scars and leaving me crawling out of the ruins, seeking more.

I ignored the jabs of pain when he lifted me, my legs circling his hips, our kiss desperate and needy. Lowering me back onto the bed, his weight pressed down on me, fitting perfectly between my legs. My hips rolled into his, craving more, desperate to feel him. Pushing at his pants, I slipped my hand between us, my palm wrapping around him, my thumb rubbing over the head, feeling the slick bit of pre-cum.

A deep moan came up his throat before he climbed off of me. His focus was intense as he yanked off his pants, freeing his hard cock, and chucked off his boots. Instead of crawling back on me, he lowered himself to his knees, yanking me closer to the edge of the bed. His hands wrapped around the sides of my underwear, dragging them down, being careful around my wound. He spread my legs, and I felt the zing of people being all around us, able to see everything.

His teeth nipped at my inner thigh, his tongue sliding up and grazing my folds. I dropped my head back, my nails curling into the bedding, my teeth sawing into my lips.

"Look at me." He sat back, waiting until my eyes were on him. He grabbed an opium pipe on a side table next to the bed. His gaze never left mine as he lit it, inhaling deeply. Tracking his every move, he spread my legs wider, his lips trailing all the way up my thigh, humming hungrily against me. His mouth covered my pussy before he blew the smoke into me.

My body jolted, and a rush of euphoria shredded a loud, long moan from my lips as his tongue licked through me. He took another hit, his tongue sliding in deeper, propelling more of the opium deep into my core.

"Oh, gods," I cried out, heaving, my spine arching in utter bliss, my hips rocking desperately against his mouth. My brain could no longer compute. All I understood was pleasure. Need and desire swirled through me with dizzying speed.

Sucking and nipping, his mouth consumed me whole. Flames burned up my spine, my orgasm already sprinting too fast to the edge. I never wanted this to end. I wanted him to feast on me forever.

"Warwick!" I groaned. Noises heaved from me; cries I had never heard before. His hands clutched my ass, my legs over his shoulder, yanking me closer to him and devouring what was left. My mind was a swirl of colors, us fucking on a bloody field, walking through a battle, dead people all around us.

The Grey.

The Wolf.

The cry from my lips as I slammed brutally into my orgasm seemed to echo through the room and crashed out into the world above. Through the high, I could feel the link braiding back, skimming over my skin and brushing at my soul. His presence around me, inside me.

His mouth still on me, he sucked in sharply, feeling it weave through us both.

The bond turned my satiated body into raw need. Twisting it with so much desperation, no drug could touch it.

"Warwick," I growled. Grabbing his head, I yanked him up. The moment he was on his feet, I shoved him flat on the bed, crawling over him.

His eyes glowed, his cock so hard the veins strained against the skin.

"Brexley," he snarled as I straddled him. I could hear the desperation tight in his vocals. "Fuckin' ride me, woman." His hands clamped down on my hips. I grabbed him, positioning him at my entrance, feeling my legs shake with need.

"*Ko-vacs.*" He grunted, his grip yanking me down as he slammed into me.

"Fuuucck!" I heard us both bellow. It was almost too much. The high of opium and the rush of our bond turned me into a ferocious fiend. Raw, feral, and unbridled. I couldn't seem to ride him hard enough.

We were loud, savage, and brutal.

I could feel eyes on us; I could see people getting off with us. Their moans and cries only created more energy between us—like a wave that would never stop breaking over the rocks. We could never get enough, never get close enough.

"Fuck, princess," Warwick hissed, slamming up into me, hitting me deeper.

"Don't ever stop." I tipped back, changing my position slightly, causing him to bark out, his eyes rolling back.

"Never," he huffed, his hand smacking at my ass, sending tingles through me.

"Warwick…" My nails clawed into his chest.

"I know what you want, princess." As soon as he said it, his shadow glided up behind me, nipping at my ear. *"To have us both."*

I whimpered, feeling Warwick's other hands glide over my skin, cupping my breasts, the feel of his skin pressing into me from behind, his mouth biting into my neck.

Our rhythm slowed into deeper and longer strokes, desire and lust curling my head back into the shadow. It wasn't completely solid yet, but the more I let go of my thoughts, gave over to us, the more real it became.

*"Brexley,"* he whispered in my ear, his palm trailing down my spine, pushing me slightly over. I rolled deeper into Warwick, his fingers digging into my thighs as I felt his other tongue slide down my back, parting me from behind.

"Oh, gods…" I breathed out, my lids fluttering, my gaze connecting with aqua eyes, as I felt his tongue go deeper.

"This might still hurt." Warwick clutched my face, pulling my chest against his, kissing me deeply. "Relax." That's when I felt him press his cock into me from behind.

I gasped roughly, my nerves burning, air locking in my chest as he pushed into me.

"Holy fuck." Warwick's head tipped back, a loud moan coming from him as he slipped his finger over my clit, rolling his thumb over it.

Feeling Warwick's shadow push deeper into me, spinning my head and spreading euphoria through my veins.

I cried out, rocking between the two bodies pressed into me, sparking the savage part of me back to life. Warwick sat up, reaching deeper, his mouth sucking on my breasts as his shadow fucked me from behind, his lips nipping at my neck.

I gave myself over to it, indulging in the utter bliss.

No guilt or death.

No torture or pain.

No prisons or test labs.

It was just us.

We would have to face it all soon enough, but right now, we took pleasure, we stole joy, we robbed grief of its hold on us.

*"You like that, princess?"* Warwick's spirit grunted in my ear, hitting harder and faster. *"Me fucking your pussy and ass."*

"Yes," I heaved, feeling the buzz of heat, the edge of oblivion coming for us.

Warwick snarled, flipping me over and propping me up on my hands and knees.

"I need to feel the real thing." He grabbed my hair, yanking it back as he pushed into me, my hands clawing and scratching at the bedding. Feeling the real thing seemed like he was splitting me apart. "Holy fuck... holy fuuuuuccckk," he moaned.

"Warwick!" My eyes watered. Through the pain, my muscles burned with desire.

*"I got you, princess."* His shadow's tongue slipped into my pussy, sucking on my clit.

I bellowed as he yanked me up to his chest, his hand circling my neck, pounding into me as he devoured my pussy.

"Oh, gods... oh, gods..." My body shook violently.

His shade moved in front of me. Feeling just as real as the other, he positioned himself, sandwiching me between the two, before thrusting into my pussy.

I couldn't even scream. My nerves were ravished and shredded by him filling me so deeply. I could almost feel them rubbing together, clawing down my bones. I cried out, my body almost going limp. The two Warwicks pressed me between them, our bodies rolling and moving together.

Pleasure.

Pain.

Warwick's tempo picked up, his hand gripping my neck tighter, squeezing until sparks burst behind my lids. Screaming, I felt myself explode. Warwick's shadow moved, his mouth lapping at my folds as I came, making me orgasm so hard my sight blinked out.

Fire bulbs flickered, a few bursting, sprinkling glass down from the ceiling, a rumble of thunder, a breeze sweeping through the stagnant underground room, dispersing the thick clouds of opium. Loud moans echoed through the room in unison, the energy from everyone's release at once only heightening ours.

Warwick roared, his hot cum spilling inside me so much it gushed down my thighs. Our chests heaved together, our muscles quaking. It took several moments for us to even be able to breathe, frozen in overwhelming ecstasy.

"Fuck, princess... that was... fuck..." Warwick exhaled heavily against my neck. "I love my dick still coming inside you while I can taste your release on my tongue."

No words found their way to my lips. No brain activity besides the rush still zooming over me, the heat of our skin, the violent trembling of my body. I could feel the withdrawal already setting in. The need for more. My addiction to him.

Warwick pulled out slowly, more of his claim sliding down my leg.

His hand cupped my cheek, twisting my chin to him, and he kissed me fervently. Lowering me down on the bed, he gathered up my shivering form, pressing me into him, my head on his good shoulder.

"How's your headache now?" He sounded smug and cocky, making me snort. I couldn't say he didn't have the right to be after that, and I knew our wounds were mostly healed. I felt no pain anywhere, just absolute gratification, my muscles melting into him.

The buzz of activity started seeping around us, making me very aware of the people near us. My mind stumbled back on what we went through, the kids who were killed, what happened with Caden. To us.

"Stop it." He wagged his head, his eyes shutting briefly. "We can talk about everything later." *Dammit, he knew me too well.* "Right now, we need actual sleep."

"Sleep, huh?" My hand rubbed over his chest, following his tattoo.

"At least a couple hours before I wake you up to fuck, take a shower and fuck you again, and maybe get food before I screw you up on the butcher block upstairs."

"As long as we can use the meat hooks."

He let out a laugh, peering at me, the sound spreading a giddy smile on my face. "Just my level of kink."

"It's why you love me," I said without thinking, feeling chagrin flood my cheeks, a rebuttal coming up my throat.

"Yeah." He grabbed my chin, forcing me to look at him, his heated gaze on me. "That must be it." His mouth brushed mine. "Now sleep."

As if he ordered my body to let go, I shut my eyes, falling into oblivion. The opium in me and around me sedating me quicker.

Letting down all my walls.

*"Brexley Kovacs."* The ancient, inhuman voice from the fae book slithered into my head as if it had been waiting in the shadows for me. *"The girl who challenges nature's laws. Your power calls to you…"*

Images flashed into my mind as it pulled me further into the darkness.

"Am I seeing things, or does that monstrous thing look even more like a python?"

*Chiiirrrppp!*

"Right?" The familiar voice plucked me from my sleep. "It's moving… you see it right?"

160

*Chirppppp!*

"*You* touch it! I'm afraid it might actually bite me."

Lifting my lids, I spotted Opie perched next to Warwick, staring bewildered at the bottom half of his naked physique, his finger out like he was about to poke a snake, while Bitzy's hands clutched at the air particles, a lazy smile on her face. High as a kite.

I let out a groan, tucking my head back into Warwick's chest. Our bodies tangled where we passed out after the last time he woke me up.

My mind felt syrupy. Thick and hazy with images and sensations—fucking amazing ones—but something else ticked the back of my mind. Like wisps of fog, I could feel but couldn't grasp them. Something right out of my reach.

Between the opium and Warwick, I conked out, only to be stirred awake later to him plunging inside me. Only half awake, our bodies rocked deep and slow together, feeling like an erotic dream, sweeping me up in a long unfathomable orgasm, which hit so hard it knocked me out cold again.

"If you touch it," Warwick muttered, his eyes still closed. "*I will* bite you. In half."

*Chirrrrrp!*

"No, I don't think he meant it in the good way." Opie stepped back slightly. "Though you'd think he'd be a little more grateful. He seemed quite happy with where my fingers were earlier."

Warwick exhaled deeply. I couldn't help but laugh.

"Master Fishy!" Opie bounded over Warwick to me, letting me get a better view of his outfit.

"Is that butcher paper?" I blinked, trying to clear my eyes. Everything felt foggy here; the contact high made everything seem unreal, as if reality was the mirage on the horizon

"Do you like it?" Opie spun. He had made a tiny kimono out of butcher paper, which only reached his hips. It was tied with silk, and he wore a thong in the same embroidered fabric I had seen draped on this bed. His hair was in a high bun with sticks you skewer meat with and poppy buds braided through his beard. Bitzy wore silk bottoms, a tube top in butcher paper, and poppy buds dangling from her ears.

"We got soooo bored waiting for you to wake up." He patted at his kimono. "I wanted to work the contrast of hard and soft." His eyes flicked between us. "But I think you guys beat me to it…" He shook his head. "Does that thing ever unstiffen?" He eyed Warwick's exposed body. "I feel it's gonna strike at any moment."

"It's going to. And if you don't leave soon, you will see it in action." Warwick grumbled, running his hand over his face, his other hand squeezing my leg sprawled across him, pulling me over him.

"We've been searching nonstop for you! Do you know what we've been through to find you?"

*Chiii-rp!* Bitzy hiccupped.

"The detour to pretty boy's mushroom garden was your idea."

*Chirp, chirp!*

"I did not get caught up in his hoover machine for two days! Total lie!"

*Chirp! Chiiirrrppp!*

"One day! And it was a complete misunderstanding." Opie stomped his foot, then turned back to me with a huge smile. "We've been so worried about you, Fishy!"

*Chiiirp.*

"Don't lie. You were worried too."

*Chirp!*

"I could tell. It was on the inside."

Bitzy tried to stick up her middle fingers, but she got distracted by the movement, wiggling them and giggling. *Chhhiiirrppp.* She sang dreamily, plunking down on her butt, her lids fluttering.

"Honey, the kids are high again," I joked, sitting up. Reaching down, I grabbed a silk cover off the end of the bed to cover myself, the bottom part cut into strips.

"Say no to drugs, kids." Warwick still hadn't moved, laying on his back, no care in the world to who could see every inch of him. I guess with him, why would he want to cover up? The man was a legend in every way.

*Chir-ppp.* Bitzy curled one finger up at him as she tipped over, passing out.

"Good talk." I patted Warwick.

"I tried." He shrugged, yawning, his eyes finally opened. Scouring his face again, he pushed himself up.

"Watch out! The big bad wolfie is on the prowl!" Opie exclaimed, pretending to shield his eyes, but ogling the legend through his fingers. "That thing could knock out small villages!"

Warwick scoffed, stretching his arms up to the canopy, leaning in toward me. "Shower's crap here, but at least it will get all the bodily fluids off." He winked.

"Gross."

"I meant blood and plasma from the lab." He lifted a dark brow. "What were you thinking, Kovacs?" He dipped further, his mouth trailing over mine, nipping at my ear. "Think I promised I'd be fucking you in the shower."

Heat burned my cheeks, sliding down my limbs and between my legs. "I think you did."

He took my hand, pulling me up and walking us toward the door. I turned back to my friends.

"No opium or drugs of any kind while we're gone." I pointed at Opie. "Especially for that one." I pointed at Bitzy, her mouth open, snoring.

"No drugs!" He saluted me. "And I will not under no circumstances make this bed… or clean in any way. Nope. I don't feel any kind of urge at all. Just because it's disgusting and covered in some crusty stuff I don't even want to think about. Nope, I won't touch anything."

The bed would be made before we left this room.

Warwick walked us through a door leading to a very rudimentary bathroom with open toilets and showers.

Something we were used to.

Turning on the shower, Warwick pushed me against the wall, letting the cold water rain down on us, his physique pressing into mine. Grabbing a bar of soap, his hand glided over my body, rubbing soap over my breasts as his fingers slipped between my folds, not caring about the three other people in the room taking a shower. Their eyes were so dilated and droopy, I didn't think they'd noticed anything.

Biting down on my lip, my body responded instantly to his touch. I went from needy to desperate in a matter of seconds.

I curved into his hands, craving him. He picked me up, my legs wrapping around him as his cock rubbed through me.

"How—?" I croaked, arms around his neck, my teeth biting and tugging on his bottom lip. "How can I still be this desperate for you?"

"Because…" He hitched me higher, his mouth crushing mine before he continued. "We defy nature, Kovacs. We break every law." His words hit me as he slammed me down on him, my mouth gaping in a loud cry, while bits of my dream flashed through my head.

*"The girl who challenges nature's laws. Your power calls to you…"*

The fae book had come to me, had reached out to me as it had done once before, flashing over images of a cabin, of a fireplace and sofa, of a dark forest outside.

"Fuck. Fuck!" Warwick pounded into me, pinning my spine to the wall, his grip on my hips bruising, but I only wanted more. Harder.

163

Without a word, he complied. Brutal and unforgiving, he nailed into me, the images getting more distinct, every detail becoming solid. My body gave over to the raw pleasure, my vision sparking and shattering.

"Kovacs!" he bellowed, releasing inside me as my pussy clenched around him brutally, my nails raking down his back, tearing into his skin.

Flashes of an object flared to life, charring more of the box it was in.

The nectar.

Heaving in and out, I clung to Warwick, both of us struggling to catch our breath, my core still constricting around him.

His gaze met mine.

"The nectar," I rasped out.

He nodded, confirming he had seen the same thing.

"I know where it is."

# Chapter 17

The cold rain and wind whipped harshly across my face, the motorcycle cutting around another bend up the mountain. The sun was already below the horizon, the dense trees intertwining thick fog through the branches, chilling my bones. Tucking tighter against Warwick, I tried to absorb more of his body heat against the freezing November rain.

Having no sense of time for weeks now, Warwick and I didn't come up from the opium den until early evening, having slept through most of the day. After getting something to eat, Gawel helped us get clothes and "obtain" a bike before we headed in the direction the book had shown me. How the nectar got so far from the Madách Tér in Savage Lands where it was left, I had no idea.

The book had shown me a picture of a map, the location. The closer we got, the more the landscape became familiar, and the more I had the urge to turn around, which had me thinking, I knew exactly where it landed.

*"A spell is guarding the place."* Warwick's shadow said to me, the roaring wind and bike too loud to talk over. *"It will try to steer us away. Just concentrate on what it showed you. Nothing else."*

The night crept in closer, and the howls of wild animals could be heard in the distance. Tugging the pack I borrowed from Gawel closer to my body, I felt the weight of my friends inside, probably still passed out.

They ignored my no drug rule and considered the mushrooms they had brought with them a "vegetable."

Warwick turned the bike down an old dirt lane, overgrown and barely a road. I knew this place. The longer we went down it, the more the need to turn around grew. Everything in me screamed we were going the wrong way. We must leave.

Warwick blew out, his hands crunching down on the bars.

"Keep going," I forced out when I really wanted to say turn back. Breathing in and out, the compulsion to leave itched at my muscles, my head pounding with the pressure.

Warwick let out a strangled grunt, pressing the throttle on the bike, picking up speed.

From a distance, I saw a trail of smoke curl above the trees. Killian's cabin.

"Faster!" I leaned over Warwick, pressing his hand harder on the gas, punching the bike forward. You could feel the sensation of going through cobwebs, a pulse of extreme power.

Then it snapped. Like a cascade, relief washed down on me, relaxing my muscles, allowing my lungs to move in and out for a moment.

The bike screeched to a stop, yards away from the cottage, both of us tensing, spotting a silhouette stooped on the front step of Killian's cabin.

"It's about time you got here." The person shuffled out from the shadows. "The book gave you good directions then?"

Unblinking, I stared at the twisted figure in bewilderment.

"Ta-Tad?" I stuttered, still not believing my eyes. "What are you doing here? I-I thought you were dead."

"Some probably wish I was." His gaze went to the side of the cabin before he came back to us. "Come, it's cold and wet out here. I'll explain everything inside." He motioned us to follow him, already going back indoors.

Climbing off the bike, Warwick and I looked at each other. He wagged his head with a snort. "Life is never boring with you."

He strolled for the doorway.

Something clicked in, seeing other figures moving toward the entry. "Warwick..." I called out, turning his attention back to me. My mouth formed the words to prepare him as a shout pierced the night air.

"Uncle Warwick!" Simon came tearing out of the cabin, racing for him.

Warwick knew they were alive, but as I did, he compartmentalized what needed to be dealt with first and would think about the rest later. He had no time to really think about his sister and nephew, or at least he never expressed it to me if he had.

166

His frame jerked, his brain connecting to where we were and who was running for him.

A guttural noise came from the big man, his response snapping him to action. Leaning down, his arms open, he swept up his nephew in a bear hug, clutching Simon to him like he would never let him go. His lids batted at the emotion, his chest heaving with a mix of agony and relief, probably reliving the moment he thought they were dead. Never to see them again.

The little boy clung to him, squeezing his uncle so tight.

"Warwick!" Eliza came running out, wrapping her arms around her brother and son, the family holding on to each other.

Warwick never showed emotion, not to anyone outside his circle, and barely to those inside it. But seeing him with his sister and nephew, the deep love he felt for them was palpable, filling my eyes with tears.

Eliza glanced over his shoulder, a watery smile for me.

I smiled back, letting them have their moment.

Eliza wiped at her eyes and stepped back.

"Gods, we were so worried," she choked, a wet laugh mixing in her throat. "I'm so happy you guys are okay."

Warwick swallowed, nodding, not able to respond in words, probably thinking the same about them. But I knew Eliza didn't need to hear words. Warwick didn't need to speak for you to feel how much he cared.

In my life, I realized words could be twisted, used as lies, trickery, and bait. A person's true character was in their actions, the truth spoken through doing, not saying.

Warwick set Simon down, the little boy already tugging on his hand, a whirlwind of energy and words, wanting to show his uncle some bugs he captured and toys he had.

As Simon yanked Warwick toward the house, his gaze snapped back to me, his eyes catching mine with intensity.

*"You coming, Kovacs?"* His voice was private between us.

*"Don't I always?"* I winked, catching up with them.

Eliza had been right about me.

I was part of Warwick's very exclusive circle.

His family.

"How did you make it out that night? Is my mother, okay?" My feet paced back and forth in front of the fire, my brain rattling off a million questions.

"Where is the nectar?" I could feel its power nearby. The call to it kept my legs moving back and forth. I could also feel the hum from the fae book. "You have the book here too… how?"

"Sit down, my girl." Tad watched me calmly. "I will explain everything."

My hands ran through my damp hair, my back-and-forth stride over the tiny space not slowing. Nibbling my lip, I forced myself to perch on the chair opposite Tad, my knee bobbing. The need to move, to follow the pull, was almost too much.

*"Breathe, Kovacs."* Warwick's command brushed my neck, my eyes flicking to the man on the sofa.

Simon cuddled up between his uncle and mother on the sofa. Zander rested on the back behind Eliza, his eyes constantly drifting to her. Neither of them showed any extra attention to the other so far, but I still could pick up a vibe, a familiarity and closeness between them.

"It's here, isn't it?" I clasped my hands together, my gaze drifting toward the back area of the cabin, feeling it coming from there.

"It calls to you." Tad nodded his head, with what appeared like distress. "Its power continues to grow. As yours does." His gaze darted between Warwick and me with a slight frown. "The connection between you two has as well. It is remarkable. I have never seen anything even close to it in my lifetime."

A nervous gurgle rolled my stomach.

"Before, it seemed as if webs were between you two, but now it's so thick, it has become a wall. I saw him next to you a moment ago as solid as the man sitting on the sofa." Tad shifted in the wingback chair. "Which I feared."

"Feared?" I sat up straighter.

Tad's mouth thinned. "You asked how the book got here?" His fingers pressed into the arms of the chair, adjusting himself again. "It called to me. Came to me in a dream and showed me everything that happened the night you were taken. It understood the danger being left for anyone to find. Also, the item left in the bag with it."

The nectar.

"A coin can't even drop to the ground in Savage Lands without someone already pocketing it. But a book there is useless, no more than fuel for a fire. Everything worth anything to them had been ransacked. I was lucky to get there in time, to be able to shroud it until it was safely retrieved."

Though I knew it was safe, I still let out an exhale, thankful Tad got to it before it was burned or found, especially by HDF.

"The nectar grew brighter each day, then one night it flared with an abundance of magic, burning the box it was in."

My cheeks heated. Yeah, I recalled precisely why and when it happened. The night Warwick came to me in the shower. And by the glint in Tad's eyes, the curve of his mouth, he presumed what caused it.

He gripped the arms of the chair, pushing himself forward. Eliza and Zander instantly reacted, getting on either side of him to help him to his feet and grabbing his cane, like it was habit to them now.

"Thank you." Tad patted their hands, leaning heavily on his staff, a soft familiarity between them all. He turned to me. "Come."

I bounded up, eager to see the nectar with my own eyes. To be near it.

Warwick was right behind me. The heat from his body and the nearness of his massive frame sent warmth skating down me.

Eliza told Simon to stay inside as Tad led us out the back kitchen door. The rain had turned into a misty haze, and clouds rolled past the moon in slivers of light. It was enough to see a large stone firepit with chairs and benches around to enjoy the blaze on a nice night.

When I got closer, I noticed the firepit was boarded over, a thick wave bubbling the whole thing. Magic.

"You have the nectar outside in a firepit?" Warwick's deep timbre raked across the ground, his cheek twitching.

"It is heavily spelled." Tad frowned, still holding onto Eliza's arm, stopping at the lip of the firepit. "That was the compromise."

"Compromise?" I stepped next to him.

Ignoring my question, he muttered a chant under his breath, the spell over the pit dissolving at his command. The instant it dissolved, the magic hammered inside my chest. Sucking in sharply, Warwick grabbed onto me, keeping me steady.

"Shit…" I breathed, my limbs quaking under the intensity. It was at least double the power I had felt from it the first time.

Zander shoved the wood plank off, displaying a scorched wooden box lying in the middle.

Struggling to capture air, I gulped a few times. The lure to it now was almost painful.

"Wow." Tad blinked at me, awed, and fear sprang in his blue eyes. "You recall how I could see a hint of your aura last time?" Tad turned his head to me.

Again, another ball of nerves swayed my stomach. "Yes?" I swallowed nervously. "Is it gone again?"

Tad stared at me for a moment, then moved to Warwick. "Yes and no."

"Huh?"

"Individually, I can't see either of your auras, but the aura between you two? It's the same gray reflective color I noticed before." He nodded at Warwick and me, a strange chuckle in his throat. "They are so thick it's impossible to see anything else. I think they've been there for a long time, but it wasn't noticeable. Not like they are now. But it's nothing compared to what you have with this." He motioned to the firepit, moving my focus to the power I could hear thumping from inside, no longer a whisper, but a cry.

"The power between you and nectar is unbelievable." Something in his tone jerked my head back to Tad, his throat bobbing.

"What?"

"It's as though you are its battery source. The more you connect, the stronger it gets."

All liquid evaporated from my mouth, my chest clenching.

He didn't need to tell me the most desired object in the world, one which could crumble civilizations if put in the wrong hands, was the last thing you wanted to get more powerful.

"What does that mean?" Warwick's shoulders hunched forward, his lids lowering in a glower.

"It means stop discharging the grenade launcher, big bad wolfie!" A voice came from my pack. Hands and feet climbed up onto my shoulder. Opie's outfit and hair were in disarray, a bit of mushroom and poppy flowers stuck to his cheek, looking like he just stumbled back from an all-nighter. "Wow, I'm already out of breath. That was a steep climb." He leaned over his knees, sucking in and out dramatically.

Everyone stared at the brownie on my shoulder.

"What?" He stood, straightening out his kimono. "Am I wrong? The legend's got too much punch in his spunk. Cake in his snake. Too much batter going into her vatter."

I cringed.

"Nizzle drizzle in his—"

"Oh, my gods, stop." I palmed my face.

Opie shrugged, peeling the bit of mushroom from his cheek and eating it.

"As disturbing as that was, he might not be too far off," Tad replied.

"What?" Warwick huffed. "This is my fault?"

"No." Tad shook his head. "It's the energy you create together, which strengthens not only your bond but fuels the nectar as well. As if there is too much, so the nectar siphons off what you can't hold."

"They do *pump* their magic juice into it." Opie plunked down on my shoulder, snickering in my ear, completely loopy. I really had to cut them off of drugs. Though it actually made sense. Our energy together affected everything around us: ghosts, humans, fae, electricity, the air.

"You're telling me we have to stop having sex?" Warwick snarled, his neck straining. "Not gonna fucking happen."

"I'm just telling you what I observe." Tad shrugged his shoulder.

"What about when I burn through the magic? It's happened a few times now… and our connection goes quiet." I gestured to Warwick. "Does it lessen its power?"

Tad tilted his head. "We noticed it wane and go quiet, but each time it flared back, it was even stronger." Tad shuffled on his feet, a nervous tick stressing his eye. "You both are growing more powerful. I can feel it." Tad's hand squeezed his cane until his knuckles were white. "But the nectar is growing much faster. I think it's siphoning the magic your body can't handle and taking it on. Just as it did when you were born." Tad's wariness was written on his face, peering down at the nectar, studying it as if it would unlock its riddles to him.

The nectar thumped like a heartbeat inside the box, pulling me closer to it, whispering to me. I needed to hold it, to have that part of me back. Maybe it would tell me its secrets. I could understand what this all meant.

Leaning, my hand reached for the box, a jolt going up my arm, my finger about to skim the lid.

"Do. Not. Touch. It." An emotionless voice said every word as though it were a battle. I jerked my head up with a gasp, my eyes taking in the outlines flittering out from the forest trees, their cloaks the color of the shadows.

"When I spoke of compromise?" Tad gripped his staff harder. "They were the concession. They wouldn't allow me to bring it here without them."

I stood immobile as seven figures moved in as silent as ghosts, the woman in front taking my attention. Her skin was pallid and thin, boney hands holding on to her scythe.

"M-mom?" I stared at her, panic and fear gripping my gut. My mother and her clan stood before me; the life in them drained away, leaving what was left…

Necromancers.

# Chapter 18

"Br-ex-ley." Eabha struggled over my name, her mouth moving stiffly as if it took all her concentration to speak.

Emotion choked me, making it hard to swallow. "I-I don't understand." I scanned through the entire clan, seeing the small differences. The life which warmed their cheeks and plumped their flesh was evaporating. The fact my mother spoke at all told me they weren't completely gone.

Yet.

"What is happening to them?" I bounced from them to Tad, demanding an answer.

Tad sighed, his spine sagging more under the weight.

"They are returning to their original state."

"But how? Why? I brought them back. My magic saved them."

"Black magic is conjured from the darkest of magic. It goes against nature. Goes against a Druid's magic. To use it… there are consequences. Ones that can never be erased." His hand rubbed at his twisted spine, reminding me my mother had struck Tad with black magic the night of the fae war. He was the most powerful Druid alive, and yet he could not fix his condition. "What their father did is a sin they will carry forever."

"But I thought…" I stared back at my mom, grief knotting my heart as she watched me blankly.

"I don't know all you are capable of, my girl, but you shouldn't have been able to alter the scars of black magic at all. The fact you did?" He shook his head, keeping the rest of his sentence to himself.

My eyes welled with tears. Before I even got to know my mother, she was being taken from me. As a kid, I dreamed of her being part of my life, of knowing her.

"You bring people back from the dead," Tad said.

"Exactly!" I screamed, anger climbing up into my chest, ready to explode. "Then I should be able to save them!"

"They were never alive or dead." Tad's statement slammed into my gut. "They are in the in-between."

Like the ghosts who slipped away from their bodies. I couldn't bring them back or conjure a person from the grave back to life.

I shook my head in denial, moving to the pit where the nectar was. "I don't care. I will try again. I will do it every day if I have to!"

Fingers wrapped around my wrist, boney but firm. I sucked in sharply at my mother's sudden nearness. How quickly she moved.

"N-o. Dau-gh-ter." Her expression was blank, but I noticed a flicker of sorrow float through her eyes. "Thhiss iss our currssse to bear."

"I can do it," I pleaded. "Please." A pained noise came from me, my focus going over to my aunt Morgan, cousin Liam, to Sam, Rory, Roan, and Breena. The family I was supposed to get to know, to have in my life, to laugh with and maybe see on holidays. "I can't *lose* you, not again."

Eabha's hold tightened, her gaze showing me something was still there. "I feel s-so lucky to have m-met you." She reached up, her skeleton hand cupping my face. "Pr-proud of you. You. Are. Ammm-a-zing. Jussst like your f-father."

Tears spilled down my cheeks, my head wagging in rejection of this outcome, while my heart broke into pieces.

"I love you, Mom." A sob wrenched up my throat.

The only reaction I got was a squeeze from her fingers before she stepped back with her clan. Aunt Morgan dipped her head at me, then they melted back into the woods.

Grief clawed my lungs, forcing me to take small, stunted breaths, trying not to fall to the ground.

Warwick didn't speak, but I felt him move behind me, his shadow grazing inside me, telling me without a word to take what I needed.

Stepping back into him, I used his physical body to keep me standing. The cruelty of getting my mother back to lose her before I had any chance to know her crippled me.

Tad turned, shuffling toward me, his mouth opening when a threatening growl came from Warwick behind me, vibrating into my back.

Tad dipped his head. "We'll be inside when you are ready."

Eliza and Zander helped Tad, all three retreating into the cabin, leaving us alone. The tap of raindrops dripping from leaves padded the damp earth. The pulse of magic from the nectar seemed to echo in the spot my mother had just left.

I could feel them near, forever guarding, forever close to me, but forever beyond my grasp. A family I had wished for, dreamed of.

"Brexley," Warrick muttered against my ear. The sound of my name on his lips cut across my chest, where a guttural sob formed.

Raging pain.

Agonizing fury.

A tempest of anguish screamed from my soul. I was so tired of pain, of loss. I wanted to destroy. I wanted the world to feel what I did. To end it once and for all.

The nectar continued to pound inside the box, every thump telling me to take it, that it could end my pain. Give me the power to bring life to my family again and take the lives of those who had hurt me.

"No." His arms went around me, stopping me from reaching the nectar.

"Get off of me!" I shoved against him, wailing and thrashing. Anyone stopping me felt like a threat. Blocking me from what I needed. I couldn't take another breath if I didn't act. If I didn't open the container. "Let go!" I rammed my elbow into his stomach, only getting a huff from him.

"Go ahead, fight me, Kovacs. Hit me. Take it out on me." His grip on me tightened.

Devastation turned off logic. Violence rose in place of my suffering, desperate to cut out the hurt.

With a cry, my spirit dipped inside him, siphoning energy from him. Using his strength against him, I rammed my head back into him, cracking against his nose. His hold loosened, allowing me to slip out of his arms. Swinging around, my arm flew out, clipping his chin, stumbling him back more. Adrenaline howled in my veins as I pounced for him. He spun, getting out of the way, a feral smile pulling his mouth as blood ran down his nose.

"Come on, princess, show me what you got." He patted his chest.

Snarling, I lurched to the side, swinging out my leg and kicking his hip. He let out a grunt, the wildness in his eyes sparkling.

174

"I'm waiting for you to actually challenge me, Kovacs."

I leaped back for him, my fists hitting, my feet striking out. Noises like a wounded animal howled in the air, and I knew they were from me as I slammed my fist into his gut.

Ire flared in his eyes as I struck his face.

My fisted hands pummeled his torso and head, splitting more cuts across his face, bruises puffing around his cheek. Loud cries shredded from my throat, going from rage to a whimper.

Warwick clasped my wrists together. Twisting me around, he locked his arms around me, pressing his body into mine.

"Let me go…" I only halfheartedly tried to fight him before I felt my energy break, crumbling into sand. He pulled me to him tighter, my legs caving under me, my back bowing forward, as the grief overwhelmed me. He held me as my sobs broke out in crashing waves. He embraced me tightly, like he was wringing the pain out of me. And I let him, falling into him. Using his steady frame, his warm arms. His love.

Slowly the cries quieted until the crickets and drops of water filled the silence.

Lifting my head, I turned to him, my eyes finding his. More grief covered my face as I took in the damage I did. Reaching up, I touched the cuts, rubbing my thumb over the bruises.

"I'm so—"

"Don't even, Kovacs." He cut me off, his hand covering the one on his face. "I'll heal. Plus…" his arms went around me, touching our foreheads together. "This is fucking foreplay for us. Just wait for what I'll do to you later."

I tried to smile, but it was empty, and I leaned my head into his.

"You okay?" His mouth brushed my hairline.

"Yeah." I felt the lie burn on my tongue.

Tucking loose strands behind my ear, he didn't respond, not buying it either.

*Chirp! Chirp! Chirp!* High-pitched squeaks came from the backpack I still had on.

"You? I feel like blended brownie batter!" Opie came stomping back up to my shoulder, this time Bitzy on his back, her eyes glaring, her middle fingers sticking up high. "Next time, can we watch from the sidelines, not be part of your mating ritual?"

"Oh, shit." A laugh, I wasn't expecting, burst out of me, my hand slapping over my mouth. I had completely forgotten they were still in my backpack.

175

"Yeah, we did that too." Opie folded his arms in a huff. "Though you might mistake *it* for brownie batter, I guarantee it's not."

*Chirpchirpchirpchirp!*

"She *really* doesn't like you right now," Warwick smirked.

My eyes widened, another crazed laugh fizzing up my throat as Bitzy chewed me out, but it grounded me, brought me back to what was in front of me. The things I could control. I was far from being okay about the situation with my mother, but once again, I didn't have the luxury of time to work through it. It was for another day. We had too much to do. All our friends were still in Věrhăza. And a war none of us were ready for was on our doorstep.

One day, all of it would come back for me, and something deep inside was terrified of that time, but today was not it.

Warwick let go of me, his gaze on me, his fingers winding through the ends of my hair.

"You ready?" He tilted his head to the cabin.

Taking a deep breath, I nodded.

"You go first."

"Why?"

"Because I'm fucking hard as a rock and really don't want my nephew to see that the only thing I want to do is fuck you against the wall," he growled at me.

"Oh." Heat coursed through me, wanting to do the same. Memories of the night before were still fresh in my mind.

"Might have to take a walk later. I already know the walls are too thin for what I have in mind." His hand went to my back, putting me slightly in front of him.

"Well, we might be competing with another pair later anyway," I smirked, winking back at him. I didn't know for sure what was going on between Eliza and Zander, but the chemistry was thick between them.

"Wait. What?" Warwick stopped, unblinking at me. "Who?"

I smiled coyly, strolling for the door.

"Kovacs?" he strained.

Peering back at him, something caught my eye in the forest. I couldn't see her, but I could feel my mother's gaze on me, an innate awareness of her.

Gritting my teeth together, I grabbed the handle of the door, about to step in when I swore I heard a whisper across the back of my neck.

*"I love you too, daughter."*

Killian's top-shelf whiskey slid down my throat, the smooth burn warming my belly and numbing the pain I was trying to lock back in a box. It also ebbed the call to the nectar, and the possessive need to run back outside and snatch it up, to take what was mine.

"Obviously, you all escaped High Castle after we left," I prompted Tad. He sat in his chair across from me, pillows stuffed behind his back, keeping him propped up.

"Yes." He smiled warmly up at Eliza when she set a cup of tea down on the table next to him.

She returned to the sofa, where Simon had cuddled up to his uncle, not wanting him out of his sight. The little boy tried so hard to stay awake. Zander, as usual, stayed out of the way, but I noticed he was always near Eliza, helping her with the tea or watching her anytime she moved.

"I remember little as you well know; I was not really coherent when you departed."

Tad had been shot by HDF several times, bleeding out. I had been sure he'd die on that hill.

"When I woke up, all the soldiers either escaped or were dead, and my wounds were already starting to heal." He took a sip of tea, his hand trembling slightly with old age. "Eabha and Morgan healed me enough. And I was able to do the rest." He lifted his cup to me. "Which I feel is all thanks to you."

I wanted to believe my mother wouldn't have left Tad to die, but even if she only helped him because of me, I was grateful, whatever the reason.

"When did they start to change back?" I rolled my glass between my hands, my knee bouncing with energy, though I felt so drained and exhausted.

"Ahh… you are testing my recollection." Tad took another swallow before setting it on the table. "I find it easier to recall something over two hundred years ago than a few weeks ago." He closed his lids as if he was filing through his memories. "Now I think about it, it was right after the night at High Castle when I noticed a slight shift in them."

"Is it my fault they are turning back?" I barely heard my voice leave my mouth, guilt weighing down on me, feeling in some way I was to blame.

"As you know, magic and nature are a balance. They used a lot of magic barricading us against the attack that night. Then saving me." My mind recalled the blood-red aura I saw streaming from the clan as they murmured a spell, putting up the protective shield to save us. "You certainly have a link to your mother through the nectar since it is a part of her as well—why she will always protect it. So, there might be some truth to your fear, but their magic as witches wasn't infinite. There is always a cost for using so much magic."

"The cost for protecting us... me... was their human lives?"

Tad didn't respond, his blue eyes telling me all I needed to know.

My head bowed, the burden of everything growing heavier. Another thing I had to shove away when other things were more critical. Things I could change. Taking a deep breath, I focused on another topic.

"Warwick and I just came from Istvan's labs. We know what he is doing." I glanced over at the Legend. His arms stretched over the back of the sofa, one ankle crossed his knee, Simon snuggled into his side, sound asleep. Warwick appeared relaxed, not a care in the world, but I could feel his energy, the intensity with which he peered back at me. If anyone walked through the door, he would be up, already slicing into their throat before we even registered movement.

The Wolf was always ready to fight. To kill his prey. Protect his family.

"It's far worse than anyone knows. His reach and connections extend farther than I think most of us thought. Prague, Ukraine, Romania, and probably many more countries are with him now. Soldiers from all these places are taking the pills, making them fae-like. Istvan is building the largest army anyone's ever seen, while getting powerful leaders under his control."

"He also has fae working with him," Warwick added.

"What do you mean he has fae working with him?" Zander jolted.

Right. I forgot how much they were unaware of. "Boyd, for one," I stated.

"Boyd? He's working with Istvan?" Zander exclaimed.

"Are you really surprised?" I countered.

Zander blinked, taking in my question. "No, I suppose not." He scoured his head.

"Also, Killian suspected someone on the inside blew up the palace." I swigged down the rest of my drink, setting the glass down. "He was right. It was Iain."

"Iain?" Zander stood up from his perch on the end of the sofa. "No way... I trained him. He was satisfactory at best and not the brightest bulb. There is no way he could pull that off."

"Clearly, he was smart enough to fool you, pony-boy." Warwick shot

Zander a look. "He was playing you. It was all an act so no one would suspect him."

"I don't believe you."

"It's true." I pressed my palms down on my jittery knees. "He was at Věrhǎza."

Zander's forehead crumbled. "As a prisoner?"

"As a guest," I replied.

"I don't understand." Zander shook his head.

Warwick scoffed, ready to respond to that comment, but stopped when I shot him a glare.

"Iain was working as a spy, like you, but just not for someone we would have thought." I stood, not able to sit still for another moment. "For Prime Minister Leon."

"What?" Eliza shook her head in disbelief. "He was working for a human leader? Why the Czech prime minister?"

"Because he is the son of Sonya. One of the old Seelie queen's ladies-in-waiting." Warwick responded to his sister with a knowing look.

"Sonya?" Her mouth fell open. "That insufferable bitch who is shacking up with Leon?"

A groan bayed from Zander, his hands scrubbing his face. "They want her to sit in Killian's seat."

"Yep." I leaned on the mantle. "A front to deceive the fae, while Istvan and Leon grab more control, eventually flipping the power struggle and taking over."

"Basically, we're heading for another fae genocide." Eliza leaned her elbows on her legs, rubbing her face. "I don't understand people like Sonya, willing to hurt their own kind. For what?"

"Power and money." I shrugged a shoulder. "Sadly, coming from her other son, Lukas, she's always been this way. She will turn on anyone to get where she wants to go. But I feel Sonya thinks at the end of this, she will come out on top. I see her turning against Leon and Istvan once she's seated."

"Sounds like her." Eliza frowned. "We've heard about her for a long time. She comes from old noble blood from the Otherworld—ones who believe they are the rightful heirs to power. Now her being with Leon makes sense."

"If she thinks it will get her to what she wants in the end, there are no limits to what she will do, like Istvan."

"Our number one priority, though, is getting everyone out of Věrhǎza. Every day we wait, more could be dying. Tortured, starved to death. Let's just say Věrhǎza makes Halálház seem a little less horrendous."

"Really?" Zander blanched, our gazes meeting. For one minute, I could see we both were thinking of the moments we spent together in the holding pen before I was forced out into the Games. The support he gave me, the terror I felt, both of us thinking I might never come out again.

"Istvan has turned it into a labor factory for making fae bullets and sewing uniforms. All preparing to take over Hungary. But he won't stop there. He will take control of the entire Eastern Bloc, and if he figures out how to use my blood or gets his hands on the nectar, he'll go after the Unified Nations."

"And let me guess, he has your blood." Eliza sighed, sitting back on the sofa again.

"Yes." I nodded. "We set him back a little when I blew it up, and we escaped the hell hole, but I guarantee he still has some of it."

"Blew it up?" Tad pipped up. "What do you mean?"

I hesitated.

Warwick curved his brow at me. *"You gonna tell him, Kovacs?"*

"I got very upset, and I don't know—sometimes power comes out of me. It destroyed the entire lab." And killed dozens of men who were in the tanks.

"Was that the first time?" Tad eyed me cautiously.

"No." I stared down at the borrowed boots on my feet, which were two sizes too big. "I also slaughtered dozens of wild animals with my magic when we were put in the pit to fight them."

Tad's eyebrows went up.

"It's why we need to get them out of Vĕrhăza now." I shifted the topic back, not wanting to get into the details. "And since you spelled it. I need your help to undo the spell."

Tad studied me for a long time, the crackle of the fire snapping in the background, along with the hums of Simon's soft snoring.

"You think it would be so easy?" Tad tried to adjust his back.

"No." My arms went out. "But we have to try. I won't let them die in there like that. Can you do it? Can you unspell the prison?"

Tad sighed, his mouth pinching together.

"I can only do it from the inside. I would have to be taken as prisoner and get in to do it."

"What?" Eliza sat fully up. "No."

"There is no way I can unspell some of those enchantments without being right there. I purposely made them that way, so no one could even bend or twist them."

"That would have been good information to know earlier," I muttered to myself, thinking how cocky I was, imagining I could pull down Tad's enchantments.

"There is no way you are going in." Eliza stood up, her hands on her hips. "Absolutely not!"

"El…" Zander reached for her, his hand touching her back, his figure moving close behind hers.

"He can barely get out of bed. I will not let him go back in there, especially under Istvan. He will kill him!"

"Hey, hey." Zander's voice was low and soothing. "It's okay."

She turned to him, taking a deep breath, not noticing Warwick was catching every single nuance of their interaction. His gaze burned into them, a nerve in his cheek twitching, his jaw locking. He was about a second away from lurching up and tearing Zander's hand off his sister.

"Look." I tried to distract him. "I wish we could keep Tad far from there too, but thousands of lives are counting on us. Do you want Ash or Killian to die in there? Kitty? Sloane? Almost the entire Sarkis army?" I flinched at the last part, fighting to keep back the haunting memory at bay.

Sarkis was leaderless now.

"Of course not." Eliza folded her arms.

"Brexley?" Zander ambled closer to me, concern etching his face. "What aren't you telling us?"

"Andr—" I cleared my throat. "Andris." My nostrils burned with tears. "He and Ling are both dead."

"What?" Zander jerked back as if he had been shoved. "Andris is dead?"

All I could do was bow my head.

"Istvan killed him?"

"Yes," Warwick growled.

"No," I replied at the same time.

"Istvan is the reason Andris is dead," Warwick stated, his gaze drilling into me. "Ling, Zuz, and Maddox too."

"No." I shook my head. "I am."

*"No, you aren't. Do not put that on yourself,"* Warwick's shade hissed next to me, but my focus stayed locked on the man. I wouldn't hide from the truth.

"Istvan pitted Andris and me together in the Games."

"Oh, gods," Zander uttered. He knew what that meant better than anyone. Only one walked out.

Sorrow started to worm back up, wrapping around my esophagus.

"The blame is on Istvan," Warwick spoke. "He had Andris thrown into a firepit, burning him alive." Eliza gasped, putting her hand over her mouth. "She was only putting him out of his misery."

"Brex…" Eliza twisted to me. "I'm so sorry."

I didn't want to think about it. I didn't want to discuss it.

"I will do everything I can to get the rest of his people out. Everyone in that hell." I lifted my chin, clamping tightly down on my emotions.

"We can't do it alone." Tad slumped deeper into the chair, appearing exhausted. "The prison is too much for just us to take on. And it will take me some time to break all the spells. What we need is a distraction."

"Now that *I* can do," Warwick smirked, his hand absently running over his nephew's head, the boy sleeping soundly through all this.

"We need more than bombs. They are a good diversion, but not enough. Bombs won't hurt the prison since they made sure to build it deep." I tracked back and forth over the rug. "What we need is an attack on the prison. For all the HDF to be so focused outside the walls, then they won't realize the prisoners are breaking out from within."

"And where do you plan to get these people to attack?" Warwick lifted his arms. "We're not swimming in numbers here, Kovacs."

"But my uncle is." I faced the group, the fire flaming behind me. "The leader of Povstat should probably be aware of what his prime minister and fae mistress are doing." The plan formed in my head. "He has a lot to lose too. His people are also in the prison. If Istvan wins, the entire Eastern Bloc goes down. Prague has just as much stake in this as we do."

Everyone let it soak in, a sober mood descending on the room. Tad barely staying awake.

"So, we head to Prague tomorrow after dark." Warwick nodded, rising from the sofa, picking up Simon with him. "We can plan in the morning, but I think right now, all of us could use some sleep."

Eliza moved to take her boy, but Warwick shook his head. "I got him."

She smiled, motioning for Warwick to follow her down the hall.

"I can't believe Andris is dead. And Ling." Zander stepped to me when they left, wrapping me up in a hug. "I am so sorry for your loss. Andris was a true hero." He squeezed me, patting my back. "Get some rest. You can take Killian's room at the end of the hall. Warwick can sleep on the porch like a good doggie."

I batted his arm with a bemused chuckle. "Better be careful. I think he noticed."

"Noticed?" Zander stepped back.

"Please, I see the way you look at Eliza. And so does he."

"We're just friends." He tried to deny it, but his cheeks colored.

"Sure," I scoffed. "He's gonna kill you anyway, so you might as well go out being more than friends."

Zander made a noise in his throat as if I were being silly, moving over to Tad.

"Come on, let's get you to bed." Zander helped Tad up to his feet. The old man shuffled past me and stopped, peering back at me.

"You are a mystery to me, my girl. What you are. What you are capable of." Tad's eyes narrowed, as if he were trying to see into me. "Which at one time I would have found exciting. There is not much I don't know. However…"

"However, what?"

"I'm beginning to fear you."

# Chapter 19

My eyes jolted open as if someone screamed my name, my heart smacking against my ribs. Darting around, my sight adjusted to the dark room, a sliver of moonlight streaming in from the window. The silence in the cabin echoed in the dead of night.

Restless, my muscles ached to move, an unexplainable need to get up spread through my limbs. Propping up on my elbow, I peeked over at the huge figure lying next to me. Warwick was naked, sprawled out on his back, arm tucked under his head, one leg butterflied, only a sheet covering his lower half, his face relaxed in sleep.

Nibbling my lip, the need to climb on him, waking him up with my body, with my mouth, and take all this unsettled energy out on him almost triumphed. He had made sure I had fallen asleep absolutely boneless, claiming me on Killian's bed like he wanted our scent and moans to mark this room forever, making the fae lord very aware of who had me.

The frame creaked as I slowly slid off the enormous bed, the pads of my feet touching the soft fake fur rug. It might be a cabin, but Killian still made sure it was fit for a lord. It was simply decorated with only a king bed, nightstands, dresser, and small walk-in closet, but the textiles, chandelier, and unique carved wood furniture were top-notch.

Grabbing Warwick's discarded shirt from the floor, I pulled it over my head, the hem reaching my thighs, before finding a robe and slippers of Killian's hanging on the hook next to the ensuite bathroom.

Sneaking down the hallway, I pretended to be heading for the kitchen to get a snack, but both my mind and gut knew where I was headed. Pausing at the back door, I tried to deny it, willing myself to turn around and climb back into bed with Warwick. It was pointless. The draw continued to pull me to the door and out.

Fog misted the damp ground, rolling and coiling through the trees, and the dense wet air filled my lungs and nipped at my skin as I stepped outside. Stars shone brightly, and only a few clouds rolled across the moon, leaving the night fresh and cool. Step by step, I proceeded closer to the firepit. The thump in my ears grew louder. My fingers wiggled with the need to touch it, to feel the power in my hands, to have that piece of me back. The connection to it was intense, almost hard to define. It was akin to a witch's familiar, an extension of myself, a bond no one else could possibly understand. It protected me, saved me, and completed me. When the wall fell and Aneira was killed, it took a lot of the magic that could destroy any other person, fae or human, baby or adult, and shielded me.

Lowering myself to the lip of the firepit, I stared down at the harmless-looking box. The only sign something was off was the scorch marks tattooing the lid. Shifting closer, my hands shook. I could feel the force slipping through the box tangling around my fingers and pulling them down farther to it. It wanted me to take it, to combine our powers as if it craved my magic as much as I craved it.

*"We need to destroy it; it's beyond dangerous. This tiny substance is the most powerful thing in the world. The damage it can do."* Andris's voice whispered through the back of my head, but I shook it away. I could never destroy it. It was part of me.

The nectar didn't speak to me the same as the fae book, but the lure to it screamed loudly in my head, sweat beading at the base of my spine.

The tips of my fingers grazed the box. Images flicked on the cusp of my mind, going so fast I could hardly decipher them.

Thunder crackled in the clearing sky, as wind swept through the trees, rustling the leaves together.

A vision of a battlefield, blood and death littering the ground, the air smelling of the sweetness of magic and the acrid tang of blood. But this time I was alone, covered in gore, but what I felt—the power and magic—electrified me inside. No high could rival it; no thrill could compete. It was euphoria. Something you would chase for the rest of your life to feel again.

I wanted more.

*"No."* A scythe cut down, just nipping at my fingers, hitting the top of the box.

185

With a cry, I fell back on my ass, fear cutting through the trance I was in, my gaze leaping up to a hooded figure standing over me. My mother's black, emotionless eyes pinned me to the ground. My heart hammered, fear biting at the back of my neck, telling me something was off.

*"You must resist."*

A cry caused me to scramble back through the mud, the understanding dawning that she had spoken, but her mouth never moved.

*Holyshitholyshit.*

A speck of humanity left in her made her flinch. *"You hear me?"*

Sucking through my nose, my head nodded. "H-How?"

Eabha watched me blankly for a long time before her voice skated around me.

*"When you brought us back, something must have changed. Necromancers communicate through a link. You must bear the curse more than we thought."*

I knew I did. With Warwick and Scorpion, it was a huge part of our connection. I had begun to experience it with Andris before he died.

"But why?" I stopped myself, swallowing and closing my mouth. *"Why now?"*

*"After you brought us back, we were witches again."* Each word was very stiff. *"We no longer communicated through a link."*

Yet, now that they were becoming necromancers again, they did. And maybe because I brought them back, I was looped in this time.

*"My link to the nectar allows me to feel it, to feel you. The nectar calls to you. Wants you. I can sense the power growing within you both. Power that should not exist. You must resist, daughter."* She positioned herself between me and the box. *"Do not think any sentiment for you will win over my duty. If I must, I will stop you too."*

The instinct to fight her, to take what was mine, made me rise to my feet. She tightened her hold on her weapon. Figures stirred at the edge of the forest—the six other necromancers letting me know they would not hesitate.

*You bow down to no one.* The thought climbed from the pyre in my gut. My breath was short, my gaze locked with my mother's. Tension sparked between us, my hands flexing at my sides. It would only take a shove, and I could reach the nectar before she could even get a swing in.

With every breath, the need only grew. My muscles twitched.

"Kovacs." Warwick stood on the porch step in his boxer briefs. To the outside world, they would only hear him say my name, but I felt all the colors, tasted all his worries and alarms.

186

Like the weapon my mom was holding, he sliced through the hostility between Eabha and me, pushing me back with a staggered exhale. The sensation to go for the nectar was still there, but reason painted everything in a different shade. I had been about to fight my mother. About to challenge seven necromancers.

"Kovacs?" Warwick called to me again, traveling closer as I stepped back to him, instantly easing the tension from my body.

He glanced at Eabha, giving her a nod, his hand going to my lower back, ushering me back into the house.

Shutting the door behind us, I expected him to barrage me with questions, but he didn't. Warwick walked me silently back to the bedroom, peeling off the dirty robe and tossing it to the ground. He spun me to face him, yanking the shirt I borrowed over my head, his fingers digging into my hips as he walked me backward to the bed. Tossing me back onto the mattress, he growled, stripping off his boxers as he climbed over me, settling between my legs. Grabbing my wrists, he yanked them above my head almost to the point of pain, arching my back, desire erupting through me. A small moan left me as his grip tightened on my arms, pinning them to the headboard.

There was no buildup, no teasing. His eyes burned with anger as he thrust deep and ruthlessly into me. I choked out a groan at the severe onslaught of him, filling me so much I couldn't breathe. He pulled out and slammed back into me. The jolt was similar to being electrocuted. My back bowed, my breasts heaving as he set a punishing pace. I couldn't feel his shade. It was only him, and he was making sure I felt every brutal thrust into me. The bed creaked and banged loudly, wood splintered, but he only went harder. Sounds hurled out of me, drowning under his retribution. He branded his fury into me, stamped his fear, tearing and burning me down to ashes. It was a battle he would not stop until he obliterated me, even if I waved the white flag.

"Oh gods…" I cried out, clenching around him.

"You ever…" He pounded, the sound of him entering me, the wetness slapping the walls, the hit of his hips against mine, played like a crescendo. "Do that again…" He clenched his teeth, hitting so hard and deep, my eyes rolled back. "If you feel that pull again, you take it out on me. You got it, Kovacs?"

Another splinter of wood.

"Answer me," he snarled.

"Yes, yes!" I would have agreed to *anything*. "Warwick!"

He let go of my arms, grabbed my thighs, and yanked me up and into him. The shift curled my toes, locking up my body as he released inside me. The cries couldn't be held back as I continued to spasm and convulse, my pussy milking him to the point it almost hurt.

"Fuck!" His head went back, pushing to the hilt as he emptied himself before he collapsed over me.

We lay there, his weight heavy on me, but he made me feel solid. Anchored to this world.

After a few minutes, he sighed heavily, rolling off of me. I couldn't move, completely annihilated, knowing sleep would find me quickly now.

Hauling my body half over his, his lips brushed my head. "I can feel it call to you." I knew his anger had been out of fear. I was scared too. Not of the nectar so much, but it was one of the most powerful objects in the world. If it fell into the wrong hands…

Drifting off to sleep, I thought I heard the fae book's voice brush by my consciousness.

*"You defy nature, girl. How do you know your hands are not the wrong ones?"*

Then the voice was lost in the abyss as I slipped into darkness.

*"Noooo!"*

A cry lurched me upright out of a dead sleep, my startled vision landing on Scorpion's shade at the end of the bed, his face twisted in horror. Then in a blink, I was in the prison, standing next to him. Cries and commotion took my attention to the middle of the mess hall. Guards surrounded Killian and Sloane on the floor, their movements similar to prowling animals, clubbing them both, their screeches not sounding human at all.

Several guards held Rosie back as she screamed and thrashed against them.

*"Killian!"* I heard myself scream out, though no one could hear me except Scorpion.

Something was really wrong with the sentinels. They howled like hyenas and chimpanzees, hitting and wailing their arms, dropping the spiked clubs on the two men over and over, with no restraint or skill.

*"No! Stop!"* Aggravation and fear boomed through me, knowing there was nothing I could do.

A soldier struck Killian on the back with the spiked club, curving

Killian's spine. A cry he couldn't stop barked from his lips. Blood colored his yellow uniform brown.

The guard lifted the baton over his head. A gasp spiked in my throat as I recognized Samu. His features were contorted, almost inhuman.

"No! Stop!" Sloane roared, leaping for Killian.

"Sloane, no!" Killian bellowed as Sloane landed over him right as the club came down.

The crunch echoed through the mess hall. The sound of crushing bone and torn flesh.

I heard my scream shredding through my body as I watched blood and gore spray from Sloane's head, his skull caving in.

Denial of what I was seeing kicked me in the stomach, burning acid up my esophagus. Staring numbly in disbelief, my eyes locked on Sloane's unmoving body. The stoic soldier who had taken me to Halálház, whose faithfulness and respect for Killian turned him into my ally. I couldn't call us friends, but I could no longer say we were enemies. Not by a long shot.

Whimpers and cries of horror sprinkled the room.

All I could do was stare, my mind not wanting to register what I just saw.

"Enough!" Boyd's voice cut through the mess hall. "What is our rule about the next fighters who are battling in the upcoming Games?" Boyd spoke to them as though they were imbeciles. "Your master won't be pleased!"

*"Kovacs."* Both Scorpion and I twisted to see Warwick behind us in the prison, his attention jumping from the spectacle in the middle to me. I knew I could pull them both in together at once, especially when my emotions were high.

"Go." Scorpion whispered to me, nodding his head to him.

Tears clotted my throat, my head shaking. *"No."*

Scorpion stood at the end of the bed, looking between Warwick and me. *"Get us the fuck out of here."*

Then the connection was cut.

My body moved before I even could think, like I could crawl back into the scene and be back in the prison. I frantically tried to connect back to Scorpion, but he had blocked the bond, not letting me in.

"Stop." Warwick grabbed me. "You can't help them that way." He yanked me back into him. Holding my jaw, he forced me to look at him. "You *can't* help them being there right now. We help them by getting them out."

Tears of fury and sorrow filled my eyes. "War-wick." My voice cracked, the images raw and brutal in my mind.

"I know." His eyes darted between mine, already knowing what I was going to say, but the words still came out in desperation.

"We *have* to get them. I can't lose anyone else."

"And we will." His hands moved into my hair, cupping the back of my head, his determination set on his face. "We. Will."

His strength dried up my tears and swallowed my grief. Tilting my chin up high, I stared into his powerful aqua eyes, determination set. Failure was not an option.

There was no limit for us.

We would walk into the valley of the shadow and death.

And they would fear *us*.

# Chapter 20

"Our plan is to leave when the sun sets and reach Kutná Hora well before midnight." Warwick sat at the table, Simon munching on a *túróstáska* next to him, sweet cottage cheese smearing over his face. "Hopefully be back here with an army by the next nightfall."

"You think your uncle will help?" Eliza leaned against the kitchen counter, sipping her coffee. The early morning light cast the room in a foggy glow. Zander and Tad sat at the other end of the table, drinking tea and eating their own filled pastries.

I nodded, my feet moving back and forth across the kitchen. Mykel had to know the stakes; even his own prime minister was part of this. And to be honest, we couldn't fight or get our friends out of Věrhăza without him. I still feared he would turn me down, saying it was too much of a risk for his people. He already lost four top soldiers and a powerful demon because of me. One of them permanently.

"Kovacs," Warwick grumbled under his breath, his hand reaching out to stop me.

Agitation was making me want to tear out of my skin, my feet pacing relentlessly. I couldn't sit still, and knowing we had hours before we left was even more aggravating. Every second we waited was torture. The images of what happened in the prison made me want to shred through Věrhăza and kill every soldier there.

191

Warwick gripped the outside of my thigh, his eyes meeting mine. *"Breathe,"* his shadow spoke against my neck. I tried, but it wasn't helping.

"No. You can't. It's too dangerous." Zander stood up, strolling back to the counter to pour more hot water into his cup, the side of his body fully touching Eliza's. She didn't move away. "Things have changed really fast in the last few weeks. The roads out of the city are being watched by soldiers."

Warwick's chest puffed; his lids narrowed on them. "Excuse me, pony-boy?" His tone vibrated with ire. "Roads were always dangerous with bandits and fae soldiers. They have never caught me yet."

"It's no longer fae soldiers out there, but HDF."

My boots came to an actual stop. "What? HDF on the fae side?"

Zander bobbed his head, leaning on the counter next to Eliza.

This country was no stranger to fascism, but it was always crazy how quietly and fast it happened. While ordinary people were just trying to get through the day and survive, it was occurring right under their noses. Istvan was hiding in plain sight and fully taking over. Inch by inch, he was declaring his authoritarianism rule, and it would get to the point there would be no way of stopping it.

"What about the side roads?" I asked. "At least until we hit the border."

"I don't know now, but they still seemed unguarded when I checked around last week. It will add at least two more hours and a lot more danger from bandits."

"We'll take our chances." Warwick glared at Zander.

Zander pressed his lips together but relented. "Okay, but I'm going with you. It's far too dangerous to be alone on those roads."

I couldn't disagree. The trouble awaiting us on those roads was probably only getting worse, and being on a single bike was begging for trouble. Two bikes still were easy prey, but we didn't have a lot of options until we reached Povstat.

"Then, I'm going too," Eliza stated, setting down her cup firmly.

"What?" Warwick and Zander exclaimed in unison.

"Fuck, no."

"Absolutely not."

Eliza's jaw rolled, shooting a look at each man.

"Do not treat me as if I were some helpless girl. Especially *you*." She pointed at her brother. "You were the one who taught me to fight. You know what I am capable of."

"Liz…" Warwick exhaled out his sister's pet name. "I'm not saying you can't fight, but you need to stay here with Simon." He glanced at his nephew.

"I can watch him." Tad rubbed the boy's head. "I'm not totally helpless. And I know where all the cookies are hidden," he whispered conspiratorially. Simon's eyes lit up, and he nodded enthusiastically.

"No." Zander's tea splashed as he rammed it down on the counter. "I won't allow it."

Eliza's body jerked, her eyebrows arching high, her head tilting, indignation perfuming from her.

"Oh, shit," Warwick scoffed under his breath.

"I'm *sorry*?" She turned fully to Zander, her voice twinging with outrage, with the same stubborn determination I saw on Warwick's face so many times. "I didn't know you could tell me what to do."

"I'm not. I'm just—" Zander floundered.

"Being a *horse's* ass?" She folded her arms. He gaped and huffed through his nose, his eyes looking around wildly like he wanted us to throw him a lifeline. We let him drown.

"Don't *ever* tell me what I can and cannot do," she seethed. "You *do not* know me. And possibly won't ever."

Zander jerked, pain flickering in his brown eyes, hearing the true meaning of her statement.

"I'm sorry," he breathed. "It's just the thought…"

"Of what?" She huffed. "I knew horses were set in their ways, but I didn't think you were sexist."

"It's not that."

"What then?"

"If anything happened to you!" He threw out his arms. "The idea of you getting hurt." He shook his head. "Of *losing* you!"

The room went silent. Eliza froze, her mouth parted.

"What we've been through together in the last month…" He let his shoulders expand, raising him up over her. He was a kind man but still had a dominance to him. There was a reason he had been a soldier for Killian and Andris. "I didn't expect it, actually tried to stop it, but I can't. I care about you. *A lot.* I adore Simon. I want this…" He motioned between them. "To be *more*."

Warwick's chair screeched over the wood floor. Before he could get up, I shot him a look.

*"Stay out of this."* My shadow's hand went to his chest, pushing him back down.

Air huffed through his nose, his body tight, ready to leap up and knock Zander to the ground, but he stayed put, his knuckles almost splitting from squeezing them so hard.

Eliza rubbed at her head, a crazed chuckle coming from her mouth, but I saw a grin curling her lips.

"Even more reason for me to go." She looked boldly up at him, the smile growing.

His brows crushed together in confusion.

"I care about you too." She placed her palms on his chest. "And I don't want anything happening to you. You need someone to watch *your* back."

Zander's eyes went back and forth between hers, joy glowing in his eyes, his lips spreading in a smile.

*"A ló farát!" Horse's ass.* Warwick shoved out of his chair, grumbling more obscenities under his breath, his hand running through his hair. *"Lófaszt!" Horse's dick.* He stomped outside, slamming the door behind him. His curses still could be heard in the distance.

"O-kay." I sucked in, clapping my hands together. "We'll let him walk it off."

While Warwick was out chopping wood to leave Tad and Simon fuel for the fire, I went over the plan with Eliza and Zander again, leaving out the exact location of my uncle's base for safety reasons. If they didn't know, they couldn't tell if they were caught and tortured.

"We need to leave by sunset, though I'm concerned we won't get far. Our motorcycle barely made it here. We need to steal a better one."

Zander scoffed, "This may be a hideaway cabin, but it's still Lord Killian's, and he likes his toys. It comes fully stocked."

Later that evening, Zander led us out to a garage hidden away in trees and brush, disguising itself, showing us exactly what he meant.

"Holy shit." I gaped, my attention going down the row of shiny metal.

Killian might be humble inside the cabin walls, but he didn't spare any expense on the secret garage hidden near the house.

Four motorcycles, a jeep, and a land cruiser gleamed under the lights. All top of the line. I'd expect nothing less from Killian.

Zander strolled deeper into the garage, flipping open a large locker built into the wall.

I blinked.

"Fuck, I'm hard," Warwick muttered next to me, making me snort. Though I probably had to agree with him.

The entire cabinet was filled with weapons. Handguns to rifles, knives to swords, dynamite sticks to grenades. Killian was stocked and ready for battle if any enemy were to breach his land.

Warwick went straight to the bikes, his hand sweeping over the curves of the sleek black design, his eyes glossing over with reverence. I had no doubt Killian got these from the Unified Nations. They were too well made for anything in the Eastern Bloc. "Never thought I'd want something Killian had." He trailed his palm up the engine of the motorbike.

I leaned against it, popping up my eyebrow. Warwick stood, his form looming over me, his voice gravelly. "Good thing you were never something he had, Kovacs."

"Think so?" I taunted, thinking back to when I kissed Killian on the veranda, when Warwick's shade had stepped in.

He gripped my hair, holding my head in place. "Well, then I've taken both from him and will ride them long and hard until they know they are mine." He rumbled against my lips, spearing desire between my legs, and hitching my breath, a snarl lifting my lip. "Don't even pretend you aren't dripping right now and wish I could fuck you on this bike. I can feel your pussy throbbing, princess." His teeth nipped my bottom lip, tugging on it, the feel of his tongue sliding through my folds before he backed away, leaving me grappling and horny as he sauntered over to the weapons cabinet.

*"Fuck you,"* my shadow murmured in his ear.

He let out a laugh, turning and winking at me. He really was insufferable, but damn he was right.

Eliza and Zander were already loaded up with guns and knives, rolling a bike out of the garage. Being a horse shifter, Zander could be his own transportation, but not for that length of time and speed.

All of us were in similar outfits, black on black. Eliza let me borrow some of her clothes, Warwick taking whatever Killian had in the closets. His clothes fit Warwick extremely tight, showing off every muscle in his thighs and the unbelievable arc of his ass.

I loaded myself with weapons, stuffing my boots with blades, and proceeded to the sleek bike, climbing on behind Warwick. Wrapping my arms around his middle, I let my shadow slip into his trousers, my tongue licking up the vein in his cock.

"Fuck!" He hissed, jolting at my imaginary touch.

I withdrew with a conspiratorial grin, leaning into his ear. "Ride long and hard, Farkas."

The cold night bitterly sliced at my skin, the hair under my beanie flagellating my face like thin whips. Clouds kept most of the sky hidden, the wind howling in my ears as the motorcycles made their way down the road, nearing the borders of Hungary, Austria, and Slovakia. Though with Markos's new reach, I no longer trusted we'd be safe from the HDF once we passed the borders.

A tingle walked up my spine, shivering the back of my neck. Turning my head over my shoulder, all I saw was Zander and Eliza behind us, their single headlight the only other occupant on the road. I shifted on the seat, feeling the itchy sensation, unsettled and jumpy from the time we left Killian's property and got onto the motorway.

Keeping my gun cocked and ready in my grip, as my gaze constantly darted around, feeling at any moment something was going to jump out at us. But miles and miles went by, and there was no hint of anything. We were so close to the border, with only a mile left.

Breathing out, I leaned my face into Warwick's back, giving myself a moment to soak in his warmth. My face hurt from the cold, every part of me willing us to cross into Slovakia.

One moment was all it took.

Tiny sounds crackled in the air, the bike skidding as the tires deflated under us, slipping and sliding us off the road. I caught sight of a spike strip lying across the dark road.

Blinding headlights burst in front of us right at the border, the squeal of tires pitched the air as three motorcycles next to the car lurched for us.

"Ambush!" Warwick bellowed back at Zander, steering the unusable bike into a ditch near old train tracks. Leaping off together, we started shooting double-handed at the unknown assailants, trying to guard Zander and Eliza. Zander stopped before hitting the spike strip, driving off the road on the other side, Eliza already shooting.

If our bike was working, we could have easily cut across the grass and headed for the main motorway, but now we were stuck.

A growl of an engine jerked my head behind us; another big truck with three motorcycles was coming up behind us.

Dread rolled in my gut.

"Warwick?" I dragged his attention to the group closing in on us. "This doesn't feel like a raid party."

"No, it doesn't." He swore under his breath. Holstering one of his guns, he yanked a weapon off the back of the bike, which reminded me of his claw-cleaver he had lost along the way. "Cover me."

I nodded, my finger on the trigger as the first three motorcycles got closer. Warwick didn't even wait. Barreling toward them, he swung the cleaver around with a roar. The sound of the blade slicing through flesh and bone hit my ears, followed the gurgling cry of a man before a head rolled onto the pavement. His bike tipped over, sliding across the road, sparks spewing up into the sky.

Shouts and cries came from the other men, bullets volleying at us. Eliza shot another one in the head as Warwick spun again, slicing through the arm of the last man, the limb splatting onto the ground next to my boots. With a guttural scream, he fell from the bike, bleeding out before Eliza shot him in the head.

Ice flooded my veins, terror filling my stomach when I spotted the symbol on the clothed arm laying at my feet.

The patch I had sewn on countless uniforms in Věrhăza. HDF.

Panic urged me to glance back at the truck heading for us, motorcycles in front of it. It wasn't a normal vehicle. It was an armored truck. Istvan's.

"It's HDF!" I yelled at everyone. I attempted to pull at my powers as I did in the pit, but to little avail.

"Go! Go!" Warwick waved at Zander and Eliza. "They don't want you. Get across the border."

"We aren't leaving you!" Eliza screamed back.

The armored truck in front of us roared to life. I could see only a single driver inside, heading for us. It struck me only because HDF were always in pairs.

"We'll be right behind. We'll run for it." Warwick replied as gunfire came from the approaching riders.

"No!" She burrowed down, stubborn as her brother. The girl was no stranger to a gun, looking like a badass.

"Dammit, Eliza, go!" he bellowed, pointing to Zander. "Go!"

Zander nodded, revving the engine, urging Eliza to get on the back.

She glanced between us, sorrow reflecting in her eyes, before she ran for the bike.

"Eliza…" I called to her, her head twisting to me. I took a breath. "Sedlec Ossuary," I said the name of the church Povstat hid under. The sacred knowledge that could destroy every life inside if discovered by the enemy. She would have known eventually, but something told me to tell her now.

She nodded, climbing on the bike, and Zander tore over the grass, heading for the main motorway. Gunfire from the oncoming attackers blasted at them.

"Come on!" Warwick spun for the rail tracks next to us, running down them, splitting the focus of the attackers. Sprinting right behind him, I felt the same prickle skate over my skin, warning me. Something I had felt before.

"War—"

Before I could get his name out, two shots rang out. Something hit my chest with a slam, tearing the air from my lungs, dropping my legs. Warwick stumbled with a roar, then fell next to me. I peered down, ready to see blood, to know this was the end. But sticking out of my chest was a large dart, pumping a drug into my veins.

Even worse than death was knowing your attacker wanted to keep you alive.

My world swayed and rolled, and dots encroached my peripheral as I slumped to the ground. My ears picked up the echo of footprints as I started to lose consciousness.

A face came over me. Sucking in fear, I stared up at the hazing details of him.

Kalaraja, the lord of death, smirked down at me.

"Ms. Kovacs." The familiar nasally voice scratched at my ears. "Did you forget? I *always* get my man. And in this case, my woman too," he said before shooting another dart into my stomach.

The sound of his cruel laugh followed me down into the pits of darkness.

# Chapter 21

Bangs and cries echoed and boomed.

Pain throbbed through my bones, and the feeling of something choking me strangled my neck.

Body odor, urine, and the dank smell of earth clipped at wings of hope, understanding before my brain did where I was.

My lashes lifted, blurry and confused, to see the cold, hard ground under me. My vision took in the bars, the watchtower, the backdrop of thousands of cages filled with prisoners.

Sitting up, the beat of my heart picked up in wild flutters.

Věrhăza.

"Welcome home, Brexley. To your *final* one." The voice made me want to throw up. Istvan stepped into view, his arms behind his back, strolling at a leisurely pace outside my cell. His face was bruised and cut, still showing signs of what I did to him in the lab, only clarifying what I already knew. He was still human. Istvan was waiting to take the formula, using everyone else as guinea pigs. He would not risk his own life until it was perfected. "I can say, of all the things I imagined your life would lead you to, what you would grow up to be? This was not it." He lifted one arm to me.

Automatically, I peered down, a narrow trail of air squeezing down my esophagus. Around my neck was an electric collar. The uniform they had put me in was no longer gray.

Stacey Marie Brown

I wore black.

The color of nothing.

To Istvan, the color was a stain on me, my scarlet letter. Even if he was wrong about what I actually was, it didn't matter. This turned me into even more of a traitor to HDF soldiers. They would go out of their way to target me because they would feel tricked, as if I knowingly duped them with my evil glamour, pushing aside the fact that they'd known me since I was a baby and watched me grow up.

"Do you like it?" He nodded as I touched the collar. "It is very rare and hard to get, but I only wanted the best goblin metal for you."

*Fuck.* Not only could he electrocute me at any time, but goblin metal was almost impossible to break through and could be used the same as poison to all fae if it got into your bloodstream. It even affected humans, causing them to be lethargic and sick. They put goblin metal in fae bullets as well as iron. He wanted to contain my magic, keep me from doing what I did in the lab and the arena again. Because I was different. Like the faux-fae, my powers worked down here.

"All I have done for you." Istvan shook his head. "Raised you, fed and clothed you, gave you the top education and training, treated you as one of my own."

"You mean like property to sell to the highest bidder." I snapped, rising to my feet, the drug in my system making me wobbly. "To use as an experiment. You used your wife and your own son as test subjects!"

Istvan's boots stopped as he faced me, his mouth pinching in anger.

"Do not bring Caden into this. I only wanted the best for him. To be the greatest," he replied evenly, trying to control his anger. "But the same as you, he seems to be another huge disappointment. I realized I can no longer save him."

"What did you do to him?" Fear coated my throat. "Where is he?"

Istvan didn't answer, his blank expression giving nothing away.

"Tell me!" I demanded, my veins filling with ice.

"Caden is no longer your concern."

My molars crunched together, trying to hold back the emotion burning my throat and eyes and tearing into my heart.

"Is he dead?"

"If you had cared so much about him and not your *fae lover*, you wouldn't have left him, would you?" I could feel the buzz between Warwick and me, knowing he was not only alive, but close by. "The boy you had declared only months ago you loved *so deeply*. How easily you

200

turned away from him. But why should I be surprised? Fae are so fickle and cruel."

My chin wobbled. "Andris was right. You have no capacity for love."

Istvan jolted forward, grabbing the bars, his movement making me step back.

"Everything I did was for my family, my people."

"Really?" I scoffed. "Locking Rebeka in a cage while you moved on to a young, vapid bitch for a political move was for her? Killing hundreds of fae and *humans* was in their best interest?"

"Yes!" he exclaimed. "Because what I am doing is for millions, not just a few. We are taking back our world. Fae need to be exterminated permanently."

"Do the fae who work for you know that?"

"Sometimes you have to make alliances with the enemy to get where you need to."

They probably felt the same about him, but when did it get to the point Istvan's power became absolute?

"You are no longer one of those. Your life would have been safe if you did what I wanted, but since your blood has been proven useless for what I want... you have to be removed." He pulled his arms behind his back once again, regaining his control. "The nectar is within my grasp. Everything is going exactly as I hoped."

Not a muscle moved, not a twitch. I deflected his proclamation like a shield, trying to show no reaction.

Was he lying? Probably. I felt an inkling of terror, knowing Istvan so well. There was nothing he wouldn't do to get it.

"Kalaraja." He said his name with admiration. "He is exceptional at his job. He can track down anyone or *anything*."

I kept still, giving nothing away, but my pulse pounded in my eardrums.

"It wasn't a coincidence my men were waiting for you at the border. You were being followed and watched from not long after you escaped. For a few coins, someone tipped us off you were spotted at a seedy opium den. Kalaraja took it from there." He tapped at his mouth, his lips curling, his feet moving again. "You know a few soldiers escaped from High Castle the night we found you, telling stories of a box and seven necromancers guarding it with their life." He let out a chuckle. "I admit I didn't believe them—until we got reports of exactly seven necromancers being seen traveling through the night, disappearing suddenly in the Gerecse

Mountains to a particular area which was spelled to keep out intruders. Land owned by the last fae lord, which Killian would inherit. What was even more peculiar is you went to the same spot."

*Don't react. Don't react.*

His demeanor suddenly shifted, yanking himself up to the bars. "I know what is there, Brexley. What you are hiding." He hissed between his lips. "It will only be a matter of time until I break through the spells and retrieve the nectar. And be sure I will; it will be *mine*."

Flinching at his crazed voice, I took in shuddered breaths.

"Thank you for making this so easy. Even if you have been nothing but a thorn in my side, you ended up giving me the best gift ever."

He cleared his throat, standing up straight and tugging at his jacket, heavy with awards. He twisted his head, flicking it as if calling someone.

Footsteps pinged the metal, my stomach knotting when Boyd stepped behind him. His eyes glinted with revenge and hate, smugness on his lips.

"Make sure the prisoner is ready for the Games tomorrow night," Istvan spoke in his formal tone.

"What condition does it need to be in, sir?" Boyd stared at me with glee. "I mean, if she steps out of line?"

"She needs to at least be standing and able to put on a good show. I have guests to entertain and persuade tomorrow."

Boyd's lips twisted. "Of course."

Bile flared in the back of my throat. Istvan had left a substantial gray area. Permission to push the boundaries for the guards. Istvan was waiting to punish me, to teach me a brutal lesson for what I did. He used to do that a lot with Caden and me, to the point we caused ourselves more torture waiting for it to happen.

I had no doubt I'd pay for what I did to his lab, for the experiments he lost, and most of all for the disappointment of not giving him the results he wanted. Because of the embarrassment I caused him with the other leaders, he would make me feel every wrong I did to him.

"Same with her fae lover," Istvan snarled. "He turned out ineffective as well. I care even less about his well-being."

That meant Caden hadn't become the legendary warrior Istvan was hoping for.

"Even better, sir." Boyd's grin widened.

Istvan dipped his head, signaling an end to their conversation, starting to walk away.

"Oh, and Brexley, your companions with you earlier?" His upper half twisted toward me. "They were severely wounded before they crossed the border. Be assured, they are now dead."

When Boyd and Markos were out of sight, my vertebrae hit the wall, and I slid down, my head pressing into my knees. The stabbing pain from imagining Zander and Eliza dead was a rope around my heart, but I couldn't feel more. Death happened so much now it made me numb. Another thing to brush under the rug and deal with later.

There were two things that did have me paralyzed with terror. One, no one was coming for us. Without Tad or Mykel's help, we had no way out of here. I was never one to believe in fairytales. I never thought someone would come in and save me in the end. Life wasn't that way. It didn't care if the bad person won. Though I guess deep down, there was always that part, like a hopeful child listening to her father read stories of good triumphing in the end, you wanted to believe.

The second thing, which was the most devastating, Istvan knew where the nectar was. It was a matter of time before he got his hands on it. Tad and the necromancers were powerful, but I had no doubt Istvan would get his prize. He had no line he wouldn't cross, no low he wouldn't go to. And the only thing blocking Istvan's thousand-man army once he broke through the spells were seven necromancers, a little boy, and an old man.

A shrill alarm rang through the air, triggering my breath to quicken, anxiety kicking in. The cell doors rolled open, the clank juddering through my bones. Climbing to my feet like a conditioned dog, I stepped out onto the walkway, trudging to the restroom with the others in my row. I was two levels above where I had been before, the number of prisoners multiplying daily.

Walking into the bathroom, with the inmates doing their business, I struggled with the feeling like I'd never left to being in denial I was back. Warwick and I knew we might need to get on the inside, but it would have been planned with Tad. This time we were just more inmates in the system, about to be used as animals, pitted against each other to survive. The odds would be stacked highly against us.

"Little lamb?"

My head jolted to the side, my eyes already filling at hearing such a familiar voice. Seeing her signature blue braid trailing over one shoulder, contrasting with the red uniform, I moved without thinking.

"Kek!" My arms flew around her. Kek was always small, but now I could feel her bones. They were starving fae of food and their magic, which might have helped keep their strength up. The more I peered around, the more I noticed how gaunt the inmates were here, no matter what color uniform they wore.

"Hey! No talking or interaction of any kind." A young soldier I didn't know barked from his position against the wall.

She squeezed me tight before we both pulled away, her gaze going to my black uniform and back up with wide eyes. "Uniform change?"

I snorted.

"Fuck, little lamb, I didn't know if you were alive or dead. What happened?" she whispered, jerking her head for me to follow her to the open toilets.

"Long, long story." *And we're truly fucked.* I left the last part out. "What about in here?"

We both sat, looking outward, talking low to each other.

"It's gotten worse. So much worse since you left. The Games are three times a week now. There are constant beatings and torture. People are getting killed daily. Killian's guard was executed yesterday."

"I know." I swallowed, the memory of Sloane's crushed face haunting my mind.

Her head darted to me.

"Learned it from Scorpion."

"Right. I forgot you can be here through him." She wiped, pulling up her pants. "That won't stop being weird, by the way." I followed suit, going to the sink next to her. "It's not all." We washed our hands. "The guards..." She lowered her voice even more. "The ones here first. The ones you knew?"

"Yeah?"

"They've beco—"

"Hey!" Another unknown guard came behind us, slamming Kek into the metal mirror. "What the fuck did we tell you? Stupid fucking demon." He put his gun to her temple. "No talking or interacting. Now move the fuck along."

He shoved her forward, walking her out of the bathroom as another guard pushed me to the exit.

"I'll take it from here." Boyd stopped us right at the door, his gaze moving salaciously and hatefully over my body. Grabbing my arm, he yanked me forward, not waiting for the sentry to respond. "It's so good to have you back with us, Kovacs. Can I say I missed you? This place just wasn't the same without you." His fingers bruised my bicep as he tugged me forcefully to the mess hall.

Heads turned, eyes burned into me, a few gasps filled the mostly silent room. All the guards lined up against the wall were new. None I recognized from HDF. They all wore the new uniform, their faces fresh, their eyes focused.

"Look, you're already creating such a stir in your new outfit." He stopped us in the middle, turning to face the room right as four guards with guns walked in a massive form, his height reaching far above their heads, an electric collar around his neck as well. His stormy gaze met mine.

*"Warwick."* I felt my mind call to him more than I used our connection; the goblin metal around my neck made it harder to link to him. A flood of air exhaled from my lungs seeing he was okay. I could feel him around me, double-checking I was in one piece too. A nerve twitching in his jaw told me he was fighting the barrier of his own goblin collar.

He wore a black uniform as well, as if he had never left Halálház. I remembered when I saw the man in black for the first time across the room my first morning. The power of his glance was similar to a lion looking over his pride. The idea of even getting near him at once terrified and exhilarated me. It still did.

"Hey, assholes! Look who's back!" Zion jumped onto the food counter, holding out his arms like a carnival conductor. "Aren't we so happy to have the great legend and the princess of HDF back among us? Oops, I guess her tiara has fallen. Do I spy a different color uniform? Guess the princess has been outcast."

"Zion, shut the fuck up," Boyd snapped at him, clearing his throat, his grip on me tightening. "But he is right about them being outcasts. The black uniform means they are nothing. They fit nowhere. This is the only warning you get. You speak or even look at one of them, you will be punished. *Severely.* They are lepers here. Ghosts. They do not exist to you." Boyd let go of me. "So, when I do this." His fist slammed into my cheek, pain exploding through my nerves, the force hurling me to the ground. "You don't react!"

*"Kovacs!"* Warwick called for me at the same time I heard him bellow, lurching for Boyd. One step and electricity hummed and crackled in the air. He jolted, his body twitching and straining under the electrocution, dropping to his knees before they relented.

Yells and pleas to stop came from all sides of the room, building up a commotion.

"Hey! Hey!" Boyd screamed, standing over me. "What did I say?" He pulled an object out of his pocket, pushing the button. My muscles jerked and spasmed, my teeth grinding together as pain rushed over me in a steady stream.

The room went silent.

He let the button go, my body easing, but I stayed curled up, trying to breathe.

"The more you respond, the more I will punish *them* and you." Boyd shoved his boot into me, highlighting the power he had. The control. "Want to live? You treat them worse than shit on your shoe."

Glancing over at Warwick, his gaze was already on me, his neck and face strained. I tried to reach out, but I couldn't. Everything in me was fried and empty, my powers traumatized by the electrocution.

A bell sounded.

"Well, look, boys and girls. Breakfast time is over before you even got any." Zion snapped his fingers in an 'out of luck' gesture, jumping down from the counter. "Don't worry, we'll keep it right here waiting as your supper. You can thank them." He motioned to us, causing more hate and tension to build with those who didn't know us.

"Get up!" Boyd dragged me to my feet, my head spinning, my muscles trembling.

Warwick rose next to me as shoulders slammed into me, knocking me forward, prisoners moving past. "Kill you myself, bitch." Hisses and threats were muttered at me. Funny enough, not one went near Warwick, still too afraid of The Wolf.

Once again, I had the target on my back.

Boyd hand delivered us to the factory floor, relishing in every knock and hit I took along the way.

"Sit." He shoved me down at a sewing machine. "You have a lot to catch up on. And you can't leave until you finish your quota for every day you were gone."

I clenched my jaw, trying to keep my thoughts inside. That was over a week's worth. A typical day's quota took over ten hours to do.

"Now you better behave, listen to your instructors, and play nice with others." He patted my head condescendingly before he leaned over, his mouth brushing my ear. "Things have changed slightly in your absence. We have a new way of earning extra credit here." He stood, strolling away.

Picking up a needle, I glanced through my lashes at the people around the table. Nora was at the far end, Kek and Birdie in the middle, and Rosie and Hanna closer to me.

It was a relief seeing them all, but when I dared another glance up, it was Rosie who peeked over, her face curving enough for me to see it.

My heart leaped up into my throat.

One side of her face was black and blue, her lip split and puffy as if she had been punched hard and repeatedly. The sickness only grew when I could make out bruise marks around her throat. Hanna and Birdie also appeared as if they had been beaten. And all I could hope was they had only been hit. Nothing more. Except something in Rosie's gaze drove bile up my throat. A hollowness that had nothing to do with starvation. She turned quickly back to her work, Hanna and Birdie doing the same.

Every few stitches, I would do a fast glance across the room. I didn't recognize even one soldier. All new faces, and brand-new uniforms, as though the HDF I knew had been wiped away.

Stretching my attention to the men's side, I noticed their population had grown even more in the week. There were new women prisoners, but it was clear one sex was dominating the prison.

Warwick had been put on the worst job, shoveling coal into the fires and cleaning the ashes out, sweat already rolling down his face, his skin red and blistering.

The only person near him was Kitty. She looked horrible. Gaunt, with a busted lip and sagging shoulders. She had given up keeping her shirt on, and it gutted me. They had finally broken her. She kept her head down, putting the ore into and out of the stove.

Ash, Scorpion, Wesley, and Lukas were spread out by the machines, cutting and shaping metal into bullet cases.

No Killian.

*"Where is he?"* My shadow jumped to Scorpion, struggling to become totally solid, my energy still on the fritz and fighting the goblin metal.

"Fuck." Scorpion jumped, hissing out under his breath, his head cocking to me.

*"Where is Killian?"*

Scorpion glanced around, his mouth pressing together before he bowed his head, pretending to work. His shade standing next to me at the sewing machines, as if he felt the extra strain it took for me.

*"Probably in the hole. He lost it after what happened. They kicked the living fuck out of him and dragged him away."* Scorpion's gaze went to Hanna and Rosie, then to the ground. His jaw rolled, fists clenching. *"He was trying to protect them. Especially her."*

I already knew what *her* he was talking about—the image of Rosie being held back screaming. That sinking feeling dropped again, swirling the drain.

207

*"Things got much worse here. Those old guards you knew became feral."*

I had seen it before I left, the wildness that took them over.

Scorpion glanced down the way again.

"What?" I muttered.

*"And I think something's wrong with Hanna."*

My attention went straight to her. This time I really saw how restless she was, fumbling with the stitching like she had lost her basic skills.

Istvan had given her the pills too. Only for a day or two, but what if it was enough? The change happened quickly with Killian's group.

Scorpion's shade grunted, our link cut, drawing me back across the room. A guard belted him with a club, telling him to pick up his pace.

I gritted my teeth, feeling the acid burn into my nose and back down my throat. Fury gurgled in my stomach over the pain and torment my friends have gone through, the sexual, mental, and physical abuse they have endured.

A group of three guards sauntered in, pulling my focus. Their egos entered before they did. I had never seen them before, but they trotted in as if they owned the place, zeroing in on one person.

"Kurva!" A dark-haired boy of around twenty called to her, fae essence puffing up his chest, reminding me so much of Kristof, the same arrogant entitlement.

Rosie sucked in, but her body reflected nothing as she continued to sew.

"I called you, *picsa.*" He came behind her, grabbing her head.

Rosie would always be pointed out, be the one treated as if she deserved being abused because of what she had done for her livelihood. A man forced her into that life so she could survive, and now they blamed her for it. Just because Rosie had sex for money in the past didn't mean this was no big deal. It was still rape.

He tugged on Rosie's hair, pointing across the table to Hanna. "My friend Petro wants you. And Josef here wants you, Blondie." He nodded at Birdie. He clutched Rosie's scalp, getting her to rise. "Now move!"

"No!" Nora cried out, rising from her seat, her hand reaching for her daughter as Petro yanked Hanna up. Another guard pulled out his baton, striking her on the back of the head.

*"Anya!" Mom.* Hanna screamed as Nora flopped over her sewing machine, knocked unconscious.

Birdie was forced to her feet, her hands in balls, her face locked like stone. Josef's hands were already rubbing over her breasts.

208

I couldn't let this happen.

Standing, I felt my lungs pumping with rage. "Don't fucking touch them," I seethed.

The three men stopped, turning around, shocked someone had the audacity to say something.

"Excuse me?" The main guy blinked at me, then paused. "Well, well, hello." His gaze ran down my body and over my face. "You are fucking stunning. Think I'd rather have your mouth around my dick anyway." He shoved Rosie into the table, strolling to me. He was about an inch shorter than me, but he tried to puff himself up. "Must teach you some manners. Punish that mouth for speaking when it wasn't told to—you got a lot to learn, new fish."

"Fish?" I slanted my head, curving one brow. "You are mistaken." I smiled tightly. "I'm a fucking piranha."

As if Warwick felt what I needed before I even knew what I was going to do, he poured his strength into me, moving me quicker than usual, fluid and precise. My knuckles struck his throat. He stumbled back, choking for air, his fingers clawing at his throat. I jumped forward, ramming my fist into Josef, blood spraying from his nose, the force knocking him to the ground as Petro leaped for me. Spinning, my boot kicked him right in the crotch, dropping him instantly.

Yells boomed off the high ceiling, twirling me back toward the room. Guards from everywhere in the vast warehouse ran for me, weapons drawn.

I saw Warwick out of the corner of my eye, starting to run to me, the heavy cinder shovel in his hands, but he stopped short, his attention on the doorway.

I tried to follow his gaze when electricity zapped through my body, locking me in place as agony tore and sliced through every nerve and muscle. My frame crashed to the ground, flopping and jerking, spitting and choking.

It stopped, and I gasped for air.

Boots struck the ground, a face peering over me. "Can't even make it an hour." Boyd's smug smile blurred in my vision. "He said as long as you're standing *tomorrow* night." He hit the button again.

My body shut down, protecting itself from the onslaught of utter agony.

Like that should be anything new.

# Chapter 22

*"Kovacs."* My name was called through an inky goo. The pull was like milk being poured into coffee, the creamy haze lightening the syrupy darkness. The obscurity had protected me, a barrier to the pain that invaded my muscles, like an exposed wire through my entire body. I became aware of weight restraining my arms and legs, the cold, hard stone digging into my bones, and the smell—a particular odor which clung to the walls, the scent branded my memory.

The hole.

*"Kovacs?"*

My eyes flew open to Warwick leaning over me, his shadow flickering with the effort. Sucking harshly, I sat up, hoping this was all a nightmare and I'd wake up in bed with Warwick. But the man who reached out and touched my face wasn't the real one, nor were we in a nice comfy cabin.

Chained and in hell, the suffocating stale air of the hole roped around my lungs. This time there were no loud noises or flashing lights, which I found odd. Just darkness. I had to breathe in and out in slow pulls to curb my panic. Only a little light from the cracks around the door gave any break to the solid blackness, allowing me to see marginal details of the man crouching in front of me.

*"Beginning to think you enjoy being chained up, princess."* Warwick's shadow ran his thumb over my busted lip. Petro had gotten a solid hit in before I took him down. *"Stop being a fucking hero every moment."*

210

I could feel the difference, his presence barely solid, sweat beading at his forehead.

"I couldn't sit back and watch. I couldn't let it happen to my friends," I muttered to him, sagging into the wall. The manacles around my legs and arms gave me barely any room to move.

"Talking to yourself, Ms. Kovacs? Or do I assume someone is here I can't see?" A voice jerked me, rattling my chains. My heart thumped with a spurt of adrenaline, not expecting anyone else in here with me. "You have returned. It may sound selfish, but I'm glad. I know you are at least alive."

It sounded somewhat off, but I knew that voice.

"Kil-Killian?" Shock and happiness twirled like a tornado in my tone, my eyes squinting, trying to see through the dense darkness for a shape against the wall. "Oh, my gods... you're okay."

"Okay is a relative term."

Rolling my lips, my head bowed, "I'm sorry what happened to Sloane."

Killian didn't respond, but in his silence, I could feel all the emotions he didn't want to speak. The hurt, guilt, anger, and grief. Killian didn't just lose an elite soldier. He lost a friend.

From the moment I met him, and maybe even before when I sat high on top of HDF, staring over at his palace, as if I knew he was standing on his balcony peering in the dark back at me, I could feel a connection to Killian I couldn't explain. It was different from Scorpion and Warwick, but was there just the same.

He cleared his throat, finally speaking, and I could hear a slur in his speech, as if he was struggling. "What did you do to get in here?"

My mind flashed to when Killian and Sloane were getting attacked by the guards, Rosie being held back, her face already showing signs of being hit. But now I could put a name to the soldiers I saw holding her. It was the same ones who came for her today.

"I have a feeling, doing the same thing as you."

He went quiet again.

"And they call us the monsters," he uttered quietly amid the scraping sounds as he adjusted against the wall. "Is she—are they all right?"

"I hope so." We both knew how it was here. We probably only delayed their pain, not actually stopping it. And maybe trying to stop it only made it worse. Once I stepped out of here, I had no doubt I would be their new target.

*"If one of those fucking cowards touches you or them..."* Warwick snarled.

"What are you going to do? You'll end up down here too." I knew my logic was off, since I had the same response. But I couldn't stomach anything more happening to Warwick. What they did to him down here last time was enough. And now there was no line Boyd or any of them couldn't cross. Istvan gave them the all-clear.

"Is Scorpion here with you? I'm still unsure how it works."

"Uh… No." I peered up at the beast standing over me now. "Did I not also tell you I have a connection to Warwick?"

"Warwick?" Killian sighed with annoyance, "Of *course*, you do." His chains jingled. "I see you have a type, Ms. Kovacs. I'm gathering I am too housebroken and refined for your taste." It wasn't an insult to me, but directed at Warwick.

*"Bet you fuck that way too, prick."* Warwick snarled. *"You couldn't handle her. This one is feral, especially when she fucks. And in your bed."*

"Warwick." Even though Killian couldn't hear him, a blush still warmed my cheeks.

"Let me guess, he's calling me some uptight asshole?" Killian let out a dry, empty laugh. "Very predictable, Farkas. A tiresome response. Plus, you have no idea what I'm like or what I've been through. I don't think it is *me* she would become weary of over time."

A low growl scraped over me.

*"He's trying to get a rise out of you."* For a moment, I was in his cell far above the hole, watching him pace back and forth.

"You chained up with one of your boyfriends didn't already get a rise out of me?" he grumbled out loud, running his hand through his tangled hair. His mood had nothing to do with Killian but everything to do with what went down in the factory.

*"I'm okay,"* I muttered to him.

He snorted, scouring his face, then stared off into the distance, cries and bangs howling through the penitentiary. "No one's coming for us."

*"Then we find another way,"* I repeated the statement he had said to me once. *"We don't play by the normal rules, Farkas. You and I make our own."*

His head snapped back to me, his eyes darkening, drilling into me with intensity. It was another example of how Warwick could strip me bare, peeling me down to only the basics. The part of me that would crawl through carnage and challenge death head-on.

The screech of door hinges severed our link, shooting my gaze to the solid cell door of the hole. My body automatically curled against the wall, knowing nothing good came when it opened.

As light pooled in, my eyes darted over to Killian, a gasp filling my throat while nausea sloshed in my stomach. Chained to the wall, his shoulders slumped, he looked haggard and depleted of strength. But it was his face that took the brunt of his punishment. It was pulverized, swollen with bruises and wounds. I could see why he was struggling to speak clearly. With the iron collar around his neck and being starved and depleted, he wasn't able to heal himself in any way close to what he normally could.

Several figures stepped in, taking back my attention. I shifted even tighter to the wall when I recognized one of them. Boyd.

"Chain him up here," Boyd ordered two soldiers, dragging a man to the wall across from Killian. Shackling him up, a guard stepped out of the way, granting me a view of the prisoner.

I swallowed back a small gasp.

Tracker.

Exhaling sharply through my nose, shock tapped my head into the wall, not expecting to see him. But then I recalled how much Tracker enjoyed being alpha, which didn't go over well in here.

I didn't remember seeing him at all today, but I also hadn't looked for him, which made guilt nip at me for how easily I forgot him.

Tracker snarled at the guards, yanking against the thick manacles.

Boyd smirked like he was nothing more than a puppy pretending to be a vicious dog.

"As you can see, we've changed things." Boyd mainly addressed me, his smirk growing, his arms open to the men on either side of me. "We realized it gets so lonely all by yourselves down here. So why not share, watch, and join in each other's experiences."

Pressure pushed down on my ribs, limiting my air as understanding crashed down on me. This was even more sick and twisted. They would force us to watch the others get tortured.

"You enjoy having company, *majesty*?" Boyd strolled to Killian, sneering out his title. "Not so desolate down here?" His tone mocking, he crouched down close to Killian. "How does it feel to be a nobody now? The one bowing to *me*?" Boyd grabbed his head, wrenching it hard, thumping it into the wall.

"Stop!" Straining the shackles, dread webbed over my chest. "Leave him alone." My words were pointless, but I couldn't stop myself. The need to protect Killian, knowing he couldn't take much more, rose within me. The powerful fae leader I knew was slowly corroding away. This place was meant to do that, to gut you like a pumpkin, leaving you a cut-out, sinister

213

shell of yourself. A walking ghost no better than the skeletons the necromancers could animate.

Boyd tilted his head to me, turning back to Killian. "Look at that. The fallen princess wants to *protect* you," he cooed with derision before laughing. "You'd probably let her, huh? Hide away to save your own skin." Boyd stood up, spitting down on Killian. "Look at you now, *Lord Killian*."

Killian's nose flared, his jaw straining, but he gave Boyd nothing back.

Boyd huffed, swinging his head back and forth. "Just so you know, a real leader is taking your throne. She will ensure fae supremacy, our right to rule, and you will die here. Alone and forgotten, only a blip in the history books, a paragraph easily skipped."

"You say it, but you work for a *human*." Killian's violet eyes flicked up at his old employee.

"He *thinks* I work for him," Boyd snarled. "His ignorance is even worse than yours. In the end, humans will fall. They will be the ones who have to go into hiding."

Sonya was planning a coup against her own lover. I was starting to believe it was her scheme all along. What if becoming Prime Minister Leon's lover had always been a plan? To get herself into power while learning everything she could about her foe. Literally sleeping with the enemy. If it were true, then damn, Istvan had nothing on her. She was far more intelligent, devious, and conniving than anyone realized. She was in the *long* game. One that took patience and precise timing.

I hated her, but I had to give her points for being by far the better player in this game. The snake waiting in the grass while the others fought to the death, not noticing the real predator ready to make the final kill.

"You're willing to betray your own kind to only help yourself," Killian slurred, his puffy eyes in slits. "You are a disgrace to the fae."

"You really want to say that when you're the one chained to the wall like a dog?" Boyd grabbed his head again, smashing it back, before kicking Killian in the side over and over.

"No! Stop!" The cuffs cut into my wrists as I tugged forward. The agony of watching Killian get hurt felt ten times worse than if Boyd was hitting me. This version of the hole would break me faster, tear me in two. Anger, fear, and sorrow churned in my gut, stacking log on top of log, building a fire inside.

"Stop!" A bulb outside of the room cracked as a small gush of wind howled down the corridor. The guards waiting for Boyd outside yelped with fear, yanking his attention away from Killian.

"What the fuck was that?" He swung around at nothing. As quickly as it came, it disappeared, sweat dripping down my temple, my head pounding.

His gaze darted to me, pinning me with suspicion. He had been there and seen what happened in the Games the night when I killed the wild animals—when wind and lightning from nowhere crackled through the arena.

Fear made most lash out in anger. He knew fae magic was blocked down here, so confusion forced his brows into one line, and he tightened his shoulders with ire, stomping closer to me. Boyd had been here long enough to have made the connection. No other human who had taken the pills showed any sign of magic similar to this. They had fae-like strength and seemed to possess stronger shifter qualities, but not magic able to create storms. Storms that could kill.

He leered over me, his eye twitching with rage.

I heard the strike before I felt it. The slap of skin and bone smacking against the walls, my head hitting the ground as pain streaked across my cheek, blooming behind my eye to my ear.

Killian yelled, but his voice was lost as Boyd leaned over me.

"I cannot wait to watch you die tomorrow night. My only regret is I won't be able to do it myself." His hand squeezed my already swollen jaw. "I will make sure, Kovacs, that you, the legend, and your fae lord die of long, excruciating deaths. You will hear my laughter and cheers echo in your ears until your final breath."

He pushed me harder into the ground before standing up, turning around, and walking through the exit. The door shrieked as he slammed it behind him, blackness engulfing the room like a suffocating blanket.

"Brexley?" Killian croaked out.

It took me several swallows, tasting the metallic taste of blood. "I'm okay." Pushing myself up, my face throbbed, still feeling the echo of his hand. "Are you?"

"Fantastic," Killian muttered dryly, a small groan as his chain rattled when he moved.

"You are seriously a magnet for trouble." Tracker scoffed, and I knew he was speaking to me.

"So I've been told." I flinched, sitting fully up, my head falling back against the wall.

Killian chuckled under his breath.

"Like you can talk." I shot at him. "Or you." I flicked my chin at Tracker though he couldn't see me. "What are you in here for?"

215

"Fight," he replied quickly. I waited for him to expand, but he didn't. There was a lull before he spoke again. "Funny, the last time we were all together was in that church, talking about finding some mythical nectar, with your men pointing guns at our heads."

"The good ol' days," Killian replied wryly.

"I'll bet it was for you, *fae*." A streak of unregulated anger swiped out, which surprised me, before I heard him take a deep breath. "I can't believe you actually found it." All the anger vanished, a thread of awe in his voice. "I have to admit I didn't think it was real at first, but Mykel was adamant. Does he know about it? That you found it?"

Cradling my throbbing cheek in my hand, a pang of guilt dipped my head lower.

"No." My lashes batted together, trying to keep the emotion out of my throat. "I never had the chance… and we were actually headed to Povstat when we were caught." Where Eliza and Zander were probably gunned down and perished.

"What's wrong?" The rub of fabric against the wall rustled as Killian moved. "I can hear something is wrong in your voice."

Staring into the void, I gulped back down the bile in my throat.

"Eliza and Zander."

"What. About. Them?" Tension and worry escalated with each word.

"They were with us." I forced my tears back, fisting the fabric of my pants.

"Where are they *now*, Ms. Kovacs?" Killian turned back to using my last name, his timbre clipped. "Please tell me they got away."

"I don't know." I dug my nails into my pants, rolling my fingers in tighter. "Istvan told me they had been fatally shot, but we haven't found them yet."

Killian inhaled sharply. I knew he had grown to care about them, even if one was supposed to be a hostage and one a spy against him. "What about Simon? And Tad?"

"They are back at the cabin—safe."

He let out his breath.

"Wait. Wait." Tracker exclaimed with surprise. "You might have a group heading to Povstat right now?"

Gritting my teeth, causing more pain to shoot down my nerves, I blinked up at the ceiling, though I only saw darkness. "I hope…" Or they could be dead, and no one was coming for us.

"Mykel could be heading here *right now*?" Tracker emphasized the last part.

216

"Again, I don't know." *Please, please say they got away. They are alive.*

"But it's possible." It wasn't really a question. "Will you give the nectar to Mykel as you said you would?"

"I never said I would give it to him."

"Because you made a promise to me, Ms. Kovacs," Killian stated.

"Under duress…"

"Semantics."

"I'm still not fae, Killian. I am not bound to a promise."

"You're not human either, so once again, let me say, stop acting like one," he replied, his voice going low. "Maybe I don't need the nectar. I can *possess* you."

"Good luck with that," I huffed but couldn't deny the heat rushing up my spine from his claim. Killian and I would always have a spark. "But guess what? I fulfilled my obligation. You already have it."

"What?" Tracker burst out instead of Killian. "He has the nectar?"

"Tad found it after we were taken. Guess where he took it?"

"The cabin," Killian muttered in relief.

"Yeah, and you also inherited seven necromancers along with the Druid."

A dry laugh came from Killian. "Of course. I'm not even together with you, and I'm the one invaded by your whole family."

I snorted out a laugh. "Well, at least they're another layer of protection. With them and the Druid spells, no one can just walk in and take it." The moment I uttered the last few words, something clicked in my brain, a piece of the puzzle I didn't even know I was missing.

Freezing in place, the realization grew, expanding through my gut and up my throat, cutting off my air. Short, harsh breaths shot in and out of my nose, my chest clenching in panic.

"What's wrong?" Killian's voice reached me.

"Oh, gods…" My mouth gaped, the idea clicking in with astonishing horror.

"What?" Killian's shackles clanked.

Suddenly I could feel Warwick and Scorpion both near me, my fear pulling their shadows, my emotions pushing through the goblin magic as if it were paper.

*"Kovacs?"* Warwick moved to me.

*"Brex, what is it?"*

Terror jammed my vocals as I peered up at the two men. I couldn't move as my theory became more and more solid, kicking me in the gut with utter clarity. How did I miss this?

"*What*, Brexley?" Killian growled, also picking up on my fear.

"They *can* just walk in." My throat swelled, making it hard to get out my words.

"Who? Walk in where?" Killian's pitch was strangled, as if he sensed where this was going.

"I can't believe I never connected this." My brain looped and spun with my revelation.

"*You better fucking explain what you are talking about now,*" Warwick demanded.

"The human guards down here have all taken the pills, giving them fae qualities, right?"

"Yessss," Tracker replied with suspicion. "So?"

"This entire prison is spelled with Druid magic, so fae can't use their powers in here. But that doesn't apply to the human-fae soldiers because they aren't made from natural magic. Or me. It hurt, but I was still able to do it." My eyes met Warwick's, and his widened with understanding, and I whispered. "We pushed through it."

I heard Killian breathe in sharply, probably putting the dots together.

"I don't understand. What's that have to do with anything?" Tracker asked.

"Because..." Killian exhaled heavily. "My property is spelled with Druid magic. *Nature's* magic."

"And?" Tracker sounded annoyed.

"It means..." he trailed off.

"It means those barriers keeping fae out and dissuading humans from going there doesn't apply to Istvan's new soldiers." I bit on my lip, trying to hold back a cry. "They *can* walk right in."

# Chapter 23

Thick, weedy silence webbed the small room, the information sinking in with a weighty understanding. If Istvan figured this out, we were doomed.

Kalaraja was fae. He would assume what he felt was blocking them all. But if they knew those fae-human soldiers could push through the spell, it would be all over for us. Not even seven necromancers and a Druid would be able to stop the force Istvan would send their way.

*"Baszni!"* Warwick roared at the ceiling. His voice boomed through the cell, echoing down the hall to me as if I could hear his cry also coming from his cell far above.

Scorpion dropped his face in his hand, hissing and cursing under his breath. As my boys paced and swore in front of me in aggravated stomps, the two others in my cell were still.

"Just because we figured it out doesn't mean Istvan will." I tried to sound hopeful. "And who knows, maybe I'm wrong."

*"We don't have that kind of luck, princess,"* Warwick grumbled.

I let out a dry laugh, which probably sounded crazy to the two who didn't see who I was responding to.

"Let us hope," Killian said under his breath.

"I want to make sure I understand this." Tracker's chains clanked to my right, tipping my head in his direction. "The people who have taken these pills can just walk right onto his property and take this nectar? Same with those who had been in the tanks?"

"I think so." I was pretty sure my theory was correct. "It's not easy, mind you; Druid spells are still insanely powerful." Before, I had thought I could "bend" Tad's spells on this prison and get us out. I was wrong. I couldn't break them, but it didn't mean if I pushed hard enough, I couldn't walk through them. Similar to the faux-fae, my magic seemed to still work down here. "I think it's possible because his spells are part of nature, a balance. They don't recognize artificial or anomalous magic… something that shouldn't occur."

*Like me.*

*"Brexley Kovacs, the girl who defies nature."* The memory of the fae book's voice repeated in my head. From the beginning, it knew I wasn't right, that I shouldn't exist. But I did. I wasn't manufactured, but I wasn't normal or accepted fully by fae magic either.

As usual, I sat in the in-between.

*The Grey.*

The power deep within me whispered up. It was something I feared because, also deep down, I could feel it bubbling and churning like a cauldron. Forging and building. My energy was enough on its own, which sent chills of fear and excitement down my spine, but I could also feel the nectar. The webs connecting us weaved tightly. The power we contained, and the violent beauty which hid within our skin, crept up from the depths, wrapping and weaving itself up my vertebrae. It felt beyond me. Powers of old were restricted inside my body's limits.

What could we do once we were together?

*"Brexley."* As if he could sense my thoughts, feel a shift in me, Warwick leaned over, his fingers gripping my jaw. My name on his lips was a trail of gravel across my skin, a nip behind my ear, a harsh grip on my soul. The brutal surge of pleasure built, the lick sliding through my legs.

Sucking in harshly, I blinked, my eyes coming even with Warwick's. He didn't say anything, his gaze locking me in place. To earth. To myself.

*"Oh no… no! I've already watched you two fuck and felt it* countless *times. I have never-ending blue balls being connected to you two nymphos."* Scorpion tangled his fingers in his hair with an annoyed grunt. *"My dick is raw from how much I jack off."*

Warwick's aqua irises never left mine, his eyebrow hitching up in a smirk, creating heat to glide down my body.

Tracker shifted with a mutter under his breath.

"Ms. Kovacs…" Strain tugged at Killian's vocals, the jangling of him adjusting. "Do you mind?"

*"Yeah, we're all feeling it."* Scorpion huffed.

*"Tell* both *your boyfriends they can fuck off."* Warwick rumbled in my ear.

I was so tempted.

"Go," I whispered to him. "I'm fine. This is draining you. I need you at your full strength."

Warwick didn't budge.

"There's nothing you can do right now."

*"I beg to differ. There is a lot I could do right now."*

Everything in me clenched with need. To experience that high, to feel my body heal, and to forget the horrors of life while we drowned this entire prison in blissful pleasure.

"Go," I tried to say firmly, as my mouth twisted in a salacious smile.

Warwick stood up, his gaze on me about to make me change my mind.

"Go? Go where? Who are you talking to?" Tracker asked, perplexed.

"I'm assuming to a *legendary* asshole," Killian scoffed.

"Actually, both are here." I winked up at Scorpion. "But it kinda works for both of them."

Warwick and Scorpion both shrugged in agreement.

"Ahh... of course they are." Killian clicked his tongue. "You do have quite the harem, Ms. Kovacs."

Warwick held out his arms in a *"right?"* expression.

I glared at him.

*"Um, I was actually brought here against my will."* Scorpion lifted his hand.

My glower turned to Scorpion. He winked back at me before he broke the link, disappearing.

"What the hell are you guys talking about?" Tracker's aggravated tone snipped in the darkness.

I flicked my chin at Warwick, telling him to leave.

A low vibration came from his chest before he leaned forward, his fingers sliding through my hair as his mouth crashed into mine. His lips claimed mine with a fierceness, marking me, owning me, and then he was gone. Leaving me stumbling on solid ground.

"Asshole," I muttered.

*Bang. Bang.* The hollow echo of pounding metal was followed by Tracker yelling. "Hey!" He kicked at the door again. "Hey! Open up! I have to piss."

"What are you doing?" I hissed.

"I have to go to the bathroom," Tracker replied like *duh*.

"Stop it!" I exclaimed. What the hell did he think? That's how it worked down here? There would be no repercussions for this? Tracker was arrogant, but I never believed it outweighed his common sense. He was top tier in Povstat. You didn't get that far being stupid.

His boot continued to kick at the door, and I heard commotion stir down the hallway.

"*Hülye fasz!*" *Dumb fuck.* Killian shot at him. "Shut. Up."

It was too late. The lock on the door clanked over, and it swung open, making me flinch with the light from the passage. A handful of guards stepped in.

"What the fuck?" The lead one had a bald head and ripped arms. Again, I recognized none of them. What had happened to all the guards I knew?

"I have to piss, asshole." Tracker lifted his head, glaring at them.

"Oh, do you? What's wrong with right here" The guard shot a look at Killian and me, making sure we were watching before he reached down, clutching Tracker's shirt, yanking him to his feet as far as the chains allowed him. "Maybe I'll make it easier for you, get you to piss on yourself right here, or break your dick so you have to piss out of a tube?"

I saw no fear on Tracker's face, his gaze centered on the guard. "I have to use the latrine. Now!"

I flinched, expecting the first hit.

The bald guy let go of him, hesitating longer than I thought he would before he struck Tracker, crashing him back down to the ground. The guard's boot kicked him in the stomach. Spit sprayed from Tracker's mouth. "You want the latrine so bad? Okay, we can do that. Little field trip, huh, Tracker?" Baldy stepped away, something in his tone dropping lead into my gut. "Uncuff him," he ordered another. A young kid, all of about seventeen, jumped forward, unlatching Tracker's chains. Three other guards gathered around him, grabbing his arms and hauling him to the door.

Fear seized my chest, understanding if Tracker was taken from this room, he wouldn't come back.

"No!" I shouted, lunging forward, my cuffs cutting into my wrists and ankles. "No! Please!"

Tracker wiggled and yelled as they dragged him out, the door slamming back on us. His cries echoed and howled all the way down the hallway. Then he went quiet.

The sudden silence felt like a bomb. Shock rendered me still, taking in what had just happened.

Neither Killian nor I spoke. I couldn't. A certainty in my gut told me he wasn't going to return. Maybe I wasn't close to Tracker, but it didn't take away from the trauma of losing another person so mercilessly. Another to brush under the rug, to lock away in a box until the day I would have to face all the death, pain, and sorrow head-on.

It was building up, overflowing, and swelling. I feared the day everything would explode, raining down bloody bits of my soul.

"They might not kill him," Killian finally spoke.

We both felt and heard the lie. This place didn't give reprieves. Those were saved for the victims Istvan wanted to torture with even crueler deaths.

Tracker was nothing but a number.

Time ticked on and on. With each passing hour Tracker didn't return, the heaviness of his fate burrowed down on me. Hunger, pain, boredom, and grief were sinking me further into myself.

"Brexley?" Killian had called my name several times now. "Talk to me."

I didn't want to give up hope, but I was losing the battle within. The truth stared me boldly in the face. No one was coming for us. So many were dead. And since I didn't see a way out, many more of us would follow. Maybe it would be a blessing. If Istvan found the nectar, this country, and probably the world, would be hell on earth anyway.

"Don't give up on me, Ms. Kovacs. Not now."

"What's the point?" I hated the pitiful break in my voice.

"What is the point of all of it?" he responded. "Remember what your uncle said the one night in the square? *Love, friendship, and family. They are the reason to fight for all of this. The single true point of life. The rest is bullshit.*" He quoted Andris's sentiment.

My head dropped to my knees, tears burning behind my lids, my mouth pinning together to keep my sob back. The memory of my uncle was sharp and raw. A cruelty no torture could touch. My father's death had destroyed me, but there was a purity in that pain, a hole I could fill with his memory.

Andris's loss? I had no way of coping with it. No way of untangling the guilt and blame from my love. My hands dripped with his blood. My heart was scarred by my actions. It didn't matter if he begged me to, or it was the right thing to do. I was the one who killed him. I was the one to carry the weight.

"Brex, you have all of it. Love, friendship... a *family*."

I wiped my damp eyes on my pants, tucking my knees tighter to my chest.

"And I will remind you, the moment you are bored with the Neanderthal, I'm right here."

I stifled the laugh bubbling up my throat. "Really? Cause it looks like you are plucking at another *flower*."

Killian huffed at my cheesy pun.

"Please. What I did was what any decent person would do."

"Uh-huh."

"You are in here for the same thing. Standing up against those sick bastards."

"You sound a little defensive there, Killian," I taunted.

"She's not only insufferable, but human also. I have no interest in her or any others."

I recalled when the book took me to the past, when the sexy pirate and stunning dark-haired woman were in the tunnel with him. His feelings for her were written all over his face, his heartbreak and hurt.

"Who was she?"

"Who?"

"The girl I saw in the tunnel when the fae book took me back. I think you called her Kat."

Killian audibly sucked in.

"She's no one."

"We are probably going to die in this hellhole. Tell me something of your past. I saw your face; I know you were in love with her."

He was quiet so long, I assumed he was rebuffing me, but then he softly spoke.

"We grew up together. She was my best friend... my first love." He cleared his throat. "She did not feel the same. Not the way I felt for her."

His interaction with her made even more sense.

"Where did you grow up?"

"Where didn't I? I have made sure people only see the ruler I am now. The high fae leader." His tone went formal. "But I wasn't always. I came from poverty. Worked, fought, and bled to get myself to where I am now.

My title wasn't passed down to me. I *earned* it. Though some might say I stole it. What can they expect from an ex-pirate?"

"Pirate?" I wheezed out. I assumed the other guy was in the passage, but it was hard to look at Killian and think of some dirty, brutal, immoral pirate—though I was willing to give it a try.

"I grew up on the sea, Ms. Kovacs. Was trained under the most famous, ruthless pirate there was. Taught me a lot about this world. How it runs. How to play the game."

My mind went to the sexy dark-haired man I saw in the tunnel with Killian, remembering the girl called back for him.

"Was it the Croygen guy I saw?"

Killian didn't respond, but something in his silence led me to believe it was.

"I would love to hear stories about you as a pirate. Your scandalous adventures on the sea."

"That, Ms. Kovacs, is for a different time and place."

"I look forward to it."

"You *should*."

The clatter of the door unlatching yanked our attention to the door. Our chains clanged over the wall and floor as we recoiled back, preparing ourselves for the hell that was coming for us. Fear gripped my insides, fluttering my lungs as several figures stepped in.

Boyd took lead.

"How are we all doing?" Mocking. Cruel. His eyes danced back and forth between us. "Have to say, *my liege*, you really have let yourself go."

With the light flooding in, I could see Killian better, and it made my chest tighten. The iron wasn't letting him heal, his wounds still raw and bleeding, puffy and looking infected. The fact he had stayed awake and coherent this whole time with me, was concerned about *me*, spoke volumes of his strength and determination.

Killian couldn't take another beating. I could. I had to turn Boyd's attention to me.

"What's your excuse then?" I lifted my eyebrow.

Boyd's head cut to me, nerves jumping along his neck, his boots stomping toward me.

"No!" Killian thrashed against his cuffs. "Come at me, *gennyla'da!*" *Shitbag.*

Boyd's strike banged my head against the wall, but I didn't feel it. The

225

burning rage inside me scorched out all pain. I turned my head back to him, the taste of blood on my tongue, and grinned.

"You hit like a human." Even in the dim light, I could see Boyd's face turn scarlet, his jaw grinding, hands fisting. I got what I wanted. His focus and anger were entirely on me.

Killian's yells faded into the background; my only attention was on Boyd, waiting with a smirk for him to attack.

He did not disappoint.

Blow after blow, he seethed and spit, his rage consuming him. My mind quickly pulled me away from the assault, feeling his kicks and hits as if I possessed some strange protective shell around me. The heat inside only grew, numbing me from all outside pain.

"Boyd! Stop!" Another guard yelled at him—the bald one who took Tracker out. "The general wants her able to perform. Stop."

Boyd looked as though he were about to punch the guy, but he stepped back, breathing harshly, his glower back on me. Blood dripped from his knuckles, and I didn't know if it was mine or his.

"The only reason I'm stopping, bitch, is because what's ahead of you is even worse." Boyd straightened his uniform, sneering at me. "Mark my words, you are going to die tonight, slow and excruciating... and the last voice you will hear will be mine."

# Chapter 24

When the guards unchained Killian and me, hauling us out, I knew what was ahead. Where they were taking us.

It was time for the Games.

My heart pounded with each step, the air shifting when we reached the tunnel leading to the arena. Energy hung in the air like serrated knives, the crowd's chants resonating down the passage, a call for blood. For death. Anything to distract from their own despair and anger. How easily we all turned on each other, becoming the monsters they deemed us—cannibals eating our own instead of coming together and attacking the one starving and torturing us.

My gaze shot over to Killian, really taking him in—pale, sweaty, gaunt, and broken. The iron robbing him of his energy to heal, sucking the life from him.

"Kil—"

"Don't worry, Ms. Kovacs." A forced smile ticked up his lips, bleeding with a sorrow he couldn't hide. "I'm ready to face whatever comes my way." As though he was ready if death came for him too. "I will always fight until the very end."

"Take the collar off of him," I sneered back at Boyd, the chants outside the tunnel growing louder and louder, the pounding of feet and clapping hands, the bright light of the ring shining into the passage.

Boyd tilted his head.

"Look at him. You know the iron is killing him. Give us at least a chance out there. Doesn't it make for a better show anyway?"

"It's not my decision." Boyd moved through us, unlocking the gate with giddy cruelty. "Nor do I care."

*Clank.*

The sound of the gate opening instantly tripled my pulse, a reminder of the traumas of all the times I had been here before. The clank of the key echoing in the lock, the certain pitch the gate made when it opened, felt as if nails were being hammered into my spine.

How many times would I be able to go in and walk out? One of these times, I wouldn't.

And tonight, might be the time I didn't.

Or worse, Killian doesn't.

"I thought you two would be happy." Boyd's mouth curved, his shoulder pushing the gate fully open. "You get to reunite with all your friends." He waved behind us. My eyes followed his gesture to the arena.

My body wanted to curl up on itself, to scream and wail, denying what I saw.

Once again, Markos put in every single person who mattered to me. The thought of only me and Killian was horrendous enough, but seeing all my friends, *my family*, I knew what Istvan had in store was much worse. And our numbers had already dropped significantly.

Kitty, Ash, Scorpion, Rosie, Wesley, Birdie, Lukas, Kek, Hanna, and to my horror, even Nora stood in the pit.

A large figure moved in front of them; his jaw twitched as his eyes took in my beaten face.

*"Warwick."* I called his name privately between us, my legs already moving to him. His arms scooped me up, crushing me to his chest, his mouth claiming mine hungrily.

I knew instantly what he was doing, the warmth of his shadow, the magic we weaved together, poured into my veins, healing and strengthening me. Taking one look at Boyd's work, he was getting me battle ready.

Breaking the kiss, he growled against my lips, his thumb sweeping over the bruises and cuts on my cheek. *"Whatever* it takes, princess. Fucking survive."

Slow clapping whipped my head to the balcony. Warwick set me down, my body turning toward the reason we were all here.

Istvan, in his finest uniform, stood over us, arrogance cutting his features sharply. Olena, on his left, had the same haughty expression.

Istvan's guest list had doubled.

Ivanenko, the Ukrainian Leader and father of Olena, who I had met several times at parties, where he always propositioned me, stood on the other side of his daughter. On Istvan's right were Leon, Sonya, the Romanian Prime Minister Lazar, and his sociopath son, Sergiu. The man I was supposed to marry.

His dark eyes narrowed on me with a mix of utter disgust, hate, and fury. The aura of violence and cruelty inside him wafted from him, making me realize how lucky I was fate took my life down a different road.

Smirking at Sergiu, I stepped closer to Warwick. I might be a prisoner, tortured, beaten, and about to die, but my life was still a million times better than being forced to be his wife.

"If you told me a year ago the girl I took in, raised, loved, and cared for as a daughter would stab me in the back?" Istvan's voice snapped my attention to him. "Would stand before me now with her fae friends and her half-breed lover? I'm not sure I would have believed it. Though, I guess that is my own fault. Deceiving and backstabbing run in her veins."

Istvan placed his arms behind his back, pacing a few feet. "I should be furious with you, Brexley. What you did to my lab, my experiments." Clicking his tongue, he tsked me. "I should have someone come down there now and slit your throat."

A snarl reverberated next to me, Warwick's frame rigid and threatening. Out of the corner of my eye, I saw Ash and Lukas step up next to me, could feel Scorpion behind me, and I knew Killian was also near.

Istvan's mouth pinched in amusement, watching them move in around me.

"I see who the alpha of the pack is." His eyes glinted. "What a waste. You could have been a remarkable leader."

"I already am." I took one tiny step in front, showing I didn't need anyone to guard or protect me. "You just don't like it because I'm no longer a chess piece you can move around, marry off, or train as a spy to take over the rule of more countries." I made a point of looking at Lazar and Sergiu.

Istvan's jaw rolled, his head lifting higher as Prime Minister Lazar shot Istvan an angry, confused look.

Istvan only grinned down at me. It knotted my stomach. His smile was one I recognized when he knew something more than the other person. When he knew he had you.

*Stacey Marie Brown*

"What is this all for? Your ego? Sick entertainment? Is this what leaders do now? Sip champagne and nibble on gourmet cheese while watching people die? Oh right, it's *exactly* what you all do. Hide behind your protective walls, flaunting your money and power in lavish parties like some dick-measuring competition while people starve in the streets. You use the poor as slaves in your factories while taking all the profit. Kids are dying of disease and hunger every day, and you do nothing."

"Oh, Brexley." Istvan wagged his head. "You silly, *naïve child*. Power is the *only* thing that matters. The only thing that can change this world, which I plan to do. To be the one who leads this world back to the way it should be. The way it was meant to be. *One* ruler, *one* species."

Leon and Alexandru both jerked to Istvan. They stiffened, shifting their feet in confusion as they looked at each other and then to Istvan, clearly wondering where this was going. Ivanenko did not respond, though I spotted a glint of self-satisfaction in his eyes.

"And thanks to you." Istvan motioned to me, his own smugness smearing over his face. "It happened quicker than I ever would have thought." He didn't react to the two other leaders, their nerves turning them defensive and angry. It only added to Istvan's dominance. "You told me all I needed to know." He nodded to a guard standing behind him. Noise and movement happened behind him, more guards bringing someone from Istvan's private passage out onto the balcony, the progression slow and cumbersome.

As if a roped looped around my neck, the sound of my heart drummed in my ears, my entire world flipping over.

Istvan stepped slightly to the side, letting the guards haul the person forward.

My legs dipped as a scream stuck in my throat, complete terror locking it back, not wanting to believe what I was seeing.

Crystal blue eyes pinned me down with strength as his body swayed with fragility, his mouth muzzled to prevent him from being able to speak.

Or utter a spell.

"No." I shook my head, but there was no denying it.

Tad.

Istvan had his arms tied and gagged to prevent the Druid from chanting or doing any spells.

Before I could even take it in, I saw Istvan lean down, lifting something up from below the railing, a mop of black hair and blue-green eyes.

"NOOOO!" Warwick boomed, his voice bouncing and cracking against the walls, ringing the arena in his rage, lurching forward.

Istvan perched Simon on his hip, holding the boy awkwardly, as if he had no idea what to do with children. He ran his fingers down the boy's tear-streaked cheek.

"I wouldn't, Farkas." Istvan's tone stopped Warwick in his tracks. "They are so fragile at this age. So easily hurt."

"Don't you fucking touch him," Warwick grunted through his teeth, every syllable a warning.

"That's up to you now, isn't it?" Istvan's challenging threat very clear. "This is such an impressionable age. He might make a good HDF soldier with the right guidance and family. Since he seems to be an orphan now." Istvan's insinuation about Eliza's fate was clear.

Warwick heaved with rage, his body twitching with the need to destroy. To attack the threat on his family.

"I want my uncle Warwick." Simon wiggled and fussed, trying to get away from Istvan.

Istvan set him down. "Your uncle has done bad things. Do you know what happens when you do bad things? You get punished."

Simon glared at Istvan, moving closer to Tad. Tad put his arm around him, pulling him into him, letting Simon hide in his robes. Only then did I feel a minuscule bit of reprieve from Warwick. It didn't lessen the threat, but I felt better knowing Tad was with him. Simon wasn't completely alone up there.

The shock of seeing them was weaning, letting logic settle in, filling my head with the notion they had been caught and what it meant.

"Oh, gods..." Oxygen slipped from my lungs, whirling my head. "You got in." My voice barely made it out, sticking on the dry patches in my throat.

Istvan's superior smile zeroed in on me poignantly. "We *walked* right in."

My lids fluttered, dark spots seeping into my vision.

*"It means those barriers keeping fae out and dissuading humans from going there don't apply to Istvan's new soldiers. They can walk right in."*

He had heard me.

"H-How?"

"Not how." His lip curled with arrogance, cruelty glinting his eyes. "But *who*."

He turned his head as Tad and Simon were pushed farther back, and a man in a new HDF uniform stepped forward, his spine straight with proud arrogance, his eye puffy with a deep healing bruise.

A long gasp tore from my throat.

"Holy fuck," Lukas exclaimed behind me.

Both of us gaping, my brain struggled to climb over this hurdle, to accept what I was seeing. Connecting the dots that led me to who was standing up on the balcony with Istvan.

Tracker.

He peered down at me, a hint of a sneer on his mouth.

"I-I don't understand." I did, but I didn't want to believe it.

"What better way to get information from you than send in someone you trust. Especially feeling guilty for leaving him to *die*." He patted Tracker's arm. "Tracker here has been quite an asset to HDF. Though he hasn't been with us long, his initiative and devotion to the cause have made him one of my most valuable soldiers." Istvan's words had Tracker beaming with pride. "It was his idea to be put in here and in the hole with you, to get all the information he could. It was his idea to look authentic." Istvan nodded to Tracker's bruised eye.

My attention darted to Tracker as he self-righteously smiled down at me. Little moments came back to me, like the guard calling him by his first name. They didn't usually do that, especially with someone like Tracker. He'd only be known by his number. And how he suddenly needed to go to the bathroom.

*"What's strange, besides the bizarre dreams of being in some water tank, is waking from my coma. I've never felt better in my life."* I had never caught on. Only the rich were put into the tanks. Especially not some ex-Povstat elite, unless Istvan had plans for him. Hanna didn't even get that treatment.

*"Friends are never as faithful as a person whose whole world is in your hands."*

My lids shut for a moment, going back to the moment he stepped into this prison. It had all been a lie. A setup. Every conversation had been to get information from me. He had been a spy for Istvan all along. Tracker was a prime candidate to flip—arrogant, angry, inferiority complex, lost, and feeling betrayed. Istvan swept in and preyed upon that, giving him a leader to follow. A reason to blame and a reason to worship and be indebted to him. He made him equal to fae.

I had walked right into it, believing he was still loyal to Mykel.

*"Zrádce!"* Traitor! Lukas screamed in Czech. "You piece of shit! I'm gonna fucking kill you!" Lukas raged, Ash and Kek holding him back.

"I was shown the way. Awoken to the truth," Tracker snapped back at Lukas. "Even your mother and brother see the truth. Maybe it's you who is the traitor."

"It didn't take you long to be brainwashed. Though I'm not surprised, not like you were robust in that department anyway." Kek jeered, her eyebrow cocking up in a knowing expression. "Upstairs *or* downstairs."

Lukas and I both swung to look at her, and she shrugged one shoulder.

Oh, gods, I didn't want to know.

"Shut the fuck up, *demon*," Tracker snarled, ramming his body against the railing. Istvan put a hand up, and Tracker instantly stepped back, quickly obeying his new master.

"Tracker quickly saw how manipulated he had been before, saw the error of his ways, believing the false lies fae spouted about us all being equal as they murdered us in droves," Istvan spoke down to us. "After his *own* group turned their backs on him, left him for dead in the streets, choosing fae over him, he now sees where his loyalties lie."

"What about Ava? Didn't you care about her? Sab? Blade? Jak and Lea?" Lukas listed off his comrades in the Povstat's first unit. "Were we not your friends?"

"Friends?" Tracker huffed. "No. I realized we were never *friends*. And it didn't go above my notice to see I was the only human in the entire squad. Mykel's preference was *very* clear. And the only reason I was there was because I was the best out of all of you."

"Now you are even better." Istvan nodded at him, the same look on his face I recalled when he was pleased with Caden, making a bad taste slide down the back of my throat.

"It wouldn't have been long before Mykel replaced me with more *fae*." Tracker hissed out the final word like it was a foul taste on his tongue.

Tracker's ego and sense of entitlement were prime for Istvan to warp and control. A perfect candidate to bend and mold. Shape into the image you wanted.

I would never bend.

"If you hate fae so much, why were you so willing to become one?" I fired at him.

"I will be even *more* powerful." His chilling confidence prickled at my skin.

"That you will." Istvan shared a knowing grin with him, and my stomach sank. "Great things are ahead of you."

"Istvan, what is going on?" Leon shuffled, both he and Alexandru grouping together, unsettled by the shift in the atmosphere.

"Leon, why don't you shut the fuck up and hide behind your fae mistress as you normally do?" Istvan dismissed him.

Leon's eyes went wide with shock, his mouth puffing, his cheeks ruddy with embarrassment and anger. "How *dare* you!"

"I said shut up!" Istvan's voice cut through the space. "Both of you have been nothing but a nuisance to me. And now I no longer have to play nice."

Ivanenko and his daughter peered at each other haughtily, and I understood a great shift was happening.

"I do not have to stand here and be disrespected like this." Lazar huffed, ire creasing his features.

"You do, and you will, Alexandru." Istvan gleamed with power. Every word to these men was said with dominance. He seemed relieved he could finally pull down the veil of pleasantries. "Things have *changed*."

Tracker retrieved something from a messenger bag, lifting it up into view.

My entire universe stopped, oxygen seizing in my lungs.

In his hands was a box, singed and burnt on the corners and across the lid. I recognized every mark as if it were a tattoo on my skin. I knew they had it, could feel it, but seeing Tracker place the nectar in Istvan's hands... Reality slammed into me like a tsunami. Terror churned and swallowed me whole. Taking no prisoners. Perception of time and space blinked out of existence, my brain not computing the certainty of this moment.

Istvan had the nectar.

He had his men walk in and take it because of one single flaw *I* let slip out to the wrong person. One of the most powerful substances in the world was now in the hands of the most narcissistic, psychotic, evil asshole because of me.

"What is that?" Leon huffed, though Sonya stood stock-still, her eyes locked on the box. "I've had enough of your games, Markos." Leon turned for the exit. Sergiu tapped at his father, wanting to follow, but Lazar stopped him, his head shaking.

"Take another step, Leon, and it will be your last." Istvan's focus stayed on the box in Tracker's hands as he spoke.

Leon's eyebrows pushed together, glancing at everyone else as if he were saying, *are you going to put up with this?* The rest didn't move as if they sensed what Istvan held, could feel its magic, whether they were human or not.

"This is ridiculous!"

"For once, just shut up and listen before you open your trap," Sonya spat, irritation and disgust on her face, like she also no longer had to play nice to him.

He went still, shocked by her reaction, taking in Lazar's and Sonya's tense figures.

But they no longer mattered to me; all I saw was the object in Istvan's hands.

I could feel it calling to me. The possessiveness of someone taking part of you—it was violating and wrong. The power thrummed from the box, a drumbeat in sync with my pulse. It wanted me to seize it back. To have what was rightfully mine. It went past ownership, a magic significant to only me. Oxygen heaved from my lungs, a growl slipping through my gritted teeth. I felt and saw nothing else.

*"Kovacs,"* Warwick called my name, the feel of him skimming over my skin, dipping beneath. His real hand tried to pry mine open. Peering down, I noticed blood dripping into the dirt from my hand, my nails slicing deep into my palm from my grip.

*"It's mine."* The force with which it called to me, the need to take it and protect it from *anyone* else who wanted to touch it, trembled my muscles.

*"I know,"* Warwick replied evenly, his deep voice keeping me from actually leaping up to the balcony. *"We will get it back."*

Istvan's fingers clutched the lid, slowly opening the box, his eyes scanning over the object inside. A smile curled his lips, his eyes flashing, the shine of greed and power glowing on his face. His shoulders were set back, his spine straightening; his confidence created the impression he was getting taller. Arrogance and superiority filled the space around him.

"What is that?" Leon looked in the box, his nose wrinkling up, his overconfidence ramming up against the tension growing among them. I was starting to think Sonya pulled the strings behind the scenes, giving Leon his ruthless reputation. I didn't doubt he was, but his own arrogance had dulled his common sense, made him believe he was untouchable. "This is what you are all trembling over? Some solidified honey or whatever it is."

"Nectar," Istvan replied, a giddiness in his tone I had never heard before.

*"This* is the mythical nectar?" Leon exclaimed before bursting out in a throaty laugh. "You have lost your mind. Not only is it just a fairytale, but you expect me to believe that gross lump of goo is all-powerful? It is sap you probably harvested from a tree—"

"Do you not feel its power, Leon?" Istvan's hand quaked as he lifted toward the nectar.

I didn't even realize I had reeled forward until I felt Warwick and Ash both grab my arms.

"Are you that obtuse? Ask Sonya if she thinks the nectar is a myth. Even Lazar seems to understand what I have."

Leon glanced at Sonya and Lazar, both resembling statues. While Sergiu seemed to want to follow Leon's example, his father's grip on his arm was the only thing keeping him from stomping off like a toddler. Ivanenko and Olena glowed with authority and supremacy. Ivanenko, through his daughter, was on the side of power. And I couldn't deny Ukraine was by far a more formidable ally in strength and power than Romania or Czech.

Istvan sucked in a sharp breath before pulling his hand back, nodding his head at Tracker. Tracker shut the lid.

"Sonya, let's go." Leon beckoned her as he would a dog, still continuing down his obstinate road. When someone is used to being the alpha, or at least acting the part, they couldn't seem to get when it was time not to be an idiot. "I'm done with your games, Markos." He marched for the door.

With an insignificant flick of Istvan's chin, HDF soldiers shuffled in, blocking Leon's path.

"Move!" Leon bellowed. "How dare you block my way. You still work for me."

*Bang!*

The shot rang out, piercing the walls in surround sound. Lazar and Sonya barely reacted, while Sergiu screamed out as Leon's body dropped to the ground. Blood pooled from the hole between his eyes.

"You are wrong, Leon. They work *for me*," Istvan retorted. The shift in power, in leadership, was like a light switch, guards moving in and around Sonya, Lazar, and Sergiu, holding them at gunpoint.

"Leon was warned." Istvan snapped around to the remaining leaders. "So, let it be a warning to you… *things have changed*," Istvan declared, his head held high with no doubt. "I am your king now."

Olena moved closer to Istvan with a cruel smile, and her head held with the same conceit and surety. She was his queen.

Ivanenko may not like Istvan being over him, but being on his side with his daughter gave him even more power and control than he had before. He could basically rule and dictate out Istvan's laws as a sub-king.

The king could only do so much, so Ivanenko had made himself basically second in charge.

In one swift move, not only did Istvan have Romania and Czech, but he had Ukraine as well. Three huge power-seated countries. It wouldn't be long before he took the rest of the Eastern Bloc. Only China might contest; the rest were too poor with insufficient military power to fight.

"What?" Sergiu spurted. "Father, are you going to let him get away with this?"

Lazar grabbed his son's arm again, his head jerking with a "shut up" motion.

"Your son is an idiot, Alexandru." Istvan tucked his arms behind his back, strolling a little closer. "And if he ever took rule over Romania, your country would perish. You should thank me for letting your name go down with you—in honor, instead of embarrassment."

"You should talk." Alexandru seethed through his teeth. "Where is *your* son, Markos?"

Istvan dipped his head. "Yes, I know all too well about having a disappointing son. But unlike you, I do not pretend he is otherwise. Truth is, I no longer need him as a successor."

Acid formed on my tongue upon hearing his claim. It was true. With the nectar, he would live a fae's lifetime. He could rule for centuries to come. My stomach turned with thoughts of Caden and how we left him, not knowing if he was alive or dead now.

"Though, in six months, I will have one anyway. A boy." Istvan went to Olena, touching her belly. "A *true* son and heir over my realm."

Oh, gods. Olena was pregnant? Now that I was looking, I could make out a slight bump under her dress.

Olena glowed with a proud smile, her hand over his, rubbing her baby bump with smug glee. She was now permanently tied to Istvan.

If I was doing the math right, it meant she had gotten pregnant around the time of her engagement to Caden. Even back then, Istvan had been contriving and strategizing backup plans, seeding another heir from the woman supposedly marrying his son. He could have declared the child as Caden's or claimed the baby depending on what happened. Rebeka's fate also was in flux back then too. He had all of it laid out, ready for multiple outcomes.

Now, Caden had become the spare. The one no longer needed.

"I think you see what I will do to keep the strength of my reign. So, sit back and enjoy the entertainment I had planned for you this evening." I didn't even see Istvan's signal before servants carried out throne-like chairs for him and Olena. More servants came with trays of food and drink, while many guards kept their weapons pressed into Sonya, Alexandru, and Sergiu's heads, ensuring they knew they were no longer guests, but hostages. Leon's dead body still lay there as people stepped over him as if he were nothing. A reminder of how fast this game changed and how easily you could be taken out of it.

Istvan and Olena sat down in their seats, Ivanenko perched on a more subdued chair slightly behind them, so he didn't forget where he stood in this.

"Cheers, my dear." Istvan clinked glasses with Olena. With refreshments in hand, servants waiting for their orders. The pair looked the epitome of a haughty king and queen, gazing down on their peasants.

"How is the view, darling?" Istvan patted Olena's hand, the other one on the box Tracker had placed on a table next to him. His gaze stayed down on me. Tracker stood behind his chair. Not quite a prince's position, but where an elite guard or right-hand man would be. "Are you ready for some fun?"

"More than you know, my love." She nuzzled into him, staring up at him like a crown was already on his head, herself the queen of all.

"I can imagine you are…" He chuckled almost conspiratorially. "Go ahead. Do the honors."

"What the fuck?" Warwick muttered, suddenly jerking his head back toward the fighters' tunnels, his forehead wrinkling, his body stiffening as if he sensed something. Before I could follow his gaze, Olena's voice sang out like a giddy schoolgirl.

"Guards, bring them out!"

I was starting to think she wasn't as vapid as she looked. The bitch was conniving and manipulating.

The side gates squealed behind me, where Warwick had his full focus. His forehead creased, twisting me around to follow his gaze.

"Fuck." I heard Warwick mutter before two figures were shoved out roughly onto the dirt, their bodies hitting with a thud.

Oxygen ripped from my lungs, the ground once again crumbling under my feet.

A woman and a man. Threadbare clothes, dirty and beaten.

"Oh, gods…" My mouth hung open as I watched one look around in utter fear and confusion, while the other seemed to understand what was happening, his brown eyes looking straight at Warwick, his forehead wrinkling in a mirror of confusion before his gaze jumped to me.

"Caden," I muttered in shock, my gaze jumping to the woman next to him. "Rebeka."

"Let the Games begin!" Olena's voice cheered out.

# Chapter 25

"Rebeka!" Nora's cry for her friend rang across the arena, jerking Rebeka's head. Her mouth dropped at seeing her oldest friend approaching her wearing a prison outfit.

"Nora?" Rebeka's voice cracked as she got to her feet. Rebeka had always been trim, but now she was emaciated. Her silky hair was dirty and knotted, her beautiful face cut up and bruised. A far cry from the regal woman I grew up with in designer clothing, expensive perfumes, who held a queen-like demeanor.

"You're alive." Nora clutched her arms, her head shaking before she hugged her friend.

"Wha-what are you doing here?" Rebeka's question was drowned out by a loud clatter, the sound of a machine cranking.

"Oh shit," I muttered, knowing that resonance as if it was embedded into my nightmares. My attention snapped to the floor of the pit. Cages were quickly rising from below, shrieking noises and howls coming from them, making me positive they were filled with wild animals again.

The cages clicked in as they became level with the ground, shapes moving quickly and frantically, their cries growing louder and more piercing.

*"Same as last time?"* Scorpion's shadow stood between Warwick and me, though he was across the pit from us.

"Yes…" My response tapered off as I made out what was inside the pens. Everything changed. My plans, my thoughts—they sunk to the bottom, drowning in the abyss.

"Oh, my gods." Terror cracked through my system.

"What are those?" Ash's shock stepped him back.

"Holy. Fuck." Warwick uttered.

Wild. Feral.

But it wasn't animals inside.

It was all the old guards. The ones I knew from HDF who had taken Istvan's first dose of pills.

My attention was locked on the men. Or what used to be men. All of them now acted more like rabid animals. I had noticed the decline before, feared they would take on whatever fae essence they were given.

My deepest nightmare had come to fruition.

The doors to the cages swung open with a clank. The figures inside instantly scrambled out. Low to the ground and ready to attack, they still had enough human in them they didn't go down on all fours.

Joska was the first out, getting himself in front. The already large guy puffed his chest, beating on it as a gorilla would, rallying the dozens of beast-like men behind him.

He was the alpha.

"Joska?" Caden wheezed, taking in his old classmate. Then his gaze went to Samu, not too far behind. "Samu?"

Joska's and Samu's heads snapped to Caden, a sneer hitching on their lips, responding to their names.

They understood him.

A howl from Joska pierced the air, sending chills down my spine. He grabbed the cage he came out of, his arms flexing. Grunting wildly, he snapped off a metal bar, his dark eyes landing on me. Recognizing. Despising. The feelings Joska had for me before seemed to only heighten in this state.

He howled again, ramming his fist with the metal rod into the air, rallying up the group behind him, ready to attack. One by one, they each broke a bar from their cage, displaying their excessive strength, shaking their weapons with his.

Then they did something that sunk terror into my gut. Spreading out, they started to move around us like we used to do on sweeps. It was methodical. Planned.

"Shit." I stepped back, oxygen slipping from my lungs, my gaze snapping from Caden to Hanna, their eyes coming back to me with the same horror and understanding. They saw it too. The old guards seemed to still have enough cognitive understanding of a human but double the strength of any fae I'd ever seen, with animal instincts to kill. They were far worse than the wild animals.

There were ways to counter a sweep in the real world by breaking through one side, spilling out of the circle. Here there wasn't anywhere to go. No breaking free.

The only chance was to get their weapons from them and spread out as we did last time, lessening the power they had as a group. With Joska the leader of the pack, most followed his cues. They wouldn't be as strong alone. Depending on what fae essence they took on, some would be better than others at fighting.

As if Joska knew what I was thinking, he let out a yowl, the entire throng running for us like we were on a battlefield. They moved so fast our human reactions couldn't keep up.

"Mom!" Hanna's voice shrilled through the stadium. Nora didn't even have time to turn as Samu chucked the metal rod in his hand like a javelin.

The jagged point struck its mark, spraying blood over Rebeka's face. It was so fast, Nora stared unblinking at Rebeka, her body not registering what had happened. Her mouth opened to speak, blood drooling from it.

"Nora!" Rebeka screamed as Nora's body finally crumpled to the ground.

"Mooooommmmmm!" Hanna wailed, moving forward. Wesley grabbed her, holding her back as she thrashed. "No! Let me go! Mom!" she sobbed, her body sinking in despair against him.

Caden dove past Rebeka, shoving her out of the way as the soldier-monster hurtled for us, ripping the bar out of Nora, his training was conditioned in his body, seeing an opportunity and taking it.

We had no time to register or mourn Nora's death, the throng of monsters coming straight for us.

Pushing through the goblin metal, I reached out to Warwick and Scorpion. *"Take out the weakest links. Get their weapons. Scorp, you go after the back group. We will take on Joska."*

Scorpion nodded, getting in front of Hanna while Wesley tried to get her to her feet. For a moment, I didn't know if she would, but she was a trained soldier down to her core. You learned to compartmentalize. Do your duty. Grieve later. Killian and Rosie grouped with them.

"Ash!" I nodded at another tier of monsters. He instantly reacted. Kek,

241

Kitty, Birdie, and Lukas ran with him, not waiting for the hybrid monsters to attack first.

"What the fuck is she doing?" Caden gripped the bar he stole, his head jerking toward the tiny blonde running for one of the largest monsters out there, one who seemed more rhino than human.

"Oh, holy shit." I knew exactly what she was doing. Birdie's slight frame scaled up the back of him like she was a squirrel before the creature even understood she was there. Climbing onto his shoulders, her legs wrapped around his neck. I had seen her use that move on a guy who had to be part giant and win.

He clawed and bucked, trying to get the girl off of him, but Birdie held on, contracting her legs and crunching down on his esophagus. The man's face turned purple before he fell to his knees. She didn't relent, her thighs like a boa constrictor. The man's eyes flipped back, tipping over, slamming into the ground. The brutal impact tossed her into the dirt, rolling her over to us.

Coughing out a groan, she got up.

"I won't lie and say that wasn't frightening and oddly hot at the same time," Caden huffed, his head shaking.

"Oh, pretty boy, if you think that was scary…" she brushed herself off with a wink, "your little vanilla world couldn't handle what I actually do *in bed*."

Caden jerked slightly at her statement. A smile curved her mouth as she whirled back around, facing the wave of monsters coming at us.

We met them halfway, Samu's fist slicing across my cheek, probably the only time he ever got a hit in first, and that was because he wasn't human anymore. With a growl, I slammed my elbow into his gut, causing him to stumble back. My heel plowed into him, tossing his ass onto the ground.

He snarled back, his eyes darting over to Caden. His body pointed toward him. You could feel and see the animosity, jealousy, and hurt because Caden never befriended him. He wanted him to pay.

Jumping for him before he could move, a force knocked into me, hurling me back into the wall like a freight train. My head slammed into the wood, spinning my mind. Blood trickled down the back of my neck, my lids lifting to see Joska only feet from me. Anger and rage heaved in every breath he took. His eyes narrowed on me, his lip curling, raising the pole in his hand, chucking it straight at me.

Adrenaline and fear exploded through my muscles, jerking my body down farther. I felt the bar skim my head, grazing the top of my scalp and sticking into the wall behind me.

*Holy fuck.*

An aggravated roar filled the arena, Warwick plowing into Joska, both men crashing hard into the dirt, rolling together. Joska bellowed, his unbelievable strength matching The Legend as his teeth bit down on Warwick's neck. Wagging his head violently, he tore into Warwick's flesh.

"No!" I screamed, scrambling up, yanking the spear out of the wall. My fingers wrapped around the metal, Warwick's bellow filling the arena. I didn't think; the only instinct was to save him.

Running up behind Joska, my arms went up. "Move!" I screamed at Warwick.

He shoved Joska over as I dropped the bar like an ax into his back. The sound of bone, muscles, and matter slurped as the spear drove between Joska's shoulder blades. Joska reared back with a yowl, Warwick scrambling out from underneath him as I yanked the bar free. Saliva dripped from Joska's mouth as he turned to me, his bloody, meaty hands grabbing for me. I rammed the rod through his throat, feeling the pointy end embedding in the dirt, the reverberation jarring my muscles. Blood sprayed over my face, the metal tunneling through his neck.

Joska's brown eyes stared at me. Gurgling, his mouth opened, pooling blood onto the ground.

Warwick got to his feet, his face and arms cut up badly, but I knew he'd heal.

Birdie dropped another guard, using her uniform top to strangle him, his body going limp right next to us. "Two down. You only have one?" She smirked.

"Remind me to never piss you off." Caden retorted, moving to us.

"This? Please. You should see what I do when I'm actually angry."

Right then, a grunt came from Joska's dead body, swiveling us back around. His eyes popped open, his hand reaching for the pole, his lips snarling as he yanked it out of his neck with a growl.

"Holy shit." Birdie leaped back. "He's still fucking alive!"

Joska snarled as he rose, his death stare only on me. The other guards we thought we killed were twitching awake as well.

The darkest dread sank into my chest. Not only were they stronger because of the drug, but they were even harder to kill… if not impossible. They healed rapidly, and from what I remember in Killian's lab, they didn't register pain.

Joska roared, causing all the others to respond in a chilling cry. A warrior's death cry.

"Kovacs!" Warwick shoved me away as Joska sprung, the harpoon coming for me.

*BOOOOOOOM!*

The earth shook violently, flinging us all to the ground. My spine hit the dirt as screams from the stands and pit curled up with the distant explosion. Right away, another explosion quaked the prison so hard, clumps of the ceiling fell, the lights flickering out.

"Kovacs!" Warwick rolled over me, his body barricading me from falling debris. The generator lights kicked on, the room glowing in dim light. His aqua eyes captured mine, and I had a strong sense of déjà vu of us when Halálház was bombed.

When my uncle saved us.

"What the fuck was that?" Caden coughed and hacked next to us, the sprinkling of dirt still trickling down. He tried to protect his mother from most of the debris, panic, terror, and grief lining her dirty face. Birdie was on her other side.

Birdie's gaze lifted, meeting Warwick's, a slow hint of a smile on their faces.

"*Distraction*," they both uttered at once.

"You think...?" Hope bubbled and churned. Could Mykel be here? Could Eliza and Zander have reached them? This was nowhere near the destruction of Halálház, but we were far deeper underground this time. Could my uncle be saving us again?

Shrieks of confusion and fear rang out in the dome. Even the feral beasts set to attack us sensed danger, all running for the cages for protection, their survival instincts kicking in.

Warwick climbed off me, pulling me to my feet, Caden and Birdie following, both helping Rebeka stand. She looked lost, terrified, and numb. In the last few weeks, her entire world had overturned. Something I completely understood. Though I had been trained to battle, she had not.

"How do we get out?" Caden asked. "My father has made sure this place is secure. And it's been spelled."

Spelled?

My head whipped to the balcony. Through the commotion, haze, and darkness, my eyes went to the balcony. Soldiers were rushing Istvan, Olena, and Ivanenko out through the tunnels. In Marko's hand was the box of nectar. Behind the newly self-instated royals, guards moved Sonya, Lazar, Sergiu, Simon, and Tad.

The Druid we needed to break the spells... *from within.*

They were headed for the only way out of here. The factory floor, where their escape vehicles waited, and the gate which could free us.

I turned around, shouting at anyone who could hear me. "Get everyone to the factory floor! Grab anything you can for a weapon." My shadow told Scorpion the same thing across the arena. "Now!"

Ash, Lukas, Kek, and Kitty were the closest, their heads nodding at my command.

"Go!" I ordered Caden and Birdie.

"What are you doing?" Caden's brow wrinkled in that familiar, concerned way, when he had no clue what I was up to.

"I can't let him leave." With the nectar, with Simon or Tad. Whirling around, I already sensed Warwick sprinting with me. We understood without speaking. With everyone funneling to the factory above, we would get waylaid. And with Simon and the nectar on the line, nothing would stop either of us from getting to them.

Warwick raced ahead of me, leaping up to the first level, far above, pulling himself up and climbing onto the rail before leaning down and yanking me up with him. Repeating, he drew me up to the next level until we reached the balcony. The moment my feet landed on the concrete floor, I rushed toward the tunnel, almost tripping over Leon's corpse. The sounds of our boots clipped the floor, our breaths in sync.

I could feel the nectar, but with the goblin collar around my neck, it denied me the ability to pull anything from the source, to even dive into my own powers.

Terror sat on my shoulders, biting into the back of my neck, but I couldn't let myself acknowledge it. If I did, it would cripple me. Tear all courage from under my feet and render me useless.

Everything was against us, but hope was a powerful weapon. When you had something to fight for, it made you believe anything was possible.

The tunnel ended at the stairs leading up. I could hear sounds from above echoing down. Orders were barked out, car engines turning over.

Panic made me spring up the steps faster. The thought of Istvan escaping, of everything slipping through my fingers, hurled my feet to take them two at a time, my heart rapping wildly against my chest.

Warwick and I barreled through an open door into the factory. The generator lights gave enough light to see the hundreds of HDF soldiers who worked at Věrhǎza darting around. Six armored trucks were lined up, their headlights on, engines revving, as the guards hurried the various parties into them. My eye went to the last vehicle. White hair and a robe sliced through the sea of dark uniforms like a beacon, a little boy being heaved into the truck before him.

"Tad!" I bellowed his name, hurtling toward him like a bullet. I knew it would bring more than his attention to me, but I couldn't pause. If I hesitated before he was put inside the car, they'd be lost to me for good.

His head whipped around, eyes finding mine through the vast, dimly lit room as if he knew exactly where I was. His mouth was gagged and arms tied. I saw his head dip as guards followed his gaze, trying to locate me. It was in that moment our gazes stayed locked, and I swore I could feel the lifetimes in it.

Guards started moving in our direction, and everything was in slow motion until I saw Tad wink. Then everything flipped into chaos.

Tad, with his frail, curved frame, barreled into the guard holding him, causing him to stumble to the ground out of pure shock, while Tad slammed his head back into one behind him, cracking his nose and wiggling out of their grip.

Warwick reacted first, already sprinting for them. He leaped quickly onto a guard not ready for him, snapping his neck, the body not even dropping to the ground before Warwick stole his rifle, knocking the next in the head while swiveling around and shooting another.

Damn, that man turned me on.

Running, I dropped to my side, sliding into a guard. I rammed my heel into his knee, snapping it the wrong way. The guard screamed, falling to the ground in agony. Swiping up his weapon, I leaped up, bashing it against his head, then twisting and firing at several more coming at me. Cutting down anything moving for me, I wiggled my way toward Tad, slipping up behind a guard who was trying to shove him in the car.

*Bang!*

The bullet went through his head, the weight taking both of them to the ground.

"Tad!" My nails tore at the heavy weight over him, pushing the dead body off him. I heaved a sigh of relief when he blinked up at me, his face smeared with blood. My fingers yanked at the cloth around his mouth.

"Excellent timing, my girl."

"Go! Go!" I heard a soldier yell, cutting their losses at the back. The large gate creaked open, and behind me, I could hear masses of people climbing the steps to the factory floor, the inmates about to flood the area.

Istvan's car lurched forward, the nectar about to disappear from my grasp.

246

"Help me up!" Tad groaned as I got him to his feet, his mouth already moving, a low chant closing his eyes.

"Simon!" I yelled as someone in the passenger seat leaned back, grabbed the door, slamming it closed. The door locked. "No!" I yanked at the handle as the armored truck tore away.

"Simon!" Warwick bellowed, heartache and terror weaving through his gruff cry, his feet tearing off after the vehicle, jumping onto the back, riding with the caravan like a stowaway.

I felt my chest splinter as the truck drove through the exit. The magic around the gate was spelled to keep us prisoners inside. It recognized Warwick as a fugitive, zapping an electrical current through his body. Warwick jerked and convulsed as voltage went through him, pitching him back onto the cement with a thump.

"Warwick!" I ran for him. The commotion from the inmates streaming in, attacking the guards left to fight, was muted in the background. Dropping to my knees, my hands touched his face, sliding down to his unmoving chest.

No heartbeat.

No breath.

No life.

# Chapter 26

"Warwick!" I slammed my hands down onto his chest, feeling heat simmer inside me, a flame catching on fire. "Don't you *dare* leave me. Whatever it takes."

Letting myself dive into him, I shoved against the goblin metal trying to contain me, sweat dripping down my forehead as it battled and pushed back, feeling the murmur of my powers whispering in my ears, bubbling up from the depth, telling me something I couldn't quite make out.

Thunder purred around me, a crack of lightning, wind brushing my cheek in a kiss.

"I forbid you to die, asshole." Slipping under his skin, I pushed even deeper, wrapping around his heart while I pumped on his chest.

Warwick seized forward, gasping in breath, his eyes moving around until they landed on mine. His nose flared, taking another deep inhale, swallowing. His hand cupped my face, pulling my forehead to his, his voice raking through the gravel and dirt.

"*Sotet démonom.*"

A gasp of relief huffed from my lips against his, my lids closing briefly. "Don't ever fucking do something so stupid again."

"What's the fun in that?" He tried for humor, but his features were streaked with worry as he sat up. "Simon."

"We'll get him." I stood, yanking him with me.

Magic hissed and sparked at the gate as if it was lashing out, twisting me to it. I could feel the energy in the spell fighting and lashing back. My neck craned around to see Tad walking up to the gate. Magic emitted from him like thousands of glowing webs. Eyes closed, muttering, his body weaved, barely staying up. His forehead creased with pain and determination as if he were in a battle himself. Just because he put them in place didn't mean they were easy to pull down. He probably had to use immense energy to do both. And I was understanding more and more that magic had a life of its own, a true give and take.

Warwick and I rushed around him, making sure he stayed protected as he worked, shooting at any soldier who got close.

The fight in the factory grew louder. Gunshots and screams rang out as more and more inmates funneled into the room, though the HDF guards were fully loaded with weapons and fae-like strength, keeping the odds still in their favor.

Soon, the feral-fae would follow the commotion.

The room spun with chaos, spiking fear and adrenaline throughout the space. You could taste it on your tongue like a bitter pill and smell a pungent odor. It was a living, breathing entity. Anxiety banged my heart against my ribs, as with every second, Istvan got farther away from us.

Tad wobbled, his face straining as he struggled to get each word out, sweat beading down his face, his concentration entirely on his counter spell.

Letting out a cry, he spit out words. A loud crack popped the air, blowing back at us, the force slamming Warwick and me to the ground. Tad took the brunt, and a strangled bellow came from him as magic swept over him. Then it dissipated, leaving only threads of electricity humming in the air. His body crumpled to the ground.

"Tad!" I crawled to him.

Breathing heavily, he stared at me, his face pale. "I'll be fine. Go, my girl. Don't let him get away. Get the boy."

"Come on!" Warwick grabbed my arm, yanking me up as he was already racing for the gate. Grabbing the reinforced metal, his muscles flexed and strained, a guttural roar heaving from his chest as he pulled on it. The metal shredded and pitched as he forced it open, a grunt scraping up his throat and tearing more crevasse into his vocal cords.

*Snap!*

The hinges on the gate broke, the gate falling open. Yells and even more gunfire roared up in both cheers and protests behind us. Gunfire pinged off the walls at our heads as we ran in, our feet moving us to safety. For now. I knew many would follow behind us. Prisoners and guards.

Fire bulbs lit every dozen yards, giving us enough to see where we were going. The tunnel steadily inclined toward the surface; the rumble of vehicles could still be felt under our feet.

We weren't too late.

"Hurr—!"

*BOOOM!*

The tunnel quaked with rage, swallowing Warwick's sentence. Earth heaved under our feet, tearing down the ceiling on us.

"Kovacs!" he screamed, his physique crashing into mine, taking us both to the ground. His warm, massive frame covered mine as chunks rained down, tucking us up against the wall. He shielded me as the heavy pieces lightened into a patter.

Coughing and hacking, we slowly lifted our heads, seeing the destruction before us. A lot of the ceiling had collapsed.

A person on foot could still pass through, but cars wouldn't be getting in or out anytime soon. And if they were in the tunnel, they probably would have been crushed, or at least stopped.

"Simon," Warwick whispered his name, the same thought coming to him.

We were both back up, panic pushing us past feeling any pain from the falling rocks, bruising and cutting at our skin. Scaling over boulders, mounds of dirt, and cement, we treated the tunnel as an obstacle course race. One we had to win.

Up ahead, natural light spilled into the darkness, growing brighter the closer we got, permitting my eyes to make out more shapes.

"Warwick…" I gulped, pointing about a hundred yards ahead of us. Brake lights glowed through the wreckage. The armored cars withstood the destruction but were buried under the cave-in, trapping them.

Sneaking up, our guns primed, I noticed a few car doors left open. My pulse thumped against my neck as Warwick and I checked each car, finding them empty, the strum of disappointment playing in my stomach, terrified they had gotten out and were past catching now.

"Fuck!" Warwick hit the final car we checked, anger at his own failure to protect Simon.

Pops of gunfire streamed into the tunnel from outside, prompting us to look at each other, hope filling up the air between us like a balloon. Our legs bolted forward, scaling the final stretch of rubble blocking our way.

The sun was lowering on the mountain, splashing the sky with deep blues and purples, the tips of the forest around the Elizabeth Lookout Tower painted in oranges, reds, and browns. It was only a split second, breathing in the fresh, crisp air, piercing my lungs with a delicious stab. Most people didn't appreciate the simple things, the gifts of true freedom. The feel of the cold air snapping at your exposed skin, filling you with vivacity. The sight of nature thrumming with life, the rich colors of the sunsets, birds chirping in the sky.

But in this case, gunfire as well.

Darting out of the excavated tunnel, we crept out toward the commotion, perching behind an old stone monument.

"Holy shit." I gawked. Down the one lane which led in and out of this place, a barricade of cars and SUVs blocked the road, preventing an easy escape. And behind the cars, my eyes caught familiar faces.

Tears of relief sizzled behind my lids.

Eliza, Zander, and Mykel.

Warwick's head dropped for a moment, his cheek twitching as he took a moment. He didn't show anything more, but I could feel it everywhere. Relief. Happiness. Pride.

His sister was alive. Not only that, but she finished what we could not. She found my uncle and got us help.

The relief was short-lived. Not far from us, the ground was leveled and primed for new buildings, cutting into the forest. A few structures were being built with a partial thick stone wall, giving a little coverage for at least a hundred HDF soldiers shooting back at Povstat. Istvan clearly had plans to make this into a fortress, assuring we would never be able to escape. I had no idea a whole battalion was above our heads this whole time.

"Go!" Istvan's voice shot my attention to him, finding him behind a section of the new wall. He waved Tracker on, pushing Olena and Ivanenko to follow him. His faithful lapdog kept crouched, running off behind the tower with the wannabe queen and her daddy behind him, leaving Istvan and Simon with four other guards. All the others were fighting to hold the line against Povstat, Istvan throwing orders and commands to the forces.

No longer were Sonya, Alexandru, and Sergiu with him. They undoubtedly dashed off into the forest the moment they could, while Istvan and the guards were distracted.

My fingers crunched down on my weapon, spotting the box in his hand, his other hand on the back of Simon's neck.

He deserved to die. He had caused so much suffering.

My finger pushed firmer on the trigger.

"No." Warwick shoved my gun off the target. "You might hit Simon."

251

I was an excellent shot, but Warwick was right. Simon was too close to him. At any second, one could alter a hair, and I'd hit the little boy instead.

"Plus, this shit is personal," Warwick growled. Crouching, he slid around the stone monument, moving slowly... a predator stalking its prey.

I followed right behind. We kept low, knowing at this distance Mykel's army wouldn't be able to decipher between our black prison outfits and HDF's dark uniforms.

Gunfire volleyed loudly between HDF and Povstat, bullets hitting the tower and the ground around us. Adrenaline coursed through my blood, sweat trickling down my back as I defended us from behind. Even over the shooting, I could hear distant echoes from down the tunnel telling me other inmates and probably guards were headed this way soon, about to add to the turmoil and confusion.

Blood would spill.

Warwick crept behind our targets like a silent killer, darting up to the nearest officer in a blink. His hands clutched the guard's neck, snapping it as I slammed my pistol into the back of another one, both of them dropping.

The rest of them turned to us as we pounced on the last two guards. *Pop! Pop!* Their guns fired. I dropped down, slamming my fist into a sentry's crotch. Groaning, he leaned over in agony as I jumped up, my elbow smashing into the back of his neck with a crack, flattening him to the ground. The final guard crumbled under Warwick's fatal blow.

Istvan's eyes widened in fear as Warwick prowled for him. Scrambling back, he grabbed a knife, making the box with the nectar in his arms tip, the item inside tumbling to the dirt between us.

A breath. A blink. Time stopped as Istvan and I stared at each other. And just as fast, it broke.

Surging for it, Istvan's boot kicked it out of my way, driving the blade into Simon's skin. The little boy cried out in pain and shock.

Warwick and I froze.

My gaze snapped up to the knife edge cutting into Simon's neck, the blood trailing down, soaking into his t-shirt.

"Back up! Touch it, and I kill him," Istvan snarled, desperation shaking his hand wrapped around the knife, his movement more frantic. "Don't for a moment think I won't."

"You do..." Warwick's body vibrated with untapped fury, his teeth clenching together. "And I will tear you apart bit by bit, making sure you feel every single moment."

"I said back up," Istvan yelled, pushing the blade in deeper. Simon gulped, as he tried to hide the terror, struggling to be stoic like his uncle.

Warwick stepped back, his nose flaring.

"You have been a thorn in my side from the moment I took you in." Istvan adjusted Simon, inching closer to the nectar. "Little did I know the real truth your father was keeping from me."

My attention snapped up to Istvan, something in my chest curling with dread.

"I thought it was the pills making you different. That changed you… but it wasn't." He sneered. "Benet knew what you were all along. Is it why he was in alliance with Povstat, his brother *Mykel*?"

I sucked in, my shoulders going back at hearing Istvan reveal my uncle's identity and relation to me.

Of course. "Tracker." My lip lifted. "Wise to trust someone who so easily turns on his last leader?"

Istvan's head went back in a laugh. "You think I didn't know the whole time about Mykel? Who he was?" He tilted his head at me in pity. "Oh, Brexley, so naïve. I knew your father, even unbeknownst to Andris, was working with fae and fae sympathizers, starting a coup against me."

"What?" I jolted.

"I had Kalaraja follow your father, found the secret cabin he had in *Gödöllő*. How do you think we were so prepared to attack you the night you went there?"

Realization dropped in my stomach, burning like acid.

"Your father gave up everything for you. Turned his back on his morals, his people… *me*."

That was what Istvan hated the most. My father no longer wanted to follow him, no longer thought Istvan was a capable leader.

A sneer came up on Istvan's face. "So, I killed him."

The world stopped on a pin. No longer could I see or hear anything around me.

"What?" I whispered, my breath going in and out, barely touching my lungs.

"I was the one who sliced his throat on the battlefield that night. His last image as he choked on his own blood was my face. So easy. Everyone assumed he was killed by fae, which only made the troops more bloodthirsty to destroy the fae. It worked out perfectly."

He killed my father. He destroyed my entire world.

Everything I believed in was set on fire, burning me up with unbridled grief and fury. Every day I lived with Istvan, he looked at me and knew. Every tear I shed for my father, the heartbreak and grief... it was all because of him.

The level of betrayal had no bottom, an endless pit of rage and hate, bubbling up like black lava, scorching everything in its wake.

*"Kovacs..."* Warwick spoke low with no emotion, only warning.

Everything around me felt far off, as if I were in a snow globe, shielded from the world. The call to the nectar laced and weaved through me, tangling me into it, giving me no choice. Singing into my veins like a siren, the song lured and drew me into its power. To destroy him. To level everything.

All the pain I had hidden away and ignored roared up with a vengeance. Suffering, agony, sorrow, pain... Istvan had caused so much of it. Even now. Through my lashes, I gazed over the area around the Elizabeth Lookout Tower. Mykel's army clashed with HDF as more inmates and HDF soldiers spilled from the tunnel.

Simon sucked in as Istvan tipped the blade deeper into his throat, snapping me back to Markos, his eyes wild. Desperation made people unpredictable. Dangerous.

But *I* was the most dangerous thing of all.

Moving, I gave neither one of them time to react as I swiped up the nectar, the power instantly pulsing in my hand. Power shot up from my gut as if the nectar summoned it, rage taking over as my howl impaled the sky.

Wind wailed through the trees, breaking the branches, twisting in the sky like a hurricane. Thunder rolled; lightning crackled in the clear evening sky.

*"Kovacs!"* I heard Warwick yell at me, like he was trying to pull me back. Hold on to what was left of my sanity.

I had none left.

All I felt was wrath.

*"I love you so much, Brex."* The memory of my father's voice spoke in my head. *"There's nothing I won't do for you. You are my entire soul."*

The picture that sat on Istvan's desk, the strain on my father's face, came back to me with more clarity. Did Istvan keep the picture as a cruel taunt to me? A sick memento of my father? All the times he made snide remarks about my father's loyalty.

*"Know if anything happens, I will always look out for you. There is nothing I won't do to keep you safe. Your uncle is watching over you too. We will all protect you."*

254

My father knew. He understood what might come for him.

Not fae, but Istvan.

Wrath rolled through me, impaling and devouring, the weight around my neck a tiresome burden, which was supposed to keep me contained. Though it was nothing to me. A burdensome ornament. A decoration.

My fingers curled over the goblin metal collar. Muscles flexing, I yanked on it, the metal groaning under the stress.

"What are you doing?" Istvan jerked back, throat bobbing. A loud grunt strained my vocals and face as I pulled harder. The choker snapped, clanking to the ground. He yelped, stepping back.

Wind whipped at my strands, lightning zipping across the sky, kissing the tips of the trees. I feared the power, the magic I felt bubbling inside for a long time. I had kept away because I was afraid to fully accept it. To test the limits of my magic.

What a dark Druid and light Seelie queen could create. Not good and bad, only gray.

I wasn't afraid anymore.

There were no limits.

I was everything and nothing. And nobody in the world, present or past, was the same as me. I was born in war, created from magic, constructed from a queen, and conceived from a curse.

I walked the line of life and death.

Took life and raised it.

I was *The Grey*.

The wisps of ghosts from afar heeded their queen's call, ready for combat and to defend me. The nectar in my hand seared through my nerves. The highest high burned with bliss as it overtook me. Power consumed and devoured. Every broken piece inside me forged together, standing stronger against the flames, never bending to others.

My gaze went to Istvan. Terror opened his eyes wide, his fear tasting like candy on my tongue.

He killed my father.

I never got to say goodbye.

He took Andris from me.

The deep betrayal, grief, and anger carved into my chest. He destroyed the best part of me. Took my family, my security, home… love. Ling, Maddox, Nora, Albert, Zuz—he took them all by his hand or mine by force. So much death, torture, and agony originated from him. He conditioned me to become the very being he trembled in front of now.

All the pain and misery I had been stuffing away erupted, spilling out in waves of grief. I felt every death and loss over again; the emotions piercing me so deeply, my insides twisted as if they were burning into embers.

*"Kovacs!"* I heard Warwick's voice break through, the intrusion only pissing me off more. Slamming the door closed between us, the screams and cries of more being hurt around me exploded inside me. One of those screams could be Mykel or Eliza… someone else dead because of Istvan.

A bolt of lightning cracked down close to Markos, the wind howling louder.

"Brexley, no!" Another voice bellowed; Tad's bowed figure hobbled up into my eye line. Ignoring him, I squeezed down on the nectar, dropping any barriers to it.

It rushed inside me, filling me with so much power time no longer existed. White light burst from me, the ghosts taking an order I no longer had to speak.

Attack. Kill.

They acted quickly, my invisible soldiers reaping souls, reveling in the pained and scared screams from the victims they claimed, cut down by unseen hands.

Another lightning strike hit the ground, leaving charred marks in its wake, energy impaling out of my body like daggers heading for Istvan, for anything in my path. The nectar seared me from the inside, burning its way through every vein and muscle, cauterizing what was left of my pain.

It scorched.

It destroyed.

And it felt amazing.

"Brexley, stop!" Tad moved in front of Istvan and Simon, his arms up, his voice throwing out a spell. Before I could stop, my magic slammed into him. I watched it hit the old man, funneling only to him as if he had directed it to him, taking the brunt of my power, avoiding Simon and Istvan. The force flung him up in the air like a doll, pitching him back into the dirt. His body spread out on the ground, just as my mother had done twenty years before, twisting his body with black magic.

Like a slap, the trance I was in shattered into pieces, breaking over me with awareness and horror. What was I just about to do? Simon was an innocent child, and I hadn't even thought past my hate for Istvan. Tad protected him.

"Tad?" I whispered his name, his form not moving.

Inching closer, air locked in my lungs. His eyes were open, but they did not blink. They stared vacantly at the sky.

"Oh. Gods. No. Tad!" I heard myself cry out, my body no longer able to hold me up, the nectar falling from my hands in a dull, charred lump. Crawling over the ground to him, I knew already. I felt it.

Emptiness.

"No!" Warwick bellowed behind me, and I twisted enough to see him, Istvan already escaping into the forest with Simon, Warwick disappearing after them.

I could no longer feel Warwick. The connection was scorched, leaving me empty. Cold. Floating in darkness without an anchor. Full of guilt, rage, devastation, and terror.

Staring down at Tad, his empty eyes gazed blankly up at the sky. Absent of life. Of the power which was woven in the earth, his life older than the trees next to us. He had lived thousands of years. My friend. My companion in Halálház.

Now he was gone.

*Because of me.*

He saved Simon's life, protected him.

*From me.*

I killed him.

"Oh, gods…" I scrambled back on my feet with a sob, devastated at the truth of what I had done, what I was capable of.

Sounds drew my attention up. Only handfuls of people still stood, staring down in shock at the dead bodies scattered across the terrain. My attention fell on dozens and dozens. I recognized one of the dead near me. Jan, the grumpy coffee guy at Povstat. Dead. Without a mark on his body.

My hand slapped over my mouth as I stepped back in utter horror. My call to attack didn't discriminate. I gave no order as to who. They killed on both sides. My magic didn't decipher between guilty and innocent. There was a mix of HDF soldiers, Povstat soldiers, and inmates slain over the ground. Some were dead from gunshot wounds, but most were not.

I had killed them.

The hundred souls I had taken swirled around me, adding to my undead army. Terror gripped my throat like fingers, my eyes dropping back down again to the body at my feet, comprehending what I had truly done. My magic took a hundred innocent lives, and it was potent enough to murder one of the most powerful Druids in the world.

I had almost killed Simon.

The gut-wrenching shame burned a sob in the back of my throat, Andris's warning murmuring in my head.

*"Brex, it's beyond dangerous. This tiny substance is the most powerful thing in the world. The damage it can do. Do you know what could happen if people found it? What if Istvan discovered it?"*

It wasn't Istvan he should have been afraid of.

It was me.

I was the monster.

I had no control and no idea how much more damage I could do. My heart and brain couldn't come to terms with my crimes, with what I had done. What I was capable of...

I stared down at the lifeless nectar, empty of magic. But I knew it wouldn't be long before the power came back. And I wanted it to. Like a drug, I had tasted the high... the power. I wanted more.

I didn't trust myself to be anywhere near it.

Scanning the area, I saw some grieving over their loved ones or thinking of the young men whose parents back at HDF would learn their child was no longer alive.

My feet retreated a few steps, the panic and need to run jarring my bones. I was too dangerous. I no longer walked in the gray... I had fallen into the darkness.

The threat, the danger.

Little did I know the whole time...

*I was the villain.*

# Chapter 27

## Warwick

The squeal of tires came around the tower, heading for where Istvan ran into the forest with Simon. The moment they got into the car I had no chance of getting my nephew.

"No!" I bellowed, terror firing my rage, tearing my boots across the land.

A door slammed, tires squealed, and through the trees, I spotted an SUV speeding away. Tracker was behind the wheel, Istvan in the passenger seat, and shadowy outlines of Olena and Ivanenko in the backseat.

Panic heaved my muscles as my energy waned. The hum I always felt to Kovacs was gone. I could feel everything inside me scorched into cinders, the pain almost crippling, but I couldn't stop. I wouldn't lose Simon.

"Simon!" I bellowed, pushing my legs harder, sweat beading down my face.

A sniffling sound stopped me in my tracks.

"Uncle Warwick?" Simon came out of the forest, blood still leaking into his shirt. His face crumpled as he ran to me.

Falling to my knees, I wrapped him up in my arms, relief heaving from my lungs, pulling his tiny frame into me.

259

He was safe. And I would never let anything hurt him again.

I gripped him so tight, not wanting to let him go.

"I want Mom." He sniffled into my chest.

"Okay, big man." I squeezed him tighter, sighing deeply. "Let's go find her."

I rose, lifting him up into my arms, his head falling on my shoulder.

Suddenly, pain wrenched across my chest, a grunt heaving through me, and I dropped us both back to the ground, my body curling over.

"Uncle Warwick?" Simon's voice sounded scared as I clenched my teeth through the shredding pain.

I had felt our link burn out before; I knew how it felt when she used my energy.

This was different.

Hollow. Empty. As if all the color in my world was ripped from me.

I bellowed out a roar.

"Uncle Warwick!" Simon cried out. "What's wrong?"

Sucking in, I pushed back the agony, standing up and taking his hand. The moment we hit the edge of the forest my gaze went to the spot I had left her.

Gone.

Panic rose in my throat, my hand clasping Simon's tighter, pulling him with me as I jogged back to the spot.

"Kovacs?" I gritted out. More and more, I felt off, my gaze taking in the sea of dead bodies on the ground.

"Mom!" Simon yanked free of my grip, running across the terrain where my sister stood. Her shock morphed into tears as she scooped him up, hugging her son to her body in utter relief and love. Zander and Mykel stood nearby.

"Warwick!" Ash's voice hit my ear, and he ran to me, Scorpion moving to me as well, but my attention didn't make it past Tad's body on the ground. The horrified shock. Tadhgan was dead.

She was able to kill the oldest and most powerful Druid alive.

Most of the carnage on the ground was from her too. I could taste her signature, smell her magic like I was tuned only to it.

"Fuck, princess, what did you do?" I muttered, reaching out for her, but feeling nothing. "Kovacs!" I screamed, echoing off the sky, bouncing through the trees as if it was chasing after her. The link was burnt out, an abyss that echoed forever. I couldn't even feel a buzz between us, spearing alarm in my lungs, the darkness already yanking me down to my most basic instincts.

Kill. Avenge. Destroy.

"Where is she?" Scorpion's voice peaked with dread, sensing it too, but not as I did. I knew it with every fiber of my being.

"Gone." I stared out at the forest, the sun dipping below the horizon, knowing she was somewhere out there, every second getting farther and farther away.

"Better watch out, princess," I muttered to myself. "I'm coming for you."

If she thought she could run, could hide from me, she was mistaken.

I hunted and tracked down my prey.

I was the threat, the danger.

I was *The Wolf...*

**Shadow Lands is Available Now!**

*Thank you to all my readers. Your opinion really matters to me and helps others decide if they want to purchase my book. If you enjoyed this book, please consider leaving a review on the site where you purchased it. It would mean a lot. Thank you.*

# About the Author

*USA Today* Best-Selling Author Stacey Marie Brown is a lover of hot fictional bad boys and sarcastic heroines who kick butt. She also enjoys books, travel, TV shows, hiking, writing, design, and archery. Stacey is lucky enough to live and travel all over the world.

She grew up in Northern California, where she ran around on her family's farm, raising animals, riding horses, playing flashlight tag, and turning hay bales into cool forts.

When she's not writing, she's out hiking, spending time with friends, and traveling. She also volunteers helping animals and is eco-friendly. She feels all animals, people, and the environment should be treated kindly.

**To learn more about Stacey or her books, visit her at:**

**Author website & Newsletter**: www.staceymariebrown.com

**Facebook group:** www.facebook.com/groups/1648368945376239/

**TikTok:** @authorstaceymariebrown

**Instagram:** www.instagram.com/staceymariebrown/

**Facebook Author page**: www.facebook.com/SMBauthorpage

**Sex, Lies, & Blank Pages Podcast:**
https://linktr.ee/sexliesandblankpages

**Goodreads:**
www.goodreads.com/author/show/6938728.StaceyMarie_Brown

**Pinterest:** www.pinterest.com/s.mariebrown

**Bookbub:** www.bookbub.com/authors/stacey-marie-brown

# *Acknowledgements*

The love for this series has seriously been beyond anything I expected! Thank you all so much for living the Savage Lands Series as much as I loved writing it!

**Kiki & Colleen at Next Step P.R**. - Thank you for all your hard work! I love you ladies so much.

**Mo & Emily**—You both make it readable! Thank you!

**Jay Aheer**—So much beauty. I am in love with your work!

**Judi Fennell at www.formatting4U.com**—Always fast and always spot on!

**To all the readers who have supported me**: My gratitude is for all you do and how much you help indie authors out of the pure love of reading.

**To all the indie/hybrid authors out there** who inspire, challenge, support, and push me to be better: I love you!

**And to anyone who has picked up an indie book and given an unknown author a chance**.

**THANK YOU!**

Printed in the USA
CPSIA information can be obtained
at www.ICGtesting.com
LVHW022151141023
761116LV00005B/121